Next Exit, Use Caution

CW Browning

Cover design by Dissect Designs / www.dissectdesigns.com
Book design by Clare Wroblewski

CW Browning
Visit my website at www.cwbrowning.com

First Printing: 2019

ISBN: 9781795788250

Author's Note:

This book is dedicated to wine – without which my sanity would not have remained intact.

Next Exit, Use Caution

"Though they plan evil against you, though they devise mischief, they will not succeed."

~ Psalm 21:11

Prologue

Downtown Singapore Mainland

A warm breeze carrying the hint of orchid blossoms drifted across the large balcony. The sun had set an hour before, cloaking the city in a hot and humid darkness that offered only slightly lower temperatures from those dominating the daylight hours.

Viper raised her eyes from her laptop and glanced across the balcony to the man lounging in the shadows a few feet away. He was dressed in dark khaki cargo shorts and a black tee-shirt, stretched taut across his broad chest. Her heart thumped of its own accord and she pressed her lips together in reaction, ignoring the leap in her pulse.

"What if he doesn't show?" she asked.

The man smiled faintly in the shadows.

"Then I hunt him down."

"So much for our relaxing getaway."

Viper stretched and closed her laptop, reaching for her bottled water.

"Is that what this is?" Hawk asked, straightening up and going across the flagged stones with lazy, measured strides. He moved like a panther, and Viper knew he was just as dangerous. "Yesterday you were scouring the embassy, looking for ghosts. This morning you were gone before dawn and came back with a new wound on your neck. Not much of a getaway."

Viper shrugged, the corners of her lips tugging upwards.

"Old habits," she murmured apologetically.

Hawk stopped next to the chaise lounge where she was stretched out and looked down at her, his blue eyes glinting in the low light from the lamps on the rooftop.

"I'll take care of this as quickly as possible," he promised, "and then we can get back to enjoying the evening."

Viper smiled up at him and set the computer aside, swinging her legs off the cushions and standing in one fluid motion.

"You can only take care of it as quickly as the target allows," she said. "Personally, I'm not holding my breath."

"Neither am I," he admitted, turning to look across the street at the high-rise opposite. "There's about a seventy percent chance he'll show, but when is anyone's guess."

Viper followed his gaze to a dark window directly opposite them.

"Who is he?" she asked, curiosity getting the better of her.

Hawk glanced at her.

"A Chechen separatist," he said slowly. "I've been watching him for a little over a year. It's just pure luck I spotted him on our way from the airport."

"Is it?" she asked softly.

Their eyes met and he shrugged.

"Probably not."

Viper nodded, turning toward the small table holding the remains of their dinner.

"Charlie?" she asked over her shoulder, reaching for a slice of mango.

"Who else? He's the one who sent us here."

"Good point." She turned to face him again, biting into the mango. "I can't help feeling there's something else going on though."

Hawk looked at her.

"Like what?" he asked.

"I don't know," she murmured, shaking her head. "You know how he is. Singapore isn't just a whim. We're here for a reason, and I think that reason is more than just an ex-soldier."

He stared at her for a long moment, his lips drawn into a grim line.

"Something connected to Asad?" he asked finally. "Or the leak in Washington?"

Viper's mask slid into place and she shrugged, popping the rest of the mango into her mouth.

"I don't know, but when I find…"

She stopped abruptly, her eyes widening as Hawk lunged in front of her, turning his back to her as he did so. For a split second, his broad shoulders blocked her view. Then, suddenly, they moved.

She never heard the shot that threw him backwards. Viper reacted with pure instinct, reaching out to grab him as they both fell hard on the stone balcony. She grunted when they landed and immediately pulled herself from under his weight. Rolling onto her stomach, she low-crawled straight to his rifle, set up a few feet away. She didn't need to hear the shot to know where it must have come from.

Reaching the rifle, she set her eye to the night-vision scope and scanned the building opposite, rolling over windows quickly until she found the one she wanted. Viper watched as a man slung a soft rifle bag over his shoulder, turning away from the open window.

Viper exhaled slowly as she squeezed the trigger. The man opposite fell a second later as the 7.68 round blew apart his skull. She watched him fall, then shifted back to the window Hawk had been watching all night. It was still dark. No threat there.

Viper closed the bipod legs attached to the rifle, lifting the gun and rapidly disassembling it with sure fingers before placing the pieces in an open case nearby. A moment later, there was no evidence a rifle had ever been present on the edge of the balcony.

Viper turned then, and her heart surged into her throat. Hawk was lying perfectly still, blood soaking his abdomen and spreading across the stones beneath him.

Chapter One

6 Days Earlier – Somewhere over the Pacific

"Tell me again why we're going to Singapore," Damon suggested, seating himself across from Alina with a glass in his hand.

"If I knew, I'd tell you," she said, amused.

Damon Miles sipped his beer and watched as she plugged an external drive into the side of her laptop.

"You're the one who opened a box with two fresh passports and reservations to a swanky downtown hotel on the mainland," he pointed out. "How do you not know why we're on a 22-hour flight to South Asia?"

"You're the one who had a private jet on stand-by in Philadelphia," Alina retorted, not looking up. "You tell me."

Damon grinned.

"I make it a habit to keep transportation on stand-by whenever I end up in Jersey. Things have a habit of getting dicey there."

That got her attention and she looked up with a laugh.

"You make it sound like a bad thing. You know you'd get bored if it was any other way."

Alina Maschik stretched her arms, rolling her head to loosen her neck, a smile playing on her lips.

"I don't think I will ever get bored with you." He raised his glass in a silent toast. "Yesterday I was in Washington DC defusing a bomb, and you were in Maryland eliminating a target. Now we're on a plane headed to Singapore. Not exactly a dull moment anywhere in there."

Damon watched as she closed the laptop and set it aside, reaching for her glass of water.

"We certainly seem to keep busy, don't we?" she agreed

thoughtfully. "To be fair, this wasn't my plan when I got back to the house last night."

"What was?"

"A hot shower, take-out, and bed, in that order."

Damon leaned his head back with a yawn.

"My kind of plans," he murmured. "I should have waited to give you Charlie's box."

"It certainly wasn't convenient timing. Kasim is still at large on the East Coast, and I think Stephanie wants my head on a platter."

Damon raised an eyebrow.

"Why? She and Blake can handle clean up. It's their job."

Alina looked at him, amused.

"I'd love to hear you tell her that," she said dryly. "I was thinking more along the lines of her personal struggle, not the professional one."

Damon lifted his head again and looked at her steadily.

"And what about you?" he asked softly. "Stephanie's not the only one who lost someone."

Viper's unemotional mask slid into place and she set the glass of water down with a clink.

"John wasn't mine to lose," she said briskly. "I told you, I'll handle it in my own time."

"Actually, what you said was that you'd take care of Asad, and then take care of you," he pointed out, unfazed. "You've taken care of the target, but I don't see you taking care of yourself."

"We got straight on a plane. I haven't had time to take care of anything, let alone succumb to pointless grief."

"It's not pointless if it helps you heal." Damon sighed and finished his drink, setting the empty glass down. "I know you're still trying to process John's death. I also know you'll go after the person who killed him. Let me give you some friendly advice, from one professional to another: get your head straight before you do. If you don't, you'll miss your target and you might get yourself killed in the process."

Alina considered him thoughtfully for a moment.

"If I didn't know better, I'd think Harry put you up to this," she murmured. "Or are you just taking a leaf out his book?"

Hawk's lips twisted and he leaned his head back, closing his eyes.

"I've never had the patience for the kind of head games Harry plays. He can keep his psychology. I just call 'em like I see 'em."

Viper watched him for a minute in silence.

"Don't worry about me," she finally said, her voice soft and deadly. "I haven't missed my target in three years, and I'm sure as hell not starting now."

Madrid-Barajas Airport

The private lounge for first class passengers was nearly empty this time of night and the lone occupant had the room to himself. He dropped his carry-on onto a recliner before turning to walk over to the refreshment area. He picked up a bottle of water and grabbed a copy of the day's paper before returning to his chosen seat. A flat screen TV displayed flight information, while another one, on the opposite wall, broadcast the news channel. He glanced at the news, reading the running ticker across the bottom of the screen, and shook his head.

Moving his carry-on, he sank down into the chair and glanced at his watch. He had half an hour before boarding; just enough time to scan the paper.

He sat back comfortably with his water and his paper, ignoring the drone of the news commentator on the TV and the occasional sound of the PA system outside the lounge.

A flight attendant came in behind him and moved silently to the desk at the back of the room. The man heard him, but never lifted his eyes from the paper. No longer alone, he turned the page and continued to scan the headlines.

"What appears to have been a coordinated mass attack on the United States was thwarted yesterday afternoon when US Federal authorities seized several bombs placed from Washington, DC to Boston," said the newscaster on the TV, drawing the passenger's attention.

He glanced up at the TV.

"While the exact number of bombs is unknown, authorities are treating it as a terrorist attack. Salvatore Consuelo reports from New York City."

The camera switched from the news studio to a man standing on a busy walkway in Manhattan.

"I'm standing outside the Cathedral of St. John the Divine, in Manhattan's Morningside Heights neighborhood, where, just yesterday, FBI discovered a bomb in the back of a car. This was just one of several uncovered yesterday along the East Coast, causing speculation of a widespread and coordinated attack on US citizens. Details about the attack are not being released, but a spokesman for the FBI did state the agency had advanced knowledge of the plot and acted to neutralize the situation. If the attacks were successful, they would have occurred on Palm Sunday and, at least here in New York City, there was a large crowd gathered for an event celebrating the launch of Holy Week. Other cities were also targeted with Philadelphia, Washington, DC, and Boston confirmed, but the number of bombs remains undisclosed. So far, no one has claimed responsibility for the attempted attack."

The passenger stared at the TV, the paper in his hands forgotten. Multiple cities? And Philadelphia was one of them?

He lowered his eyes to the paper again, staring at it blindly as thoughts swirled around his head. A terrorist attack on US soil had been foiled at the last minute, and one of the country's top assassins just happened to be in the Philadelphia area this week.

Viper.

The name was like poison, echoing like a death knell in his ears. When it passed the lips of the dying man in a hospital bed four days ago, he didn't believe it at first. What would an FBI agent know about an assassin of Viper's caliber? How would he even know the name? So few did. It was impossible, or so he thought at the time.

He changed his mind a few moments later when he passed a stranger in the corridor, heading toward the room he himself had just vacated. When he turned back to look, he met cold, dark eyes that shot a warning clear through him. In that instant, he knew he was staring at the mysterious and illusive Viper.

It was *not* impossible.

The man's lips tightened grimly. He'd heard whispered tales about the infamous assassin. They all had. The US government's elite assassin had reached almost god-like status in the underworld. They said she never failed. Viper had a 100% success rate. There were others, most notably one they called Hawk, but Viper became notorious the moment her own government put out a contract on her.

The passenger shook his head. He didn't normally listen to rumors, but the contract had been real enough. He received it himself, reading it before the offer was rescinded a few hours later. Talk at the time was that she had already been terminated when the contract went out. Clearly it wasn't true. She was alive and well. He'd seen her four days ago.

What the hell did the FBI agent have to do with her?

"Sir? I can board you now if you'd like," the flight attendant said, breaking into his thoughts.

The passenger snapped his attention back from his thoughts to find the newspaper crumpled in his fists. He released his hands, folding the paper before standing and tucking it under his arm. He picked up his bag and nodded to the attendant.

"Thank you," he murmured.

The attendant nodded and waited for him to present his passport and boarding pass. The man watched as he was checked into the flight, then took his papers back with a nod before turning to walk out of the lounge and into the long corridor leading to his gate.

In the intervening days since the hospital, he'd managed to convince himself that he imagined it. That the look from the stranger was just a look from a stranger, and the man was delusional with pain killers when he whispered the name. He even began to relax, and stopped looking over his shoulder. After all, why would an international assassin be on US soil to begin with?

A foiled terrorist attack changed all that. If Viper was working, and her target led her to the United States, she would follow. They were trained to stalk their targets, and it didn't matter where. If the target went, they followed.

Once again, the passenger pressed his lips together grimly. He wasn't arrogant enough to think an assassin as skilled as Viper wouldn't recognize him. She had looked straight at him, and his whole body had reacted with warning to the look in those eyes. There was no way she could possibly know who he was, but even so, it was dangerous just to have been seen by her. They were professionals, and professionals didn't forget a face.

Who *was* the FBI agent to her? That was the key. If he could find out how she knew the man in the bed, he could begin to understand just what he had gotten into when he took the job that landed him in the same hospital as Viper. Then he just might have a chance of avoiding the impending doom looming over his head with every step he took.

The man in the bed. He was the key.

Seletar Airport, Singapore

Alina glanced at her watch as she strode through the crowds, a messenger bag slung across her body. The swarms of travelers were familiar and comfortable to her, concealing her in their midst as thoroughly as camouflage in the jungle. The positions of the security cameras had already been noted, and Viper moved through the airport quickly, seamlessly avoiding each camera with timing and precision. It was second-nature to her, something she did automatically. As far as CCTV was concerned, she was invisible.

She and Damon had parted company on the tarmac after leaving the plane. He went into the airport first, heading for the car rental desk to procure transportation. She held back for a few minutes before following and turning in the opposite direction. They would meet at the car.

Alina felt her phone vibrate in her back pocket and she pulled it out, glancing at the screen. Stephanie again. This was the fourth call in twenty-four hours. Pressing her lips together, Alina slid the phone back into her pocket. She felt just enough guilt at leaving without a word that she would send her old friend an email once she got to the hotel. She just wasn't sure what she would say. How could she explain disappearing just when Stephanie needed her the most? The truth was out of the question, yet nothing else could possibly be acceptable.

Why does everything have to be so complicated? she wondered, side-stepping a toddler who darted in front of her without breaking stride. She missed the days when she was answerable only to herself.

Viper glanced up as she turned the corner. The doors were ahead. She pulled the clean phone she used to communicate with Damon out of her jacket pocket and texted him. Suddenly she just wanted to get out of the crowds, and to their hotel where she could shower and take a few minutes to think. So much had happened in the past week, and Alina had the sinking feeling it was just getting started.

Damon dropped his bags into the trunk of the sedan and closed it, glancing at his watch as he moved to the driver side door. Alina should be exiting the airport. When they landed over an hour ago, they tossed to see who would get the car and who would ensure there were no surprises waiting in the airport. He won.

Sliding behind the wheel, Damon grinned to himself. Before he strode away from her on the tarmac, Alina warned that she would get her own transportation if he showed up with a compact roller skate.

He started the engine. He assumed a brand-new Audi would be acceptable.

Damon backed out of the parking spot and the smile left his lips. Traveling in a pair was more complicated than he had anticipated. He could count on one hand the number of times he and Alina had traveled together, and on those few occasions they always parted company as soon as they landed. Staying together presented a whole new set of challenges. They couldn't simply disappear. They had to coordinate together and, while they were on the same page as far as their security habits were concerned, it was a challenge working with another person. Hawk shook his head. This was only going to get more complicated before it was over.

But he wouldn't have it any other way.

He puzzled over the thought briefly as he waited in the line of traffic leading to the exit doors of the airport. He was surprisingly comfortable with the fact that he just flew halfway across the globe with Viper, without knowing why Charlie had sent them to Singapore. A month ago he was in Tbilisi, Georgia, with no idea he would be summoned to join Viper in the States. Hell, he didn't even know she was stateside again. The last he'd heard she was in Cairo. A single message from Harry changed all that.

Now Charlie had changed it again.

Damon inched forward, watching the doors of the airport. Passengers flowed out in waves, getting into taxis lined alongside the curb. Now everything had changed. He shook his head, still trying to wrap his mind around all that happened in the past week. One thing was certain, there was no turning back now. For better or worse, he and Viper were in it together for the long haul. His lips curved. She might not fully accept it, but there was no going back to the way things were. The faint smile was short lived, and Damon sobered quickly.

He had her now, and he would die before he let her go.

The clean phone in his pocket vibrated and he pulled it out, glancing at the screen. She was on her way out. Glancing in the rearview mirror, he pulled over, cutting off a slow, lumbering bus. He had just come to a stop at the end of the curb when he saw her emerge from the building in the middle of a crowd of chattering tourists. Her messenger bag was slung across her body and her duffel was tossed over one shoulder. Damon watched as she turned to look in his direction and started toward the car.

Why did Charlie have her traveling again?

The thought popped into his head as he watched her weave through the crowds toward the car. Two weeks ago, she was pursued across Europe by enemies who shouldn't have known she even existed. Charlie sent her home to lie low while he tried to determine if they had a security leak. As far as Hawk knew, that leak was still concealed in Washington.

A troubled frown drew Damon's eyebrows together. What was important enough to risk Viper's cover again? And how the hell was he going to protect her?

"I guess Charlie isn't worried about us keeping a low profile," Damon said, stepping out onto the balcony.

Alina smiled, turning her head from where she stood at the iron railing overlooking the water. They had checked into the hotel an hour before to find a balcony suite with a stunning view of the bay had been reserved for them. Damon dropped his bags and disappeared to examine the hotel, leaving her to the luxury of their room. After a long, hot shower, she was feeling refreshed and more human. The sun had set, and the lights glittered brightly against the dark waves below.

"I'm not complaining."

Damon walked up behind her, slipping his arms around her and looking at the view.

"Why do you think he did it?"

Alina leaned her head back on his shoulder, gazing out across the water. The air was heavy with the scent of flowers from the many trees in bloom around the city, and the breeze blowing off the bay was gentle. She took a deep breath and felt the tension flow out of her.

"I don't know," she said slowly. "I'm sure we'll find out soon enough. He didn't say anything when he gave you the box?"

"Not a word."

They stood in comfortable silence for a few moments, staring out over the water. The pressure of the past week faded into the distance and a feeling of contentment washed over her. Suddenly she didn't care about the events that had led them here, or the terrorists still at large in the United States. All that mattered was that, for the first time, she was standing on a balcony in a foreign city, and was not alone. How many times had she unwillingly longed for Hawk to be with her, overlooking one city in a line of many? Now here they were, his arms wrapped around her, with the exotic beauty of Singapore surrounding them.

Alina was loathe to move, reluctant to break the spell.

"Have you ever been here?" Damon asked. His voice was soft, as if he too was unwilling to disturb the moment.

"Once, a few years ago."

"It's one of my favorite cities," he said. "I wish I got here more often."

Alina smiled.

"It's beautiful. You can give me a tour while we're here."

Damon tightened his arms around her and dropped a kiss on the side of her neck.

"I'd love to," he whispered. "I've wanted to show you my cities for a long time."

Alina turned in his arms and raised her eyes to his. They were like cobalt sapphires. She slid her arms around his neck.

"What other cities do you love?" she asked. "What would you show me?"

Damon smiled and rubbed his nose against hers.

"I'd start with Amsterdam. You told me once you'd never been."

"That's still true. I don't get into Europe as much as I'd like. Charlie seems to prefer me in the Middle East these days."

"You're effective there, just as I'm effective in Russia and the Baltic region."

"With this long hair, you fit right in," Alina said, toying with it. "Where else?"

His smile was slow and wicked.

"Lima, Peru. You didn't stay long last time."

Alina burst out laughing.

"Ouch."

"Istanbul is on the short list," he continued, "and, of course, Moscow. What about you? Where would you take me?"

Alina thought for a moment.

"It's not a city," she said hesitantly.

Damon raised an eyebrow, his eyes probing hers.

"Where then?"

"Montpellier, in the South of France."

Damon stared at her, fascinated.

"The South of France?"

"I lived there for a few years," she told him, surprising him. "I often went across the channel to Cornwall."

Damon smiled softly.

"France it is," he murmured, brushing his lips against hers.

They lingered, and by the time he raised his head, they were both breathless. "We'll start with Singapore, then work our way around the world."

Alina inhaled deeply and lost herself in those deep blue eyes, content to dream of a future that was far from guaranteed.

"It's a plan," she agreed, "but first, I'm starving. What are we doing about dinner?"

Damon pulled her tighter against him and lowered his lips to hers again.

"I think room service."

Chapter Two

Philadelphia International Airport

Stephanie Walker glanced at her watch and looked up at the arrivals board. Angela's flight had landed thirty minutes ago, but there was still no sign of her coming from baggage claim. She sighed and turned to walk back to her waiting spot near the doors. The past forty-eight hours had been non-stop and stressful. Stephanie just wanted to pick up her old friend, take her home, and then go home herself. The couch was calling to her, and she had every intention of answering.

She shook her head, her eyes on the doors. After narrowly averting a coordinated bombing attempt, Stephanie had been sucked into the debriefing at FBI headquarters with her boss, Rob Thornton. When she was finally finished, she left exhausted and disheartened. Far from being grateful for her assistance, her boss was angry with her for ignoring her leave of absence to get involved. If it weren't for Special Agent Blake Hanover, she wasn't even sure she would still have a job. In fact, Stephanie wasn't all that sure of anything anymore.

Blake Hanover.

Despite her grim mood, Stephanie smiled. He had stayed by her side the whole time, asserting that he was the one who pulled her into the investigation for an extra pair of hands. He calmly pointed out to Rob that when he had placed Stephanie on LOA, Rob didn't take her badge or weapon. Therefore, Blake argued, he was well-within his rights to ask for her assistance in his investigation. Rob had finally backed down. As far as her boss was concerned, the whole operation had been Blake's brainchild, and Stephanie was content to let that stand.

By the time Blake headed back home to Washington, DC for some much needed rest, Stephanie was sad to see him go. Somehow he'd become a rock for her in the harrowing events of the past week. Her only consolation was that he had promised to return.

Passengers began to exit through the doors in front of her, carting carry-ons and rolling bags behind them, pulling Stephanie from her thoughts. Towards the tail-end of the first wave, she spotted her friend.

Angela Bolan pulled a trolley loaded with bags and Stephanie's eyebrows soared into her forehead. The amount of luggage on the trolley made it look as if she had been away for months when, in fact, it was only two weeks.

"Steph!"

Angela caught sight of her and waved, heading in her direction. Stephanie couldn't stop the grin that spread across her face. Angela's honey-colored hair was perfect and she was dressed in designer jeans with Jimmy Choo's on her feet. How she was managing the laden cart in the four-inch stilettos was beyond Stephanie's comprehension, but she was doing it, and she looked like a model at the same time.

"You're insane," Stephanie informed her as Angela came to a stop in front of her. "What are all those bags? You were only gone for two weeks!"

"I went shopping in Miami." Angela threw her arms around Stephanie and hugged her tight. "How are you? You look like hell."

Stephanie hugged her back, fighting back tears that suddenly flooded her eyes at the embrace of one of her oldest friends.

"I feel like hell," she admitted.

Angela pulled away and looked at her searchingly before linking one arm through hers and grabbing the trolley again with her other hand.

"You should have told me as soon as it happened," she said, starting forward with Stephanie. "I would have come straight back. Why did you wait until yesterday to tell me John died?"

"Honestly, I didn't think to," Stephanie answered, guiding Angela through the busy terminal toward the exit. "There were so many other things going on, and it just didn't occur to me. I'm sorry."

Angela glanced at her.

"Well, you know I was never John's biggest fan, but it's shocking just the same. What happened?"

"I'll tell you in the car. It's a long story."

"At least Alina was here," Angela said as they stepped outside. "That's something. How's she taking it?"

"I have no idea."

Angela stared at her.

"What do you mean you have no idea?" she demanded. "Haven't you seen her?"

Stephanie sighed and pulled away from Angela as they came up to the pedestrian cross-walk leading across the street to the short-term parking where she had left her car.

"Yes, but you know how she can get these days. After the accident, it was almost as if she'd already decided John was going to die," Stephanie said, starting across the road as the crossing lights turned white and the traffic paused. "I don't think she ever expected him to pull through. When he...passed...she didn't show any emotion at all, at first."

"At first?"

"I saw a little of the old Lina for a second, but then it was gone." She shrugged. "Honestly, I don't think she's facing it yet. She's been busy...working."

Stephanie's voice trailed off. Angela had no idea what their friend did for living. As far as she was concerned, Alina was a security consultant who traveled a lot and was rarely home. While Stephanie believed it was mistake to keep Angela in the dark as to Alina's true identity, that was a fight she hadn't been able to win.

"Well *that'll* change now I'm back," Angela muttered. "She can't work at a time like this. I'm sure her company has bereavement leave and I'll make sure she takes it. For God's sake, she and John were engaged once upon a time. She's got to be feeling some kind of way about it!"

"I think she's more angry than anything," Stephanie said slowly as they reached the other side of the road. "I don't know why I think that, but I do."

"Anger is one of the steps of grief, so maybe she's transitioning." Angela stopped on the sidewalk and wiped her hand across her sweating forehead. "Is the car very far? I'm dying here."

Stephanie laughed despite herself.

"You're the one who went shopping in Miami, and then wore heels onto the plane. Seriously, what were you thinking?"

"I didn't think you were going to park a mile away from the terminal!"

"It's not a mile. It's in this lot, a couple of rows from here."

Angela grunted and began walking again, lugging the trolley behind her.

"What about Mr. Hunk O' Mysterious?" she asked. "Has he been around lately?"

Stephanie grinned. Mr. Hunk O' Mysterious was what they

called Alina's reticent military friend, Damon Miles, behind his back. Angela was convinced that the two had unresolved sexual tension between them, and Stephanie was inclined to agree.

"Actually, yes," she said. "He's been in and out all week, from what I can understand."

"Really?" Angela drawled, her eyes dancing. "Where did he stay? Did he stay with her?"

"I have no idea."

"Ugh!" Angela rolled her eyes in exasperation. "You're supposed to find this stuff out for me!"

"I can't find something out if they're not sharing," Stephanie protested, laughing. "Short of showing up at her house in the middle of night, how am I supposed to know if he's staying there?"

"I can see I'll have to take over. You're hopeless. I'll figure it out."

"Good luck," Stephanie said. "I don't even know if he's still here. In fact, I'm not even sure she's still here."

"What do you mean?"

"I've been trying to reach her, but she won't answer." She pulled out her keys as they started down the row toward her maroon Mustang. "I haven't heard from her since Sunday. I think she might have been called out for work."

"Did you stop by the house?" asked Angela. "Maybe they're holed up having sex like rabbits."

"Angie!"

"What?" she grinned. "It's what I'd do if I could get someone like him to look twice at me."

Stephanie shook her head, laughing reluctantly.

"I'll give you that one." She pressed a button on her key fob and beeped her alarm off, then opened the trunk. "I haven't had time to go by the house. If I don't hear anything by tomorrow, I'll swing by."

Angela nodded and grabbed one of the bags from the trolley, lifting it into the trunk. Stephanie grabbed another bag and they had the trolley empty in no time. Looking around, Angela shrugged and pulled the empty trolley off to the side.

"You're not going to leave it there, are you?" Stephanie demanded.

"I'm certainly not carting it all the way back to the terminal. Someone will come get it."

She went around to the passenger side door and got in, leaving Stephanie to shake her head.

"So tell me what happened," Angela said as Stephanie slid behind the wheel and started the car. "Don't leave anything out."

"John had an accident street racing the Firebird," Stephanie said slowly. "The front tire blew. He flipped and slammed into a tree."

"Why was he street racing?"

Stephanie glanced at Angela as she pulled out of the parking spot. She had to be careful what she said. Angela could never know much of what happened. Not only was it classified, but it would also reveal that Alina most definitely was *not* a security consultant.

"One of his friends was killed a week before and John didn't believe it was an accident. He started poking around, looking for answers. His main suspect was a street racer and he was following a lead; or so we think."

Angela was silent for a moment.

"Do we think John's accident was just an accident?" she asked quietly.

Stephanie's lips curved. Angela was a lot smarter than she looked.

"No. The blow-out was caused by a bomb in his wheel well."

"What?!"

Angela stared at her, shocked. Stephanie nodded grimly, pulling into traffic heading for the airport exit.

"Turns out he was right about his friend. He was murdered, and when John started asking questions, they went after him as well."

"Did you catch the bastards?"

"No." Stephanie scowled. "They both disappeared."

"Son of a…what's being done to find them?"

"That's what I want to know," Stephanie muttered.

Two days ago, Alina had assured her Dominic DiBarcoli and Tito Morales, the two responsible for John's crash, would not get away. Yet Stephanie had heard nothing since. While she suspected both men had been detained, or worse, by her old friend, she didn't have confirmation. As far as she knew, they were both still at large.

Angela shot a searching glance at her.

"Why don't you know?" she asked. "In fact, why aren't you at work? It's the middle of the day on a Tuesday."

Stephanie sighed and took the exit ramp onto I-95 north.

"I've been placed on leave of absence," she said reluctantly. "It happened just after John's accident."

Angela stared at her.

"What? Why?"

"The Bureau is running an internal investigation on John. I was guilty by association. My cases were reassigned and I was advised to take some time off."

"On what grounds? You're not the one who was street racing!"

"I know. Rob wouldn't say anything except it wasn't disciplinary." Stephanie switched lanes as she merged onto the highway and pressed the gas pedal down. "Then John died and now he says I need the time off to rest and cope. Something's going on, but I haven't been able to figure out what yet."

"What the hell, Steph!" Angela exclaimed, throwing her hands up in the air. "I go away on business and all hell breaks loose. What else happened? And don't tell me nothing because I'm not stupid. I watch the news. I know there were bombs found in DC, Philly, New York and Boston."

Stephanie looked at her, amused.

"Yes, there were, and yes, I was there in Philly. And no, I can't tell you anymore than you already heard on the news."

"Was that what John was poking around in when he got himself killed?" Angela asked bluntly.

Stephanie was startled.

"What?"

"Please don't treat me like an idiot," Angela said. "You know me better than that. It really doesn't take much to realize street racers don't go around putting bombs into other racers' wheel wells."

"Fair enough," Stephanie said grudgingly. "Yes, that's why John was targeted. Some of the street racers were smuggling products up and down the East Coast, and some of those products were bomb parts."

Angela nodded and looked out the window, absorbing all the information.

"Does Lina know John was targeted by someone?" she asked after a long silence.

Stephanie glanced at her, hesitating for a second.

"Yes."

"She's not angry, then," Angela said decidedly. "She's furious."

Stephanie nodded.

"Yes."

Angela sighed and stretched, rolling her head a few times.

"What's going on with the funeral?" she asked.

"His body was just released this morning. Our ME did an autopsy. He was waiting on a tox screen to come back."

"Have you spoken to his parents?"

"Yes. They're flying in Thursday. They were waiting for his

body." Stephanie's voice broke and Angela looked at her sharply. "Now we can work on funeral arrangements. I don't know if they'll have the funeral here or take him back to California."

"I would think they would have it here," said Angela. "He lived and worked here. Just because they retired to California doesn't mean he should be buried there."

"That's not our call," Stephanie said quietly. "Absent a will, they're the ones who get to make the decision."

"He had a will," Angela said unexpectedly.

Stephanie looked at her sharply.

"What?"

"He drew it up a few years ago," Angela said. "I have the name of the attorney at home. He gave me the name in case..."

"What?"

"Well, in case something like this happened."

Stephanie stared at the highway in front of her, stunned. It had never occurred to her John would have a will, or that he would tell Angela about it. She knew for a fact his parents were unaware of it.

"You could have told me that sooner," she muttered.

"You could have told me he was dead sooner."

Stephanie choked back a short laugh.

"You're really not going to let me slide on that one, are you?"

"Nope."

Stephanie looked at her.

"God I'm glad you're back," she said suddenly.

Angela glanced at her and reached out to squeeze her arm.

"Me too," she agreed. "You said on the phone Blake was staying with you. Is he still here?"

"He went back to DC last night. He'll be back for the funeral, if not before."

"Why don't you come stay with me?" Angela suggested. "So you're not alone."

Stephanie shook her head.

"Thank you, but I have to face it on my own," she said slowly. "Blake helped a lot and I'll miss him, but the worst of the shock is over."

Angela studied her profile for a minute, then shrugged.

"Well, you know where I live if you change your mind." She leaned her head back on the headrest. "In the meantime, I have some Ativan if you need it."

"Already got it covered, but thanks."

Chapter Three

Washington, DC

Michael O'Reilly climbed out of his truck and slammed the door, nodding to the tall man waiting for him on the sidewalk.

"That was quick!" the man called.

Michael beeped his truck locked and strode toward his old friend.

"I wasn't wasting time after a call like that," he replied, reaching the sidewalk. "Where is he?"

Blake Hanover motioned to the building behind him.

"Inside," he said, turning to walk toward the entrance. "It was pure luck I was in the office when the call came from Metro PD. I just got back late last night."

"How's Agent Walker?" Michael asked, opening the door and holding it for the other man.

"Not good," said Blake. "I'm going to arrange to work out of the Philly office for a few days. I didn't like leaving her alone."

Michael glanced at him.

"That bad, huh?"

"She's trying to hide it, but the whole thing has been a blow." Blake led the way down a sterile corridor, navigating the city morgue like the seasoned FBI agent he was. "Have you talked to your Black Widow?"

"Not since Sunday," Michael answered, a frown crossing his face. "I haven't been able to get hold of her."

Blake glanced at him.

"That doesn't sound good."

They reached the end of the corridor and Blake pushed open a door, holding it for Michael to pass into the large room beyond. A technician in a white lab coat was waiting for them.

"Agent O'Reilly?" he asked.

Michael nodded and pulled out his Secret Service badge, holding it up for examination. The technician studied it for a moment, wrote something on his clipboard, then held it out to Michael with a pen.

"Sign on the last line, please," he instructed, "next to Special Agent Hanover."

Michael scrawled his signature and the technician took the clipboard back.

"Follow me."

Michael glanced at Blake and turned to follow the technician through another set of doors at the far end of the room. Blake fell into step beside him, and they were silent as they entered a sterile room lined with freezers on one side. Tables were arranged in a row across the center of the room, all of them empty except for one.

"Here he is," said the technician, walking up to the lone occupied slab. "Hanover said you might be able to confirm his ID."

"Possibly."

"If you can, it would be a relief. I need to make arrangements for the disposal of the remains if he is a devout Muslim."

Michael nodded and stopped next to the steel table. The outline of a body was visible, concealed beneath a sheet. The technician looked at him.

"Ready?" he asked.

"Yep."

The technician pulled back the sheet and Michael stared down at the bloated, discolored face lying lifeless on the table.

"They pulled him out of the Potomac this morning," said Blake. "He floated up near the banks in Georgetown. Cause of death was a stab wound to the neck. It went right through the carotid artery. Death would have happened in seconds, or so I'm told."

Michael was silent, staring at the face as thoughts swirled through his head. The wound to the neck was precise, the weapon entering at exactly the right angle.

"Any other injuries to the body?" he asked.

"Just the wound to the neck," the technician replied. "There aren't even any defensive wounds."

"So he was either surprised or knew his attacker," Blake said. "Is he one of the terrorists you were tracking?"

"Yes." Michael looked away from the face and glanced at Blake. "He's one of them."

The technician replaced the sheet, concealing the body again.

"Do you know his name?" he asked.

"No, but I know someone who does," Michael answered, turning away from the table. "It's safe to start making your arrangements. He's definitely a devout Muslim."

Next Exit, Use Caution

Blake followed Michael back into the larger outer room.

"That's one down," he said in a low voice. "You said there were three? We think Viper took care of one already. Do you think she's responsible for this one too?"

"I don't know," Michael answered, striding toward the door to the outer corridor. He pushed open the door and stepped into the corridor. "I just don't know."

"It's a very professional wound," Blake said, following. "Who else knew they were here, and could do that?"

"The list is longer than you'd think," Michael replied grimly. "I'll see if I can at least get his name for you."

Blake glanced at his friend.

"What's wrong?" he demanded.

Michael looked at him, but was silent until they got outside in the fresh air.

"Something just doesn't feel right about the whole thing," he finally said, stopping and running a hand through his short hair. "I know what Viper does. She's an assassin. The wound, the target, everything is just what an assassin would do. Except I don't think she would have dumped the body into the Potomac. It's not clean enough for her. She's been trained to leave no trace. A body floating in a river is a really big trace."

Blake pursed his lips for a moment.

"Fair enough, but a body isn't that easy to dispose of. What else would she do with it in the middle of the Capitol?"

Michael shook his head with a frown, his eyes troubled.

"I don't know," he admitted, "but this just isn't sitting right."

Blake studied him thoughtfully for a moment.

"You think there's something else going on?"

Michael thought about the background Viper asked him to do on one of Washington's elite.

"Yeah, I just don't know what."

Dawn was lightening the sky outside while the city still slept. Alina opened her eyes and stretched, rolling over in the bed. She propped herself up on her elbow and looked down at Damon, tracing a faint scar on the side of his neck. The injury happened three years ago, in London. He told her about it the first time she saw him at her house in Medford, New Jersey, last year. Alina tilted her head. Now why did she suddenly remember that?

His dark hair had flopped over his forehead and a five o'clock shadow darkened his jaw. She smiled and brushed a long, dark lock out of his eye before lowering her lips to press them softly against his.

"Mmmm." His blue eyes opened and he smiled at her. "Good morning."

"Good morning." Alina smiled softly. "I don't know if I can get used to this. I'm not sure how I feel about waking up next to you."

Damon raised an eyebrow, amusement lighting his eyes.

"Is that so?" he drawled, pulling her down on top of him. "Let me help you make up your mind."

Alina laughed as his lips captured hers and he rolled her onto her back. She was just wrapping her arms around him when a cell phone rang stridently through the room. Damon groaned, tearing his lips from hers.

"It's yours," he muttered, shifting off her.

Alina rolled over and reached for her phone, glancing at the screen.

"It's Charlie," she said, propping her weight on her elbow with her back to Damon. "Yes?" she answered.

"You made it to Singapore, I see," Charlie said, his voice brisk. "I got the check-in notification. Did you have any problems?"

"No. The hotel was a surprise. What's the occasion?"

"It's one of my favorites," said Charlie easily. "Fantastic view of the water."

"Yes, it is. Why are we here?"

"Not very subtle, are you?" Hawk murmured behind her.

"There's someone there: someone you need to find," Charlie said cryptically.

"Who?"

"He used to be a soldier. He's made Singapore his home now. As you know, it's one of the financial hubs of the world. Tread carefully, but move quickly."

"How quickly?"

Alina bit her lip as Damon slid his hand over her thigh, leaving goosebumps in his wake.

"The reservation is for three days."

"Do you have a name?"

"That's what you have to find out."

Alina rolled her eyes.

Oh, is that all?

"Understood. What's happening with Kasim?" She swatted Damon's hand away. "He's still at large somewhere with two of his cohorts."

"One of his cohorts. The other one just floated up in the Potomac," Charlie said after a moment. "I don't have much information yet, only that he was stabbed in the neck. For now, the FBI and DHS are looking for leads on Kasim. When you're finished there, we'll re-evaluate."

"They can't handle him. You know that."

"I don't want him handled yet."

Alina stilled, her body stiffening.

"What do you mean?" she asked softly.

"I want to make sure what we stopped is all he has planned. I'm monitoring the situation."

"You think there's something more?" Alina frowned. "What does Sgt Curtis say?"

"Not much. He passed away unexpectedly," Charlie said dryly. "He *did* infect himself with the Ebola virus, and his organs shut down faster than expected."

Alina pursed her lips.

"That's unfortunate," she murmured. "What about the medical personnel who were exposed?"

"They're being monitored by your Dr. Krupp, or at least, their blood is. He's working on it."

Alina ran a hand through her hair and sat back against the pillows. Damon was watching her with those unfathomable eyes of his, and she carefully avoided meeting their gaze.

"And the antidote in the hospitals?"

"Already pulled." Charlie sounded amused. "Stop worrying about what's happening here. I sent you to one of the most beautiful and exotic cities in the world. Enjoy it."

Alina glanced at Damon, devastatingly gorgeous with his sleep-tossed hair and stubble on his strong jaw.

"Oh, I am."

She disconnected and reached over to set the phone back on the bedside table.

"Well?" Damon prompted.

"I have three days to find someone he thinks I need to find."

"Ok. Who is it?"

"He didn't say."

Damon stared at her.

"What?"

She shrugged.

"All he said was he used to be a soldier, and that this is one of the financial hubs of the world."

Hawk frowned.

"He wants you to focus on the banks," he stated.

She nodded.

"Yes, but why?"

"What did he say about Kasim?"

Alina repeated what Charlie told her and Damon listened, his lips pressed together thoughtfully.

"Do you think they have another plan?" he asked when she was finished.

"It's possible," she said slowly. "I wouldn't rule it out, but I also wouldn't lay bets on it. Asad was the brains of the two. Without him, Kasim is just a bomb-maker."

"Don't underestimate him," Hawk warned softly. "He got this far."

Viper looked at him for a long moment.

"I know. That's why I want to get back as soon as possible."

Damon smiled slowly, his eyes gaining a mischievous twinkle she was learning to recognize. It made her pulse leap and her heart skip beats.

"Don't be in such a rush," he murmured, lowering his head to press a soft kiss on the base of her neck. He smiled against the rapid pulse there and kissed a leisurely path up to her lips. "We have three days. Let's make the most of them."

The man watched as the nail technician placed both his hands in warm, citrus-scented water. She nodded to him and turned to talk to her co-worker at her side while his nails soaked. Leaning his head against the high back of the massage chair, he closed his eyes.

When he had arrived back the afternoon before, he was already planning his flight back to the United States. It was the only place he could find the information he needed. He had to go back to Philadelphia. His intent was to get home, book a flight, sleep, and leave again today.

The airport had changed all that.

His lips pressed together unpleasantly. He was walking out of the baggage claim area when he saw her, moving purposefully through the crowds. She was avoiding the cameras skillfully, and he knew it would be pointless to pull the CCTV footage from the airport. She wouldn't be on it.

Viper was too good for that.

He couldn't deny it had been a shock to see her there, in his home city, clearly having just arrived. She was careful, he would give her that. She not only avoided all the cameras and security, but she swept the whole terminal, looking for signs of ambush or surveillance. The entire sweep was accomplished in less than thirty minutes. She was nothing if not efficient.

The man suppressed a sigh. The only reason she didn't see him was because, through pure chance, he saw her first. It was simple enough to grab a baseball cap and reading glasses from one of the small gift shops, and transform his appearance into something she wouldn't look at twice, especially when he knew exactly what she was looking for. They were trained to see the same things, search out the same warning signs. Government agencies were all so boringly identical. Same clothing, same haircuts, same undercover disguises. Hell, most of the civilized countries even used the same surveillance vehicles. The colors and models changed, but the MO remained the same. Stupid.

He frowned, opening his eyes to stare at the ceiling of the salon, painted a mellow cream with tree branches stenciled in decorative clusters. Of course, he wasn't a government man, just as she wasn't an official government agent. She had seen him, though, and he knew she wouldn't forget his face. Short of plastic surgery, there was no way to hide from her now, not really. He might be able to slip past her once or twice, but if Viper ever got a good look at his face, he knew he was done.

And now she was here, in Singapore.

The frown eased as the nail technician lifted one of his hands out of the water and dried it before starting on his nails. He watched as she began filing, starting with his pinky.

There was only one possible explanation. She was here for him.

How the hell did she find out who he was?

The man returned his eyes to the ceiling thoughtfully. All his contracts were anonymous. He never knew who hired him. He didn't want to know. He was very clear in his terms. If the client began to slip and give him too much information that would indicate their identity, he stopped them. The less he knew about the people paying him, the better off they all were. It was a mutually beneficial arrangement that his clients appreciated, knowing their identities were safe. He had never had a reason to doubt the wisdom of not knowing who hired him. Until now.

Discovering how a lowly FBI Special Agent was involved with an elite, international assassin would be much easier if he knew who wanted the FBI agent dead badly enough to pay him twice his normal rate. The man shook his head to himself. He should have realized there was something wrong with the size of the fee. No one paid that much for a simple Federal agent, not without a good reason.

The technician finished with his left hand and lifted his right one out of the water. He looked down again and watched as she dried it and reached for her filing block again.

First things first: he had to find Viper, and he couldn't do it himself. It was too risky. If she saw him, it would be over. He had to find her before she found him, and he had to move quickly. There was a reason she was called Viper. She moved silently, struck swiftly, and never left survivors.

Or so they said.

The man watched as his nails were shaped and tidied. There wasn't a lot for the technician to do. He made it a point to have a manicure once every two weeks, and took very good care of it between sessions.

He would use Wesley. Wesley was a local man with a promising future. He knew how to move without being seen, and observe without doing anything rash. Viper wouldn't look twice at him. He had the misfortune of being one of the most nondescript people the man had ever seen. Not very helpful with the ladies, but extremely useful for his line of work.

The man leaned his head back again, satisfied. Wesley would find her. If he was fortunate enough to get a clear shot, he would tell him to take it. Maybe he would get lucky and Wesley would take care of Viper for him. His lips twisted sardonically.

Doubtful, but a man could hope.

Chapter Four

Viper slipped unobtrusively out of the private office on the fourth floor of the US Embassy, moving quickly down the deserted hallway. According to the calendar on the desk, the employee who worked there was on a two-week holiday in Athens, leaving the office deserted. Getting in was almost too easy, she reflected as she headed toward the stairwell. No wonder the country's security was in such disarray. Gaining access to the Marine and Army databases was decidedly harder, but again, not impossible. At least, not when you knew what you were looking for and how to bypass the firewalls.

Her lips tightened as she disappeared into the stairwell. After spending three hours poring over pension and disability records, she had found three potential candidates on the mainland, and two on neighboring islands. She would start with them.

Moving down the stairs, Alina wondered what Hawk was up to. He had left after their breakfast of coffee and fresh fruit, saying he had something to take care of. She sighed now as she jogged down the steps. They both clearly had their own goals today, and that was unlikely to change even if they continued to spend significant amounts of time together. Neither of them were used to working as a team, and at least in this instance, they had separate agendas.

Reaching the ground floor, she pushed open the door with her shoulder and moved into the back corridor of the embassy. A frown crossed her face as she thought about the cryptic phone call with Charlie this morning. Why was she here? Last week she was on lock down in New Jersey, under orders to stay out of the international arena until Charlie could find the leak that led to her being pursued through the Mediterranean. Now he sent her half-way around the world. Why the sudden change?

Viper was well aware of the vastness of intelligence Charlie had access to. If there was one thing she had learned over the years, it was that Charlie knew things that no one else did, and he used that knowledge with impunity. It was part of the beast he had created with the Organization. He knew more than his assets, and he manipulated and directed them as the need arose, to keep US soldiers and citizens around the world safe. Knowledge was his weapon, and he wielded it ruthlessly. Viper never questioned it. This was the way her world worked, and her role in it was very clear. He passed select pieces of intelligence on to her, and she eliminated the targets accordingly. She did not question the orders. She performed her own research, her own planning, and her own execution. All he did was provide the initial intel. Viper had never had a reason to question his motives.

Until now.

She paused outside the entrance to the public area of the embassy and took a deep breath. Exhaling, she opened the door and slipped into the bustling lobby. She lowered her face and partially turned her head, obscuring her features from the camera pointed at the door. Moving confidently away from the door, she crossed the marble floor and moved through the embassy toward the entrance. No one spared her a second glance. She was just another face, making her way out after completing her business.

Two weeks ago she was identified in Damascus by people who should never have known she was there. She was pursued through Greece and Italy, again by agents who shouldn't have known of her existence. Charlie had a leak in his Organization, and while he was working to uncover it, his assets were at risk across the globe. Viper had known this when she stepped onto the plane with Hawk forty-eight hours ago. They both knew their survival was solely in their own hands. A leak in Washington knew much more about asset movements than was safe, and their very anonymity was in question. Now, for the first time since this nightmare began, Alina found herself questioning everything, even this trip.

Charlie was up to something, and he dispatched her and Hawk to Singapore for a purpose. It wasn't her job to question it, but Viper found herself wondering what was so important he was risking not just her, but Hawk as well. Was this ex-soldier really so critical that Charlie was willing to expose them?

She nodded to the Marine guard at the door and stepped outside into the hot, muggy afternoon sun. A few minutes later she was passing out of the gates and striding away from the fortress-like embassy. She hailed a cab a block away and gave the driver the first address on the mainland. The questions and doubts swirling in her mind were pushed aside. For the time being, they were immaterial.

It was time to start hunting.

Hawk watched in the store front window as his target stepped out of the restaurant on the opposite side of the street and turned to walk the single block to his hotel. He waited until the tall man was halfway to the corner before turning and leisurely strolling along the sidewalk, two bags from designer stores in either hand. He was just another tourist out wandering the shopping district while his significant other spent his money. He glanced into the next store window, his eyes watching the man as he paused on the corner and waited to cross to his hotel.

When Hawk got the text from Charlie this morning, telling him Sergei Kuriev was heading to Singapore, he actually chuckled to himself. For once it appeared he knew something before Charlie. It was with great relish he had responded that Sergio was already here. Hawk had seen him in the street on the way to their hotel.

The man crossed the road, and Hawk turned to watch as he strode to the entrance of the hotel and disappeared inside. Pressing his lips together thoughtfully, Hawk turned and continued his leisurely stroll, crossing the street and walking along the pavement, his sharp blue gaze picking out the doorman and security in the alcove of the hotel. He turned his head and looked up, then stopped and turned to face the building next to him. To any observer he appeared surprised that the building was another hotel and not a store, and he turned to wander back the way he came. A small smile played on his lips as he crossed back to the other side of the street again.

He knew just how to get to the illusive Chechen warlord. Now he just had to convince Viper that she wanted to go to another hotel for dinner tomorrow night.

Damon strolled along the street, maintaining his slow pace even though his target was no longer in a position to see. It had been easy enough to find him. Sergei had a very specific routine which he followed every morning, no matter the weather or how late he was up the night before. Last night, while Alina ordered room service, Damon went online and found the only two restaurants that included Syrniki on the menu. This morning at eight o'clock sharp, Sergei walked into one of them, dressed in running pants and a windbreaker, fresh from the gym. Habits were maintained, even when away from home. His target was nothing if not predictable.

Damon continued down the street and turned the corner. He wondered if Charlie had intel that Sergei was going to be here before he sent them to Singapore. They knew when they got on the plane in Philadelphia that Charlie was sending them halfway across the world for a reason. As it turned out, he had two reasons. Hawk swore that man was omniscient.

If he could do that, why couldn't he find a leak within his own Organization?

When he left the hotel this morning Viper was getting ready to go out, and it hadn't escaped his notice that she wasn't wearing her back or ankle holsters. That meant no weapons, which meant she was going somewhere she couldn't take them. He didn't like the idea of her wandering around unarmed when they had no idea who might be watching.

Hawk frowned, his own weapon sitting comfortably in his holster. There were only a handful of buildings with security measures stringent enough to make her leave her ever-present .45 behind. The Embassy seemed the most likely destination. He glanced at his watch and turned to hail a cab. Charlie told her to look for a soldier, and the Embassy was the quickest way to do that.

A cab pulled up and Damon got in, giving the driver the hotel address. As the car began to move, he turned his attention out the window. So much for a relaxing few days with his Jersey Girl. At this rate he wouldn't be able to show her anything of the city. He sighed silently.

One day, he promised himself. One day they wouldn't be bound to a brilliant spy-master. One day their time would be their own.

And he had every intention of grabbing that time with both hands and not letting go.

Blake Hanover held the leash with one hand while he unlocked his front door with the other. Buddy, his fifty-pound pit bull, stood next to him on the doorstep with his tongue hanging out. After leaving the city morgue earlier, Blake went back to the office and worked on his report from Sunday's bomb escapade. It was past six before he left the office to run some errands. As a result, it was pushing nine o'clock before he got home. When he walked in, Buddy was practically standing with his legs crossed.

Blake opened the door and Buddy shoved past him into the house. He followed, closing the door behind him.

"Ok, ok," he muttered as Buddy pulled on the leash, trying to get through the living room to his water bowl in the kitchen. "Give me a second already!"

Blake reached down to unhook the leash from his collar, straightening up as Buddy started for the kitchen. Suddenly the dog pulled up short, a low growl coming from deep in his throat.

Blake froze. Buddy was staring into the dining room, his whole body still and tense, his top lip curling back. Without thinking, Blake reached for his gun, unsnapping his holster as he moved forward slowly.

"What is it boy?" he murmured, moving next to his dog.

Buddy glanced at him, then returned his attention to the dining room. The growling had stopped now that his master was beside him, and Blake dropped a calming hand on the top of his head.

"Easy."

He pulled his weapon out of his holster and moved forward silently, sliding the safety off as he went. Reaching the door to the dining room, Blake kept his back to the edge of the wall and looked in. A quick glance was enough to assure him that the room was empty. Empty, but not undisturbed. A frown settled on his lips as Blake stared across the room at the open window.

That window was always closed and locked.

Blake glanced behind him and watched as Buddy sat down, staring at him.

"Some guard dog you are. You're just gonna sit there and watch?"

Buddy's response was to yawn widely and stretch out his front legs, resting his large head on his paws. Blake grinned and shook his head, moving past the dining room to the kitchen. He listened to the deafening silence in the condo, straining to hear the slightest sound that would indicate an intruder, but there was nothing.

Blake looked around the kitchen, noting that nothing had been moved since he dropped his mail on the counter before taking Buddy out. The stack of mail was just where he left it, undisturbed. He moved on toward the bedroom at the rear of the hallway, his pistol ready near his shoulder. Despite the silence, his heart was pounding in his ears as he moved silently into his bedroom. He reached out and flipped the light switch on the wall.

No intruders jumped out at him. The room was just as it had been this morning. Blake wasn't a man for clutter. A queen-sized bed, mission-style dresser, and one bedside table were the only furnishings in the large master bedroom. There was nowhere for an intruder to hide and, once Blake glanced behind the door, his shoulders began to relax.

He strode over to the open closet door and glanced into the walk-in closet. It was empty.

Turning, Blake looked around the bedroom with a frown. Nothing was out of place. He strode out of the bedroom and across to the bathroom. After checking behind the shower curtain and in the linen closet, he holstered his gun and moved back down the hallway.

Buddy was still stretched out on the floor outside the dining room, watching him with his big, dog eyes, and Blake moved past him into the living room. He looked around. The TV was still mounted on the wall, the entertainment system was still on the rack beneath it, and his laptop was still plugged in and sitting on the desk in the corner.

"What the hell?" he muttered. Buddy whined and Blake looked at him. "Yeah, I don't get it either. Come on. Let's get you some water."

Blake went into the kitchen and picked up Buddy's empty water bowl, carrying it to the sink. Buddy padded into the kitchen behind him, waiting for him to set it down. Blake obliged before going back to the living room. He went straight to his laptop and opened it, unlocking the security layer quickly. While Buddy noisily drank his water in the kitchen, his collar jiggling and jangling in his enthusiasm, Blake sat before his computer and opened up a security program. By the time Buddy wandered back from the kitchen, he was staring at the video footage from the cameras he had installed throughout the small condo.

Buddy flopped down next to him, but Blake didn't even notice. He was too busy watching as a man dressed in dark jeans and a black hoodie jimmied open the dining room window and climbed through. The hood on his sweatshirt was up, concealing his face from the camera in the dining room. He moved straight into the hallway. There the hall camera showed him looking into the living room for a moment before he turned and headed down the hallway toward the bedroom. The intruder glanced into the kitchen as he passed, but never broke stride. The hall camera lost him when he went through the door, but the bedroom camera picked him up as he walked in. He paused inside the doorway, looking around slowly. A moment later, he disappeared into the walk-in closet and the bedroom camera lost him.

"What the…"

Blake muttered a few choice words as he stared at the silent footage, waiting for the intruder to reappear. A minute later he did, heading straight out of the bedroom.

He left the way he came, never stopping anywhere else in the house.

Blake sat back in the chair, staring at the laptop screen, bemused.

Who the hell broke into a house and didn't take anything?

Blake scowled and closed his laptop, standing up. He turned and strode down the hallway to the bedroom, Buddy following amiably. Going straight to the closet, he pulled the cord to turn on the overhead bulb. What was the guy doing in here?

Blake looked around, studying everything. His clothes were hung neatly on the bar circling three sides of the closet, all spaced perfectly as his OCD demanded. The coated wire modules installed on either wall beneath the clothes for extra storage were untouched, the various boxes and storage bins right where they should be. The gun safe at the back of the closet didn't appear to have been tampered with. Nothing was amiss.

The intruder came in here for a reason. Something had to be different. Blake stared at everything again, starting on one side and concentrating on a section at a time. He was halfway around the closet when he tilted his head suddenly.

There!

Just as his clothes had to be perfectly spaced apart on the rail, so did his shoes on the shoe racks. Blake would love to be able to blame his time in the military for this particular OCD of his, but in all honesty, he could not. For as long as he could remember, he would obsess over the spacing between his apparel. If the spacing wasn't even or, heaven forbid, two articles of clothing actually had the audacity to touch, it drove him crazy until he fixed. In Afghanistan, some of the guys would move his gear half an inch, laying bets on how long it took him to notice.

Now his OCD had unexpectedly paid off.

Blake turned and strode out of the bedroom, going back to the living room quickly. Reaching the desk, he picked up his work bag and pulled out a pair of latex gloves. He pulled them on as he strode back to the bedroom. Re-entering the closet, he moved forward and picked up a snow boot that was about an inch too close to the hiking boot next to it. He glanced inside as he picked it up and frowned. Turning it upside down, Blake's eyebrows soared into his forehead as a plastic bag fell out and hit the carpet with a soft thud.

Blake set the snow boot down and bent down to pick up the

plastic bag. He opened it slowly, careful to disturb it as little as possible.

Inside was a pile of sealed plastic baggies filled with white powder.

Michael frowned and pressed end on his phone as the call went directly to voicemail. He laid the phone down on the island in his kitchen and turned to open the fridge. He'd been trying in vain to get through to Alina for two days now. Each time he tried, the call went straight to the impersonal, computer-generated voice telling him to leave a message. Where was she?

He studied the contents of his refrigerator with more interest than they warranted, and after a moment, closed it again with a sigh. He didn't want anything in there. He was just restless.

Michael turned to leave the kitchen, swiping up his phone as he went. On Saturday night, he left Alina's in Medford to go to his parents' house in Brooklyn. The next day he tracked down a bomb in the back of a kid's car, saving Manhattan from countless fatalities, while Viper went after the terrorist that planned it all. That was the last he had heard from her.

Michael scowled and went into the dining room where his laptop sat on the large farmhouse table. According to Blake, Stephanie Walker had spoken to Alina later that day on the phone, but no one had heard from her since. Where was she?

His phone rang suddenly, making him start, and he turned it over to look at the number. He raised an eyebrow and answered, glancing at his watch. It was past ten o'clock.

"Hello?"

"Hey Mike, you still up?" Blake asked.

"I answered, didn't I?"

"Is everything ok over there?"

Michael frowned.

"Yes, why wouldn't it be?"

"I just got home from taking Buddy for a walk. Someone broke in while I was gone."

Michael's eyes widened in surprise.

"What?!"

"The dining room window was open. It was closed when I left."

"What did they take?"

"Nothing."

Michael frowned.

"Nothing?"

"Not a thing."

"Are you sure you didn't leave the window open?" Michael asked after a moment of silence. "People don't just break in and not take anything. How do you know someone was there?"

"After your girlfriend made herself at home in my house last year, I installed hidden cameras. And they really are hidden."

Michael smiled reluctantly.

"Fair enough. What did they pick up?"

"Some guy in a hoodie entered through the dining room and went straight for the bedroom closet. He came out a minute later, then left."

"And he didn't take anything?"

"Nope. So, I checked the closet."

"And?"

"I found something that wasn't mine," Blake said grimly.

"Do you want me to guess?" Michael asked after another moment of silence.

"The dude put a brick of heroin in one of my snow boots."

"What?!"

"The only reason I found it was because he didn't put the boot back in exactly the same spot," Blake said, his voice tight. "Thank God for my OCD."

"Who would have thought *that* would turn out to be useful?" Michael agreed, getting up and taking a restless turn around the dining room. "Blake, this isn't good. You didn't move it, did you?"

"'Course not. I left it there and took pictures, then called you. What the hell is going on?"

"I have no idea. Who have you pissed off lately?"

"You want a list?"

Michael grinned despite himself.

"Let's try this, where are you in your investigation on the Casa Reinos Cartel?" he asked. "Could they have done it?"

"Who knows," Blake sighed. "I guess it's possible. I have to call it in to my boss, but I have no idea what to tell him."

"The truth," Michael advised. "That's your only option. Show him the video and tell him exactly what happened."

"Do you realize what could have happened if I didn't install those cameras last year?" Blake demanded after a moment of silence.

"You'd be joining Agent Walker on the inactive duty roster," Michael said. "Call your boss. The sooner you report it, the better. Whoever planted it will probably call in an anonymous tip. You want to beat them to it."

"I know." Blake sighed. "Just when I thought things were settling down after the weekend."

"Do you want me to swing by?" Michael offered after a second.

"No, I'm fine. I'll call it in now. He'll send some agents over and you'd just be in the way," Blake said.

"Well, let me know what happens. I'm working from home all week."

"Will do." Blake paused. "Hey Mike? Be careful. I'm not convinced this is the Cartel. It's not their style."

Michael frowned thoughtfully.

"You think it might be connected to those bombs?"

"I'm just saying pulling a dirty trick like this is more consistent with the general population of DC than the Cartel or random terrorists."

Michael thought of the unusual request Viper made of him over the weekend to investigate one of the staple figures in the town and his frown deepened.

"I'll take care of me," he told his friend, "you just make sure you take care of you."

Chapter Five

Downtown Singapore Mainland

Alina glanced at her watch and pressed the button for the twentieth floor. Her messenger bag was draped across her body and she adjusted it absently as the elevator doors slid closed. She was late. When Hawk texted her to meet him for dinner, she was on a bus, returning from a fruitless trip into one of the more remote corners of the island. She was striking out with all the addresses she pulled from the Embassy yesterday. Viper didn't know what Charlie was looking for, but none of the men she had found thus far warranted any interest. Just the opposite in fact.

And yet, she must have rattled someone. Alina frowned as the elevator rose swiftly and silently. The local man who had been trailing her all day was nothing if not persistent. Who was he?

The elevator came to a seamless stop and the doors slid open. Alina stepped out, glancing around, and her eyebrows rose. Instead of the hotel restaurant she was expecting to see, she found herself standing in a lushly carpeted hall with suite doors widely spaced apart. She pulled her phone out of her pocket, quickly texting Hawk.

Do you want me to guess?

She started to the right, glancing at the nearest door and noting the number. She was half-way down the hall when her phone vibrated in her hand.

Last one on the right.

Alina shook her head and strode to the last door in the corridor. She opened it and stepped through, glancing around as she closed the door behind her softly. She was standing in a spacious living room suite with a couch and two chairs arranged around a modern glass coffee table. On the far side of the living room, sliding doors fronted a large balcony and she could see Hawk standing outside, his hands on the stone balustrade.

Alina moved forward, pulling the messenger bag over her head and dropping it onto the coffee table as she passed. A glance to the left revealed wide double doors open to show a king sized bed in the master bedroom. She shook her head again and stepped out onto the balcony.

"Let me get this straight," she said. "You got a balcony suite in a completely different hotel just to have dinner?"

Hawk turned to look at her, a grin spreading across his face. "The room service comes highly recommended."

Viper caught sight of his rifle case near the edge of the balcony and everything was suddenly clear. The only question was, why was she here?

"In that case, how can I refuse?" she murmured.

On one side of the balcony, a chaise lounge overlooked the pool beside the hotel. On the other end were two wrought-iron chairs and a table for any guests who preferred to eat their meals outside. A set of unlit candles sat in the center while two wine glasses and a bottle of wine were off to the side. The highly glossed wall of the hotel acted as a mirror, and Alina caught sight of herself in the reflection as she walked toward the table.

"If you're working, why are we having dinner?" she asked, glancing at the wine.

"I don't know if I *will* be working," Hawk answered readily, turning back to look over the city. "It depends on whether or not the target cooperates."

Viper glanced at him, then at the high-rise hotel across the street. She pursed her lips thoughtfully, but remained silent. Their jobs were their own, and his was none of her concern.

"Is this your idea of showing me the city?" she asked, joining him at the balustrade. "I'm not sure it lives up to the hype."

"Don't underestimate me," Damon murmured, his eyes dancing.

Alina bit back a grin and glanced up at the man beside her. She was having more fun than she'd had in years, she realized with a start. Things were certainly more interesting with him around.

"Oh, I never do," she murmured. "When is dinner?"

He glanced at his watch.

"It should be here any minute."

Alina watched him as he turned and went over to the table to pick up the bottle opener next to the wine.

"Good. I'm starving. I haven't eaten since breakfast."

"Neither have I," he admitted, pulling out the cork. "Any luck with the ex-soldier?"

"Not yet." Alina walked over as he poured the red wine, accepting one of the glasses from him. "I'm working on it."

"Here's to a speedy resolution." He raised the other glass in a toast.

Alina smiled and drank.

Stephanie dropped her purse and keys onto the dining room table and turned to go down the short hallway to her bedroom. She wasn't back to work yet, but she had just spent the whole morning in the office cleaning out John's desk and fielding questions from co-workers. Her boss Rob was unusually understanding and took her out to lunch before she headed home, John's personal effects in two boxes in her trunk.

Stephanie kicked off her heels and dropped onto the side of the bed, exhausted. The thought of simply laying down and going to sleep was almost irresistible, but after a moment, she got up again. Going to her dresser, she pulled out a pair of jeans. Hiding from it wouldn't change anything. John was gone. Nothing was going to change that.

Angela gave her the name of the attorney handling John's will, as promised, and Stephanie had left a voicemail for him this morning. She still had to call his mother and advise her of the existence of a will. That was a call she wasn't looking forward to making. While she had always liked Mrs. Smithe, there was no denying the past few phone calls with her had been rough.

After changing into jeans and a tee-shirt, Stephanie went back to the dining room. She was just heading into the kitchen to get a soda when her cell phone rang inside her purse. She sighed and reversed direction.

"Hello?"

"Hey Sunshine," Blake's voice greeted her. "How's it going?"

Stephanie smiled despite her melancholy mood.

"It's been better, but I'll get through it. How are things in DC?"

"About the same, actually," he said. "You first. What's going on?"

"Nothing serious. I just got back from cleaning out John's desk." Stephanie turned to go back to the kitchen. "Just a long, emotional morning. How about you?"

"My house was broken into last night."

Stephanie gasped.

"What happened?"

"I took Buddy for a walk late last night and while I was gone someone broke in and planted a brick of heroin in my closet."

"Wait…what?!"

"Yeah," he said grimly. "Luckily I installed cameras last year after your Black Widow broke in and left a gun on my dining room table." Blake paused. "Actually, now I think about it, no one seems interested in stealing from me. They all just want to leave me presents."

Stephanie choked back a laugh and pulled a can of soda from inside her fridge.

"Not a bad problem to have," she murmured, "although, I'm not sure I'd call a brick of heroin a good present. Were you able to ID them?"

"The guys at the office are reviewing the video now. None of the cameras picked up a clear image of his face. He had his hood pulled up, so I'm not expecting much."

"What did your boss say?" Stephanie asked, going into the living room and dropping onto the couch. She propped her bare feet up on the coffee table and sat back. "Do you have any idea who would want to set you up?"

"I've got a few, but who knows which one's right, if any," he replied. "We're waiting to see what happens with the anonymous tip we're sure is coming."

Stephanie shook her head, staring across the living room thoughtfully.

"The Casa Reino Cartel seems like the most likely culprit," she said slowly. "You've been a thorn in their side for months."

"I think they would just put a bullet in me."

"Oh, please don't say that," she muttered. "I can't hear that right now."

"Sorry," Blake apologized. "Hey, how do you feel about dogs?"

Stephanie blinked at the sudden change in subject.

"They have four legs and go outside to poop," she said.

Blake laughed.

"That's it?"

"They generally have good noses?" Stephanie offered, at a loss. "I don't know. I've never had a dog."

"Would you be opposed to my bringing Buddy up with me?" he asked. "Given the turn of events in the past twenty-four hours, my boss agrees it might be a good thing for me to work out of the Philly office for a few days. I'd rather not leave Buddy here again so soon after the last trip."

"Will he want to come?" Stephanie asked, glancing around her living room.

"I don't know. Let me ask him." Blake sounded amused.

Stephanie laughed.

"Well, I don't know how dogs are! Angela's cat gets very stressed out if you try to take her out of her house," she said. "How do I know dogs aren't like cats?"

"Dogs are nothing like cats," he assured her. "Trust me. He'll be fine."

"Do I need to get anything? Bowls? Food?" Stephanie asked, resigned.

"I'll bring all that. Thanks. I appreciate it."

"When are you boys descending?"

"Tomorrow?"

"Ok. Let me know when you think you'll get in," she said, "and keep me posted about the situation down there."

"Will do."

Stephanie hung up and dropped the phone onto the cushion next to her. Suddenly, the day looked a little brighter. She didn't question it. She just accepted that Blake coming up made her happy. Well, Blake and his pit bull. She looked around the small living room again.

This was going to be interesting.

Senator Robert Carmichael glanced at his phone and surreptitiously slid it back into his pocket. He was seated in his chair on the floor, listening to the roll call vote winding down. It was not a highly publicized vote. It was expected to follow party lines and, as such, the President was expected to sign it into law within the next few days. All in all, not a very interesting day at the office, but a required one nonetheless. Once it was concluded, he could leave the Capitol Building and head to his favorite restaurant for a late lunch. There he could give some thought to the situation he suddenly found himself in.

A frown crossed his face. He wasn't sure when this enterprise went so drastically off the rails, but he suspected that it was around the same time Special Agent Blake Hanover began questioning what really happened to that FBI agent in New Jersey last week. Until then, everything was running along smoothly. Everything was on schedule and he was slated to make an absolute fortune on the stock market. Then it all went sideways somehow. Within the space of a week, Robert had two dead street racers, one of which was an FBI agent, and he was watching his guaranteed windfall from a calculated stock purchase disappear before it was ever realized. Just like that, months of planning went down the drain.

Even then he could have recovered with little damage if it weren't for Dominic DiBarcoli's sloppy handiwork. The frown turned into a scowl. The man had simply become too arrogant for his own good. Dominic thought he was invincible, when nothing could have been farther from the truth. Witness him getting stabbed to death outside the Willard.

Robert pursed his lips thoughtfully. While he hadn't arranged for that particular incident, he had to admit he was a bit relieved to read about it in the paper the following morning. Someone had very obligingly taken care of Dominic for him, making that one less thing he had to worry about.

The vote came to an end and Robert stood up, nodding to a colleague as he moved toward the closest exit. Now he just had to worry about Blake Hanover.

That was decidedly trickier. Why was he so interested in the death of Special Agent John Smithe anyway? Robert shook his head as he moved out of the chambers and into the wide corridor. How did they even know each other? John Smithe worked out of the Philadelphia office and Blake worked in DC. There was no reason for their paths to have crossed at all, but they obviously had. Blake was in New Jersey last week questioning Dominic about the whole thing. That was a problem, and a big one.

Blake Hanover had made a name for himself in the short time he'd been in DC. He was respected in the law enforcement circles, and he was a damn war hero to boot. Hell, he was awarded the Bronze Star. He wasn't some random over-achieving agent who could be bought with money or promises of promotion. He was a man who, by all accounts, lived his life by a code of conduct most had forgotten existed. He was a damned Boy Scout.

Robert's lips tightened. Getting to Blake Hanover was tricky, but not impossible. He'd already laid the groundwork. By tonight any standing Special Agent Blake Hanover had in this city would be questioned. Once his reputation and character were tarnished, it would be a simple matter to roll up any doubts anyone might have as to the death of John Smithe in New Jersey. Once that was removed, there would be no reason to look twice at the death of Dominic DiBarcoli. More importantly, no one would think to look at what, exactly, Dominic had been doing when he met his Maker, or who he was doing it with.

That was the main key. Robert had to ensure he was as far removed from Dominic DiBarcoli as possible, and that meant removing anyone who could conceivably connect the dots back to him.

Robert stepped outside into the sunlight. Not only had he lost a fortune, but if anyone ever connected him to Dominic he would lose his position in this town, and possibly even his seat in the Senate. He had come too far to have everything stripped away from him over the little matter of a few dead men who should never have been connected in the first place.

Chapter Six

Something was wrong. Terribly wrong.

That was Damon's first conscious thought as black nothingness disappeared and awareness returned. He was lying on something that felt suspiciously like a bloody uncomfortable bed, and five-star hotels did not have uncomfortable beds. He took a deep breath and frowned as the smells of antiseptic and sterile plastic filled his nose. What the hell?

Damon opened his eyes, trying to focus on...what was that? Was it a shower curtain? No. The fog in his brain cleared as he came fully awake. It was a partition. Damon turned his head on a white pillow and looked around. He really was in a bloody uncomfortable bed, covered with a functional sheet and a warm blanket, both white. An IV was taped to his left arm, inserted into the back of his hand. The line ran to a bag hanging from a tall, metal stand next to the bed.

Where the hell was he?

Damon tried to sit up and gasped softly as sharp pain sliced through his body. He let out a groan and sank back against the pillows. As soon as he relaxed, the slicing stopped, replaced by a dull, throbbing ache.

Hawk took a deep breath and forced himself to focus. What was the last thing he remembered? He'd start there. Maybe then he'd get some idea of how the hell he was lying in what seemed suspiciously like a hospital. Except he didn't do hospitals. They couldn't, he and Viper. It was too dangerous. So where was he?

They were on the balcony of the hotel.

The thought came to him suddenly. They had eaten dinner, and he was waiting for Sergei to put in an appearance at the hotel across the street. He was staying there with part of his entourage, and Hawk had been watching, waiting. Damon closed his eyes, his brows pulled together in concentration. That's right. He was waiting for his target to show, and Viper had been sitting on a lounge chair working on her laptop. She got up and went over to the table where the left-over dinner was laid out. They were talking about something, but

Damon couldn't remember the conversation. Then what? How did he get from a balcony with Viper to...wherever here was?

Voices interrupted his thoughts, and Damon listened as they entered the room.

"...doing very well," one said. "He's very fortunate. It could have been much, much worse. Whoever patched him up before he got here saved it from being more serious. The wound was cauterized, which stopped the bleeding and prevented infection from setting in."

The partition was pushed aside suddenly and Hawk's eyebrows soared into his forehead. A doctor had pulled the curtain aside, a wrinkled but clean white coat hanging over blue scrubs. It wasn't he who managed to surprise Hawk, however. Given the preceding conversation, he was expecting another doctor.

He was not expecting Charlie.

He stared at him, at a loss for words, and Charlie's gray eyes stared back calmly.

"Ah, you're awake," the doctor said, glancing at the monitor. "How do you feel?"

"Like hell," Damon replied, his voice hoarse. "Where am I? What happened?"

"You're in a trauma center in Virginia," Charlie told him. "This is Dr. White. He's been taking care of you."

Damon stared hard at Charlie, then turned his attention to the doctor examining a clipboard at the foot of his bed.

"Doctor," he murmured in acknowledgment.

"You've had quite a couple of days," Dr. White said, looking up. "You've been kept sedated, so I'm not surprised you're confused. What's the last thing you remember?"

Damon glanced at Charlie. He nodded, his unflappable calm reassuring.

"You can speak freely," Charlie said. "He's one of our surgeons."

"One of our..." Damon sputtered. "I didn't know we had surgeons."

Charlie smiled faintly.

"There's a lot you don't know."

Damon shook his head and looked back at the doctor waiting patiently for an answer.

"The last I remember, I was standing on a balcony in Singapore," he said. "What happened? How did I get to Virginia?"

"You were flown here," Charlie answered. He looked at the doctor. "Well?"

"He's certainly not showing any confusion outside of what's to be expected," Dr. White replied. He walked over to the side of the bed and leaned down. A small flashlight appeared in his hand from nowhere and he shone it into one of Damon's eyes, then the other. "How's your head? Does it hurt?"

"Everything hurts," Damon muttered, "but not my head especially. Why?"

"You had a mild concussion when you arrived," Dr. White said, straightening. "Not surprising, really. You have a pretty good-sized lump on the back of your head."

"I feel like I've got more than a lump on my head."

Charlie let out a guffaw at that.

"A little bit more, yes," the doctor said with a grin. "You don't remember anything?"

"I told you, the last thing I remember was standing on a balcony, looking at..." Damon's voice trailed off and his eyes widened. His heart started to pound and he suddenly went cold. "Oh my God," he breathed, looking at Charlie. "Where is she?!"

"Whoa, careful!"

Dr. White moved swiftly, holding Damon back against the pillows as he pushed himself upright with his arms. Even in his weakened state, Hawk was much stronger and Dr. White shot a look at Charlie as he struggled to subdue the suddenly frantic man.

"Calm down," Charlie barked, his voice acting like a bucket of ice water on fighting cats. "She's fine. Who do you think got you here?"

Damon sighed in relief and sank back against the pillows. Dr. White shook his head and stood up, straightening his coat.

"Good God, man, do you want to start hemorrhaging?!" he exclaimed. "You just got closed up an hour ago!"

Damon looked from him to Charlie and back again.

"Would you care to fill me in on my injuries?" he asked, forcing himself to speak more calmly.

Dr. White glanced at Charlie, who nodded back.

"It was a high-powered rifle," he said, "although, you look like you already knew that. The round entered your left side and nicked your large intestine before glancing off a rib, going through the muscle and exiting out the side. All things considered, you're one lucky son of a bitch. If the bullet had been just a little to the right, you wouldn't have made it here."

Damon stared at him.

"That's it?" he demanded. "It was a through and through?"

"That's it. You hit your head pretty good when you fell, but like I said, you're one lucky SOB." Dr. White scribbled something on his chart and hung it back on the foot of the bed. "I want you to stay calm until we get your blood pressure back to normal, so no more outbursts. I also want to monitor for infection, so we'll be taking blood regularly. No moving too much and no food yet. How's the pain? I can have the nurse put something through the IV if you like."

Hawk waved a hand impatiently.

"The pain is nothing," he said. "I've had worse. How soon before I'm cleared to leave?"

"Barring any complications, you should be up and around again in two to three weeks."

"Two to three…that's not going to work for me," Damon protested. "I can't just lie here for weeks!"

Dr. White looked at Charlie.

"This is where you come in," he said humorously. "I'll leave you to deal with it."

He turned and left the cubicle, leaving the curtain open, and Damon heard a door open and close beyond his line of vision. He turned his attention to Charlie.

"Where is she?" he demanded.

Charlie sighed and looked around. Spying a chair outside the cubicle, he stepped past the curtain and pulled it over to the side of the bed. He settled into it, crossing his legs comfortably.

"She's in DC right now, then it's my understanding that she's going back to New Jersey," he told him, sitting back. "Tell me what happened in Singapore."

Hawk stared at him for a moment, then shook his head.

"I don't know. I was waiting for Sergei Kuriev. She was standing about a foot away when...I saw a reflection in the hotel wall behind her. It was only a freak stroke of luck I saw it. There was a helicopter flying overhead and the lights glinted off the rifle. It lit it up like a beacon in the mirror finish on the side of the hotel."

Charlie studied him for a moment.

"You saw all that in a reflection?" he asked softly.

Damon shrugged.

"I wouldn't have seen it except for the light from the helicopter."

Charlie was silent for a moment.

"Then what happened?"

"Apparently I was shot," Damon retorted dryly.

Charlie's lips twitched despite himself.

"Do you think it was Sergei?" he asked.

Damon thought for a moment, then shook his head.

"He didn't know I was there," he said decidedly. "He never saw me, and none of his body guards know me."

Charlie nodded slowly.

"That's what I thought," he murmured.

"Was Viper hit?" Damon demanded. "Is she OK?"

Charlie studied him for a moment.

"She's fine," he said slowly. "For now. You heard what the doctor said. The bullet went through your side. What he doesn't know is that something threw it off target, which caused it to go through your side instead of your chest."

Hawk stared at him, feeling hot then cold.

"You mean..."

Charlie nodded somberly.

"If you weren't directly in front of her, and the shot was true, it would have hit Viper either in the throat or the head, depending on the path. Either way, she wouldn't have walked away." Charlie studied him for a moment. "Would you care to tell me why you saw fit to move yourself into the path of the shot?" he asked softly.

Damon met his gaze and a rueful smile crossed his face.

"How did you know?" he asked.

"She told me."

Damon was surprised into a bark of laughter, quickly choked back as pain gripped him with the sudden muscle contraction.

"Of course she did," he muttered. "Yes, I moved in front of her. I wasn't thinking, I was reacting. I saw a rifle and moved. What made the shot off target?"

Charlie shrugged.

"We don't know. It was a clear shot from the room the shooter was in. Viper's guess is the helicopter. She remembered it passing after you went down. She thinks the same light that showed you the rifle blinded the shooter."

"What?!"

"Dr. White was right. You've got some luck on your side, both of you," he said. "At the very least, one of you should be dead, most likely both. It was only a freak accident that saved you."

Hawk laid his head back and stared up at the ceiling, his mind whirling.

"Who knew she was there?" he demanded.

"No one," Charlie said flatly. "No one knew you were going except me."

Hawk looked at him. He pressed his lips together and was

silent for a moment.

"I can't be laid up here for two weeks," he said finally. "It's not gonna happen."

"I know."

Hawk looked at him, a glint of amusement creeping into his eyes, and Charlie sighed imperceptibly.

"Viper patched you up and took you to a private doctor in Singapore, who got you ready to travel. She had you in the air less than six hours after you were shot. She stabilized you, kept you sedated, and got you here to give you the best chance to recover quickly. It would be a shame to ruin all that effort by pushing yourself out of bed too soon."

"It's just a flesh wound."

"A nicked intestine isn't exactly a flesh wound," Charlie said dryly. "At least stay long enough to make sure no infection sets in and let the muscles start to heal. You're no good to me dead."

"I'm not going to die," Hawk retorted, "and there's no infection. Dr. White said that when you two walked in. You can't honestly expect me to hang out in bed while someone is hunting Viper. If they found out she was halfway around the world in Singapore, they'll find out she's in New Jersey."

"She said the same thing just as she was leaving," Charlie nodded. "I didn't get the impression it bothered her. In fact, just the opposite. I think she's looking forward to it."

Hawk started to laugh, then groaned instead.

"Of course she is," he muttered. "She's looking for blood."

"If she wasn't already, she certainly is now," Charlie agreed thoughtfully. "I wish she'd found what I sent her to Singapore for, but I suppose it will happen in its own time now."

"Who is the ex-soldier you had her looking for?" Hawk asked, sending Charlie a sharp look.

Charlie returned the look squarely, his gray eyes hooded.

"Someone who tipped the scales," he said obscurely.

Hawk scowled.

"Well isn't that helpful," he muttered. "And Sergei?"

"Oh, you'll have to finish that," Charlie said matter-of-factly. "However, it can wait until you're healthy. By then he'll be back in Georgia and it will be more difficult, but that's something you're used to."

Charlie stood up and buttoned his charcoal suit jacket.

"I'm glad you're not dead," he said, looking down at Damon.

Damon grinned despite his pain.

"So am I."

"Let me know if and when you decide to check yourself out. And try to give yourself every chance to heal. I don't know how long we have before Viper takes matters into her own hands. I'd rather you were a hundred percent when that happens."

"You think that's likely?" Hawk asked, startled.

"Given the look in her eyes when she left, I'd say it's very likely." Charlie paused, considering his next words. "It's my understanding the house in Medford is still secure, but I don't expect her to stay there long. Once she starts hunting - and she will - whoever arranged for the shooter to take the shot in Singapore will have another chance."

Hawk nodded, his blue eyes serious.

"Where are you with that leak in Washington?" he asked softly. "That's where this all started. That's where it'll end."

"This is larger than just a leak," Charlie said unexpectedly. His eyes met Hawk's. "I'm working on it. I need you to trust me, and keep her alive while I sort it out."

Blue eyes bore into gray, and after a long moment, Hawk nodded.

Charlie turned to leave, then paused.

"She stayed until you went into surgery," he added, almost as an afterthought. "She asked me to give you a message."

Damon raised an eyebrow questioningly.

"Well?"

"She said you owe her a tour of Singapore."

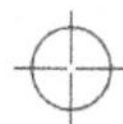

Michael groaned and opened one eye, peering at the clock on the bedside table. The luminescent blue numbers read 2:54 and he groaned again. AC/DC continued to toll bells from his cell phone and he reached for it tiredly.

"You'd better be dying," he growled.

"Not today, gunny, not today," a cheerful voice greeted him, "although not for lack of trying on someone's part."

Michael sat bolt upright.

"Lina?"

"I don't know why you sound so surprised. You've called fourteen times since Sunday."

"Fourteen…did I?" Michael rubbed a hand over his face,

trying to focus. "I was trying to get hold of you."

"Clearly. Everything ok?"

"Yeah, everything's just dandy," he muttered. "You know, aside from the bombs and the terrorists loose in the country."

There was a short silence, then she chuckled.

"Well if that's all, you can go back to sleep. That's old news."

"Why are you calling at three in the morning?" Michael asked, leaning back against his headboard.

"I just landed and it seemed like a good time to catch you."

"Just landed where?"

"I'll touch base with you tomorrow sometime," Alina told him, ignoring his question, "and you can tell me what warrants fourteen calls."

"Sorry about that," he said ruefully. "I had no idea it was that many."

"Don't worry. Stephanie has you beat by three."

Michael grinned despite himself.

"That's what you get for disappearing on us. Where did you go, anyway?"

"A little island getaway. I needed a break."

Michael snorted.

"Yeah ok, and I'm selling the Brooklyn Bridge. Have you talked to Stephanie yet?" he asked suddenly.

"No. Why?"

"Blake's got himself in a jam. I thought she could invite him up there for a few days."

A beat of silence followed, and Michael was just wondering if she was still there when she spoke.

"What happened?" she asked sharply.

"Someone broke into his house last night," Michael told her. "It doesn't look good."

"What did they do?"

"They planted drugs in his closet."

Michael's eyebrows soared into his forehead when he heard her swear softly.

"Who found them?"

"Luckily, he did. He's reported it all to his superiors and they're investigating." Michael yawned widely. "I just think it would be best if he got out of the city for a few days."

"Agreed," Alina said, surprising him.

Michael frowned.

"You're thinking something. What?"

"Nothing I can tell you now," she answered shortly. "I'll talk to Steph and follow up with you tomorrow. Thanks for telling me."

Michael blinked, surprised.

"You're welcome…why are you thanking me? Is everything ok?"

She chuckled again, the sound low.

"I'll talk to you tomorrow."

And then she was gone.

Michael sighed and put the phone back on his side table, lying back down. He stared at the clock, his mind churning. She hadn't seemed surprised Blake was being framed. In fact, if he didn't know better, he would have thought she almost expected it. He frowned. What was going on? Where had she disappeared to? And why was she suddenly thanking him for information? She'd never thanked him before.

So many questions.

As he drifted back to sleep, Michael wondered if things could possibly get any stranger. As soon as the thought crossed his mind, he groaned. It was probably just getting started.

Chapter Seven

Angela glanced at her watch and sat back with a yawn, rubbing her forehead. It seemed like a good idea this morning to come into the office at five-thirty and get off to an early start after her trip. Now however, Angela was tired of the computer screen and the stale, forced air pumping out of the vents above her head. She sighed. It was almost four-thirty. Perhaps she'd leave half an hour early. The thought had no sooner entered her head then the phone on her desk rang. Her boss was calling.

"Hi Jeff," she answered, looking at her computer screen as an email popped up in the bottom right corner. "What's up?"

"I just got off a conference call with the Miami office," he told her. "They're singing your praises down there. Good job getting them onboard with the new clients!"

"Thanks. It wasn't easy, but I managed to convince them," she said with a laugh. "I think the last round of tequila helped."

"Ha! That's not what I heard. Sounds like you had them in the conference room before the wining and dining. Keep it up! That's why we put you in this position. We need fresh thinking, and you're it."

"Well thank you." Angela clicked open the email, scanning it quickly. "I do have to request some time off though. I'm not sure when, but I'll need a couple days soon."

"Anything you need. Everything ok?"

"A friend of mine passed away a few days ago," she replied, sitting back in her chair again. "It was actually quite a shock. The funeral arrangements are still being made, but as soon as I have the day, I'll let you know."

"Oh my God, I'm so sorry to hear that. What happened?"

"It was a car accident."

"I am so sorry, Angie. Anything you need, just let me know."

"Thanks. I think I'll head out now, get a jump on the weekend. I may work from home Monday if there's nothing you need me in the office for?"

"Not that I can think of," Jeff said slowly. "Don't forget the call with New York at ten."

"I won't."

"Oh, before you go, have you heard anything more on Trasker Pharmaceuticals?" he asked.

Angela frowned.

"No, but I expect to hear from them in the next day or two. Why?"

"I've got someone coming in Monday from their head office. Guy by the name of Trent Whitfield. He says he met you in Miami?"

"Yes. He's the one who pulled the rest of their executive team onboard. He's their Vice President of Production. I didn't know he was coming. Maybe I shouldn't work from home. Do you want me here?"

"I don't think that's really necessary," Jeff said. "He's just coming to do an initial audit. Nothing official. You've done your part. He's actually flying in today, but there's a trade show in Atlantic City tomorrow he's promised to, so he won't be here until Monday."

"That's a long weekend. I don't envy him." Angela closed her email. "I'll head out then. If you need anything, you know how to reach me."

"Will do."

Angela hung up and closed the rest of the programs on her computer before shutting down. All things considered, her boss was a good man. As much as she disliked the bank they worked for, she had to admit she was enjoying her new position. Jeff was a great boss and her work kept her busy.

She reached into her bottom drawer and pulled out her purse, pushing her chair back and standing. She picked up her bag from the floor and set it on the chair while she disconnected her laptop from the docking station. Sliding it into the bag, she glanced at the top of her desk to make sure she wasn't leaving anything classified out. Satisfied her desk was clear, she hooked the laptop bag over her shoulder and picked up her purse, turning to leave the office.

Angela emerged into the late afternoon sunshine, took a deep breath, and dropped her sunglasses from the top of her head onto her nose. A brisk wind smacked her in the face and she shivered. Easter was on Sunday, but winter was holding on, gusting its icy fingers at every opportunity. She would be glad when it finally gave up and the warmer weather gained ground. She was heartily sick of the cold, especially after the balmy breezes of Florida.

She walked to the end of the sidewalk and stepped off the curb, starting across the large parking lot. It was good to get out of the office a little early. She wondered what Stephanie was doing for dinner. Perhaps she'd see if she wanted to meet. There was nothing in her house to eat, and Angela didn't feel like tackling the grocery store tonight. Reaching into her purse, she pulled out her phone and hit speed dial. Maybe she could talk her into Italian.

"Hey, I was just thinking about you," Stephanie said by way of greeting.

"Should I be worried?"

"I finally got hold of Alina and was thinking I should let you know she's still alive," she replied with a laugh.

"Where is she? Did she say?"

"No, but she said she'll be back soon. So what's up?"

"I'm calling to see if you have any interest in going to dinner," Angela said.

"Possibly. I don't have anything planned. Blake is coming in later, but he got held up in DC. What did you have in mind?"

"I was thinking Italian," Angela said, crossing over to the next aisle where her silver BMW was parked. "Maybe Toscano's?"

"What time?"

Angela glanced at her watch as she headed toward her car.

"I'm leaving work now, so anytime really," she said. "When is good for you?"

Angela pulled out her keys and pressed the fob to unlock the car. She frowned, tilting her head. Something seemed different.

"I can meet whenever you want. Do you want to say five-thirty?" Stephanie was asking.

Angela gasped suddenly as she realized what was wrong with her car.

"Oh my God!" she exclaimed.

"What?"

"My car! It's got a flat tire!" Angela stared at the front driver side tire. "What the hell?!"

"Do you have a spare?" Stephanie asked, unperturbed.

"No. They're run flats." Angela opened her door and reached in to put her laptop bag and purse on the passenger seat. "What am I going to do?"

"Call roadside assistance?"

"You're joking, right?" Angela demanded, straightening up and staring at the offending tire. "They'll take hours!"

"Well, what do you want me to do? You don't have a spare."

"How can this even happen? I have run flats!"

"That doesn't make them invincible, Ang."

"I can still drive on it, right?"

"Sure, but you'll have to buy a new tire."

"Then why the hell are they called run flats?!"

"Because technically you can go some miles on it before it conks out on you," Stephanie said, laughing.

"Well, this just sucks." Angela glanced at her watch. "I don't want to put out for a new tire. My whole life is a lie!"

"Call roadside assistance and I'll come get you."

"OK. I'm in the side lot."

Angela hung up and glared at the tire, then slid behind the wheel and opened her glove box to look for the card with the roadside assist number. After some digging she finally located it in the book that came with the car. She closed the glove box and grabbed her purse. She would call from her desk phone and wait for Stephanie in her office. She was just turning away from the car when a tall figure stepped out from the other side of an SUV a few vehicles away.

"Angela?"

Angela started and glanced up, her eyes widening in surprise at the sight of the man. He was dressed casually in faded jeans and a polo shirt, and his brown hair curled at his temples. An easy smile crossed his face as his gray eyes met hers.

"Trent!"

"I thought that was you," he said, stopping a few feet away. "I just got in from the airport and figured I'd see where I'm coming Monday."

"Jeff mentioned you were coming."

Trent Whitfield glanced at her purse, then to the BMW next to her.

"Are you heading out?" he asked.

"I was, but now I'm not going anywhere. I have a flat." She motioned to the front tire. "I was just going back in to call roadside assistance."

Trent made a sympathetic noise.

"That sucks," he exclaimed. "Do you have a spare?"

"No. It didn't come with one. It has run flats, so they say you don't need a spare," Angela said, disgruntled. "But I'm not driving on that. If I can save the tire, I will."

"If you just picked up a nail, you should be able to plug it,"

Trent said, walking over to crouch down and look at the tire. "Was the pressure low this morning?"

"No." Angela watched as he examined what he could see of the tire. "Hopefully that's all it is."

"I don't know if BMW will plug a tire, though," he said, standing again and glancing at her. "They'll probably say you need a new one."

"But what choice do I have? I don't have a spare to change it."

Trent nodded, looking down at the tire thoughtfully.

"Your best bet would probably be to call a tire store in the morning and have them tow it. Do you know a good tire place?"

Angela laughed.

"Are you serious?" she demanded. "I don't even know a mechanic. I have the dealership do all the maintenance."

Trent looked at her and his eyes lit in amusement.

"Then you're getting ripped off on oil changes," he told her with a laugh. "I'm sure someone you work with knows somewhere. Let's go in and ask."

Angela shook her head.

"You don't have to waste your time with this," she said with a smile. "This isn't how you want to spend your evening."

"Like I have anything better to do. I'm checked in at the Marriott down the road and was looking at Applebee's for dinner. Not exactly show-stopping plans."

"Yeah, but this isn't your problem," Angela replied with a short laugh. "That's a good idea about the tire store, though. I'm sure one of my friends knows somewhere."

Trent nodded, turning to look at the tire again, and Angela surreptitiously glanced at her watch. Stephanie lived about twenty minutes away. Hopefully, she was already on her way. As much as she had enjoyed Trent's company in Florida, she had left him in Florida without another thought. Now, here he was again. While she was sure he was very nice, Angela was hungry and tired and looking for a quiet evening with one of her oldest friends.

"Do you want me to drive you home?" Trent offered, looking back to her.

"Thank you, but I have a friend on the way," Angela said. "I was going to call roadside assistance while I waited, but I think you're right. I'll wait and have it towed in the morning."

"It's a shame. I hope you didn't have any plans to drive anywhere tonight."

"Yeah, it sucks, but at least I saw it before I drove away.

Otherwise, I'd be stuck at the side of the road right now."

Trent nodded, his eyes unreadable.

"That's true," he murmured. "Lucky you saw it."

Angela looked at him and the easy smile reappeared.

"Do you want me to wait with you until your friend shows up?"

"I'm fine," she assured him. "Don't worry about me."

"You have to let me do something to help," Trent protested. "I'm a Southern boy. It's what we do. We help pretty little ladies in distress."

Angela's eyes narrowed just slightly even as she laughed politely.

"But I'm not in distress! I'm just pissed off I have to wait an extra half hour for dinner!" she laughed. "Seriously, Trent, I'm fine. You go find your own dinner and don't worry about me."

He grinned and nodded.

"Fair enough," he agreed reluctantly, turning to walk back to his SUV. "I'm sure I'll see you Monday. Enjoy your dinner!"

"Thanks. You too!"

Angela watched him walk around to the driver's door and get behind the wheel before she turned and unlocked her car. She got in and closed the door, inserting the key and turning it to auxiliary so she could press the power locks.

Pretty little lady, indeed. He made her sound like a useless flower whose only function was to look good.

Pulling out her phone, Angela swiped the screen and opened her email. Hopefully Stephanie would arrive soon. She was hungry, tired, and clearly getting grumpier by the minute. At this rate, she'd be biting her own head off soon. She sighed. A nice quiet dinner and a few drinks with Steph was just what she needed. She would probably know somewhere she could call in the morning about the car, and in the meantime, all Angela could do was wait.

Chapter Eight

Viper slipped into the empty office and closed the door softly behind herself. She didn't bother with the light, pulling a slender Maglite from her jacket pocket instead. Switching it on, she quickly directed it around the dark, windowless office before moving toward the large desk.

This section of the Pentagon was deserted at this time of night and Viper sat behind the desk, pulling a slim drive from her inside jacket pocket. Bending down, she plugged it into the PC under the desk and turned the computer on. She glanced at her watch. She had about twenty minutes to find what she was looking for before the cleaning crew came through this wing. When that happened, she had to be gone.

This had to be one of the crazier things she'd done in a long time. If Hawk knew where she was, he'd either have a coronary or laugh himself silly. Alina wasn't sure which. She pursed her lips.

Hawk.

Anger washed through her anew as she thought of him, laying in a pool of blood on a stone balcony. The bullet had glanced off his rib, causing very minimal damage in the end. Once she had him stabilized and got him to the surgeon, Viper knew that the worst was behind him. The problem was that he'd been hit at all, and with a bullet meant for her. Of that, she had no doubt. If he hadn't thrown himself in front of her, it was doubtful she would be alive. Even with the bullet off-target, where it hit Damon would have corresponded to the right side of her chest.

The computer finished loading and she bent her mind to the task at hand, setting aside the conflicting emotions clamoring for attention. Now was not the time to ponder what-ifs. Now was the time to find the bastard responsible.

In less than two minutes Viper was past the security and firewall, and into the system used by the Unites States Defense Department. Harry would have her head on a platter if he knew what she was up to. As her fingers moved rapidly across the keys, Alina's lips tightened thoughtfully. Harry was still working with Homeland Security and, as far as she could tell, he was showing no signs of coming back to the dark side. Whether that was by choice or because Charlie still needed him over there was anyone's guess. The two were masters of subterfuge and had practically written the playbook for all the intelligence operations in the past ten years. It was impossible to tell what role Harry was really playing at DHS, but one thing Viper knew for sure: he'd throw a fit if he ever found out she'd internally broken into the Department of Defense.

Charlie, on the other hand, would probably just shrug and tell Harry the problem was with the security, not his asset. Viper's lips curved briefly. Charlie's attitude had shifted over the past months. His strict adherence to protocol had eased a bit, as she had seen yesterday when she left him in Virginia with Hawk. His parting words to her were to find the person responsible for the shooting. She got the impression he was not terribly concerned with how she did it.

After another minute, Alina found herself looking at a list of all current and prior servicemen and women now living in Singapore. The list was not long, and she quickly copied it onto the external drive before entering another search criterion. The next list she pulled was significantly longer. She scrolled through it, scanning the names before copying them as well. A large number of servicemen and women had bank accounts in Singapore, more than she was expecting. Alina was just about to navigate away from the page when a name caught her eye. She frowned, staring at it. Jordan Murphy.

Now why was that name jumping out at her?

Viper glanced at her watch, then opened a different database, entering the name. Multiple hits came up and she scrolled through them swiftly, stopping on one towards the end of the list. That particular Jordan Murphy was honorably discharged from the Marines four years ago. She clicked on him, pulling up his service record and glancing through it. She froze suddenly as a sharp chill rolled through her. Alina stared at the screen, her heart pounding. After a spellbound second, she copied the entire service record before she could think twice.

Five minutes later the door was closing softly behind her, the office dark and empty.

Michael unlocked his door and stepped into the house, flipping the switch on the wall. Light flooded the entryway and he closed the door, tossing his keys onto the hall stand. He set the deadbolt tiredly and turned to go down the hall to the kitchen at the back of the house. There was leftover pizza in the fridge, and a beer was calling his name.

He was passing the door to the dining room on his right when a shiver of awareness streaked down his spine. Michael frowned in reaction and turned his head, glancing into the dark room. Something caught his attention and he paused, turning toward the doorway.

"Long day, gunny?"

Michael started and stepped into the dining room, flipping on the light. Seated comfortably in a chair in the far corner was Alina, her legs crossed. She was dressed in black SWAT pants and a lightweight black jacket hung open to reveal a charcoal gray shirt underneath. She blended so completely with the shadows that if it weren't for her speaking, he would never have seen her.

"Lina!" he exclaimed, his heart pounding. "What are you doing ?!"

Her lips curved into a smile that didn't reach her eyes. It was a look he was getting to know well.

"Dropping in to say hi," she replied, uncrossing her legs and standing up smoothly. "I hope I didn't startle you too much."

Michael opened his mouth, then closed it again wordlessly. This time the smile that crossed her lips was genuine, and her eyes lit with amusement.

"Cat got your tongue?" she murmured, walking up to him. "I think this is a first."

"This is the first time you've surprised me," he retorted.

"Not quite the first time."

Michael's face darkened and he scowled at the gentle reminder of when she'd caught him unaware and knocked him out cold next to his truck.

"Well *that* won't happen again," he muttered, turning to continue on his way to the kitchen. "I'm having some cold pizza and a beer. Care to join me?"

"I'll pass on the pizza," she said, following him, "but I'll take a beer."

Michael glanced at her, surprised.

"Bad day?" he asked, going to the fridge and pulling out two bottles of beer. He turned to hand her one before reaching back in for the pizza.

"Bad couple of days," Alina answered.

Michael shot her a sharp look as he set the pizza on the

kitchen island before turning to grab a piece of paper towel from the roll on the counter.

"That's doesn't sound good," he said. "Why don't you come see my latest project and you can tell me about it?"

Alina raised an eyebrow.

"Your latest project?" she repeated.

Michael nodded and pulled a piece of pizza out of the box, biting into it as he walked over to the door leading into his garage.

"Trust me," he mumbled with a grin.

Alina followed him down the couple wooden steps into the garage he had turned into a wood shop. The smell of fresh sawdust filled the air and a tabletop rested across two saw horses.

"Another table?" she asked. "Tired of the dining room already?"

"This is for the kitchen," he said, pulling a stool out from under the work bench along the wall. "Have a seat."

Alina glanced at it.

"I'm ok," she said. "Let me guess. You know this room is secure?"

Michael grinned.

"Good guess. I used to sweep it every day for listening devices, but after the tapped phones last week, I went one step further. When I got back from Brooklyn I installed infrared sensors. No one can get in here now without my knowing."

Alina nodded and sipped her beer, moving around the table slowly.

"Smart move," she told him. "If I were you, I'd do the whole house."

"Is it that bad?"

"It can't hurt to be on your guard. Where are you with Trasker?"

"It's slow." Michael sat on the stool and took another bite of pizza. "I'm still waiting on a subpoena for the internal records. It will be a lot easier when I get that."

"You have it." Alina paused in her slow pacing to look at him. "It was signed tonight."

Michael stared at her, dumbfounded.

"How?"

"I convinced someone it was a priority," she answered calmly. "Gunny, it pays to know people like us. We come in handy on occasion."

"Us?"

"I spoke to someone and was able to make them see it my way." Alina took another drink, easily avoiding his question. "What about that other issue I asked you to work on? How's that going?"

"The subject covered his past pretty thoroughly," Michael said slowly, watching her. "Someone who's gone to the trouble he has usually doesn't want something uncovered."

Her dark eyes met his solemnly.

"I know. I told you it wouldn't be easy."

"What's going on?" Michael asked quietly. "Why did you just disappear on Sunday? And why do you have me digging into the past of a war hero?"

Alina studied him for a moment, her face emotionless, the mask in place. Michael had no idea what she was thinking, or even if she would answer, and a wave of frustration welled up inside of him. Last week she asked him to do background research on someone, without any explanation of why. She made it clear doing so was dangerous and that others had already died over it. In a moment of what he could only assume was temporary insanity on his part, he had agreed. Now he wanted answers, and it didn't look like any were going to be forthcoming.

"How much do you really want to know, gunny?" she finally asked, serious. "The more you know, the more dangerous it is for you."

Michael finished his pizza, his eyes never leaving her face.

"You said it's already dangerous for me. A little situational awareness can't go amiss."

A flash of amusement shot into her eyes and was gone just as quickly. If he hadn't been watching her so closely, he would have missed it altogether.

"Typical Marine," she murmured. "I didn't disappear Sunday. Not intentionally, anyway. I was sent away for work."

Michael raised an eyebrow.

"I thought you were already working," he pointed out. "You went after a terrorist. That *is* your job, correct?"

"Yes, and I found him. Job over."

"And right on to the next one?" Michael asked incredulously. "Don't you get a break?"

Alina grinned despite herself.

"No rest for the wicked, gunny," she said. "However, in the interest of full disclosure, I believe the assignment is related."

"Is?"

Alina's lips twitched as he latched onto that one word.

"You catch on quick," she said, lifting her bottle to her lips and taking a sip. "Things didn't turn out quite as expected."

Michael saw the tightening of her lips and the clenching of her jaw and his eyes narrowed.

"What happened?" he asked softly.

"Someone took a shot at me and hit Damon."

"What?!" Michael roared, his irritation forgotten.

Alina smiled faintly at this reaction.

"You wanted to know why I had a bad couple of days."

"Is he alive?" he demanded.

"Yes, but only through pure luck." Alina began pacing, her mask sliding back into place. "A helicopter was flying between the buildings at the time. I think the light blinded the shooter. The bullet was off-target. It nicked his intestine, glanced off his rib and came out his side."

"Thank God for that," Michael breathed, watching her controlled movements. "Where is he?"

"Somewhere safe. He's in good hands for now, but I want him moved as soon as possible."

"You don't trust where he is?"

"No," she said bluntly. "In fact, I don't trust much of anything right now."

"You're sure the shot was meant for you?"

"Yes."

Michael studied her for a moment. He knew she wasn't telling him everything and the frustration returned in a sudden wave.

"I'm going for another piece of pizza," he said, standing. "Another beer?"

"No, thanks." Alina finished her beer and handed him the empty bottle. "I have another stop after this."

Michael nodded and took the empty bottle, turning to go back into the house. He grabbed another slice of pizza and bit into it while he turned to the fridge to get another beer for himself, shaking his head. Someone tried to kill her and hit the SEAL instead. A chill went down Michael's spine again, just as it had when she said it the first time. He'd got to know Damon a little bit over the past year, at least as well as one *could* know the former Navy SEAL turned government assassin. Michael liked him, and always got the impression the feeling was returned. However, knowing he took a bullet meant for Alina had Michael feeling suddenly inadequate.

Eleven years ago Alina's brother Dave was his best friend and fellow gunnery sergeant in the Marines. He made Michael promise to look out for his little sister if anything happened to him. The day Dave

Maschik died in Iraq, Michael stepped up to make good on his promise. Unfortunately, he'd been unable to find her until last year, when she unceremoniously found him. Now it seemed that the SEAL was doing more to take care of her than Michael had yet.

Michael grabbed a bottle of water for Alina along with his beer and turned back to the garage. How the hell did it happen? Who knew where she was? For that matter, who knew *who* she was? So many questions.

He went back into the garage to find Alina near the automatic door examining one of the sensors.

"This isn't bad," she said as he came back, not turning her head from the sensor. "It will stop your average criminal."

"But not you?" he asked, walking over to hand her the water with a grin.

She straightened up and looked at him, taking the water. A small smile pulled at her lips.

"No, but not much can."

"Why do you think the shot was meant for you?" Michael asked, his green eyes meeting hers. "Why not Damon?"

"Because he threw himself in the way," she said simply, turning to walk back over to the table. She pulled another stool out from under the workbench and settled onto it, opening her water. "If he hadn't, it would have hit me."

"You said it was off-target?" Michael sat on his stool and sipped his beer. "Where do you think it would have gone if it wasn't?"

"And he didn't act like a damn hero?" Alina asked. "My best guess is my forehead."

Michael's stomach dropped inside him and he scowled.

"A sniper?"

"Yes, but not an experienced one," she answered. "The light from the helicopter would have been enough to throw them off-target if they were using a night scope. Only an amateur would have taken the shot before it passed by. A professional would have waited."

"Thank God for that," Michael breathed. "Who knew you were there?"

Silence followed that question and he glanced at her sharply. The look on her face made him inwardly shiver.

"That's the big question," she finally said, raising cold, hard eyes to his. "As far as I knew, no one."

Michael stared at her.

"What?"

Alina sighed, sipped her water, and turned to face him

reluctantly.

"I haven't been entirely straight with you," she said slowly. "There's a lot going on you don't know about."

"I figured as much," he said, meeting her gaze squarely. "I also know you can't tell me as much as I'd like."

"That's true. I shouldn't be talking to you at all."

"You do realize I have top security clearance?" he said, suddenly amused. "I'm Secret Service for God's sake. I'm cleared to protect the President."

"This is beyond security clearance, gunny." Alina got up restlessly, setting the water bottle on her stool and turning to resume pacing. "It's your safety I'm worried about."

"My safety?" Michael demanded, his eyebrows soaring into his forehead. "I'm not the one getting shot at."

She glanced at him.

"I'm only going to tell you what I think you need to know. The more you know..."

"The more dangerous it is. You said that already. Start talking."

Alina let out a short laugh despite her dark mood.

"You Marines, you all think you're invincible," she muttered. "I'm starting to think you're all just too dumb to realize your own mortality."

"Oh, we realize it," he countered cheerfully. "We just don't care."

A rare, genuine smile transformed her face and Michael watched her eyes light with amusement. His own lips curved in response. This was the Lina he wanted to see more of, not the stony, mechanical professional she'd been since she called to him from the shadows of his dining room.

"Never change, gunny," she told him. "The world needs more people like you." The smile faded from her face and she continued her restless pacing. "When you came to see me in Jersey two weeks ago, I'd just gotten back from a long trip. One of my stops was Syria."

Michael was silent, watching as she circled the table top slowly. Her mask was back in place and he had no hint as to what she was thinking as she spoke; only that she seemed to be considering her words very carefully. His lips tightened at the mention of Syria. He didn't want to consider what could have happened to her in that unstable and volatile country.

"While I was there, someone recognized me. For lack of a better phrase, my cover was blown."

Michael stared at her.

"How is that possible?"

The look he encountered from her was chilling.

"That's the crux of the whole problem."

"What happened?"

"I was followed out of Syria, then Greece, then the Italian Special Service picked it up through Italy." Alina glanced at him. "None of those people should have had any idea I was there, or even who I am."

"And now they've probably spread the information," Michael said with a scowl.

"Oh, they aren't talking to anyone," Viper said matter-of-factly. "The information died with them."

Michael knew what she did for a living but nevertheless, that left him speechless. She smiled a twisted smile at his dumbfounded look.

"Don't look so horrified, Michael. It was self-defense."

"But…Italy is an ally!" he sputtered. "You can't just go around..." his voice trailed off at the patently amused look on her face.

"I think you're getting distracted from the primary point," she said gently. "People who shouldn't know I exist knew what I look like."

Michael sucked in his breath as understanding hit.

"You think it's someone here," he stated rather than asked.

"You didn't know it at the time, but your hunch that someone in Washington was planning another terrorist attack was closer to the truth than you realized," Alina told him grimly.

"Is it someone in your organization?"

"We're trying to figure that out now," she replied. "Personally, I think it's higher up, but they could have someone in my agency. Either way, my boss is working on it."

"Apparently not hard enough. They knew where you were. And where *were* you, anyway?" Michael asked, lifting his beer to his lips.

Alina glanced at him.

"The other side of the world," she said evasively. "Whoever it is, they've got eyes and ears in very select places. No one knew we were there."

"Well someone did," Michael pointed out gently. She was silent and he sighed, running a hand over his short hair. "Ok. So someone's gunning for you, and we're pretty sure it's someone here in DC. Is that why you have me doing that background? You think it's him?"

"No, but I think he can lead me to them," she said. "It's complicated."

"Clearly." Michael finished his beer and set the empty bottle on the workbench behind him. "Answer me this. Why are you still here? And by here, I mean stateside. Why haven't you disappeared?"

"Run away?" she stopped pacing and stared at him. "You can't be serious."

"Lina, you're trained to be invisible," he said, leaning forward. "Hell, you're a ghost. Use it! Get the hell out of here and let your agency handle it. This isn't a game. They'll kill you."

"You think I don't know that?" She swung around to face him and Michael found himself staring at Viper. Any remnant of the Alina he knew was gone, and the intimidating weapon his country had produced was in her place. "If I run now, I'll never stop. I don't trust anyone right now, especially my own people, so I sure as hell won't trust someone else to find the bastard. You're right. I'm trained to be a ghost and I'll be one right here, until I find the son of a bitch."

Michael blinked at the sudden fury flaring in those dark eyes and, in that instant, saw the raw emotion driving her.

"What can I do to help?"

He gave up trying to get her to leave. She wasn't going anywhere. The only thing he could do now was try to help her get out of this alive. There was no point wasting time bemoaning the situation. There would be time enough for that later, when it was all over.

"You're already doing it. Find the money trail to Trasker, and get me all the information you can with the background search."

"And you? What are you going to do?"

Alina sighed and went back to perch on her stool, picking up her water. She took a long drink, then capped the bottle.

"I have to go back to Jersey," she said quietly. "I have John's funeral to deal with, and I need to recoup my armory while I can."

Michael studied her thoughtfully for a long moment.

"What about the terrorists?" he asked. "One of them floated up in the Potomac yesterday."

"Yes, I know. You ID'd him."

Michael stared at her, taken aback.

"How the hell do you know that?!" he demanded.

"Did you really think a terrorist could float up in Washington, DC and we wouldn't hear about it?" she asked, amused.

"But how do you know I was the one who identified him?"

"Who else could have? I'm the only other person who knows what they look like, and I know it wasn't me."

Michael blinked and grinned sheepishly.

"Oh. Good point. I ID'd him as one of the terrorists, but we don't have a name. Care to share whose body we have?"

"His name was Nasser Hussein. As for the other two, I'll take care of them." Alina stood up. "In the meantime, you just keep on Trasker and Mr. X."

"Mr. X?" Michael raised an eyebrow. "That's what you're calling him?"

"That's what he is right now," she said with a shrug. "He's the X factor in all of this. He may turn out to be nothing, or everything."

Alina turned toward the door to the house, then paused and turned back, pulling something out of her jacket pocket.

"Oh! Here." She handed him a slim box. "It's a clean phone and charger. Use that to contact me."

Michael took the box and nodded.

"I haven't addressed the phone situation, yet," he told her. "I'll deal with it later, when this is all over. For now, I'm just letting whoever tapped them think we're not onto them."

"That's the best thing you can do," she agreed. "It will give them a false sense of security and superiority."

"Exactly."

"That's why I got the clean phone. I need to be able to contact you and know it's secure. Don't use that phone for anyone else, not even Blake. The more the number is used, the less secure it becomes."

"Don't worry," Michael said, following her to the door. "I'll make sure it stays secure. You just make sure you stay alive or this will all be for nothing."

Chapter Nine

The man stepped out of the abandoned factory and into the sunlight. He put on large sunglasses, shielding his eyes from the glare, and turned toward the beige sedan parked a few feet away. Walking toward the car, he pulled out his phone and hit speed dial. The call was picked up after one ring.

"He's dead," he said flatly.

There was a pause on the line, then a sigh.

"May Allah welcome him home at last," a voice said. "Did you find the body?"

"No. It's been removed." The man opened the door and got behind the wheel, gazing at the large, deteriorating building in front of him. "The house is cleaned out and the truck is gone. Nothing remains."

"Nothing at all?"

"No. They were very thorough."

"How do you know he's dead? Perhaps they took him."

"I found where he was killed," the man said heavily. "The wire he was tied with is still on the floor and the cement is stained with blood."

There was silence on the line for a long moment.

"You're sure it was his?"

"Who else? This place is less than a mile from the house and the blood stain appears new. Asad's last contact was five days ago, on Sunday. The stain is still dark, not faded. The wire on the ground is tied in professional knots. What else could it be?"

There was another silence on the line, then another sigh.

"What do we do now? Nasser hasn't checked in since Saturday. Asad believed he was caught or killed. Now Asad is dead. If they cleaned out the house, they have everything."

The man was quiet for a long moment, staring at the building. Anger was building inside him, slow and steady.

"Not everything," he said quietly. "We can still make a statement."

"Not enough of one. We have failed."

"Not yet." The man closed the door and started the engine. "We haven't failed until we fail to avenge Asad's death."

"How?"

"We find the one who killed him."

"We don't even know where to start!" the voice protested. "It's impossible. We don't even have a name. Perhaps we should go back to Damascus. We can form a new plan. Try again."

"We can't go back," the man said sharply. "We stay and find his killer. We plan. We've come too far to stop now."

"Yes, but we don't even know who we're looking for!"

The man tightened his lips grimly. He shifted the car into drive with one hand, while the remaining three fingers of his left hand gripped the steering wheel until his knuckles turned white.

"Yes, we do. We are looking for the Viper."

Angela unlocked the door to her townhouse and stepped inside, flipping on the light. She lifted a hand to wave to Stephanie, closing the door as the Mustang pulled away from the curb. A small bell jingled as an orange tabby cat jumped from her spot in the chair. She started toward Angela, pausing midway to stretch languidly before continuing toward her mistress.

Angela bent to pet her cat fondly before straightening and walking across the living room to the stairs. She dropped her purse and keys on the side console along the wall, her cat strolling after her.

"What a day, Bella," she murmured. "I hope yours was better than mine."

She started up the stairs, intent on getting out of her work clothes and into yoga pants. She was halfway up when her cell phone began ringing and she sighed loudly, turning to go back down and grab it out of her purse. Anabelle sat on the step, watching her. After a moment she began cleaning one paw while she waited. Angela grabbed her phone and hit accept, turning back to the stairs.

"Hello?"

"You called?"

Angela sighed in relief.

"Lina!" she exclaimed. "Where are you?"

There was a short silence.

"You called to ask where I am?" Alina sounded amused. "Are you really that bored?"

"Well, no. I called to see how you are," Angela said, starting back up the stairs again. Anabelle dropped her paw as she passed and followed behind her again. "Stephanie said you're not home yet."

"I'll be home tomorrow."

"Good! How are you?"

"Fine."

"Fine?"

There was another short silence.

"What's on your mind, Angie?" Alina asked, sounding resigned.

"I know you can't be fine," Angela told her roundly. She reached the second floor and turned toward her bedroom. "John just died. Even though you like to pretend you have no emotion these days, I know that's not true."

"Isn't it?" Alina asked softly.

Angela scowled.

"No." Her voice came out sharper than she intended. "Why did you go on a trip now, of all times? Don't you know Stephanie needs you?"

There was a longer silence and Angela inwardly winced, wondering if she had gone too far. It was perfectly true, but maybe she could have been more tactful.

"I had to," Alina finally spoke. "How is Steph holding up?"

"She seems to be handling it ok," Angela said, opening a drawer in her dresser and pulling out a long-sleeved tee-shirt. "Her friend Blake is coming to stay for a few days. I think that will help."

"Blake? When?"

"Tonight." Angela opened another drawer and pulled out a pair of yoga pants. "We went to dinner and she got a call from him while we were eating. He was an hour away."

"Is he bringing his dog?"

"Yes wait…how did you know he has a dog?"

"It's been mentioned once or twice." Amusement laced her voice and Angela raised an eyebrow. "Any word on a funeral yet?"

"They've released John for burial. They were waiting on some test, apparently, but it finally came back. His folks flew in today and Steph heard back from the attorney. He's talking with John's parents, but the arrangements will get underway now."

"What attorney?"

"John had a will," Angela told her.

"What?!"

Angela blinked at the sharpness in her old friend's voice.

"What?" she asked. "Why is everyone so surprised he made a will? I have a will. It's just a smart thing to do. He told me about it a couple of years ago and gave me the name of the attorney. Stephanie is the executor."

"Steph?"

"Yes. I guess he figured it was the most practical thing to do after his parents retired out to California. She's going to try to get the funeral arranged as quickly as possible. I told her I could help tomorrow if she needs it. I have to get my tire fixed anyway, so I'll be sitting around waiting. I might as well make myself useful. I'm not sure how much we can get done on a Saturday, though."

"What happened to your tire?"

"I came out of work to a flat," Angela said. "It's weird because this morning it was fine and the car didn't indicate a low tire."

"Did you pick up a nail?"

"I don't know. Steph gave me the name of a place to call in the morning. They'll tow it and fix the tire for me, but there goes half my day." Angela pulled her shirt off and reached for the tee-shirt. "So I might as well make myself useful to Stephanie. What time are you getting in tomorrow?"

"I don't know," Alina replied.

"I would think your job would be a little more understanding," said Angela. "You've had a death. You should be home, not off on a business trip."

"I'll be sure to mention it," the amusement was back in Alina's voice. "I have to go. I'll talk to you soon."

Angela frowned as she disconnected and tossed her phone on the bed.

"Good-bye," she muttered.

She finished getting changed and turned to leave the bedroom, switching off the light as she went.

Across the street, a tall figure moved in the shadows as the bedroom window went dark. A few minutes later, it stirred again as Angela's shadow moved across the living room. The room grew brighter, light flickering through the lightweight curtains. The figure settled down again. She was watching TV.

It was going to be a long night.

Alina slid her phone into the inside pocket of her jacket and slipped into the dark stairwell. She ran up the steps silently until she reached the fifth floor. There, she paused outside the door, listening. Glancing at her watch, she cracked the door to peer through the opening. The nurses should have completed their rounds by now, leaving the coast clear for another hour. After watching for a minute, Alina stepped into the quiet hallway and moved along the worn tiles toward the room halfway down. She glanced up at the sound of laughter coming from the nurses' station around the corner at the far end of the corridor. A moment later, she slipped into the room, closing the door behind her silently.

"It's about time you came to see me."

Hawk's voice was husky and she looked across the room.

"Not all of us have the luxury of lying around in bed all day," she retorted, crossing the room.

A single light was on next to the bed and a tablet lay next to him on top of the sterile white blanket. He was propped up against a mound of pillows, the hospital gown looking pale and worn as it stretched across his broad chest. His dark hair fell over his forehead in a thick wave and his eyes were a startling blue. A glint of laughter lit them now and Alina met his gaze with a smile.

"How are you feeling?" she asked.

"Like hell."

"You look better than you did." She glanced at the monitors, noting his heart rate and blood pressure. "What's the prognosis?"

"No sign of infection, internal bleeding has stopped, and I'm all stitched up. I have a cracked rib, but nothing more." He reached out and took her hand, his fingers entwining with hers. "The doc wants my blood pressure to come back up and to monitor my white cell count before he releases me."

"How long before we can move you?"

Damon's eyes met hers and he grinned.

"As soon as I decide to move," he replied. "Charlie knows I won't stay long. I've cracked ribs before and it's no good reason to keep me out of action."

Alina nodded and sat on the edge of the bed. She had a sudden vision of another face in a hospital bed, one with pale blue eyes and contusions covering his face and neck. Her throat suddenly tightened and she pressed her lips together, pushing the fresh memory aside.

"I didn't want to bring you here," she told him. "When we landed in Dulles, I wanted to take you to a private surgeon. Charlie insisted."

"How did you get me back so quickly?" Damon asked. "The doctor said I was patched up pretty good, but a few more hours and it could have been much worse."

Alina smiled faintly.

"Charlie sent Hermes," she said. "We didn't know how bad it was. You lost an obscene amount of blood."

"I assume I have you to thank for the field patch job?"

"Yes and no. I cauterized the wound, but it was a local doctor who got you stable for travel."

Damon watched her for a moment, noting the tightness about her mouth and shadows around her eyes.

"Who was the shooter?" he finally asked.

"A local, probably hired. I tagged him before he left the room. A maid found him the next day."

"And the local police?"

"Found his rifle. Their running theory is rival gang members."

"You took care of clean up?"

"Somewhat. I was a little…preoccupied with you, so I wasn't as thorough as I would have liked. I made sure they couldn't get a match on DNA and took care of the cameras. We should be clear."

His lips quivered.

"Preoccupied?"

She glared at him.

"Don't even think about cracking a smile," she warned. "It's not funny."

His lips were sternly repressed.

"Any idea who was behind it?" he asked instead.

"I'm working on it." She glanced down at their joined hands. "I can tell you I won't stop until I find them."

"I know you won't," Hawk murmured, watching her. "What aren't you telling me?"

Alina looked up, surprised, and his lips twisted faintly.

"I'm getting to know you pretty well, Alina," he said in a low voice. "What else happened in Singapore?"

She studied him for a moment, then sighed.

"I was being followed all day," she admitted. "He was waiting for me when I left the hotel that morning. I thought I'd lost him, but clearly I didn't give him enough credit."

Damon leaned his head back on the pillows and stared up at the ceiling, frowning.

"I don't like it," he muttered. "How did he know you were there? How did he even know who you were?"

"How did Al-Jibad's people know I was in Damascus?" she countered. "How did the Italian Secret Service know I was in Italy?"

He turned his head and looked at her.

"I don't like you being back here," he said. "Someone knows way too much about you, and now you're here in their front yard."

"Same goes for you," said Alina. "That's why I want to move you as soon as you're able."

He grinned.

"Not because you want to nurse me back to health?" he demanded, his eyes dancing.

Alina rolled her eyes and, for a moment, her mask lifted and Damon glimpsed the Jersey Girl inside.

"I don't have the bedside manner for nursing," she retorted with a grin. "You wouldn't last a week."

"Then I'd just make sure you weren't at the bedside," he said devilishly, pulling on her hand. He reached out with his other arm and pulled her close, bringing her lips to his. "I'm sure we could come to some kind of compromise."

His lips were warm and firm and Alina sighed against them, bracing her weight on her arm. The kiss lengthened and when she finally pulled away, she was a little breathless.

"I've been wanting to do that since you walked in," Damon said huskily.

Alina glanced up at the monitor and smiled slowly at his increased heart rate.

"I can see that," she murmured, returning her eyes to his. She reached out and smoothed a lock of hair out of his eyes gently. "I don't think it's on the list of approved activities the day after surgery, though."

Damon grinned and watched as she moved back to her spot on the edge of the bed.

"I'm not going to start hemorrhaging with one kiss," he said. "What were you doing in DC?"

He slipped the question in smoothly and she glanced at him, grinning reluctantly.

"How did you know I was?"

"Charlie told me. He was under the impression you were going back to New Jersey from there, but clearly you had other plans."

Damon settled himself on his pillows again and looked at her expectantly. "So, what were they?"

"I made a few stops," Alina said evasively. "Nothing you need to worry about."

He raised a dark eyebrow in patent disbelief.

"Nothing I need to - listen, I may be stuck in this bed temporarily, but if you think you're going to keep me out of the loop, think again. Spill it. What progress have you made?"

Alina studied him thoughtfully, then glanced at the monitors again. Despite the fact she knew he was going to be fine, John's sudden death was still too close. The threat of losing Hawk as well had been haunting her for three days, and it wasn't going away that easily.

"I'm fairly confident that part of getting your blood pressure back to where the doctor wants it doesn't include getting upset," she informed him. "I'm just trying to help you get back on your feet faster."

"Will I get upset?"

She shrugged.

"I don't know, but I'm not risking it. Not after..."

Alina stopped abruptly and Damon studied her for a moment silently.

"Not after what?" he asked softly.

Alina wouldn't quite meet his bright blue eyes.

"I almost lost you," she said, her voice low.

Damon reached for her hand again, his fingers closing around hers strongly.

"But you didn't," he said gently. "I'm going to be fine."

"No thanks to you," Alina muttered, raising her eyes to his. "What the hell were you thinking? You literally threw yourself in front of me!"

This time it was his eyes that shied away.

"I wasn't thinking," he replied gruffly. "It was just a reaction. I saw a threat and my instincts took over."

She snorted inelegantly.

"Since when is throwing yourself into the line of fire your first instinct?" she demanded.

"Since you came along," Damon said simply, returning his eyes to hers.

Alina stared at him, caught and paralyzed by the look in his deep blue eyes. She swallowed, feeling flushed, and gave herself a mental shake.

"If this is going to become a habit, then we have a problem," she murmured. "You're not made out of body armor. You're not built to stop a bullet."

"You're still alive, aren't you?" he retorted.

Alina choked back a short, humorless laugh and reached into the inside pocket of her jacket. She pulled out her phone, laid it on the bed, and reached in again.

"About that," she began, extracting something small from the pocket. "I may still be alive, but you definitely didn't stop the bullet."

Alina held out her hand and Damon stared at the mangled bullet in her palm. She watched as understanding broke over him and he raised his eyes to her face, dumbfounded.

"Where did it hit you?" he demanded, reaching to take the lump of metal from her hand.

Alina lifted up her jacket and shirt. A square gauze bandage was taped down on her right side, just below her ribcage.

"You slowed it down considerably," she told him. "It lodged in the muscle above my intestines. Any more juice and it would have gone into my liver."

Damon glanced up from the bullet sharply.

"What?!"

She shrugged and lowered her jacket and shirt, covering the bandage.

"It didn't do any damage," she said calmly. "I dug it out on the plane."

"On the…" Damon shook his head, a reluctant grin pulling at his lips. "You left it in until then?"

"I was a little preoccupied, remember?" Alina reminded him. "The doctor who got you ready to fly offered to do it for me, but I wanted to get in the air."

Damon returned his attention to the bullet, turning it over in his fingers.

"This isn't a civilian round," he said.

Alina watched him.

"No."

"So what was a local man in Singapore doing with military-grade ammunition?"

"That's what I spent today trying to figure out," she said. "I found something that might get me a step closer."

Damon closed his fingers over the bullet and looked at her.

"Isn't this the second time you've been the final resting place for a through and through?" he asked suddenly.

Alina rolled her eyes.

"Yes."

"Last time it was Angela."

"Yes."

Damon grinned at the irritation in her voice.

"You're not having much luck, are you?" Damon laughed outright at the look she gave him, then grimaced in pain. "At least we have the bullet now. We can match it."

"I'm glad I could be of service," she said dryly.

Damon looked at her, the amusement fading from his face.

"If I hadn't moved when I did, this bullet would have killed you, off-target or not," he said seriously.

She nodded slowly.

"I know."

"As soon as you start hunting, they'll be waiting for you. They won't miss again."

Viper lifted icy eyes to his.

"You're assuming they'll get a chance," she said grimly. "They won't."

Damon studied her for a long moment before pulling her down to him again.

"See that they don't," he whispered, capturing her lips with his.

Alina felt almost as if Damon was touching her soul with the kiss, and she pulled away with reluctance. As she did, his hand tightened on hers and she looked down as his other hand pressed the bullet into her palm. She looked into his eyes questioningly as he closed her fingers over it.

"Keep it safe," he murmured, his voice low. "You asked what I was thinking when I moved in front of you? I was trying to save you."

"It could have killed you," she whispered.

"I don't care, and I'd do it again if there was a chance to save you again," he told her. "Keep that bullet as a promise from me to you. I will always put your life above my own, without any thought or regret."

Alina caught her breath and her heart pounded in her chest at the look in his eyes. She nodded slowly and leaned down to kiss him softly.

"How about we don't test that again?" she asked, lifting her head a moment later.

Damon smiled into her eyes and the smile went straight through to her heart.

"I'm sorry I didn't get to give you that tour of Singapore," he said softly.

Alina trailed her fingers along his jaw and smiled back.

"I'm not letting you off that easy," she told him. "I'm holding you to it."

"And I'm holding you to the South of France."

Damon pulled her lips back to his and Alina closed her eyes, feeling his warmth and vitality beneath her. Contentment washed over her and, for the first time since she turned and saw him lying in a pool of blood, Alina allowed herself to feel something other than emptiness. Her heart was suddenly so full she thought it might burst out of her chest. She didn't want to think about the past few days, or tomorrow, or the hailstorm they were walking into. For the moment, Alina just wanted to feel Damon's lips against hers, his arms around her, and his strong and steady heartbeat against hers. That was all that mattered.

Chapter Ten

Michael opened the can of soda and chugged about half of it before wiping the moisture off his forehead. It was Saturday, and Saturday meant hard work at his house. There was always a project underway, some more labor-intensive than others. Today's last minute project fell into that category. Impromptu wiring throughout the whole house was not for the faint of heart, especially when it had been gently advised by a top government assassin.

Michael leaned against the kitchen counter and pulled out his phone, setting the soda down. It had been vibrating all morning with notifications, but the last one brought him down off his ladder to take a break. He opened his email and read the short message again.

> Hey Gunny,
>
> We need to talk. Call the number below from a secure phone. If I don't answer in two rings, wait an hour and call back.
>
> Damon

The email came through encrypted and the phone number was for what Michael assumed was a burn phone. When he ran the number through one of his apps, it came up unknown. With an internal shrug, Michael pulled out the clean phone Alina had provided and dialed. It was picked up before the first ring had completed.

"That was quick, for a Marine."

The deep voice was familiar and Michael grinned.

"We don't waste time like you Navy squids."

There was a faint chuckle on the other end.

"This line's secure?" Damon asked.

"It better be. Alina gave it to me."

Michael picked up his soda and carried it into the garage, closing the door behind him.

"Good. Don't use it for anyone but us."

Michael rolled his eyes.

"She already gave me the spiel," he assured him. "How are you feeling? I heard you had a run-in with a full metal jacket."

"Outstanding," Damon replied dryly. "Let's me know I'm alive. When did you see her?"

"Last night." Michael perched on a stool and sipped his soda. "She filled me in on a few things. You picked a hell of a time to go and get yourself shot."

"Tell me about it. Where is she now?"

"You don't know?" Michael raised an eyebrow. "I figured you'd know more than I do. Last thing I know is she's heading home to Jersey. She has John's funeral and wants to restock her armory while she has the chance."

"John's funeral?" Damon jumped on that. "When is it?"

"I don't know." Michael frowned. "She didn't say. In fact, come to think of it, she didn't say much about John at all."

"Not surprising. She's not dealing with it yet."

Michael stared at the tabletop in progress on the saw horses, the frown still on his face.

"That's not good."

"No, it's not. I'm damned if I can get her to see it, though. How's your schedule looking these days?"

Michael's eyebrows soared into his forehead.

"Busy. Why? What's up?"

"I need your help," Damon said unexpectedly. "I'm laid up for at least a few days, and I'm not happy about her being in Jersey without backup."

"Well that makes two of us," said Michael, "but I don't think she shares our concern."

"Someone knows who she is, and so far they've been able to find her no matter where she goes. They're gunning for her, and it's only a matter of time before they zero in on New Jersey. Another set of eyes can only help."

"Agreed." Michael sipped his soda again. "What do you suggest?"

"Can you take your work to Jersey?"

Michael choked.

"What?" he spluttered.

There was short silence while he coughed and caught his breath, then Damon continued, sounding amused.

"I want you to go to New Jersey. You're Secret Service. You're trained to protect the President. This should be a piece of cake."

"The President is substantially more amenable to protection

detail," Michael retorted. "If I show up on her doorstep and tell her I'm there to handle security, she'll blow my head off."

"I doubt that," said Damon. "Although, I'd love to see her face."

"You're serious, aren't you?" Michael demanded after a moment of silence.

"Yes."

Michael exhaled and ran a hand over his short hair.

"You don't think it's a little redundant sending Secret Service to guard an assassin?" he asked.

"Guard is a strong word. Think of it more as a collaborative mission. She has her job to do, and you ensure she's not ambushed while she does it."

Michael was silent for a long moment.

"This is unreal," he finally said. "It's like something out of a movie."

"I'm lying in a hospital bed with a gunshot wound. It doesn't get any more real than this."

"What the hell am I going to tell her?" asked Michael, resigned.

"I'm sure you'll think of something," Damon said. "She'll know it's a lie, but she'll play along, if only to see what you're up to."

"And you?"

"I'll join you as soon as I can." There was a short pause. "I'm asking you and not the Fearless Fed because, to be frank, I don't know if I trust Agent Walker just now."

"What?" Michael scowled. "The two grew up together. They're like sisters."

"No doubt, but someone seems to know an awful lot about Viper, and I can count on one hand the number of people who know who she really is. Stephanie is one of them."

"And I'm another," Michael pointed out.

"I know."

The two words fell heavily and the warning wasn't missed by Michael.

"So you don't want Stephanie to know anything about this."

"I'd rather no one knew anything about this, including you, but unfortunately, I don't have much choice, given my present incapacitation. No offense."

"None taken."

"On the plus side, you'll be off the grid while you're there, so if anyone gets wind of that extra background you're running, you're safe for the moment," Damon said cheerfully.

"You know about that?" Michael asked, surprised.

"Yes. Do me a favor? Don't get yourself caught. It's hard enough keeping Viper focused after John."

Michael rolled his eyes.

"You guys really don't have any faith in my skills, do you? I won't get caught."

"That's what they all say, until they're floating in the river with a hole in their head," Damon said ruthlessly. "Viper was right, though. You're in the best position to find what we need. Just don't mess it up."

"Really, your encouragement is heartwarming."

Damon laughed.

"Hey, if she didn't have faith in you, she wouldn't have asked. When can you get up there?"

"I'm leaving for Brooklyn early in the morning to meet my parents for Easter brunch," Michael said with a sigh. "I can go to Jersey afterwards. Blake is already up there with his dog, so at least I'll have back-up if I need it."

"I'd rather you went sooner."

"Dude! I'm in the middle of wiring motion sensors all over my house. I can't just leave," he protested.

"If you leave at seven, you can be there by ten," Damon pointed out. "The later you show up, the less likely she is to send you packing. You can go to your folks from there tomorrow."

"You want me to just show up without warning late at night? Are you trying to get me killed?"

Damon laughed at that.

"She'll know it's you before you get anywhere near the house, so unless you've pissed her off in the past twenty-four hours, you're safe. The sooner you get there, the sooner you can get an idea of what's going on and report back."

The frown on Michael's brow cleared instantly.

"She's keeping you in the dark, isn't she?" he demanded, amusement in his voice. "You have no idea what she's up to."

"She seems to think she's protecting me."

"Funny how that works. Now you know how it feels to be on the other end."

"Not for long, gunny. You're going to loop me back in."

Michael rolled his eyes.

"You're lucky I like you," he muttered. "No guarantees, though. She's just as likely to keep me out of the loop too."

"You'll manage. I'm trusting you," Damon said seriously.

"Don't let me down."

Michael frowned at the warning.

"Just get yourself better and come join the party as soon as you can," he retorted.

Stephanie watched as Buddy bounded after the stick, his ears flat against his head and his lips flapping in the wind. She laughed, shaking her head. The pit bull was having the time of his life. From the time he arrived late last night with Blake, he'd been nothing but curious, friendly and playful. Really, he was a very good dog. He'd come into the apartment readily, and after spending an hour investigating and assuring himself it was safe and secure, he'd taken up residence in her living room as if he'd been there his whole life. This morning when Blake said he was going to take him for a run, Stephanie suggested the dog park. Now Buddy was running off all his energy, and she was being distracted from the heart-breaking task of planning John's funeral.

She watched as Buddy picked up the stick and ran it back to Blake, his hind-quarters shaking back and forth in his excitement. She grinned again.

And people thought pit bulls were dangerous.

"Where's the funeral home?" Blake asked, taking the thick stick from Buddy's mouth and throwing it again. The stick spun through the air, going even farther than before, and Buddy barked and tore after it. "Is it far?"

"About fifteen minutes," she answered. "I'm lucky they were able to work with me so quickly. Larry, our ME, gave me their name. They have a good reputation."

Blake glanced down at her.

"When did they get the body?"

"Larry said they picked it up an hour ago," Stephanie said. "Joanne is insisting on an open casket."

"Joanne?"

"John's mother."

Buddy was heading back towards them again, stick in mouth.

"So when's all this going down?" Blake asked. "I heard you say something on the phone about Monday."

"The viewing might be Monday night. I'm waiting to hear back from the church, but we're hoping to have the funeral Tuesday," said Stephanie. Buddy skidded to a stop in front of Blake and dropped the stick before plopping down. He sat there panting with his tongue hanging out of his mouth while he gazed up at his master adoringly. "It's been long enough. John needs to be put to rest."

"Will he be buried here?" Blake bent down and clipped Buddy's leash back onto his collar. "Come on, boy. That's enough running for one day."

"Yes." Stephanie turned to walk with Blake as he headed back toward the entrance to the park. "John didn't specify whether or not he wanted to be cremated in his will, but when I mentioned the option to Joanne, I thought she would have a heart attack. She's determined to have a viewing and full burial. They're paying for it and I don't think John would have cared either way, so here we are."

"If this is what his parent's want, why aren't they arranging it?" Blake asked after a moment.

Stephanie shrugged and her lips curved in a wry smile.

"They think it's more appropriate I do it," she replied. "Joanne's working with the funeral director on the flowers, but she said I was closer to him than they were lately, so I'd be better to plan everything else."

Blake looked at her sympathetically.

"I'm sorry, Steph," he murmured, reaching out and taking her hand with his free one. "This has to suck for you. What can I do to help?"

Buddy tried to take off after a rabbit he had spied in the distance and Blake tightened his hold on the leash, yanking him back. Buddy yelped, then fell back into step with them, watching his prey disappear into the woods at the edge of the dog park.

"Honestly, I don't know," she sighed. "There's so much, and I don't know where to start. Until I hear back from the priest, I can't really do anything. If we can have the funeral Tuesday, the funeral director already said they could have John ready for a viewing Monday night." Her voice shook and Blake tightened his fingers on hers briefly. "They'll take care of refreshments, so I don't have to worry about that, but the funeral will be an ordeal. The entire Philly office will be there, and Rob said the offices in New York, Baltimore and Boston have said they're sending representatives in. John worked with all of them at various times."

"That's normal for an agent's funeral," Blake said. "They're not small affairs."

"No, but they'll all have to be fed," Stephanie said. "Where am

I going to find a place to host upwards of 200 people with less than forty-eight hours' notice?"

"Calm down. Not all of them will stay to eat," he assured her with a laugh. "Most of them will go to the church, pay their respects and leave."

Stephanie snorted.

"You don't know Jersey," she retorted. "Funerals are an event around here, almost as popular as the viewings."

Blake stared at her.

"Eh?"

She nodded glumly.

"You'll see. The viewing will be jam packed, and most of them will go to the church the next day. Trust me. Then they'll want to know where the luncheon is."

Blake opened the gate and the three of them went into the graveled parking lot.

"So make it invitation only," he said. "Seriously, Steph, you don't have to feed everyone. Make the luncheon family and close friends only. That's perfectly reasonable."

Stephanie stopped and watched as Blake unlocked his Challenger and opened the door so Buddy could jump into the backseat.

"You don't think that's...I don't know…kind of rude?"

He looked at her in exasperation.

"No, I don't," he assured her. "It's normal. Do you know how many funerals I've had to go to? Trust me."

Stephanie nodded and felt a little of the weight ease off her shoulders.

"Well, that will help a lot," she admitted, getting into the passenger seat. "If I do that, I'm only booking for about twenty, maybe twenty-five."

"See?" Blake smiled down at her. "That's much more manageable."

He closed the door and Stephanie watched him walk around the front of the car to the driver side. Not for the first time today, she was grateful Blake came up to stay again. His common sense was something she obviously needed right now.

A cold, wet nose touched her neck and she started, laughing as Buddy plunked his chin on her shoulder.

"Do you mind?" she demanded, shrugging him off. "You're all slobbery."

Blake slid behind the wheel and grinned as Buddy tried,

unsuccessfully, to lick Stephanie's cheek.

"Sit down, Buddy," he commanded.

Buddy looked at him, then reluctantly dropped his haunches down on the backseat. Blake murmured "Good boy," and the engine roared to life.

"Don't worry, Steph," he said, glancing at her. "We'll get it all figured out. Didn't you say your friend Angela offered to help? Give her a call. Maybe she knows of some restaurants you can try."

"She's getting her tire fixed, but you're right. She'll help." Stephanie pulled out her cell phone and hit speed dial. "Maybe she can come over when she's finished and we can hammer out some details. Hopefully, I'll hear back from Father Angelo soon and we'll have a better idea of time frame."

"What about the friendly, neighborhood assassin?" Blake asked, backing out of his spot and turning toward the entrance. "Can she lend a hand?"

Stephanie glanced him.

"I don't even know if she's back in town yet," she muttered, holding her phone to her ear.

"You still haven't heard from her?"

"I talked to her briefly yesterday morning. She said she would be home soon."

"That's it?"

"Yep." Stephanie shrugged. "She didn't even ask about the funeral. Although, in her defense, I didn't give her much chance," she added thoughtfully. "I was too busy complaining that she just disappeared on us."

Blake glanced at her with a grin.

"I'm sure she loved that."

Stephanie disconnected as Angela's voicemail picked up.

"She wasn't very amused, no," she agreed. "Angie's not picking up. I'll try her again in a little bit. Are you hungry?"

"I could eat," Blake said, looking at the clock. "What did you have in mind?"

"I don't care, I just need fuel," she replied, leaning her head back against the headrest. "I feel like I'm running on empty."

"Alright. Let's get Buddy back to the apartment and go get you fed. Maybe by then you'll hear back from someone and we can start tackling arrangements."

Stephanie looked at him and smiled. He caught the smile and raised an eyebrow.

"What?"

"Nothing," she said, flushing slightly. "Just...thank you."

"For what?"

"For being here, and trying to help. I appreciate it."

Blake nodded.

"I told you I'm here for you," he said. "I meant it. Besides, you took me and Buddy in. It's the least I can do."

"That's no problem," Stephanie assured him. "In fact, I'm actually enjoying having the dog around."

"But not me?" Blake laughed. "Gee thanks."

Stephanie grinned and looked out the window.

"Both of you," she qualified. "Although, when you meet Angie, you might re-think everything."

Blake looked at her, then turned his attention back to the road.

"I doubt that," he murmured.

Chapter Eleven

A man watched through binoculars as the couple walked out of the dog park and toward the black Challenger. A large dog walked beside them and he watched as the man opened the passenger door. Pressing a button on the side of the binoculars, he snapped multiple pictures of both the man's and the woman's faces. The dog jumped into the car and then the woman got into the front seat. He lowered the binoculars thoughtfully.

Special Agent Stephanie Walker didn't look like much of a threat, but the man with her had the familiar bearing of ex-military, and then there was the little matter of the dog. The dog complicated things. It didn't matter how silent you were, dogs always smelled you coming. He wouldn't be able to get close to John Smithe's partner until the dog was out of the way. He frowned. That was if it even became necessary. With any luck, it would not.

When he landed in Philadelphia yesterday, he wasted no time. He was already over a week behind Viper. The man tightened his lips grimly. While he was playing catch-up, she had managed not only to evade Wesley in Singapore, but to blow his brains out as well. She was good. He admitted that freely, and it only strengthened his resolve to find her, and terminate her as quickly as possible.

Do unto others before they do unto you, he thought, his lips twisting wryly in amusement. He couldn't remember what movie that was from, but it was appropriate.

The black Challenger pulled out of the small parking lot and roared off down the road. The man stood up and turned to walk through the sparsely wooded area to his rental sedan. If he wanted to know how Viper knew John Smithe, he had to start with Agent Walker. With just a bit of luck, she would lead him to his target. If not, he'd try her boss. Someone had to connect the dots.

Not for the first time, the man wished he knew the name of the person who had hired him to eliminate John Smithe. He would never have taken the job if he'd known it was going to bring him into direct conflict with Viper. He frowned again. If he knew who hired him, it would be a simple matter to backtrack to the assassin. It would also be a simple matter to find out what was so important that an FBI agent in New Jersey warranted an assassination in the first place.

The man stepped out of the trees and unlocked the silver sedan, sliding behind the wheel. He supposed it didn't matter now. It was too late to go back and correct the past. All he could do was try to minimize the damage.

And Agent Walker was in a perfect position to help him.

Alina ejected the magazine from her .45 and inserted a new one, never taking her eyes from the target positioned seventy-five feet away. She raised her arms and unloaded the new magazine, watching as the grouping from this round of shots went through the center of the established grouping on the target. A minute later she ejected the spent cartridge and lowered her arms. The modifications were perfect. Now to test the range. She turned and walked a few feet to her left, turning to face the target setup thirty yards away.

When she got back in the wee hours of the morning, Alina had been restless and unable to sleep. Dawn found her working on modifying her primary weapon, the Ruger SR45 that accompanied her everywhere. Raven, her black hawk, had watched from the roof of the stand-alone garage as she set up four targets in the back yard before finally going to sleep for a few hours. When she awoke in the early afternoon, Viper was still restless, but at least now she'd gotten some sleep. That counted for much more than it seemed, as she well knew.

Sliding a full magazine into place, she raised her arms and took aim. Her lips tightened imperceptibly. She didn't have much time. The incident in Singapore had made that abundantly clear. The leak in Washington was getting bolder. She was going to have to move soon, and quickly. Whether Charlie was ready or not, they were almost out of time.

Viper relaxed her shoulders and fired a few rounds, then studied the target in the distance. She adjusted her aim a bit and emptied the rest of the magazine. Lowering her arm, she ejected the spent cartridge, studying the grouping on the paper in the distance.

She was just turning to move over to the last target, placed forty yards away, when her phone vibrated against her thigh. Reaching into her pocket, she pulled it out with a frown, glancing at the screen.

Her security perimeter had been tripped at the road.

Alina swiped the screen and touched the blinking quadrant on the phone. The frown turned to a scowl at the sight of the silver BMW turning into the dirt driveway from the road. Alina cursed softly and glanced at the targets, visible in the trees. There was nothing she could do about them in the short amount of time before Angela made it through the woods to the house. She'd just have to hope her friend wouldn't notice them. Alina slid a fresh cartridge into the pistol and flipped on the safety before tucking it into her holster at her back. Bending down, she began to gather up the empty magazines littering the lawn. The long-range test would have to wait.

A few minutes later, Angela pulled around the side of the house, tires crunching on gravel. Alina watched from the deck as she pulled to a stop next to her black Jeep.

"You're here!" Angela called as she got out of the car. She slammed the door shut and started across the lawn toward the deck. "I wasn't sure if I'd catch you or not, but figured I'd try."

Alina waited while she made her way across the grass toward the deck. Angela was dressed in jeans and a sweater with designer boots on her feet. A large expensive bag was thrown over her shoulder and Alina shook her head. As always, her old friend looked like she'd just stepped out of the pages of Vogue.

"What are you doing? Were you on your way out?" Angela asked, reaching the deck.

"No, I saw you on the security camera," said Alina smoothly. "You got your tire fixed, I see."

"Yes, I just came from the shop. They had to replace the whole tire. You're never going to believe this. It was slashed!"

Alina's eyebrow rose sharply into her forehead.

"What?"

Angela nodded and dropped into one of the Adirondack chairs on the deck.

"Yep. When they got it off, there was a gash and the guy said it wasn't from wear. He thinks some kids did it overnight."

Alina looked at her for a moment, leaned against the railing and crossed her arms over her chest.

"Is that a possibility?" she asked.

Angela shrugged.

"I suppose so. I usually park in the road outside my house. I've never had any problems before though, and as far as I know, neither have my neighbors." She looked up at Alina. "Stephanie called me in the car. Have you talked to her yet?"

"No."

"She heard back from Father Angelo at St. Pete's in Merchantville. The funeral is at eleven-thirty on Tuesday. Viewing is Monday night at the funeral home."

Alina nodded.

"Father Angelo, huh? I can't believe he's still there."

Angela raised an eyebrow.

"Do you know him?"

Alina smiled faintly. Yes, she knew Father Angelo. Eleven years ago when she ran away to join the Navy, Father Angelo was the one who encouraged her. That was a lifetime ago, when she still went to mass occasionally, and Father Angelo was more of an advisor than a priest to her.

"I used to," she murmured. "He was there when I left for boot camp."

Angela studied her for a moment. Alina got the impression she was searching for some kind of emotion on her face, emotion that Viper was very careful to keep hidden.

"Well, he's doing the funeral. Stephanie expects a crowd and at least we know St. Pete's can accommodate everyone. We're still trying to find somewhere for the luncheon afterwards. I gave Steph some restaurant names in Cherry Hill and she's going through them. Blake showed up. He's helping her."

"Yes, you told me he was coming," said Alina.

"He's staying with her!" Angela said, wiggling her eyebrows. "What do you think about that?"

"What am I supposed to think about it?" Alina moved over to the other chair and sank down, resigned. "Why shouldn't he?"

"Have you met him?" Angela demanded, turning to face her. "Is he single? Is he good-looking?"

"I have no idea. I've never met him." *Officially,* she added silently.

"Ugh!" Angela rolled her eyes. "What good are you?"

"Sorry," said Alina, surprised into a chuckle. "I've been a little too busy lately to worry about Stephanie's love life, or lack thereof."

"What about you? Has Mr. Hunk O' Mysterious been around lately?" Angela asked airily.

Alina grinned. Angela was not subtle, nor did she believe for one moment that Angela didn't know Damon had been here last week. She would have pried that information from Stephanie within minutes of landing back in Philadelphia.

"Yes."

Angela waited expectantly, frowning when no more information was forthcoming.

"Well?" she prompted.

Alina met her look blandly.

"Well what?"

"How is he?" Angie asked impatiently.

Alina's mood darkened with that question and her lips tightened.

"He's fine," she said shortly. "Before you ask, no, he's not here, nor do I expect him."

Angela studied her for a moment, then sighed.

"You scared him away, didn't you?" she demanded. "I knew it. You just won't let yourself have any fun! You need to loosen up and stop working so hard."

Alina blinked and felt a headache start pricking behind one of her eyes.

"Ang–" she began, but Angela threw up a hand, stopping her.

"No, I don't want to hear it. All you do is work. Hell, your ex-fiancé dropped dead last week and you went off on a business trip! Who does that?"

"It wasn't exactly like I had a choice," said Alina, amused. "And it wasn't as soon as he...dropped dead, as you put it. For God's sake, don't say that in front of Stephanie. She's likely to have a meltdown."

"That might be a bit harsh," Angela admitted ruefully. "Unexpectedly popped off?"

Alina burst out laughing.

"Oh Angie, don't ever change," she gasped.

Angela grinned.

"I don't plan on it," she said, then sobered. "How are you? Seriously? It had to be a shock."

"Not really," Alina said, feeling her mask slide into place. "It was a miracle he survived as long as he did."

"Stephanie said the Firebird was totaled," Angie said slowly. "Did you see it?"

"Yes."

"He restored it for you, you know," she said unexpectedly.

Alina looked at her through hooded eyes.

"Yes, I know."

"Don't try to pretend that you don't feel anything, Alina Maschik!" Angela exploded. "I know you do!"

Alina shrugged.

"I don't know what I feel," she said slowly. "I haven't really had time to think about it."

"You haven't had time to think…" Angela's voice trailed off as she stared at Alina in disbelief. "What's it like on your planet? Is the air really thin? Maybe it's deprived you of oxygen to your brain."

Alina grinned.

"I don't feel the way you think I should. So sue me."

Angela huffed.

"Pretend all you want, but I know you better than you think," she said, pointing a long finger at Alina. Then, in true Angela fashion, she abruptly changed the subject. "John's parents are in from California. Do you have something appropriate to wear to the viewing and the funeral?"

Alina blinked and a deep sense of foreboding washed over her.

"What do you mean?" she asked, almost afraid for the answer.

"Well, Lina, you can't show up in cargo pants and a tank top, which is all you seem to wear these days," Angela told her patiently. "Especially with Joanne there. You don't want her thinking her son dodged a bullet when your wedding fell through."

"I really don't care what Joanne thinks," Alina muttered, "or anyone else. What does it matter what I wear?"

"I just told you! Everyone's going to be looking at you. You're the one that got away. You have to look the part."

Alina stared at her old friend for a beat.

"What part?"

"The part of the grieving ex who is much better off now."

Alina felt one of her eyes begin to twitch.

"Am I being punk'd right now?"

"I'm serious!" Angela exclaimed. She stood up. "Come on. Let me look through your closet. Or better yet, let's just go shopping right now."

"No!"

"I'm not taking no for an answer," said Angela. Her lips settled into a bullish look Alina remembered well. It never ended well for any of them when Angela got that particular look on her face. "Come on. It'll be fun. We'll go shopping and go out to dinner. My treat on dinner."

"I'm not going shopping."

"Yes you are."

"No, I'm not."

Damon watched the nurse leave the room and returned his gaze to the TV in the corner. He watched the news channel for a few minutes before pointing the remote at it in disgust and pressing the power button with more force than was strictly necessary. He tossed the remote onto the table at his side and scowled at the ceiling. If he had to spend one more day in bed, he was going to go out of his mind. This was worse than torture, and it had only been two days!

He stared at the ceiling for a long moment. Charlie had stopped by this morning unexpectedly. Hawk suspected the visit was more to see if he was still there rather than check on his progress. He didn't stay long, but his visit succeeded in convincing Damon that he needed to get up and out as soon as possible. It wasn't so much what Charlie had said, but more how he'd said it.

Damon sighed and reached for his phone. While he knew it was Viper who had collected his things in Singapore, it was Charlie who handed him the phone, watch and firearms this morning. Thank God for small mercies.

He swiped the screen and selected Viper's number from the contacts. She picked up on the third ring.

"Yes?" she answered shortly, sounding irritated.

"Is this a bad time?"

"No. Why?"

"You sound like you want to snap someone's neck."

There was a slight pause on the line, then what sounded suspiciously like a grunt.

"The idea has crossed my mind repeatedly the past hour," she said. "What's up?"

"Absolutely nothing," Damon replied. "If I have to watch one more minute of CNN, I think I'll shoot myself again and do it right."

"I'm sure you can get the TMZ channel," Alina said, a tremor in her voice. "Or I hear the Kardashians are still on."

"I'm going to pretend you didn't just say that. Where are you?"

"In Jersey." Her voice was muffled, as if she was speaking through something, and Damon raised an eyebrow. "Where did you think I was?"

"Have you made any progress on the face behind our shooter?"

"I haven't had chance. I've been working on some

modifications for my side arms. I want to refresh my armory before I do anything."

Her voice was clear again and Damon pursed his lips thoughtfully. What was she doing?

"That's probably a good idea," he said slowly. "Charlie was here this morning. He brought me my stuff. Thank you for grabbing everything."

"Of course. The rest is with me. What did he have to say?"

"He's making some progress, I think. He was unusually interested in what you're doing right now. He said to impress on you the importance of staying out of sight."

Alina was silent for a moment.

"Did he give any indication of what kind of progress he's making?" she asked softly.

"Of course not. He did say one thing I didn't like much. Harry doesn't know what happened, and Charlie made it clear he isn't going to tell him."

The silence on the other end was longer this time.

"I don't like that, either," Alina said in a low voice. "So as far as Harry knows, we could be anywhere."

"Exactly."

Damon stopped as he heard something strange in the background, then a voice.

"Lina, I found another one. I'm tossing it over. And if you like the gray one, I found a fabulous pair of red heels that will look killer with it!"

Damon's eyebrows soared into his forehead.

"Viper?" he said softly. "Are you…shopping?"

"No!" she snapped.

"Oh, and try this on! It wouldn't work for the funeral, but I think it's sexy as hell and would look amaze-balls on you."

"Really?" he drawled. "Because it sounds like someone's passing you clothes to try on. Is that Angela?"

There was a faint sigh.

"Yes."

Damon couldn't stop a grin from stretching across his face.

"Funeral shopping?" he asked, only the mildest tremor in his voice showing his enjoyment. "I thought you were modifying your .45?"

"I was, then Angie happened."

Damon burst out laughing, wincing as pain ripped through him but unable to stop.

"Oh, I wish I could see this," he chortled. "Is she trying to dress you like a tragic widow?"

"More like a Desperate Housewife," Alina muttered. "I don't know how this even happened."

"I want pictures," Damon told her. "If you go to John's funeral looking like a cougar, I want it documented for future generations."

"Keep it up and I'll put another hole in your side," she hissed.

Damon guffawed again.

"I'll leave you to it," he relented, still grinning. Then the grin faded. "Viper, be careful. Something has Charlie worried. Watch your back. That amaze-balls outfit won't look so sexy with a bullet hole in it."

Chapter Twelve

Stephanie pressed the end button and lowered her cell phone, a deep frown on her face. She'd been going back and forth with John's attorney for the past two days, so when his number showed up on her caller ID, she had answered readily. Now she stared at the wall across from the dining room table, lost in thought. It was awkward enough that John made her the executor of his will over either of his parents. Awkward, but understandable. They accepted her role without much of a fuss, and Stephanie was sensitive to the fact they were still his next of kin. Now, however, the attorney found something else.

Stephanie sighed and set her phone down, stretching and rubbing her eyes. Even after he was gone, John was still being a pain in the ass.

She stood and picked up her empty glass, circling the dining room table to carry it into the kitchen for a refill of water. Blake was taking Buddy for a final lap around the complex before calling it a night. Stephanie glanced out of the kitchen window as she filled her glass from the filtered pitcher in the fridge. She couldn't see anything in the darkness except her own reflection.

According to the attorney Wayne, John had a safe deposit box. While that was surprising enough, the caveat John had apparently insisted on in his instructions to the attorney was downright bizarre. Stephanie was the only one allowed to access to the box. In the unlikely event she was also deceased, the box could be accessed by only one other. Wayne was reluctant to divulge the name, but when pressed, he admitted it was in the will. When Stephanie read it, she'd find out anyway.

Stephanie replaced the pitcher in the fridge and took a long drink of cold water. John's alternate for the deposit box was Raven Woods.

Stephanie shook her head and went back to the laptop on the dining room table. She shouldn't be so surprised, but she was. Stunned was more like it. She and Alina were the only two allowed access to a safe deposit box John kept secret from everyone. She sank back into her chair. If both of them were deceased or otherwise incapacitated, the box was to remain sealed.

"John, what the hell were you up to?" Stephanie muttered, dropping her head into her hands.

Wayne had the key and he was meeting her first thing Monday morning at the bank where the box was located. He'd already called the manager and they would be ready for them.

The front door opened suddenly and Buddy bounded in, followed by Blake. He looked across the room to her and closed the door, flipping the deadbolt into place.

"You ok?" he asked, turning to follow the dog.

Buddy lumbered up to Stephanie and shoved his nose onto her lap, his hind-quarters wiggling as his tail wagged furiously.

"Yeah," Stephanie sighed, lifting her head from her hands and rubbing Buddy's head. "I just got off the phone with John's attorney again."

"Everything alright?" Blake asked when she didn't continue.

"I suppose so." Stephanie watched as he went into the kitchen and heard him open the fridge a second later. "I have to meet him at the bank at nine on Monday. John had a safe deposit box, and his instructions were very clear. I have to open it as soon as possible."

"Monday?" Blake appeared in the doorway with a beer in his hand. "Can't it wait until after the funeral?"

"Apparently not." Stephanie stopped petting Buddy and sat back in her chair. "John wanted it opened without delay, as soon as he died. Unfortunately, Wayne didn't come across that particular directive until this afternoon. And before you ask, I'm the only one who can open it."

"I wish I could help you with some of this." Blake moved toward the living room. "Why don't you give me a list of things I can pick up on Monday? I can at least run some errands while you're at the bank. What time is the viewing?"

"Seven." Stephanie stood up and followed him, dropping onto the couch tiredly as he settled into the recliner. "There actually isn't much to do. The funeral home is taking care of the flowers and memorial cards, and Joanne is meeting with Father Angelo at the church. She asked if I wanted to come, but I said that's all her. Angela found a restaurant for the luncheon on Tuesday, so that's done. Really, I guess all I have to do is go to the bank, and then buy something to wear."

"See? That all came together quickly and fairly painlessly,"

Blake said, sipping his beer. "Have you heard from Alina yet?"

Stephanie glanced at him, surprised.

"Why?"

Blake raised an eyebrow at her reaction.

"You said you hadn't heard from her, that's all. What's wrong?"

Stephanie sighed and leaned her head back on the couch, propping her bare feet up on the coffee table.

"I'm sorry," she apologized. "I'm just...on edge, I think. I haven't talked to her, but she texted me about an hour ago. She's back. Angela was over there today." She grinned suddenly. "Lina says it might end up being a double funeral."

Blake grinned.

"I can't wait to meet this Angela," he said. "Between what you and Michael have said, I've got quite a picture in my head."

"I can guarantee it's nothing like the original," Stephanie assured him with a laugh. "She's pretty special. She suggested brunch tomorrow for Easter. Are you game?"

"I'm always up for food. Do you know me?"

Stephanie got up and headed back into the dining room to get her phone.

"I'll text her and tell her we're in," she said over her shoulder. "Better you get used to her before the viewing."

"You make it sound like I don't get along with anyone."

"Trust me. Angie can try the patience of a saint, and you're no saint."

Alina winced involuntarily as she poured hydrogen peroxide onto the seeping wound in her side. She pressed a wad of clean paper towel against it and sighed, glancing at herself in the mirror. It wasn't easy keeping Angela out of the fitting rooms while she tried on an endless array of clothes, but she'd managed it. She had no choice. There was no good explanation for the bandage on her side; not that Angela would believe, anyway. Alina's eyes went to the smaller bandage wrapped around her left bicep. That one she hadn't been able to hide. Luckily, Angela bought her story of flying glass from a shattered window.

Looking at herself, Alina shook her head.

"You're a mess," she told her reflection.

The bandage wrapped around her bicep was covering two bullet holes, courtesy of a through-and-through she had received last week in the process of saving a biochemical engineer by the name of Dr. Krupp. Now she was trying to ward off an infection from another one in her side. Any more and she would start looking like Swiss cheese.

Alina lifted up the paper towel and peered down at the hole in her side. It was red, and angry, and hurt like hell. It was starting to close, but it was not happy. Obviously she hadn't done a good enough job cleaning it out on the airplane. Not surprising, really. She was too busy worrying about Hawk to pay much attention to her own injury.

Tossing the wet towels into the trash can under the sink, she reached for a large, nonstick, gauze bandage and ripped open the packaging. She would give it another day. If the infection got worse, she would have to get it cleaned out professionally. That was something Viper tried to avoid at all costs. Medical professionals meant a trail, and trails were never something people like her wanted to leave behind. She held the bandage against the wound with one hand while she reached for paper medical tape with the other. Hopefully the infection was only superficial and the peroxide would do its thing. If there was any debris, or worse, metal shards inside her, she was out of luck. No amount of home remedy would touch it.

Alina had just finished taping down the bandage when her phone vibrated. Simultaneously, a very loud, high-pitched beep echoed through the house. Her security perimeter was breached. Her brows snapped together in a scowl and she grabbed her phone, swiftly swiping the screen. Viper touched the flashing icon on her phone and pulled up the birds' eye view of the property. Her eyebrows soared into her forehead when she saw the black Ford F150 entering the dirt drive from the road at the edge of the property.

Alina slid her phone into her back pocket and reached for the tank top she had tossed onto the vanity. Between her arm and her side, she was stiff and sore, and she pulled it over her head with a grimace. Once the bandage at her side was covered with the black shirt, she turned and strode out of the bathroom. As she passed through her bedroom, she glanced at the empty perch in the corner. Raven was out.

Raven was her pet hawk. Or rather, the black hawk that adopted her for his own. When she tried, very responsibly, to leave him in his home environment in South America, Raven had other ideas. He followed her out of the mountains and halfway across the country. When it became clear he had no intention of leaving her, or allowing her to leave him, she conceded. He'd been with her ever since, following her each time she relocated. Now he seemed content to watch over her sixteen-acre property. When she left to travel, he stayed behind. How he knew she was coming back was a mystery she hadn't been able to solve, but Viper admitted she was always happy to see him when she returned.

Striding down the stairs, her lips curved involuntarily. He was probably in the trees now, watching Michael approach, ready to stop him if he dared get too close to the house without Alina's permission. People were naturally reluctant to take on a bird of prey when he appeared with his claws and beak ready for business.

Alina reached the bottom of the stairs and went to the front door, throwing back the deadbolt and stepping onto the front porch just as the headlights from Michael's truck pierced the darkness of the front yard. The dirt driveway that snaked through a quarter mile of pine forest from the road turned into gravel as it broke into the clearing, curving in front of the house before splitting into two. One half curved back towards the road, while the other turned left and ran along the house to the rear. Michael pulled up in front of the porch and rolled his window down.

"You're a long way from home, gunny," Alina greeted him, stepping off the porch and up to the truck.

"Depends on which way you look at it," Michael answered with a grin. "I'm closer to Brooklyn here than in DC."

"True enough." Alina studied him through the open window for a long moment. "Is that where you're heading?"

"Not yet."

"I didn't think so," Alina said, smiling faintly. "Pull around. I'll meet you back there."

She turned to go back into the house as he rolled forward and took the left turn at the split. Viper frowned as she went down the hallway. First Angela, now Michael. All she wanted to do was get her armory restocked and loaded, ready for the war she knew was coming, and find the bastard responsible for killing John and putting a bullet in her and Hawk.

What she did *not* want to do was play happy neighbors with old friends who insisted on dropping in unexpectedly, and at the worst possible times.

Alina let out a heavy sigh as she crossed to the sliding doors leading to the deck. Unfortunately, the moment she decided to buy this house in her home state of New Jersey, she had opened herself up to this. There was no getting away from any of them now. They knew where she lived and clearly had no compunction about showing up unannounced. Viper had known this from the beginning, which was why all of their cars and electronics had been adjusted to leave no GPS evidence of their location. Once they crossed the three-mile perimeter around her property, they were effectively off-grid and untraceable. While that kept Viper's location secure, it didn't do much to prevent them from dropping in at all hours.

Stepping onto the deck, Alina watched as Michael climbed out of his truck and started across the lawn toward the house. Out of nowhere, a huge black shadow swooped down from the trees. Alina grinned as Michael let out a curse and ducked instinctively as deadly claws passed within inches of his head. After buzzing Michael in warning, Raven glided toward the deck, his black wings outstretched majestically and his eyes locked on Alina's face. She held out her arm and he landed on it gently.

"Can't you stop him from doing that?!" Michael demanded from the safety of the grass, straightening up and glaring at them. "He knows me!"

"That doesn't mean he trusts you," she retorted, smiling as Raven turned his head to stare coolly at Michael. "If it's any consolation, he does the same thing to Damon. If he wanted to attack either of you, he wouldn't miss."

"At least I know it's not just me," Michael muttered, somewhat mollified. "Is it safe to come closer?"

"Yes."

Raven watched as Michael moved cautiously toward the deck. After watching him intently for a moment, he turned on his mistresses' arm and stepped onto the railing encircling the deck. As Michael set his foot onto the first step, Raven stretched his wings. Michael froze.

"Raven, stop teasing him," Alina admonished with a laugh as the hawk finished stretching and settled down on the railing. He glanced at her innocently. "He won't bother you," she assured Michael, the grin still on her face.

He eyed the bird warily as he continued onto the deck, finally relaxing when Raven turned his attention to the trees beyond the lawn, effectively ignoring them.

"Why can't you have a dog or a cat, like other people?" he demanded, following Alina to the sliding door.

"How boring," she retorted. "Where's the fun in that?"

She slid the door open and stood aside so he could enter the house before glancing swiftly around the dark yard. Raven was settled in, watchful on the banister, and Alina turned to follow Michael into the house, sliding the door closed behind her.

"So what brings you up from DC?" she asked, walking around him and past the black marble-topped bar into the large kitchen.

"Blake," said Michael, walking to the bar and sliding onto a stool.

Alina glanced at him, one eyebrow raised.

"Blake?"

"He's staying with Stephanie. He's working out of the Philly office for a few days while the dust settles at home. He thought it would be better if he left town while they figured out who planted the drugs in his closet and his boss agreed."

Alina studied him silently for a moment, then turned to the fridge.

"Beer?"

"Thanks."

Michael watched as she opened the stainless steel refrigerator, resisting the sudden and almost uncontrollable urge to cross himself. She didn't believe him. Not by a flicker of an eyelash did she show even an ounce of disbelief, but Michael was getting to know her mask well. Viper didn't have to show disbelief. The mask was proof of it.

He exhaled silently. Damon better be right. If she wasn't willing to play along to find out what he was up to, he would be on his way back to DC within the hour, and how would he explain *that* to the SEAL?

"Angela said he was staying with Stephanie," said Alina, closing the fridge and walking over to hand him a bottle of Yuengling Lager. "Are you going to play chaperone?"

Michael grinned, taking the beer.

"Hardly. He asked me to get some information for him, and given the currently unsecured state of my phone, I had no choice but to drive up to give it to him."

Alina studied him impassively for a long moment before turning to get a wine glass out of the cabinet over the counter.

"It's late to be driving back to DC," she said over her shoulder. "Where are you staying?"

"Here?" Michael asked with a grin. "If you're not comfortable with that, I can get a hotel room. I'd planned to go to Brooklyn tomorrow for Easter with my folks anyway, so I just came up early. But if you'd rather I didn't stay here..."

"Don't be ridiculous," said Alina, setting the wine glass on the bar. "You know my spare room is always open to you."

She circled the bar and went into the adjoining dining room to get a bottle of red wine from the wine rack. Michael breathed a silent sigh of relief. He was through the door, at least.

"I appreciate it," he said. "Any word on John's funeral?"

Alina carried a bottle and corkscrew back to the bar.

"The viewing is Monday night and funeral is on Tuesday," she said shortly, cutting the foil off the wine bottle. "Stephanie was able to pull it together quickly once the Feds released his body."

Michael watched as she uncorked the bottle and poured a glass of wine. No more information was forthcoming and he frowned.

"How are you holding up?" he finally asked.

Dark, emotionless brown eyes met his.

"I'm fine. Come into the living room. It's more comfortable."

Michael picked up his beer, following her into the living room. When she headed for the recliner, he settled himself on the sofa.

"Tell me something," she said as she made herself comfortable. "What do you remember about Jordan Murphy?"

Michael stared at her.

"Jordan Murphy?"

"Yes. He was in your company when you and Dave were in Iraq."

Michael thought for a moment, bringing to mind a hazy image of an average guy with dark hair and possibly glasses.

"Did he have glasses?" he asked. "Dark hair?"

"Yes."

"Not much," Michael said slowly, his brows creased in thought. "He acted as an interpreter on occasion, I remember that. I think his mother was an Iraqi immigrant. I never paid much attention to him, to be honest. Dave might have. I seem to remember they were hanging out a lot before…"

His voice trailed off and Alina raised an eyebrow.

"Before he took a bullet through his helmet?" she prompted.

Michael glanced at her.

"Well, yeah. Why do you ask? How do you know him?"

"I don't." Alina sipped her wine. "I came across his name recently. Do you know what he did after Iraq?"

"No clue," Michael shrugged. "A lot of guys discharged after that deployment and I didn't keep up with half of them."

"He and Dave were close?"

Michael sipped his beer, leaning back on the couch and casting his mind back twelve years.

"Not especially," he said slowly. "Dave only got friendly with him in the last couple weeks before he died. Jordan was kind of a loner, if I remember correctly. I think that's why I don't remember much about him. He tended to keep to himself."

"Any idea why Dave suddenly got chummy with him?"

Michael shook his head.

"Not the faintest. Knowing your brother, he probably felt sorry for him. Or maybe they discovered something in common. Who knows." Michael looked at her. "Why the interest?"

Alina was silent for a long moment, sipping her wine.

"Just curious," she finally said, smiling sheepishly. "I came across the name and started to wonder about Dave and his buddies. That's all."

Michael crooked an eyebrow skeptically, but let it go.

"The viewing is Monday night?" he asked instead, turning the conversation back to John.

"Yes."

"Mind if I come back after Easter dinner and pay my respects?"

Alina looked at him in surprise.

"Of course not."

Michael nodded.

"I didn't know him well, but I liked him," he said. "How's Stephanie?"

"I don't know. I texted her earlier, but I haven't seen her yet."

"It's got to be tough for her, losing her partner," Michael said, shaking his head. "Especially one she knew most of her life. Is she back to work yet?"

"Not yet. At least, not officially." Alina set her empty wine glass down on the coffee table. "If you're staying for the viewing, you might as well stay for the funeral. Did you bring your laptop?"

Michael nodded.

"Good. You can work on Trasker while you're here." Alina stood up and her lips curved into that smile that never quite reached her eyes. "You won't find a more secure place to work. You might as well make the most of it."

Michael watched as she picked up her glass and carried it into the kitchen. He stood and followed with his empty bottle.

He was in.

Chapter Thirteen

Thunder rumbled, rolling in and disturbing the absolute silence present in the darkest hours of the night. Black clouds obscured the moon from view, cloaking the region below in shadows, the air heavy with the promise of a pending storm.

Angela's eyes popped open. She sat up abruptly in bed, glancing around as beads of sweat formed on her forehead and she took a ragged gulp of air.

It must have been a dream that woke her so suddenly, but she was darned if she could remember it. Angela frowned and rubbed her eyes, looking at the clock. It was almost three in the morning. She groaned and fell back against the pillows. Thunder rumbled again, low and deep, and she yawned widely, snuggling down under her covers. If it wasn't a dream, it must have been Annabelle that disturbed her sleep. Her eyes drifted closed.

Then promptly popped open again.

Annabelle!

Angela sat up again, looking around the dark bedroom. Where was her cat?

"Bella-Boo? Psss-psss-psss. Come on, girl."

Angela waited for a moment, listening. Silence. Her brows drew together in a frown and she tossed the covers off, swinging her legs over the side of the bed. Where was she? The orange tabby always slept with her mistress. If she did wander off in the night, a single call was usually enough to elicit the welcome sound of a bell jingling down the hallway.

"Bella!" Angie called louder.

A loud thump and crash downstairs broke the silence, followed by a shrill *yeeeoowwww*. The cats' cry ended abruptly and a deafeningly unnatural silence resumed. Angela's feet hit the carpet as her heart thumped out of her chest.

She looked around frantically, the blood pounding in her ears, trying to think clearly. Someone was in the house! She was trapped upstairs with nothing but her phone and...what? There had to be something she could use to defend herself.

Angela's breath came fast as she stood in the middle of her bedroom in the darkness, desperately trying not to panic. She listened to the overwhelming silence, almost paralyzed. Why, oh why, hadn't she paid more attention when Stephanie tried to talk her into keeping a firearm in the house for protection? Her excuse was she didn't know anything about guns. Now she wished to God she'd learned.

Thunder rumbled again outside and a white flash of lightning lit up the room. In the split second of illumination, Angela caught sight of her new pair of Jimmy Choo heels on the floor inside her open closet door. In an instant, the lightning was gone and the room plunged into darkness again.

Running to the closet, she reached down to grab one of the pastel pink shoes before spinning around and going to the bedroom door. Her heart was pounding and her throat was tight with fear as she stood inside the door, listening. Over the sound of her own terror in her ears, she heard the unmistakable creak of the middle step.

Someone was coming upstairs.

Angela clapped one hand over her mouth to prevent a cry from escaping as she looked around her room frantically. Terror gripped her, making her feel nauseous, but she forced herself to think. Her phone was on the other side of the room, charging next to the bed. She would never get to it and make the call in time. Her grip tightened on the stiletto heel in her hand and she moved behind the bedroom door. Her panic-stricken gaze fell on her vanity table a few feet away, zeroing in on the can of aerosol hairspray sitting next to her makeup case. She moved forward swiftly and grabbed it. Returning to her spot behind the open door, Angela gripped the high-heel in one hand and the hairspray in the other.

The floor creaked at the top of the stairs and she listened, holding her breath as blood pounded in her ears. There was a moment of deadly silence. Then, even though there was no sound to prove it, Angela knew the intruder had turned toward the master bedroom. She stared through the narrow crack between the door and the frame, her teeth clamped down on her bottom lip to keep herself from screaming as a tall, dark shadow fell across the floor outside the room.

Angela wasn't a stupid woman. She knew she had no hope of winning a fight against an intruder. She wasn't skilled in self-defense, or in fighting of any kind. Nor was she athletic enough to outrun them. Even if she had been, there was nowhere to run. The bedroom was one story up, and the only exit was the very door she cowered behind. Her only hope was to take him by surprise and hope for some luck.

Angela inhaled silently, moved her forefinger over the nozzle of the hairspray and tightened her other hand on the Jimmy Choo. The shadow moved into the doorway. It was now or never.

Bracing herself against the wall, Angela lifted her bare foot and kicked the door with all the strength her shaking leg could muster. The door flew closed with considerable force, slamming into a solid body. There was a low grunt and a loud, satisfying thud as the intruder was thrown sideways and his head cracked against the door jam.

Angela rounded the door to confront a tall man dressed in a black jacket. She only had time to note his height before she aimed at his face and pressed the nozzle on the can, holding it down.

The man threw his hands up instinctively to protect his face, but his pained exclamation told her she'd hit him right in the eyes with the aerosol spray. Dropping the can, she swung her other arm with all her might, aiming for his head. The stiletto caught his forehead and he stumbled backwards. Angela followed him, swinging again. Fear and panic gave her strength she didn't know she possessed and the stiletto found its mark again, catching the soft area where his shoulder met his neck.

This time, the heel stuck, impaled in the intruders' neck.

Angela let go with a gasp of horror as the pastel pink Jimmy Choo struck a bright contrast against the black jacket. With about half of the stiletto embedded in the man's neck, the shoe perched firmly on his collarbone, the peep-toe winking at Angela.

The man let out a strangled gasp and turned, stumbling down the hallway toward the stairs. Angela watched him go, holding her breath as he stopped at the top of the stairs. When he paused and half-turned toward her again, she panicked.

Without thinking, she ran forward and shoved. He went down the stairs head-first, but managed to grab the railing on his way, breaking his fall halfway down. He slid the rest of the way on his side, hitting the first floor with a crash a moment later. Angela backed up until she felt the wall pressing against her and covered her mouth with shaking hands, watching as the intruder laid still for a second. Then, slowly, he struggled to his feet and stumbled out of sight. A moment later, the back door slammed shut.

Angela lowered her hands and sucked in a deep, shuddering breath before turning to stumble back down the hallway to her bedroom. She went straight to her bedside table and grabbed her cell phone. Her hands were shaking and tears blurred her vision as it took three tries before she managed to successfully dial 911.

Next Exit, Use Caution

Stephanie jumped out of the car as soon as Blake came to a stop, slamming the door closed behind her. She ran across the road, ignoring the rain pelting down as the storm erupted. Flashing police lights lit up the street and the front door to Angela's townhouse was guarded by a uniformed sentry. She pulled out her badge as she ran, holding it up as she ran up the few steps to the door.

"Special Agent Walker!" she barked at the police officer.

He glanced at her badge and nodded.

"Ok," he said quickly, opening the door for her. "She's inside."

Stephanie nodded and went into the house. Angela was sitting on the couch with a fleece blanket wrapped around her shoulders, a ball of orange fur clutched on her lap.

"Angie!" Stephanie crossed the living room, ignoring the police officer standing near her friend for the moment. "Are you ok?"

Angela raised a tear-stained face.

"I don't know," she confessed, her bottom lips trembling.

Stephanie looked at the policewoman questioningly. The woman nodded to her.

"She's fine," she said reassuringly. "She's had a fright, but she's physically fine."

"Thank you."

Stephanie turned her attention back to her friend and sank down next to her on the sofa. She put an arm around Angela's shoulders and Angela leaned against her. The orange ball of fur stirred and two wide green eyes peeked up at Stephanie.

"What happened?" Stephanie demanded gently. "Where were you?"

"In bed," Angela said, taking a deep shuddering breath. She paused as the front door opened again and Blake stepped into the house, looking around. "Who's that?"

"Blake. He drove over with me."

"He's good-looking!" Angela whispered loudly. "Is he single?"

"Oh my God, Angie!" Stephanie hissed, wishing the couch could just swallow her up. "Shush!"

"What? He didn't hear me."

"Yes, he did." Blake's deep voice was filled with amusement and Stephanie didn't need to look to know he had crossed the room to the sofa. "I am."

"You are what? Good-looking or single?" Angela demanded, looking up at him.

Blake grinned.

"Both," he answered promptly, eliciting a chuckle from the policewoman. "I'm Blake Hanover. You must be Angela."

He held out his hand and Angela shook it.

"Nice to meet you."

"I wish it was under better circumstances," he said, releasing her hand. "How are you?"

"I've seen better days," Angela replied. She looked at Stephanie. "He hurt Anabelle. Knocked her right out."

"What?!" Stephanie dropped her gaze to the cat curled up in Angela's lap. "How?"

"I don't know. When I came downstairs she was just lying there." Angela's lips trembled again. "I thought…I thought…"

"Ok, it's alright," Stephanie said soothingly, glancing at Blake. His eyes were dark and somber, his lips pressed together in a grim line. "I think you need some caffeine. Do you have any coffee or tea?"

"There's coffee in the cabinet in the kitchen," Angela said tiredly.

Blake met Stephanie's look and nodded.

"I'll make it," he offered.

"Thank you." Angela watched him turn and go toward the kitchen. "The cabinet above the sink," she called after him.

Blake nodded and disappeared into the kitchen.

"Mallory!" a voice called from the back of the house. "Can you give me a hand?"

The policewoman glanced at Stephanie.

"You'll be here for a few minutes?" she asked her.

Stephanie nodded.

"Yes, go. It's fine," she said. "He came in through the back?"

"Yes. The lock was forced," the policewoman answered, turning to walk down the short hallway to the back of the house.

"You were asleep?" Stephanie asked, turning her attention back to Angela.

"Yes." Angela sighed and leaned back against the cushions tiredly. "Something woke me up. I thought it was a dream at first, but then I realized Anabelle wasn't in the room. I called her, but she didn't come. I heard a crash and I heard her cry..." Angela's voice cracked and Stephanie waited while her friend composed herself. "Steph, I've never been so scared in my life."

"I can believe it," Stephanie murmured, shaking her head.

"Did you see him?"

"See him?" Angela looked at her. "I fought him off!"

Stephanie stared at her, speechless.

"You…what?"

Angela nodded.

"He came upstairs. I had no choice. I was trapped in the bedroom."

"He made it all the way upstairs?!" Stephanie heard her voice rising but couldn't seem to help herself. "He was *in your bedroom*?!"

"When you say it like that, it sounds a hundred times worse," Angela decided, visibly shuddering. "Oh my God, what if I hadn't woken up?"

Her eyes widened at the thought and Stephanie reached out to rub her shoulder comfortingly as what color was left in her friend's face drained away.

"You did, so don't think about what-ifs," she said hastily. "Tell me what happened. You said you fought him off. How?"

Angela rubbed her hand over her eyes.

"I…sorry. I told the police officer everything, and now I can't seem to think straight," she murmured. "Just give me a minute to get my thoughts together. I'm still thinking about what could have happened if I didn't wake up."

Stephanie looked up as Blake came back into the living room. He met her glance and smiled faintly.

"Coffee's brewing," he said, coming over and perching on the edge of the coffee table. "What did I miss? I heard someone raise their voice."

"That was me," Stephanie said ruefully. "Apparently, the guy made it all the way to the bedroom."

Blake's eyebrows snapped together in a scowl and he looked at Angela.

"Are you alright?" he demanded.

"I'm fine," she assured him, flushing faintly. "I did more damage to him."

Blake crooked an eyebrow and looked at Stephanie in question.

"I don't know any more than you do," she answered dryly. "She was just about to tell me."

"Something woke me up," Angela began hesitantly. "I called Anabelle and heard the crash downstairs. When I heard the crash, I knew someone was in the house. It wasn't the kind of sound Bella makes when she knocks something over. It was bigger. Turns out it was the hall stand near the back door where I keep umbrellas and snow brooms. He must have knocked it over when he came in...or when Bella showed up."

"You said you heard her cry?" Stephanie asked suddenly. "Was it before or after the crash?"

Angela thought for a moment.

"After?" she said doubtfully. "I think? Yes, it was after the crash because it suddenly stopped mid-cry, like she'd been...silenced. Then everything was dead silent. I didn't know what to do. I don't have anything to use as a weapon. Steph, I kept thinking about how you've always said I should get a gun and learn how to shoot. I wish I'd listened now."

Stephanie's lips twisted into a humorless smile.

"I'll teach you," she promised. "I told you I would."

"You don't have anything?" Blake asked. "Baseball bat? Hockey stick? Nothing?"

Angela looked at him.

"No. I don't play sports," she told him. "Although, I like the idea of a baseball bat. Maybe I'll buy one until I learn how to shoot," she added thoughtfully.

"Then…what did you do?" Blake demanded.

"I used a shoe."

Stephanie and Blake both stared at her.

"A…a shoe?" Stephanie repeated dumbly.

Angela nodded.

"And hairspray," she added.

Blake's eyebrows soared into his forehead.

"Hairspray?"

Stephanie felt a grin pulling at her lips.

"Please don't tell me…Aquanet?" she asked, her voice unsteady.

Angela looked at her as if she had grown a second head.

"Sebastian," she said, affronted. "Do they even still make Aquanet? Please."

"Sorry."

"Can we get back to the hairspray and the shoe?" Blake asked. "What did you do?"

Angela took a deep breath and began petting Anabelle.

"I hid behind the door. When he was in the doorway, I kicked the door closed so it would hit him. While he was still seeing stars, I sprayed him in the face with the hairspray. It's an aerosol can, so I just pointed and held the nozzle down."

Blake blinked.

"That would do it."

"What about the shoe?" Stephanie demanded.

"I hit him with it."

"You hit him? You mean, you threw it?"

"Not exactly." Angela looked up to find both Stephanie and Blake staring at her expectantly. She shrugged. "I…you know…hit him with it."

"You mean..." Stephanie wondered if she looked as stunned as she felt. "You mean, you used a shoe like a...a..."

"Hammer?" Blake offered helpfully.

"Yes."

Stephanie looked at her, shocked.

"You used it like a hammer?!?!" she shrieked.

"What else was I supposed to do?" Angela demanded. "A man was in my bedroom! Uninvited! Was I supposed to just let him in?!"

"No, of course not!" Stephanie exclaimed. "But...what kind of shoe was it?"

Angela's face suddenly darkened and storm clouds gathered on her brow.

"A new one," she muttered. "I only wore them once. Now it's ruined and I'm down a pair of Jimmy Choo's."

Stephanie's mouth dropped open.

"You used one of your Jimmy Choo's?"

Blake looked from one woman to the other.

"Care to loop in the schmuck who has no idea what a Jimmy Choo is?" he asked.

"They're heels," Stephanie explained. "Very expensive, designer heels."

"You clocked the dude with a high heel?" Blake demanded, impressed. "Good for you!"

"Good for me maybe, but not for the shoe," Angela retorted. "It got stuck in his neck and now it's gone."

Stephanie sputtered and Blake opened his mouth, then closed it again silently. For a long moment, they both simply gazed at Angela speechlessly.

"What?" she asked. "Why are you staring at me like that?"

Blake found his voice first.

"Let me get this straight," he said, his voice shaking. "You nailed the guy with a door, sprayed his eyes with hairspray, and then drove a high-heel into his neck?"

"Well, it was a stiletto," Angela clarified after a few seconds thought. "It's not like it was a block heel."

"When you say it got stuck and now it's gone, are you speaking metaphorically?" Stephanie asked, trying to avoid looking in Blake's direction.

"No. It got stuck in his neck and he left. Well, after I pushed him down the stairs."

"After you...well of course. Naturally." Blake couldn't control his face any longer and his lips trembled with laughter. "You didn't happen to douse him in gasoline and toss a match his way, did you?"

It was Angela's turn to stare at him.

"Of course not!" she exclaimed. "Why would I do that?"

He shook his head, his shoulders shaking with silent laughter.

"No reason," he choked out.

Stephanie shot him a look filled with reproach even as her own eyes were dancing with amusement.

"I think I missed the part where you pushed him down the stairs," she said. "How did that happen?"

"After I hit him he stumbled down the hallway toward the stairs, trying to leave," Angela told her.

"Smart man," Blake interjected.

"But when he got to the top of the stairs, he stopped and turned back," Angela continued. "I panicked. I just wanted him out of my house."

"So you pushed him."

"Yes. He caught himself halfway down and slid the rest of the way. Then he left."

Stephanie nodded, absorbing it all, and her lips twitched. Then twitched again. Angela watched her suspiciously.

"Are you laughing?" she demanded.

Stephanie started to shake her head, but her resolve failed her.

"Yes."

As soon as the word popped out, Stephanie burst into laughter. Blake joined her and Angela looked from one to the other, frowning in consternation. Stephanie tried to tamp down the laughter, but only succeeded in laughing harder.

"I can't…hairspray and a shoe..." Blake gasped.

"Well, it was the closest thing I had," Angela protested. "What is so funny?"

Stephanie choked her laughter down and shook her head helplessly.

"It's just so...so...*you*!"

"Well I know it wasn't all professional like you and your law enforcement training, or Alina with her military training, but it was the best I could do," Angela muttered. "It worked. He left."

Stephanie reached out and hugged her old friend, her shoulders still shaking.

"It did work, and I'm so very glad it did," she said, squeezing her tight before letting her go.

"Then why are you laughing?"

"Because it's so refreshing," Blake told her, getting his amusement under control. His eyes were warm and still filled with laughter as they met hers. "That's the best self-defense story I've ever heard."

"Really?"

"Really," he affirmed.

Stephanie nodded in agreement.

"Honestly, Ang, I'm amazed," she said, her voice shaking. "For someone who has no weapons in her house, you were outstandingly efficient."

"I was terrified, that's what I was."

A loud tone from the kitchen indicated the coffee was finished and Blake stood up.

"I'll get the coffee," he said over his shoulder, a grin still playing on his lips.

Angela watched him go and looked at Stephanie.

"Did I really do good?" she asked.

Stephanie met her look and smiled.

"Yes. You did very good."

Angela nodded. Before she could say anything else the policewoman returned, striding down the short hall and through the living room with a plastic evidence bag in her hand.

"Excuse me," she said, approaching the couch. "You said you hit the intruder with a shoe. Was it this one?"

She held out the clear plastic bag. Inside was a pastel pink Jimmy Choo, the stiletto heel soaked in blood about halfway up the four-inch spike. Angela nodded.

"Yes."

"We found it in the back. You said it was stuck in his neck?"

"Yes."

"That had to hurt like hell," she said, a grin cracking her face. "Good for you!"

Chapter Fourteen

September 21 - Iraq

Hi John,

Hope all is well. I got a letter from Lina yesterday. She says you're not acting right and you barely talk to her. What's going on? Don't make me come back there and kick some sense into you. Relationships are hard, and sometimes they suck, but it's always worth it, so get your shit in line.

Now that's out of the way...Last letter I told you about the missing crates from the ambushed convoy showing up. The next day, I went back to the town on another recon sweep. One of the guys with me, Murphy, acts as an interpreter when needed. He's fluent and could pass for one of them if it weren't for the uniform. We went through the block where I saw the crates getting loaded onto the truck, but the house the crates came out of was gone. My buddy talked to a couple of the locals and translated for me. The house caught fire in the night and two men inside died in the flames. I walked away convinced my only leads to the crates were dead.

On the way back to base, Murphy asked why I was so interested in the house. I brushed it off, but I don't think he bought it. He knows something's going on, especially after I slammed on the brakes halfway back to base. There's a road that leads into the mountains there, and damned if I didn't see that same pickup truck and one of the men who supposedly burned to death the night before turning onto it. I swear it was the same guy, alive and heading into the mountains.

I'll write more later. Keep these letters safe. Things are getting crazy here.

Give Lina my love,
Dave

The low hum of the server was the only sound in the

command center as Viper scrolled through another military record. She reached the end of the file and closed it with a sigh, moving it into her cleared folder. One by one, she was eliminating possibilities as one factor or another excluded them from her search.

Stretching her arms over her head, she leaned back tiredly. Her eyes fell on a photo, partially hidden behind the monitor, and her lips tightened briefly. It was taken a lifetime ago, when she was much younger and had no idea what the future held in store for her. Alina stared at the photo and a wave of melancholy swept over her. She was standing on the boardwalk at the shore, between her older brother and her then-fiancé, laughing and carefree. Alina suddenly remembered the scent of the ocean and warm breeze on her hair as if she were there again. She had been perfectly content, surrounded by the men she loved, safe and innocent.

Now, twelve years later, she was the only one still living, and she had taken more lives than she cared to count.

She shifted her gaze to the smiling face of Dave, her brother. He was killed a few months after the photo was taken. She had been devastated at the time. Now she was furious. Through pure chance, last week she had come across the emails Dave sent to John in the two weeks before his death. Now she knew Dave's death wasn't as simple as a shot taken from an insurgent.

Now she was looking for a traitor, and her brother's killer.

Viper reached out and flipped the frame over impatiently. This was why she normally didn't keep any photos around. The past served no purpose in her present. The only thing it did was remind her of a girl she didn't want to remember, a life that held no promise for her anymore.

Viper glanced up as movement caught her attention. The flat screen on the wall displayed the dark kitchen above her and she watched as Michael walked around the island to the refrigerator. It was just past two in the morning. He'd gone up to the spare room after midnight, leaving her to her own devices. Alina descended the stone steps concealed beneath the kitchen island to her command center and there she remained, plowing through military records, searching.

Michael opened the fridge and studied the contents for a moment before reaching in and pulling out a bottle of water. Alina watched as he opened it and took a drink, capping the bottle before moving out of the kitchen. The camera in the living room picked him up in the next frame as he moved over to the sliding glass door to the deck, peering outside.

She pressed her lips together thoughtfully. He was looking for her. That meant he never went to sleep, and knew she had never gone upstairs. Suppressing a sigh, she turned in her chair, watching as he turned away from the sliding doors.

Why was he here? She didn't for one second believe it was only for Blake. He was up to something. Viper leaned back in her chair, staring at the plasma broodingly.

Whatever it was, she was stuck with him for at least a couple of days. That was inconvenient for her, and potentially very dangerous for him. Someone wanted her dead. If they happened to catch up to her while Michael was around, she knew they would have no compunction about eliminating him as well. He knew the dangers. He wasn't stupid, despite being a Marine. So why was he here?

Her eyes narrowed as he moved down the hall towards the front of the house and the stairs. At least she could keep an eye on him this way. Someone knew more about her than they should, and although Hawk thought she was reckless being back in New Jersey, Viper was acutely aware of her situation. The only way someone could know so much about her was if they were being fed the information. Only a handful of people knew anything about her past. With Michael's arrival, they were all in New Jersey. It was only a matter of time before she uncovered the mole in Washington. Once she did, she'd know who, out of her very small inner circle, she couldn't trust.

Then may God show them mercy, because Viper would not.

Alina sipped her coffee and looked out over the back yard. Dawn had broken and the early morning sun was just beginning to filter through the trees, lightening the shadows. She had slept for a couple of hours before coming out to the deck to practice her morning yoga. Now she grimaced and slid a hand under her shirt to the bandage at her side. The wound was throbbing, but the bandage was dry. Hopefully it was just sore from the workout.

She was just lifting her mug when her cell phone began vibrating on the chair behind her. Alina turned with a frown and picked it up, raising her eyebrow in surprise at the number on the caller id.

"Yes?"

She lifted her mug to her lips once again.

"Did I wake you?" Stephanie asked.

"No."

"Good. It was already ringing when I saw it wasn't even seven yet. Sorry."

Alina sipped her coffee, waiting.

"Are you there?" Stephanie asked after a second of silence.

"Yes. I'm waiting on you. I assume you have a good reason for calling this early," she replied, amused.

"Oh! Yes. I just got home from Angie's a little while ago. Her house was broken into last night."

"What? When?"

"Just after three in the morning. The guy made it to her bedroom before Angie stopped him."

Alina's brows snapped together in a scowl.

"Tell me," she commanded.

Stephanie proceeded to fill her in on the events that dominated the early hours of the morning and by the time she was finished, the scowl had deepened.

"He got away?" she asked.

"Yes, and Angie couldn't give a description other than tall and probably Caucasian, possibly light-skinned Latino. They're checking hospitals now. The guy had a stiletto heel drilled into his neck. He had to get stitched up somewhere."

Viper's lips curved.

"Were they really Jimmy Choo's?" she asked.

"Yes. Pastel pink."

The smile grew into a grin before Viper could stop it.

"How's Angela taking it?"

"She's shaken up," Stephanie said, then paused. "Wait. Are you talking about the break-in or the shoes?"

"The shoes."

"She's furious. She only wore them once."

Alina turned to gaze out over the lawn again, a low chuckle escaping.

"Leave it to Angie to fight a man off with a thousand-dollar shoe," she murmured. "Did he take anything?"

"No, and that's what has me concerned. There was no sign of a search and nothing was missing. He went straight through the house and directly to her bedroom," Stephanie said grimly. "I think it's someone she knows, or someone who's been watching her long enough to know her habits."

Alina was silent, staring into the trees without seeing them.

"There's something else that's bothering me," Stephanie continued when Alina made no comment. "Someone slashed her tire on Friday. It was only luck she noticed it before getting in and driving away. You know how flaky she can be. I wouldn't put it past her to drive a couple miles on a flat before realizing something was wrong."

"You think the two are connected?"

"I think it's likely, don't you? I'm worried about her. I don't think she should stay there alone, and I have a full house right now."

Alina glanced at the black pickup truck parked in her driveway.

"Mine's not empty," she murmured. "Michael showed up last night. He's staying here for a few days."

"You've got two spare rooms. They've both stayed there before. Can you take her?"

"I don't think that's a good idea. She's probably safer in her own house."

"What? Your house is like Fort Knox!" Stephanie exclaimed.

Viper's lips tightened slightly.

"There's a lot going on you don't know," she said slowly. "You know I'd bring her here if I thought she'd be safer, but I'm not sure."

Stephanie was silent for a long moment.

"You have Michael there," she said. "Is he safe?"

"No, and he knows that. I'm not willing to risk Angie, especially after what she went through last night."

"What are we going to do?" Stephanie demanded. "Until we find this guy, I don't want her alone in that house. He could come back, and this time he'd be prepared."

"Let me think about it and I'll call you back," Alina said after a long moment.

"Well don't call in the next few hours. I'm going to sleep. I'm exhausted," said Stephanie. "She'll be fine for some of the day. We're all going out to brunch."

"Then I've got time to figure something out."

"Why don't you come with us?" Stephanie invited. "Bring Michael. It's Easter. You can't spend it alone."

"I'll pass, thanks. I have things to do here. Michael's going up to Brooklyn, I believe. I'll tell him to call Blake. He said he has some information for him."

"The viewing is tomorrow at 7. You *are* going to that, right?"

"If I must," Alina said grudgingly.

"Yes, you must," Stephanie snapped. "I swear, Lina, you're enough to try the patience of a saint. I'll text you the funeral home and all the details."

"Fine." Alina glanced at her watch. "Anything else?"

"Yes. Don't think I'm letting you get away with not telling me why your house isn't safe anymore. I'm tired and I want to sleep, but later I want to know what the hell is going on over there."

"Go get some sleep, Steph."

The early morning sun hadn't penetrated the trees in the park yet. It was just as well. The sole occupant of the bench overlooking the river hadn't been to bed yet, and the lightening shadows were already making his post-drunk eyes hurt. He rubbed them and yawned widely. He didn't even remember the last bar. He thought there might have been a woman at some point in the evening...he shook his head groggily. No. There couldn't have been. If there was, he'd be with her, not sitting on a park bench staring at the Potomac.

What was he doing here anyway?

The man shook his head and leaned forward to spit, grimacing at the metallic taste in his mouth. What did he drink at that last stop? Whatever it was, it was doing a number on him. Or maybe he was coming down from that last high. All he wanted to do was go home and sleep it off. He sat back heavily and stared at the gray shadows around him.

He was meeting someone.

The thought came to him suddenly and he nodded sagely to himself. Of course. The suit who hired him to plant drugs in the Fed's house had another job for him. Another windfall was coming his way, which was good because he'd finished spending the last paycheck last night. Maybe this one would pay as much, if not more.

There was a brisk wind blowing off the river this morning and he watched as waves rippled across the surface, rising and falling in crests as the current swept swiftly by. He never came to the river, he realized suddenly. In fact, he hated the water. He never learned to swim and, instead of appreciating the beauty of the water, he always felt fear. It was a force he didn't understand, nor did he want to. His feet were planted firmly on land, and that was where he stayed.

Something moved behind him and he turned, peering up at the figure walking down from the wide pedestrian path at the top of the mild rise.

"You came," the man said. "I didn't know if you were sober enough to remember."

"I was pretty drunk," the man on the bench admitted with a

grin, "but I'm here."

"You look like you need to walk," the newcomer said thoughtfully. "Come."

"I need to go home and sleep it off," the man muttered, standing a little unsteadily.

The other man laughed and began to walk alongside the river, leaving the man from the bench no choice but to join him.

"This won't take long," the newcomer assured him. "I want you to do something for me. You handled the last job as we discussed, so I have another one for you. Are you interested?"

"I'm here, aren't I?"

"True." The man paused for a moment, then glanced at his companion. "Did you tell anyone about the last job?"

"'Course not. Why would I?"

"Good. That's good. That was a sensitive thing."

The newcomer stopped and turned to gaze over the river. The bank was quite low at this section and the water lapped against it a few feet away.

"Have you seen the news?" he asked suddenly. "Someone was stabbed outside the Willard last weekend."

"I saw something about it on Facebook," the man replied, stifling a yawn. He was falling asleep on his feet. If this didn't wrap up soon, he was going to pass out right here. "I don't pay attention to stuff like that. I scrolled past it."

"Smart man. Sometimes I wish I could just ignore the world around me," the newcomer said almost wistfully. "I wonder if the dead man had anything to do with the bombs."

"Bombs? What bombs?"

The man glanced at him.

"You don't know? Someone tried to set off some bombs in different cities. It failed, of course."

"Huh. No. Never heard about that."

"Lucky you." The man turned to face him. "This job I have for you is very delicate. You're sure you haven't spoken to a soul about the last one?"

"Dude, I told you no. I don't snitch."

The man nodded slowly, studying him.

"I believe you," he finally said, nodding. "That's good."

He reached into the inside pocket of his overcoat and his companion watched, his eyes sharpening greedily. Good. He was going to pay him half up front. He loved it when they did that.

"I have something for you here," the newcomer said with a

smile. "Consider it a gift."

He never got a good look at the gift, but he certainly felt it. It was a searing pain, sharp and more intense than anything he'd ever felt. Strange. He couldn't seem to move his arms to stop it. In fact, he suddenly couldn't do much of anything, including speak. His eyes widened in shock and he tried to gasp for air, but the pain was too intense.

"Don't worry," the man said soothingly as darkness overtook him. "You can sleep now."

Less than five minutes later, the man in the overcoat was back on the pedestrian path, striding away as the Potomac River welcomed the body of the man on the bench, the current pulling it under until it disappeared from sight.

Chapter Fifteen

Blake pressed end on his phone and glanced across the park to where Stephanie was playing with Buddy. The dog park was surprisingly busy for Easter Sunday. Everyone had the same idea after eating a huge Easter brunch: get outside and try to burn some of it off. He grinned as Buddy suddenly reared up and threw his front paws onto Stephanie's shoulders, throwing her backwards. His dog liked her, perhaps more than anyone else he'd introduced him to.

"Watch out!" Blake called, heading towards them. "He loves to push people over."

"I've got him," Stephanie replied, laughing. "Don't I, boy? You can't push me around!"

She looked up as Blake joined them, dropping Buddy's paws down onto the ground again.

"Everything alright?" she asked.

"Yeah. They ID'd the guy from the video in my house," Blake said, bending down to pick up a stick. "He's a petty criminal, probably hired by someone else."

"Did they pick him up?" Stephanie asked as Blake threw the stick and Buddy tore after it.

"Not yet. Tomorrow, it sounds like." Blake glanced down at her. "Brunch was awesome. I'm so stuffed."

"Me too," Stephanie admitted. "That's where we're having the luncheon Tuesday after the funeral."

"Good choice. I guess that's how Angela got us into the brunch?"

"Yep. She's very talented that way." Stephanie watched Buddy gallop back with the stick in his mouth. "I hope she's alright. I wish she'd come with us instead of going back home. I don't like her being alone after last night."

"She needed some sleep," said Blake. "She'll be fine."

"But what if he comes back?"

"In broad daylight on Easter Sunday, after being stabbed with a four-inch stiletto? Not likely."

Stephanie grinned.

"I guess you're right. It would take a special kind of stupid to do that."

"Exactly. Stop worrying."

"What did Michael say when he called?" Stephanie asked suddenly as they walked along behind Buddy.

"He was on his way to his parents. He'll stop by on his way back. He's staying with the Black Widow."

"Yes, she told me this morning when I talked to her. Any idea why he's in Jersey?"

Blake shook his head.

"Not a single one. Last I talked to him, he was buried in work. I don't know why he suddenly came up, unless it was just to do the Easter family thing."

Stephanie glanced at him.

"Do you really believe that?" she demanded.

"No."

"So?" she prompted.

"That doesn't mean I know why he's here."

Stephanie was silent for a moment, her lips pressed together grimly. Blake glanced at her and raised an eyebrow.

"What is it?" he asked. "Spit it out. You know something."

She glanced at him guiltily, a troubled frown between her brows.

"Lina said something this morning that has me worried, and now out of the blue here's Michael. All we need is Mr. Hunk O' Mysterious to show up and we'll have a full cast."

"Full cast for what?" Blake stopped and looked down at her. "And who the hell is Mr. Hunk O' Mysterious?"

Stephanie chuckled.

"He's a friend of Lina's. Angela started calling him that and the name stuck. Michael's met him. He was with us in Baltimore when..." her voice trailed off suddenly.

"When Regina Cummings sent an assassin to kill you?" Blake finished for her. He grinned at her shocked look. "I heard all about it. Michael failed to mention this other guy, though."

"Well, he was there. He's the one who stopped the assassin." Stephanie shuddered involuntarily at the memory. "I hope to God I never see that side of him again," she added. "I thought Viper was bad, but he's much, much worse."

Blake studied her for a minute.

"Worse how?"

"I don't know. Heartless. It was like he had nothing inside him but ice." Stephanie shook her head. "Viper was the same when she killed Regina. Maybe I just know her better. I know there's a soul in there somewhere. Or at least, there used to be."

"I've never met her, but I'm sure there still is," Blake murmured, amused. "Souls don't just disappear. This isn't Supernatural."

"You didn't witness them in work mode," she retorted. "It was horrible."

"Steph, people who do that, they have to turn off human emotion," Blake said slowly. "If they don't, they can't get the job done."

"I know."

"No, you don't." Blake reached out and stopped her from walking with a gentle hand on her arm. "I know what I'm talking about. When I was on active duty and deployed in war zones, I did things I would never dream of doing as a civilian. I had to. It was the job, and it was survival. I had to turn off a part of me that was naturally resistant to the training I'd received. Now I can be more understanding and humane about when I use lethal force. You have to realize that your friend is on active duty all the time. She's not in a uniform, and she's not in a battalion, but she *is* fighting a war and she is a soldier. She goes into war zones every day. She has to do what she has to do in order to survive. That doesn't mean she's heartless, or that she's lost her soul. It just means she's found a way to bury it to get the job done."

"I know that," Stephanie said. "I understand it. It's just very jarring when you actually see it."

"My guess is you were never meant to see it," he said softly.

"No, I wasn't."

Buddy barked impatiently from a few yards away and they started walking again.

"So what did you mean by a full cast?" Blake asked after a moment of silence. "Full cast for what?"

"I don't know, but it's never good when we're all in the same state," Stephanie replied. "Look what happened the last time."

"That turned out alright," he said with a quick grin, "and it certainly wasn't boring. What did she say this morning that has you worried?"

Stephanie glanced at him hesitantly.

"She said there's a lot going on that I don't know about. She doesn't want Angela staying with her because she can't guarantee her safety."

Blake frowned.

"Can't guarantee her safety? What the hell does that mean?"

"Exactly."

"I'll talk to Mike when he stops by on his way back," he said. "I'll find out what's going on."

Stephanie grunted.

"Only if he knows," she muttered. "Knowing Viper, he's probably just as much in the dark as we are."

Viper laid a Ruger SR40 down on the workbench next to its twin and reached into her cargo pocket for her phone.

"Yes?"

"Happy Easter," Damon's deep voice greeted her. "How goes it?"

She smiled.

"It goes. How are you? Do you get Easter dinner there?"

"I do, actually," he said, surprising her. "The nurse was in earlier and asked if I like ham. What are you having?"

"I don't know. I haven't given it much thought. Not ham."

"How's the armory?"

"Coming along. I just finished one of my SR40s. How are you feeling?"

"Like hell. I slept for sixteen hours."

"You need it. You're healing. Trust the process."

"Easy for you to say. You're not the one stuck in bed with nothing to do. Any progress on our shooter?"

Alina turned to leave her small armory, stepping through the door into her command center.

"Possibly. You know how Charlie wanted me to look for an ex-soldier in Singapore?" she asked, walking over to a chair and seating herself before one of the computers.

"Yes."

"Well that search dug up quite a few possibilities, one of which is a name I recognized. He was in the same unit as Dave. In fact, Dave mentioned him in a couple of the emails to John."

Silence greeted that. Alina typed on the keyboard, waiting for him to process the information.

"Do you mean to tell me that I was shot because of something that happened in Iraq twelve years ago?" Hawk finally demanded.

"Possibly."

"Son of a bitch."

"It gets better."

"Of course it does," he said sarcastically. "Tell me."

"When he was honorably discharged, he disappeared. Went off grid," said Alina, pulling up the record she was looking for. "He stayed underground for years, until he popped up last year in Madrid. That's the first record of him since his discharge. He paid a few utility bills, then disappeared again. Ask me why that's significant."

"Why?"

"According to a graveyard in his hometown of Vinland, Kansas, he was buried the same year he was discharged. Killed in a car accident."

"That explains the disappearance," he said dryly. "So who paid utilities in Madrid? Our shooter?"

"That's the question." Alina sat back in her chair. "If the shooter did take his identity at some point, that might be what tipped Charlie off."

"If he *was* killed in that car accident. Did you verify his death?"

"Of course I did. Death certificate is legit."

"So it's another dead end."

"Perhaps. Perhaps not. Someone certainly went through a lot of trouble to try to cover their tracks."

"What did Dave's emails say about him?" Hawk asked after a moment.

"Not much. They sometimes utilized him as an interpreter. He spoke the language like a native. Michael said he thinks his mother was an Iraqi immigrant. He was helping Dave, but how much he knew about what Dave was doing is obscure at best."

"You told Michael all this?" he demanded.

"Of course not!" Viper frowned. "I just asked him what he remembered about him."

"That's still too much," Hawk muttered. "Michael may be a Marine, but he's not stupid. Asking him that much is enough to get him thinking."

"Don't worry about him," she said. "I'm keeping an eye on him."

"Oh?"

"I know you think I'm being reckless, but give me some credit. I'm not bringing anyone else into this mess."

"Viper, there's something that's been bothering me," said

Damon slowly. "Since I've been lying here, I've had ample time to think."

"About?"

"These emails from your brother," he said unexpectedly. "Why are they just surfacing now?"

"What do you mean? You know why. John had them on a hidden drive in his laptop."

"Exactly."

Alina pressed her lips together thoughtfully.

"You think there's something more to it?"

"I don't know," he said. "If these emails and attachments are what they appear to be, why didn't John tell you about them? You've been back for a year, but he never once mentioned them. That doesn't strike you as odd?"

Alina was silent, staring at the overturned photo next to the monitor. He was right, of course. That was the infuriating thing about Hawk. He usually was.

"So what are you thinking?" she finally asked.

"If he was poking around in ancient history, why didn't he come to you for help? Your security clearance is higher than his ever was, and you have access to outlets of information he didn't. He knew that. Why not tell you, and have you work it as well?"

"Maybe he didn't know how to," Viper suggested, playing devil's advocate half-heartedly. "Maybe he meant to but never got a chance. I came back a year ago, but I've hardly been a staple here. I've been gone more than I've been home."

"That's weak."

"Yeah." She sighed. "It is."

Damon was silent for a long moment. When he finally did speak, he sounded as if he was picking his words very carefully.

"I know you grew up with these people, and John was a big part of your life. All I'm asking is that you carefully evaluate all the information we have and acknowledge that someone close to you is not what they seem."

"If John had an ulterior motive for not telling me about the emails, and that's a pretty big if, what would it be? What would he have to gain? John didn't know what we know. He didn't even know my cover was blown in Damascus. There's no possible way he could have known the person responsible for Dave's death is even still alive. For all he knew, they were killed long ago. A lot can happen in twelve years."

"Unless the attachments contained something that made John

believe they were still active today," Hawk pointed out.

"The attachments were destroyed in the fire along with everything else, so we'll never know."

"Maybe that's a good thing," Damon said with a sigh. "Maybe it's better not to know why John did what he did. It wouldn't change the current situation. My only reason for mentioning it is to illustrate the point that you need to tread carefully up there. Be very careful about who you trust. We don't know who else knows about the emails, or the attachments, or what they contain."

"Well if John was doing something shady in the background, he would hardly tell anyone else about the emails," Viper pointed out. "If he wasn't doing anything sketchy, then he certainly knew better than to talk about it to anyone. I see where your concern is coming from though. Something isn't adding up and until I find out what it is, I can't take anything at face value. I'd already decided that."

"Charlie isn't happy with you there. I'm not happy with you there. Why stay? What are you trying to prove? Take Raven and go back to the cottage in Virginia. Go into the mountains. Hell, go to upstate New York if you want; anywhere but there."

"Raven wouldn't like it any further north," Viper said matter-of-factly. "He doesn't like it much here, but at least the winters aren't too extreme for him. New York would kill him."

"Then go south. Don't you have property in North Carolina?"

"Not anymore. I sold it after it was compromised last summer." Alina grinned despite herself. "I could always go to your ranch in Nowhere, USA."

"Now there's an idea!"

She laughed.

"Not gonna happen, Hawk. I'm staying here, at least until the funeral is over and I can get together enough information to act on. Kasim is still out there, and now there's something going on with Angela."

"What?" Damon asked sharply. "What does she have to do with anything?"

"I don't know yet. Someone slashed her tire on Friday, and her house was broken into last night. The intruder went straight to her bedroom."

"They didn't search anything first?"

"Nope. He didn't pass Go, didn't collect $200. Just went straight for her."

"That's not good," Hawk said grimly after a long silence. "What did he do?"

"He didn't get the chance to do anything. She managed to fight him off with a stiletto heel. Stabbed him in the neck with it, apparently, and pushed him down the stairs."

Hawk was surprised into a guffaw.

"You're kidding!"

Alina grinned.

"Angie's no joke when she's threatened," she said. Then she sobered again. "The question is who is he? And why now?"

"You don't honestly think it has anything to do with...anything, do you?" Damon demanded. "How could Angela get mixed up in all this?"

"How did she get mixed up with North Korean terrorists last fall?" Alina countered. "How does she get into any of the messes she gets into?"

"Good Lord," Damon groaned. "Why is it always so complicated with you?"

"I'm starting to wonder the same thing. Right now, the best place I can be is right here. I'm not stupid. I know the risks. I also know that the fastest way to sort all this out, with the highest rate of success, is to be right in the center where I can see everything."

"And everything can see you," he retorted. "Just remember the center is usually the kill box."

Viper smiled coldly.

"Exactly."

Chapter Sixteen

Michael watched as Alina lowered her head and aimed through the night-vision scope fixed on the .338 Lapua Magnum. She was lying on her stomach in the grass, the rifle resting on a lightweight tactical bipod with the butt nestled against her shoulder. When he arrived back from Brooklyn an hour before, she'd been setting up night targets at various distances, one as far as a thousand yards. She hadn't been exaggerating when she said she wanted to refresh her armory.

He sipped his beer as she pulled the trigger and a loud crack echoed through the trees. She never lifted her head, and a second later, another shot followed. She lifted her head then and made an adjustment to the sight before lowering it once more. She was completely focused, and not paying him the least amount of attention. He smiled faintly. Now he knew what she did in her spare time.

The smile faded as he thought about his conversation with Blake and Stephanie. Stephanie was worried about Angela, and Michael had to admit he wouldn't want any friend of his spending the night alone after the ordeal she had gone through last night. He suggested Angela come to Lina's. That was when he learned Alina had already shot down the idea. He watched as she fired off a few more rounds. While he understood her position, Michael wasn't sure he agreed. After all, Angela would not only have one of the nation's most skilled assassins protecting her, but also himself. He'd been known to handle himself well in a conflict, after all.

Two more shots cracked out as she shifted to the second target, further away. Blake wanted to know what was going on. Michael shook his head and sipped his beer, watching as Alina made another adjustment. It had been a very long time since Michael withheld information from his friend, but it wasn't his information to give. Viper was under attack, and that was no one's business but her own. She had shared with him in confidence, and he wasn't about to break that confidence. Not unless he had to.

Another shot rang out.

Viper lifted her head and pulled off her ear protection, glancing back at him.

"Hey gunny!" she called.

"Yeah?"

"Come show me what you've got."

Michael grinned and set his beer down as she rolled over and sat up in the grass. He stood and walked off the deck to join her in the darkness. She had turned off the floodlights, and the yard was steeped in the kind of impenetrable shadows only possible in the country.

"Don't mind if I do," he said cheerfully. "It's been a while since I fired one of these. It's almost nostalgic."

Alina grinned and handed him the ear protection, watching as he dropped down and made himself comfortable on the grass.

"There are clean targets at six hundred and fifty, nine hundred, or eleven hundred yards out," she told him as he familiarized himself with the rifle. "Take your pick."

Michael lowered his head to the scope and picked out the nine hundred yarder, adjusting the sight to his preference.

"Dave would be proud of you," he said, his voice muffled. "He would have loved your gear."

She didn't answer and he fell silent for a moment before squeezing the trigger. The shot cracked out in the night and he lifted his head. Alina picked up her spotter scope and searched out the target in the distance.

"Not bad. You're about an inch from center. Try the 1100."

Michael glanced at her.

"It's been a long time since I made such a long shot."

"The conditions don't get any better than this," she replied. "There's no wind. Try it."

Michael lowered his head and found the long target. After some adjusting, he sighed and the shot echoed through the trees. Alina watched the vapor trail through the scope.

"Adjust to the left half a dot."

Michael did as instructed and squeezed the trigger again.

"You've still got it," she announced as he lifted his head. "Take a better look."

She passed him the scope and he peered through it. His first shot had landed on the far right edge of the target, but his second was about an inch from the center.

"Not bad for being rusty," he decided, lowering the binoculars. He pulled off the ear protection and held them out to her. "Your turn."

Viper's lips curved into that partly-self-depreciating smile that didn't quite reach her eyes.

"Just don't get all bent out of shape," she said. "I'm not rusty."

Michael grinned and moved out of the way so she could resume her place at her rifle.

"Just want to see if Dave's little sister is a better shot than he was," he replied.

Alina was surprised into a short laugh. She loaded a fresh magazine and lowered her eye to the scope. She squeezed the trigger and lifted her head.

"Nine hundred."

Michael lifted the binoculars and searched out the target. He grinned.

"Yeah, you're not rusty."

Viper lowered her head again and shifted slightly, picking out the long target. Her finger slid over the trigger and she exhaled, squeezing. Without lifting her head, she fired again.

Michael whistled.

"Doesn't get much prettier than that," he said, lowering the binoculars.

Alina lifted her head. She didn't ask for the binoculars. She didn't need them. Her shots were parallel bullseyes and she knew it.

"Well?" she asked, sitting up and lifting the rifle. "What's the verdict? Would Dave be proud?"

"Dave would be pissed," Michael told her with a grin. "I don't think he ever made a perfect shot over a thousand yards on the first try. Hell, I don't know if any of us did."

"Well you didn't have my equipment," she murmured, detaching the night-vision scope and setting it into the case next to her in the grass. "Or my experience."

"That's true," said Michael, watching as she disassembled the rifle with quick, sure movements. "I've had some good peashooters, but the accuracy on that is in a class all its own."

She glanced at him.

"I try." She finished stowing the rifle away in the case and snapped it closed. "I'm going to collect the targets."

"I'll help," he offered, standing with her.

She nodded and they started across the grass towards the trees.

"What's on your mind, gunny?" she asked after a moment. "You look like you have something to say."

He looked at her in surprise, then shook his head ruefully.

"It's that obvious?"

Silence greeted that and he sighed.

"I stopped to see Blake on my way back. Angela was with them. You heard what happened last night?"

"Yes."

"Stephanie said you don't think you can guarantee her safety if she stays here for a few days," Michael said. "Why?"

Viper glanced at him and pulled out a Maglite as they reached the trees. She switched it on and the bright beam illuminated the dark woods around them.

"You know why," she answered. "It's not safe for you to be here, but you know that. She doesn't."

"You don't think that, between the two of us, we can protect her?" he demanded, following her through the trees to the first target.

"It's not a question of protecting her physically. It's a question of keeping her out of the reality I have to live in. It's only a matter of time before someone finds me. I don't need her getting dragged into the kill box too."

Michael shook his head and started to the right, heading towards the next target.

"You're being obstinate," he said over his shoulder. "The odds of someone getting through your virtual security fence is slim. Even if they did, you'd have them tagged before they got anywhere near the house. There's no reason Angela would be compromised."

Alina pulled the target off the stand she'd driven into the ground and turned to cross deeper into the trees to her right, heading for the nine hundred yarder.

"There was also no reason for her to get shot by a sniper a year ago, but she was," she retorted as she passed within a few yards of where Michael was taking down a target. "That was also a shot meant for me."

Michael looked up.

"What?" he asked, startled. "When was this?"

"When I was hunting Topamari. The Engineer missed me and hit her. Well, he didn't miss me, but the bullet was seriously slowed down," she called over her shoulder. "It went through her shoulder and shattered her collarbone before lodging in my side."

Viper continued on her way, missing Michael's shocked reaction to her matter-of-fact explanation.

Michael glanced down at the target in his hand and noted the perfect grouping in the center before turning to follow her. He pressed his lips together grimly. He hadn't known about Angela's injury, but he was well acquainted with the toll inflicted on both Stephanie and the SEAL when Regina Cummings went after Viper. For that matter, he hadn't been exactly unscathed in that whole debacle. Now Damon was shot. No wonder she was so reluctant to allow any of them near her these days.

He followed the glow from her Maglite and weaved through the trees, frowning. Short of going to stay with Angela himself and abandoning his post as Viper's impromptu security detail, he couldn't see any way around the current dilemma.

"What if we kept her in the house, like we did last fall?" he suggested a few minutes later when he caught up to her, taking down the last target. "If she's not coming and going, the chances of her getting caught up in anything are significantly lowered."

Viper glanced at him.

"Do you really think she'll stay put?" she demanded. "She barely stayed put last time and someone was actively trying to kill her."

"I don't know," he said thoughtfully. "I saw her tonight. She's pretty shaken up."

Alina turned to head back towards the house and Michael followed. Even weighing the cons, he still believed the safest option was here. Then he could keep an eye on both of them.

"Where is she tonight?" Alina finally asked as they broke out of the trees and into the back yard.

"When I left, she was still at Stephanie's," he answered. "She was planning on going back to her house, but she was in no rush."

Alina stopped in the middle of yard and looked at his truck for a minute, then sighed loudly.

"God, I miss the mountains," she muttered. She turned to him and Michael found himself staring into the unyielding face of Viper. "I'll make the call. You go pick her up. Her car stays at Stephanie's."

Michael smiled.

"That's a good decision," he said.

Viper made a sound suspiciously like a grunt and turned to stride towards the house.

"First thing tomorrow I'm adjusting the GPS mirrors on your truck and phone," she said over her shoulder. She bent down to pick up her rifle case and scoop up the ear protection. "If I extend the GPS perimeter to five miles, we just might have a chance."

Michael followed, raising an eyebrow.

"What difference will that make?" he asked. "You already have me off-grid at three miles out."

"The extra two miles will encompass Shamong and Tabernacle," she replied. "Trust me. It adds enough real estate to make tracking your GPS a bigger pain in the ass than it's worth."

"What about Stephanie?" Michael asked, following her up onto the deck.

"I'll take care of her tomorrow."

Alina stretched and opened her eyes. The gray light of dawn filtered into the room and she laid there for a moment in a hazy place between sleep and full wakefulness. Raven stirred on his tall perch in the corner, then settled down again, closing his eyes and returning to a state of dozing. Alina yawned, stretched again and sat up. She was just reaching for the cell phone on her bedside table when a soft knock fell on her bedroom door.

"Yes?"

The door cracked open and Angela peeked inside.

"Are you awake?" she whispered.

"Yes," Alina said with an imperceptible sigh.

The crack widened and Angela slipped into the room, pushing the door closed behind her. Her honey-colored hair was pulled back into a ponytail and she was dressed in black yoga pants and a tee-shirt borrowed from Alina. She looked as if she hadn't slept a minute.

"Oh good," she said, advancing into the master bedroom. "I couldn't sleep."

Raven lifted his head and watched suspiciously as she crossed the room to the bed and plopped down on the foot of it. Once he was satisfied that she wasn't attacking his mistress, he hunkered down on his perch, watching them through half-closed black eyes.

"That's understandable," Alina murmured, moving her feet out of Angela's way under the covers. "It'll get better the further away from it you get."

Angela looked at her.

"I've never been so terrified in all my life. Thank you for inviting me. Stephanie doesn't have room with Blake and his dog there. She did offer, but I would have to sleep on the couch and Buddy sleeps in the living room."

Alina grinned. While Angela loved her cat, she had never been much of a dog person.

"I don't see that working out so well."

Angela hesitated for a moment, then took a deep breath.

"Look, I know you don't want me here. Stephanie said you

have a lot going on and you weren't sure if you could take another house guest. I'll stay out of your way, I promise."

Alina rolled her eyes.

"Stephanie shouldn't have said anything. You won't be in my way. That's got nothing to do with it."

"But you *do* have a lot going on," Angela said. "I can tell. You're distracted."

"Yes, but it's got nothing to do with you." Alina paused and sighed in resignation. "Angie, I'm sorry if you feel...unwanted. You're not. I'm just worried I won't be able to...keep you as safe as I would like."

Angela stared at her for a moment, clearly surprised.

"Why do you think you need to keep me safe?" she asked, bemused. "My house was broken into, that's all. It's not like I'm being stalked again."

Alina was silent and Angela suddenly sucked in her breath.

"You think I am?" she demanded. "Why?"

"Let's just say I'm being cautious," Alina said. "It's not normal for a housebreaker to ignore all the big ticket items downstairs and go straight for the master bedroom."

Angela was quiet for a moment.

"That's why the police were asking about the flat tire and everything I've done since I got back from Florida," she breathed. "But...who? Why? And how? I've only been back a few days!"

"I don't know. That's what Stephanie and the police are going to find out."

"Well if that's what's really going on, I'm in the safest place I can think of," Angela announced. "You have a whole security system and a Federal Agent staying here. How much safer can I possibly be?"

"This does come with conditions," Alina warned her gently. "You're not going to like it, but it's necessary."

"What?"

"You can't leave, for one. Until we know who this guy is, you can't leave this property. Michael is positive he wasn't followed last night, so if you are being watched, they don't know where you are right now. You step foot off this property and they can easily pick you up again."

Angela wrinkled her nose, but nodded reluctantly.

"If you get in some easy to prepare food, I'll stay put," she agreed. "Last time I was here you didn't have a thing in the house to eat!"

Alina resisted the urge to roll her eyes.

"I did. You just don't cook," she said. "If it will keep you happy, make a list of food and I'll arrange it."

"What else?"

"I don't want you contacting anyone outside this house or telling anyone where you are."

Angela frowned.

"That's fine for the next few days. I already took Monday and Tuesday off for the funeral, but then I have to tell my boss something. He'll need to know why I'm working from home."

"Tell him you're sick. You came down with the flu."

"What about Annabelle?" Angela asked suddenly. "I have to go get her, and some clothes, and my laptop and charger..."

Alina did roll her eyes this time.

"Angie, seriously?"

"What? I do! I'll get those, then I can hole up here for as long as it takes," she assured her. "Michael can take me. I'll be perfectly safe with him."

"For the love of...what part of you can't leave don't you understand?" Alina demanded. "Someone else can get your stuff, but I'm not being responsible for your cat's safety in a house with a hawk. You remember what happened last time Raven caught sight of her."

"It'll be fine," Angela replied. "Now I know to be more careful about latching the doors. I have to go. I don't think Anabelle will get into a carrier for anyone else. And besides, I know where everything is. It would be quicker for me to go. Why can't Michael take me?"

Viper felt her eye beginning the twitch. It was way too early for this argument.

"Right now, we know you weren't followed here. If some psycho is stalking you, he has no idea where you are. Where do you think is the most logical place for him to watch?"

"You're assuming I *am* being stalked," Angela muttered. "We don't know that I am. I say let Michael take me to get my stuff. We can drive around all day and lose anyone who might be following."

"Drive around all day?"

The twitch was getting worse.

"Sure. Michael wanted to see where the funeral is going to be, so I can take him around and show him…oh my God!" Angela exclaimed suddenly, cutting herself off. "I completely forgot about Joanne! I have to meet her at the funeral home to check flowers, then go with her to the church to meet with Father Angelo!"

Alina stared at her for a minute and pinched the bridge of her nose as a dull headache started behind her twitching eye.

"Stephanie?" she asked after a moment.

"She has to run some other errands. That's why I'm going."

Alina shook her head. It was pointless to say Angela couldn't go. That was a fight she would never win, especially if Angela was doing it to help Stephanie.

"What a mess," she muttered. "I'll talk to Michael. If he agrees, he can take you."

"And if anyone does start following us, I'm sure he'll know. He's a Federal agent, after all."

Alina shook her head, defeated.

"Yes, he is," she agreed tiredly, humoring her. "After the church, you're coming right back and staying put."

"Fine."

Angela got off the bed and left the room happily. As soon as the door closed behind her, Viper sank down into the pillows again and stared at the ceiling. So much for keeping Angela off-grid. How on earth was she going to keep her secure with all the coming and going?

More to the point, how was she going to keep her own location secure with all the coming and going?

Chapter Seventeen

Harry sipped his coffee as a bus lumbered by. He stood at the corner, waiting for the light to change. At mid-morning the rush hour was over, and the foot traffic was fairly light in the nation's capital. The light changed and Harry stepped off the curb, starting across the side street towards a small park on the other side. A brisk spring wind whipped around his bald head, and Harry breathed deeply as he reached the other pavement and started towards the park entrance.

"You're late."

The voice spoke behind him and Harry grinned, turning his head to look at his old friend.

"I know. I got held up by a singularly obtuse barista," he said. "He was simply unable to comprehend the words 'large black coffee.'"

Charlie's gray eyes crinkled at the edges as his face broke into a rare smile.

"He'll be traumatized for the rest of the day," he said, falling into step beside Harry. "Thank you for meeting me here. I'm on my way to the airport and don't have much time. Our usual place was out of the question."

Harry grunted and they stepped into the small, wooded area nestled in the bustling city.

"If you're looking for an update on Kasim Jamal, I have to disappoint you," he said as they walked along a nearly deserted running trail. "He's proving to be surprisingly elusive. We lost him after he left the old factory in Maryland, and so far, he hasn't resurfaced."

Charlie looked at him sharply.

"That was two days ago!"

"I know." Harry sipped his coffee. "I've got people working around the clock. We'll find him."

"And the other one?"

"They'll be together. They have no reason to separate now. In fact, just the opposite after losing Asad and Nasser."

Charlie was silent for a long moment.

"What about the other issue?" he finally asked. "Last week you were making progress on the questionable agents inside DHS. What's new on that front?"

"It's very slow," Harry said glumly. "I think it goes much deeper than we originally thought. Regina Cummings and her crew were just the beginning. I'm working on it, but it's taking time."

"We don't have time." Charlie stopped walking and looked at Harry. "Information is leaking out and I need to know which agency is responsible."

"Has something happened?" Harry asked, his brows snapping together.

"An operative in Brazil was killed last night," Charlie said grimly. "They were waiting for him at his entry-point in the favelas."

Harry scowled.

"Are you sure it wasn't just a bad op?"

"Yes."

Harry sighed heavily.

"Understood."

Charlie nodded.

"I know you'll do your best."

"How's Viper?" Harry asked as they resumed walking. "Has she shown any signs of strain since John Smithe's death?"

Charlie smiled faintly.

"Just the opposite," he murmured. "She's more focused than ever."

"And the funeral?"

"I understand it's tomorrow. Once that's over, I don't think we need to worry anymore. If she has any...lapse, it will be there."

"You know, she never ceases to amaze me," Harry said thoughtfully. "I was sure there would be problems when he died. She's so damned attached to those people. I thought I'd trained her better than that."

"It is only because of your training she's come this far. She has emotional attachments, but they haven't weakened her. If anything, they've made her stronger, so I won't complain."

"Hm." Harry sounded unconvinced, but let it drop. "I got a call from Agent Walker's boss today. He needs her back. She's on LOA now because I pressured it, but with John dead, I can't justify continuing it. Not when her boss is getting antsy. You asked me to take her out of play, but I can't keep her sidelined for much longer."

"The circumstances remain, but I think Blake Hanover has been distracting her," Charlie said slowly. "Go ahead and release her back to work. If she starts to dig into things above her pay grade, we'll deal with it then."

"It might not be a bad thing for her to get pulled into all this," Harry said after a moment of thought. "Our initial concern was if something happened to those people, Viper would lose focus. John died, but you say she's more focused than ever. Perhaps our concerns were premature."

"Perhaps."

Harry glanced at Charlie.

"The sooner I find Kasim, the less we have to worry," he said. "Once we find him and who brought them into the country, we can work to eliminate the threat to Viper. Agent Walker will become a non-issue. Is Hawk still stateside?"

"No."

"That could work to our favor. If he isn't around to be threatened, Viper will be even more focused on her target."

"Yes. So do me a favor? Find her target."

Harry grinned.

"Knowing her, she'll find him first."

Stephanie watched as the bank manager left the small cubicle, leaving her alone with the safe deposit box sitting on the desk before her. She sighed and sat in the single chair, pulling the box towards her. Wayne was sitting in the bank lobby, waiting. The lawyer was true to his word. When they arrived half an hour before, the manager had the forms ready and waiting for them. All that was left now was to clean out the box, take the last of John's earthly possessions, and distribute them accordingly.

She sighed again, loathe to open the box. Cleaning out his desk at work was an emotional process that Stephanie hated having to do, and now here was another necessary act of invading the privacy of her partner. Another opportunity for her to shed tears over the man who had been like a brother to her over the past couple years.

"Oh John, why did you have to die?" she muttered, staring at the steel box.

After taking a deep, calming breath, Stephanie reached out and lifted the top off the box. The first thing to greet her was a manila envelope. She lifted it out and opened it, glancing inside. Her eyebrows soared into her forehead. It was filled with cash. John had a rainy day fund. She set it aside and lifted out an old folder, worn along the edges. Flipping it open, she leafed through personal documents: birth certificate, baptismal certificate, old passports. She closed it and set it on top of the envelope, then grinned as she turned her attention back to the box. A Beretta lay next to a box of clips and ammo. John had a backup for his backups. She lifted them out and added them to the growing pile next to the steel box.

Next was an old spiral-bound notebook with a beer bottle shaped stain on the top corner and fading doodles of Anthrax and Metallica logos. She smiled faintly. A throwback to his heavy metal days. It was probably filled with names and numbers of old girlfriends. Stephanie added it to the pile without opening it. There would be time enough to examine it later.

"Well, that's a surprise!" she murmured to herself, staring into the box.

Under the notebook was a slim, external hard-drive. She pulled it out and turned it over, looking at it. John had been nothing if not technologically declined. He never kept backups and couldn't find his way out of the C: drive if his life depended on it. So what was he doing with an external drive? Did he even know how to use it? The power cord and USB cable were in the box and Stephanie pulled them out, setting them aside along with the drive. Strange.

At the bottom of the box was a white, legal-sized envelope. Stephanie pulled it out and frowned, feeling something bulky and hard inside. She opened it curiously and gasped. Tipping the envelope, she held out her hand and a ring rolled into her palm.

Stephanie stared at it. It was the engagement ring John gave Alina all those years ago. Why had he kept it? They all just assumed he'd sold it after she, quite literally, threw it at him. Despite needing cleaning, the half-carat diamond sparkled when she picked up the ring and tilted it to the light. The white gold band was twisted to look like a vine and Stephanie shook her head. She remembered how much Alina loved that ring, right up until she threw it at John's bleeding head.

And he kept it all these years.

Stephanie dropped it back into the envelope as a crushing wave of sadness rolled over her. Now John was dead and the ring would end up being sold, another piece of him gone forever.

The box was empty and Stephanie stared at the small pile representing what was left of John Smithe. The tears came unexpectedly, hot and furious, pouring down her face as she stared at the few pieces of his life John deemed worthy of a safe deposit box.

These were the things he wanted to make sure survived. These were what he wanted to keep safe, no matter what.

Stephanie raised shaking hands to try to brush away the tears, but the more she wiped them away, the faster they came. Her shoulders shook silently, and she finally dropped her face into her hands as the sobs overcame her. This was all that was left of her partner: an old engagement ring, a couple pieces of paper to say he existed, a gun, some cash, and an old notebook and hard drive. John had been so much more, but this was all that remained.

An entire lifetime in a little steel box in a bank vault.

Alina sipped her water and moved another file into her cleared folder. Leaning back in her chair, she stretched her arms over her head and rolled her head. She was about halfway through the files she had pulled from the Pentagon, and so far, she had nothing to show for it. If she didn't find something soon, Hawk just might get his wish. Without information, Viper had no defense and truly *was* sitting in the kill box, waiting to die. It was only a matter of time before the shooter found her. If she couldn't get a step ahead, she would have to return to Singapore and try again there. But this time, she'd be ready.

Sitting forward again, Alina clicked open the next file in line. She rubbed her eyes and started scanning through quickly. On the second page, she stiffened and her eyes narrowed. Not only did this one fit the profile she was searching for, but the career followed a path eerily similar to that of Hawk's.

Viper pursed her lips and reached for her water, sipping it as she carefully read through the file. Reaching the end, she sat back, stunned. This had to be him. This had to be the soldier Charlie wanted her to find. Everything about him, from his enlistment up until his discharge, caught her attention. This was just the type of soldier to garner Charlie's interest.

Alina stared at the photo on the screen, a 3x3 copy of a military photo. The face was different, but the eyes were the same as the mystery doctor she'd passed in the hallway of the hospital the day John died.

She studied him. Who was he? According to his Army file, he enlisted in Pawtucket, Rhode Island at the age of eighteen. By the time he was twenty-three, he was a Ranger deployed to Afghanistan, where he served with distinction. After two tours, he returned stateside and was honorably discharged. There his Army military record ended.

Viper slid her chair over to another PC. She opened a database and, on a hunch, typed in the name. A few minutes later, she was staring at the same photo from the military file. This time, there was a red stamp across it – DISCHARGED.

"I'll be damned," she breathed, staring at it.

The photo was attached to an admittance form. It was a form she remembered. She'd filled hers out sitting at a table across from the man who had finally talked her into applying for a special branch of the CIA she never knew existed. Viper leaned her head back, staring at the ceiling of her command center. He was more than just an ex-soldier.

He was one of them.

The silence in the long room was broken when her phone vibrated on the counter a few feet away. Alina reluctantly scooted her chair back over to her laptop and reached for her phone.

"Yes?"

"You sound very unhappy," Damon informed her cheerfully. "Miss me already?"

"Not unhappy. Mad."

A beat of silence greeted that statement and Viper could almost feel him stiffen over the phone.

"Things never end well when you get mad. Talk to me."

"Remember the soldier Charlie wanted me to find in Singapore?"

"Yes."

"I think I've found him."

"I thought you'd already decided it was the guy from your brother's company?"

"I kept looking. I still think he's involved somehow, but I like to cover all my bases," she replied. "I'm glad I did. This other one is ringing all kinds of bells and whistles. His last known address was in Singapore, as late as this past winter."

"And this makes you mad why?"

"He's one of us."

The silence was longer this time and Viper leaned forward to pick up her water, draining the bottle.

"What do we know?" Hawk finally asked.

Viper smiled faintly. His tone may be even, but she knew better. She could almost see the icy glint in his blue eyes as he switched into work mode.

"Not much. I found it right before you called. He was an Army

Ranger, honorably discharged."

"What makes you think he's one of us?"

"I pulled another file with his discharge photo. It was attached to the same application form we filled out when we applied for the Organization," Viper told him grimly. "That's as far as I've got."

"I doubt Charlie will confirm. At least, I hope to God he doesn't. I know I'd be pissed if he confirmed my status to another asset," Hawk said.

"Actually, I wasn't going to ask him."

"That's the only way to know he's one of us. How else will you...oh no. You're not thinking what I think you're thinking, are you?"

"Do you have a better idea?"

Hawk whistled.

"Wow. You've got balls," he told her. "Are you out of your mind?"

"You don't know where I was the other night," she replied dryly. "If you did, you'd know that ship already sailed."

"You're not instilling confidence in me, Viper," he muttered. "Are you sure about this? He'll flay you alive if he catches you. In fact, to be honest, I'm not sure how *I* feel about it."

"Relax. It's not like I'll go rooting through *all* the files," she said calmly. "I know which one I'm looking for. It will be quick. In and out."

Hawk snorted.

"Charlie will have you tagged before you crack the first firewall. There is no 'in and out' with our system."

"There's always a way. You just have to find it."

There was a long silence, then Hawk sighed heavily.

"Even if you do manage it, what are you hoping to find?" he asked. "We don't necessarily need confirmation he's an asset. You can just work on the assumption he is and plan accordingly."

"Charlie wanted me to find him for a reason. I can't find that reason with only half his story."

"This is getting messier every day. I don't like it. What the hell does one of our own have to do with the banks in Singapore? Why does Charlie think this involves us? And why now?"

"All good questions. Here's one more. Why the hell doesn't Charlie know where one of his assets is?"

They were both quiet for a moment, then she sighed and shook her head.

"None of this makes any sense," she said tiredly. "I feel like I'm trying to solve a riddle with every other word redacted."

"Agreed. It would help if Charlie had given you something more to go on in Singapore. Do you think this guy could be the one behind our shooter?"

"It would make sense. It's a start, anyway. If nothing else, it will lead us in the right direction."

Hawk sighed.

"I hate being stuck here. What can I do to help? Anything?"

"Actually, yes," Viper said, opening a new email. "I'm sending you a name. Can you do some background for me?"

"Sure. What kind?"

"Whatever you can find," she told him, typing an email and sending it. "While I'm hacking the Organization, you can work on the other one. See what you can dig up."

"Will do." Hawk paused, then, "I just got it. Jordan Murphy? This is the guy from Iraq?"

"Yes."

"I'll see what I can find. At least it will keep me from watching the damn TV. I can feel my brain dying in here."

Viper grinned.

"Be thankful you're not dead," she told him ruthlessly. "How are you feeling?"

"Stronger," he said. "All that sleep did some good. I'm feeling more like myself."

"Good. What does the doc say?"

"Not much. I think he's surprised I'm still here, to be honest."

"Well, get better so you can get out of there," Viper said, glancing at her watch. "I have to go. Michael and Angela will be back soon and I have some things I have to do before they come back."

"Angela? She's there too?"

Viper sighed.

"Yes. I wasn't going to let her anywhere near me, but Michael talked me into it. He thinks it's safer for her here than anywhere else."

"Oh, he does? Does he realize what kind of labyrinth you've got tangled in?" Hawk demanded. "Now you just have someone else to worry about!"

"He's taking some of the flak for me. He's with her now while she meets with the funeral director and the priest at the church. He's doing his part. And she promised to stay put after the funeral and not contact the outside world. There's really not much else I can do."

"He's tagging along while she goes to the funeral home and the church?" Hawk sounded amused. "That must be painful. When is the funeral?"

"Tomorrow. The viewing is tonight."

"Are you ok?"

"I'm fine."

"I doubt that," he said. "If you need me, you know how to reach me."

"I know," she said. "Thank you."

"I'll get started on this Jordan Murphy guy," Hawk said. "I'll let you know what I find. Do you have a name on the other one? Or are you keeping it to yourself?"

"Why? So you can poke around in that too? I don't think so."

"Viper, you say that like you don't trust me!"

"I don't," she retorted bluntly. "I want you to focus on getting better. Let me take care of the heavy lifting."

Alina could almost feel his glare through the phone.

"I just want a name to put with the idea. Just the first name, if you insist. I can't do much with a first name."

She sighed.

"Kyle. His name is Kyle."

Chapter Eighteen

Michael got out of the truck and closed the door, looking around. He was parked at the side of a wide, tree-lined street populated with a mix of large old Victorian and Colonial homes with spacious, well-groomed lawns. It looked like something out of a magazine...or a horror movie. Sleepy, picturesque town gets besieged by demons or zombies.

Circling the truck, he glanced up at the impressive gray stone front of St. Peter's Roman Catholic Church. Statues flanked the wide stone steps on either side, surrounded by flowers. A fountain around the side and to the right of the entrance offered peace and serenity with a bench and another statue. The front lawn was split in two by a walkway leading to the steps of the church with a bronze statue of St. Pete himself dominating one of the halves. On the right of the huge church was a smaller, square building that appeared to be a school. The two structures were separated by a narrow alleyway running from the street back to a parking lot behind the buildings. To the left of the church, a rather modest rectory sat at the end of path lined with rose bushes. All of the lawns were impeccably manicured. Clearly this was not a parish hurting for funds.

"That's the convent over there," said Angela, climbing out of the truck and closing the door. She pointed to yet another stone building on the other side of the school. "The nuns teach at the school. Alina and Stephanie both went there."

"Really?" he asked, glancing over to the school. "You didn't?"

"No. I went to public school, thank God," she said cheerfully. "Ask Lina for some of her horror stories sometime. She got into a lot of trouble with the nuns."

"That doesn't surprise me one bit," Michael said with a grin.

They walked along the sidewalk in front of the church until they reached the path to the steps.

"Where does that driveway go?" he asked, nodding to the alley between the school and church.

"There's a big lot behind the church," Angela explained.

"That's probably where Joanne parked. There was a spot in the street so I didn't think to tell you about it."

"No worries. Just curious."

Michael scanned the area around the entrance of the church as they walked up the path, noting the walkway running around the side in front of the fountain before leading to the rectory. He hated churches. They always had multiple entrances and exits. Even with a whole team they were a nightmare to secure, and he only had himself. For maybe the hundredth time, he silently cursed Damon for putting him in this position.

"There's Joanne," Angela said, waving to the woman hurrying up from the alley.

"Sorry I'm late!" the woman called breathlessly. "I just had to stop at Aunt Charlotte's for some chocolate while I'm in town. Bill will kill me if I go back to the hotel without any. He's been looking forward to it since we flew in."

"Don't worry! We just got here ourselves," Angela answered with a smile. "Is Father Angelo expecting us in the church or over at the rectory?"

"The church."

Joanne bustled to a stop in front of them, her bleached hair blowing in the breeze. She was a tall woman, still attractive in her later years, and full of energy. The dark rings under her eyes bespoke sleepless nights after the death of her only child, but she was putting on a good front. Michael got the impression appearances meant a lot to her.

"He's probably inside. Shall we?" she asked, starting up the steps.

Michael started after the women. His foot was on the second step when his phone started ringing. He reached into his pocket, smiling apologetically as the two women turned to look at him.

"Sorry," he murmured. "You two go ahead. I'll catch up. I have to take this."

"Ok. Just go through the vestibule into the sanctuary," Angela said, turning to continue up the steps.

Michael nodded and returned to the sidewalk.

"Thank God," he answered the phone in relief, his voice low.

"Uh-oh. That doesn't sound good," Blake said with a laugh. "What's going on?"

"You caught me about to step foot in a church for the first time in years," Michael told him, turning to walk along the sidewalk towards the fountain. "I'm keeping an eye on Angela while she does funeral stuff."

"Funeral stuff?"

"Yeah. We went to the funeral home, and now we're at the church."

"Well that doesn't sound like a good time."

Michael looked at the fountain and the statue of Mary, then continued along the path. About halfway down was another, steeper set of stone steps leading up to another door. Another entrance to the church. He stifled a sigh.

"It's not. I had to listen for over forty-five minutes while Angela and John's mother debated the pros and cons of white versus cream flowers."

"Ouch."

"Mind you, they'd already ordered the flowers. It was already a done deal."

"Then...why the debate?" Blake asked.

"I have no idea," Michael confessed, shaking his head. "It was a complete waste of time. I still don't know why they went."

"Well if it helps at all, I'm sitting in a chair outside a fitting room, holding Stephanie's purse and looking like a fool," Blake offered.

Michael grinned.

"That does make me feel better!"

"I thought it would. We went to lunch when she was done at the bank and somehow I ended up here. Why do women make us hold their purse? They carry it everywhere, every day. Why can't they take it into the fitting room? Is there some risk of a fitting room black hole opening up and swallowing it?"

"Why do women do anything they do? Like debate the color of flowers already ordered?" Michael countered, strolling along the path to the steps ahead. "Have you heard anything from Washington yet? Did they pull in the guy who planted the drugs?"

"They can't find him," Blake said glumly. "They went to his apartment and he wasn't there. The last person to see him was his roommate last night at the bar."

"They'll find him," Michael said, starting up the steps toward the side door. "He's probably sleeping it off somewhere."

"Yeah."

Michael looked up in surprise as the door above him opened suddenly and a priest appeared. He was dressed in black slacks and button down shirt, the white collar stark amidst all the black, and he looked just as startled to see Michael.

"Hold on, Blake," Michael murmured. "Hello. Sorry. I didn't

mean to startle you."

"Not at all. Can I help?" the priest asked with a smile.

"I'm with the two women meeting Father Angelo," said Michael, reaching the top of the steps. "I had to take a call, so I told them I'd meet them inside."

"Ah! I appreciate that. Many don't think to keep their phones out of the sanctuary," the priest said cheerfully. He held the door open for Michael. "They're in the front, near the altar."

"Thank you," Michael said, grabbing the door.

"My pleasure. Have a good day."

The priest started down the steps.

"You too, Father."

Michael watched the priest descend and lifted his phone back to his ear.

"Let me call you back when I'm done here," he said. "I'm about to go inside and I guess they frown on phones in the church."

"No problem. I'll talk to you later."

Michael hung up and stepped into the dark, cool antechamber. The smell of incense assaulted him as the door closed behind him and he looked around. A tall statue of a benevolent-looking man dressed in robes looked down over rows of candles with a kneeler in front of them. He shook his head and moved across the small room toward the larger sanctuary beyond.

Rows of gleaming pews stretched in either direction and Michael looked around in surprise. The church was huge. The pews were divided into four sections divided by a wide walkway, two sections in the front half of the church and the other two in the back half. A wide center aisle ran from the front entrance all the way down to the altar. Across from him, suspended above the left side of the church like an old-style box seat at a playhouse, was an organ loft. He raised an eyebrow in surprise. Not many small town churches had organ lofts. At least, not where he came from.

The lighting was muted and the cavernous sanctuary was quiet; every step he took echoing around the space. Angela and Joanne stood before the altar with a tall priest who was graying at the temples. He was dressed in the same black slacks and shirt as the priest Michael had just passed.

"Oh, Michael!" Angela caught sight of him and waved him forward. "Come give your opinion."

Michael strode down a side aisle along the right side, passing confessional booths on his way, and crossed to where the threesome stood. As he approached, the priest smiled at him and nodded in greeting.

"Good afternoon," he said, holding out his hand. "I'm Monsignor Fanucci. Everyone calls me Father Angelo. I'll be saying the mass tomorrow."

"Hello, Father," Michael shook his hand firmly. "Michael O'Reilly. It's a pleasure to meet you."

"We were just trying to decide where we'll be seated," Joanne told him. "I think the left side, but Father Angelo seems to think the right is better."

Michael blinked and glanced at the Monsignor. He thought he detected a glint of amusement in the older man's gray eyes.

"Umm..." Michael turned to face the two lines of pews stretching endlessly to the back of the church. "There doesn't seem to be much difference between the two," he ventured. "Why do you think the left is better?"

"Because everyone will be coming from the right," Angela explained. "Joanne thinks it will aid in the flow of traffic if we're on the other side."

"You have to realize that mourners will want to pay their respects to you," Father Angelo interjected calmly. "They will simply walk over, then have to come back again to go to their seats. It will create more of a bottleneck. I've officiated many large funerals, unfortunately, and have seen it happen."

Michael looked at the women.

"Makes sense," he said. "Why is everyone coming from the right?"

"John will be laid out in that antechamber you just came through," Joanne said. "So they will come from that direction."

Michael stared at her.

"Why is he going to be laid out in there?"

The two women stared back at him.

"So people can say goodbye, of course," said Joanne.

"Isn't that what the viewing tonight is for?"

Father Angelo fell into a sudden coughing fit.

"Well, yes," Joanne said, glancing at the Monsignor, "but it seems only fair to give anyone who doesn't come tonight the opportunity to…see him one last time."

Michael felt a dull throb starting in his temple.

"I see."

"Of course, if you don't have him laid out in there, we could position the coffin here, in front of the altar," Father Angelo suggested, clearing his throat. "You can still have the casket open if you prefer. If we position him here, the mourners can come down the right, pay their respects, then move up the center to their seats. We've had great success with that flow."

"Have him...right here?" Joanne asked, motioning to the center before the steps leading up to the altar. "Is there room?"

"Oh yes! And they can offer you their condolences as they walk up the center aisle. At that point, it doesn't matter which side you're on, so if you prefer the left, you can be on the left."

Michael glanced at the priest and breathed a silent sigh of relief that the older man was taking over the discussion. He turned to look up at the altar. A large statue of the crucified Jesus dominated the back wall. To the right of the altar, a door was ajar. It appeared to lead into a back room, probably for the priests. To the left was another room, encased in windows with curtains. Michael looked at it thoughtfully. What was it?

"...if you think that would be best. Don't you agree, Michael?"

Joanne's voice pulled him reluctantly back to the conversation.

"Absolutely," he said promptly, turning back to the group.

Father Angelo's eyes lit with laughter and Michael knew the priest was fully aware Michael had absolutely no idea what he had just agreed with.

"That's settled," Angela said cheerfully. "I think Alina and Stephanie should be in the front pew with you, Joanne. Don't you agree? After all, they probably knew him the best out of all of us. I can be in the second pew, with Michael and Blake."

"Yes, I don't see any reason that wouldn't be appropriate," Joanne agreed. "How is Alina? This must have been such a shock to her. John said she was back. I was hoping...well, it doesn't matter now."

Michael's eyebrows raised into his forehead of their own accord and he turned away to continue looking at the strange off-chamber with the curtains.

"The Mother's Room," Father Angelo said at his elbow.

Michael glanced at him in surprise and the priest grinned.

"I make my living observing people and what moves them," the older man told him. "You're wondering what that room is. It is for mothers with infants so they can attend mass and not disturb the other parishioners."

"Do babies disturb?" Michael asked.

"When they're unhappy, yes. It is the nature of us all, I'm afraid."

"Huh." Michael turned back to look at the expanse of pews. "It's a beautiful church."

"We are very blessed here," Father Angelo agreed, turning to look out over the sanctuary with Michael. "You're Irish? What parish do you attend?"

"Oh, I live in DC," Michael said. "I was raised in Brooklyn."

"Ah, Brooklyn. I served in a little parish there when I was first ordained. St. Michael's."

"I was in St. Matthew's," Michael said. "My parents are still there."

"Do you get back to Brooklyn often?"

"Fairly often, when work allows."

"And what kind of work do you do?"

"I'm in the Secret Service."

"Ah, another Federal agent," Father Angelo nodded and smiled. "I should have known. You have the bearing of a military man. Have you served?"

"Marines."

"I thought so. Thank you for your service. Did you know John from work?"

"In a way," Michael murmured. "We had a mutual friend: Alina."

"Oh yes! I'll be glad to see her again, even if it is under these circumstances."

Michael looked at him in surprise.

"You know her?"

Father Angelo smiled.

"Yes, of course. She attended the school here," he said. "She helped with the retreats after she went on to high school. I spoke with her a few days before she joined the Navy. I haven't seen her since. Joanne told me she is back in Jersey."

"Yes," said Michael. "She travels quite a bit."

"So I've heard. I'm glad she's made a place for herself in this world. There was a time when she was very lost."

"When Dave died?" It was Father Angelo's turn to look surprised and Michael grinned. "I served with Dave. I was there the day he died. That's how I met her. I promised Dave...well, it doesn't matter."

"That was a tragedy," Father Angelo said. "War is such a terrible thing. It tears so many lives apart."

"Monsignor, would it be possible to have the organ play tomorrow?" Joanne called from where she and Angela had moved farther down the wide center aisle toward the middle of the church. "John loved that organ when he was a boy."

"Unfortunately, the pipes are being cleaned and restored, so that's not possible," Father Angelo replied, moving toward the two women. "However, we can feed organ music through the sound system. Do you have a particular hymn in mind?"

Michael watched as the priest joined the two women, then turned to gaze slowly around the whole church. It was far too large to cover all the entrances and exits effectively tomorrow. If he had a few weeks to plan, he might be able to come up with something to ensure Alina's safety, but with less than twenty-four hours, it was impossible.

He shook his head and turned to follow the priest. The only thing they had on their side was that the majority of the attendees were Federal agents and would be carrying firearms. It would be suicide for anyone to come into the funeral with the intent to hit Viper. The odds would be heavily against them.

Unfortunately, Michael knew that odds didn't have much to do with it.

Chapter Nineteen

Kyle Anthony March slid into the driver's seat of his rental sedan, and pulled the white plastic collar off, tossing it onto the passenger's seat. He stared at the back of the church thoughtfully for a moment, then started the engine and pulled out of his parking spot in the shade of a large old maple tree.

It had been a simple matter to find where the funeral for the man in the hospital was being held. All he'd had to do was pour through the obituaries from the past week until he found the one for Special Agent John Smithe. He'd struck gold with yesterday's Courier Post.

Agent Stephanie Walker hadn't led him to Viper yet, but he was becoming more and more convinced she would. After watching her for the past two days, he'd managed to learn quite a bit. For one thing, the man staying with her was also an FBI agent, and an ex-military man to boot. That complicated matters, but didn't make them impossible. He would just have to be cautious. There was also the other woman who showed up last night. She was another complication he hadn't expected. He had thought she was going to stay at the already crowded apartment, but then a Ford F150 showed up. While the man was inside, Kyle ran the plates and discovered Michael O'Reilly was also an ex-Marine, and a Secret Service agent. Kyle was too experienced a hunter to discount so many Federal agents under one roof. Something was going on, and somehow he'd managed to land himself right in the middle of it when he took the job to kill John Smithe.

He shook his head as he pulled out of the parking lot onto the sleepy, deserted backstreet behind the church. If it was just the FBI agents, that would be one thing. John was an FBI agent, so it was only natural Kyle would run into many of them in his search for Viper. Now, however, a Secret Service Agent was in the mix, and that was something Kyle didn't like. Not only was Michael O'Reilly an unknown factor, but he was another connection to Washington. With Blake Hanover that made two people connected to the capital, and that was two too many.

Kyle rolled to a stop at the sign at the end of the street, looked to his left, and pulled onto the town's main road. He had to learn why someone wanted John Smithe dead enough to hire him. That was the key. That would tell him why so many Federal agents were suddenly involved, and why two of them were from Washington. It would also tell him why Viper was part of it. If he knew that, he had a chance.

If he could find out what John was hiding, he'd know who wanted him dead.

And Kyle knew just where to start.

Stephanie stared at Angela in disbelief.

"What do you mean you don't know where she is?!"

Angela shrugged and tossed her hair over her shoulder.

"She wasn't at the house when we got back this afternoon, and she still wasn't there when we left," she said. "She didn't leave a note or anything. I tried calling, no answer."

"So help me, if she doesn't show up, I'll never speak to her again!" Stephanie exclaimed furiously. She swung around to face Michael. "Do you know anything about this?"

Michael raised his eyebrows.

"About where she is? No."

Stephanie made a sound strongly reminiscent of a growl and dug into her purse for her phone, pulling it out a second later.

"I'm calling her," she announced.

"Good luck with that," Angela muttered, turning to walk up the sidewalk to the funeral home. "We've already tried."

Michael glanced at Stephanie, then turned to follow Angela. When they had arrived a few moments before, the small parking lot for the funeral home was already filled. While he drove around looking for the closest spot on a side street, Angela called to tell Stephanie they were looking for parking. When they finally walked up the road to the funeral home, she was waiting on the sidewalk for them.

"Does she really think Lina won't come?" he asked Angela under his breath.

Angela glanced up at him.

"I don't know," she said, glancing back at Stephanie. "Maybe. To be honest, I think she's upset she hasn't seen her since she got back. I mean, let's be honest, Alina isn't acting like herself."

Michael was silent as they mounted the steps to the wrap-around porch of the funeral home. If Alina didn't come to the viewing, Damon would have his head for letting her roam free while someone wanted her dead. He suppressed a sigh. And if he hadn't accompanied Angela all day, Viper would have had his head. Either way, he didn't come out on top.

"Son of a..." Stephanie's exclamation followed them and they both turned to watch as she stalked up the sidewalk after them. "She's not answering."

"I told you," said Angela. "Relax. She'll come. We bought an outfit especially for it."

That caught Stephanie's attention and made her pause.

"You did?" she asked. "You mean, you actually got her out shopping?"

"Yes, on Saturday. We got an outfit for tonight and one for tomorrow. I told her she had appearances to keep up."

"Appearances?" Michael repeated. "What appearances?"

Angela looked at him.

"She's John's ex-fiancé. Everyone knows it. She can't show up looking like a scrub."

"Oh, please tell me you told her that," he murmured, his eyes dancing.

Stephanie grinned behind Angela's back, amused with him.

"Of course I did."

Angela sailed through the front door with that statement and Michael looked at Stephanie. After a second, they both chuckled.

"God, I wish I could have seen it," he said.

"You and me both," she agreed. "If that's what she had to hear for a whole shopping trip, I suddenly understand Alina's reluctance to come. Good Lord."

Michael held open the door and waited as Stephanie went through before following her in. The outer door opened into a large square hallway. A round mahogany table was in the center, dominated by a huge vase filled with cream roses and assorted ferns and greenery. Laid on the table were piles of memorial cards bearing a photo of John. A small crowd milled around the hallway, speaking in low voices and greeting acquaintances.

"He's laid out in the front room, through here," said Stephanie, moving around Angela and motioning to a set of open double-doors on the right.

"Are Joanne and Bill in there?" Angela asked, swiping up a memorial card as she passed the table. "How are they holding up?"

"They seem fine. As fine as they can be, anyway."

Michael followed the two women into the front room and glanced around. This room was filled with people. All in varying shades of black and gray, they looked like a rainy day. A receiving line wrapped around the outer edge of the room, leading back to the open coffin. Chairs were arranged in rows in the center of the room and a few mourners who already paid their respects were seated, talking together in low voices. Others milled around, nodding to people they knew and looking appropriately somber.

"It's about time you showed up," said Blake in a low voice behind him. "I've been wandering around, trying to avoid getting into 'how do you know the deceased' conversations with people I don't know."

Michael turned to look at his friend, a grin crossing his lips.

"How's that working?"

"It's not. I've met just about everyone here," Blake said glumly, moving into the receiving line with Michael and Angela. "I hate these things."

"We all do," Michael replied, watching as Stephanie departed to rejoin Joanne and her husband near the coffin. "It reminds us we're mortal."

"I'm hoping things get more interesting as the night goes on," Blake said. "I've been here since six-thirty. Stephanie promised beer and wings afterwards and I'm holding her to it."

"Beer and wings?" Angela turned around, perking up considerably. "Where?"

Blake shrugged.

"Some place called...Pete's? Chicken? Chicken Pete?" he said, his brows creasing in thought. "Does that sound right?"

"Chickie and Pete's?! Oh, we're so in!"

"We are?" Michael asked, startled.

"Yes, we are. Trust me. You'll thank me later."

Michael glanced at Blake in time to see his friend grin.

"Looks like you're just along for the ride too," he said. He looked around, then nudged Michael to get his attention. "Is your girlfriend coming?"

"I have no idea, and she's not my girlfriend," Michael muttered. "No one's heard from her since this morning."

Blake raised an eyebrow and glanced at Stephanie across the room.

"That's not going to go over well with Stephanie," he said decidedly. "Where the hell is she?"

"No clue, but Angela says she'll show. She bought an outfit especially."

"An outfit?" Blake stared at him for a beat. "You're kidding."

Michael couldn't stop the grin that stretched across his face. "Nope."

Blake glanced at the back of Angela's head and nodded to her. "Her idea?"

"Yep."

"Oh, I can't wait to hear all about this," Blake said, his shoulders shaking in laughter. "See? This ordeal is getting more interesting already."

Alina glanced at her watch and strode through the shadows, almost invisible in the darkness. She was late. Stephanie was probably threatening never to speak to her again, and Angela was probably assuring her she wouldn't miss it. She had, after all, bought an outfit just for this.

She glanced down at the black pants and deep purple silk blouse. Angela had tried to get her into a pencil skirt, but Alina managed to get away with the pants instead. Not only was there no way she was wearing a skirt two days in a row, but you couldn't move in a pencil skirt. At least, she couldn't, and Viper wasn't about to risk her mobility for the sake of appearances.

Rounding the corner of the large funeral home, Alina moved along the brick walkway crossing in front of the house. She cast a sharp glance around the yard, noting the various people coming and going. The street in front of the home was quiet and well-lit, affording good visibility, and Viper looked at the few cars lucky enough to get spots directly in front of the funeral home. They were all empty.

Her shoulders relaxed slightly as her heels clicked along the bricks. She hated being out and exposed like this, but there was no other choice. Her .45 pressed comfortably against the small of her back and an ankle holster held a military combat knife against the leg under her pants. She had worked with less, in much more hostile territory. John's viewing should be a walk in the park.

Light poured from the front porch, welcoming mourners with a comforting glow at odds with the nature of the event. As she moved up the steps to the front door, Alina glanced at the few mourners smoking on the wrap-around porch. Her brain registered the fact that all but two of them were Federal agents as she stepped onto the porch and walked toward the door. The two that weren't she put down as spouses.

She noted all of this in a glance and reached for the door. Taking a deep breath, she paused for the briefest of seconds, her hand on the handle. Then, her lips tightening in resolve, she pulled it open and stepped inside.

The crowd in the hallway was immense and, as the door opened, all those near to it turned to look at the newcomer. Alina suddenly relaxed. Crowds comforted her. They were large and impersonal, and Viper knew how to navigate them with ease. Those near her turned back to their conversations as they realized they didn't know her and Alina moved through the crush easily, heading toward the large double-doors on the right.

"There you are!"

Angela's voice cut through the medley of conversations and Alina turned her head to see the brunette moving through the throng towards her.

"Stephanie's ready to have your head!" she exclaimed, taking her arm and moving through the double doors with her. "Where have you been?"

"I had some things I had to take care of."

This room was even more packed than the hall. Alina estimated close to a hundred people were crammed inside, shoulder to shoulder. Angela guided her through to the far side where the receiving line was dwindling down.

"Well at least you came at a good time. This is the shortest I've seen the line so far!" said Angela. "I think our entire graduating class showed up, not to mention so many FBI types I've lost count. Joanne's been asking for you. She and Bill will be glad to see you've arrived."

Angela deposited her at the back of the relatively short line and looked at her assessingly.

"You look fantastic," she said approvingly. "I knew purple would look good on you."

"Is that Mr. Gregson?" Alina demanded, staring at an older man on the other side of the room. "The gym teacher?!"

Angela glanced over her shoulder and nodded, turning back with a grin.

"I'm telling you, Lina, there are people here I haven't seen since graduation," she said. "Who knew John was so popular?"

Alina stifled a groan and finished scanning the crowds. She

recognized more faces than she cared to remember and her heart sank. So much for sneaking in and out unnoticed.

"He always was," she murmured.

"At least they're not all women," said Angela cheerfully. "A lot, but not all. Oh!" she lowered her voice conspiratorially. "Nipples is here. I thought Joanne was going to have a heart attack when she met her."

John's on-again off-again girlfriend had gained the dubious nickname of Nipples from Stephanie and Angela. Alina raised an eyebrow, curiosity getting the better of her.

"She? I thought that was a generic, collective term for all his girlfriends."

"It kind of was. We couldn't keep up with their names and they all fit the same profile, so it was just easier that way. This was the latest one," Angela explained quietly. "I think her name is Cami, or something like that. When she met Joanne she started crying and told her she'd heard so much about her from John. I thought Stephanie's eyes were going to roll out of her head."

"Where is she?"

Angela glanced around, then nodded toward the front of the room, near the casket.

"Over there, to the left, a little bit in front of the casket. She's the one wearing the leopard print," she whispered. "I mean, seriously. Who wears leopard print to a viewing?"

Alina followed Angela's directions and her eyebrows soared into her forehead. Nipples definitely lived up to the hype. The buxom blonde was dressed in a skin-tight, leopard print pantsuit so low-cut that the girls would pop right out if she bent over. As it was, mounds of smooth flesh bulged up against the tenuous control of the thin fabric.

"Good God," Alina muttered. "John liked that?!"

"Oh, they all looked like that," Angela said cheerfully. "I want to know what the hell she's wearing to push her boobs up like that. It's gotta be a corset. I don't care how much silicone is in those puppies, it's not natural how high they sit."

Alina felt a laugh bubbling up inside her and she tamped it down, pressing her lips together firmly. She watched as Nipples spoke animatedly to two men, long red finger nails flashing as she gestured with her hands to make her point.

"I can't look away," she murmured, transfixed. "It's like watching a train wreck."

"I know! Isn't it the worst? Aren't you glad I talked you into the new outfits? There's no comparison between the two of you."

Alina tore her gaze away from the blonde and looked at Angela.

"There's no reason for a comparison," she said. "What are you talking about?"

"Lina, you might think there's no reason, but I assure you, everyone here is looking at you and saying he was better off with you than someone like her," Angela replied calmly. "Oh look, you're almost there."

Alina looked forward to find herself three people back from John's parents. Stephanie stood next to Joanne and, as Alina glanced up, she caught her eye. She smiled faintly and Alina sighed, nodding back.

"How long has Stephanie been standing there?" she asked Angela.

"At least two hours now," she answered. "People just keep coming. I think it's starting to wind down now, thank God."

Alina moved forward, the next to go, and got her first good look at John's parents. She hadn't seen or spoken to them since she threw a cast iron teapot at their son's head twelve years ago, effectively ending their engagement. She had departed for the Navy a few weeks later, never looking back. Now here she was, next in line to offer them her condolences with John lying a few feet away in an open coffin.

Joanne looked the same, but older. Her hair was impeccably styled, her makeup perfect, and she was dressed in a black suit with a light gray shirt under the jacket. John's father, Bill, was just as tall as Alina remembered but his hair was completely white now, a stark contrast to skin deeply tanned from years spent in the sun.

Emotion welled up inside Alina suddenly like a geyser, choking her, and she pressed her lips together firmly to stop them from trembling. Memories flooded into her mind at the sight of the couple who would have been her in-laws if things had gone differently all those years ago. Suddenly Alina was remembering Joanne and her own mother, taking her to lunch after a long morning of fruitless dress shopping. Joanne was very close with her mother. After the engagement ended, Alina knew the friendship had continued. Something tightened inside her and Viper took a deep breath.

Those were memories better left behind. They had no place in the present.

"It's about time you got here," Stephanie told her as Alina stepped forward. "I've been dodging questions all night."

"From who?" Alina asked, startled.

Stephanie rolled her eyes.

"Everyone!" she hissed. "Look around. It's like a class reunion!"

Alina shook her head.

"I don't know why they even remember me," she muttered. "I was gone long enough. Don't they have anything better to worry about?"

"Alina! My dear!" Joanne cried, turning to her as the man in front of Alina moved on to Bill. "Oh, it's been so long!"

Alina found herself engulfed in a tight hug and a strangely familiar smell of flowers enveloped her. Good God, the woman still wore the same perfume!

"Joanne," she murmured, lifting her arms to briefly touch Joanne's shoulders before pulling back. "I'm so sorry. I don't know what to say."

"Thank you," Joanne smiled at her, her eyes watery. "It's just such a shock! And it was for you too. I wanted to reach out to you as soon as we landed, but I didn't know how to reach you. How are you?"

"I'm fine," Alina told her, smiling faintly. "It was a shock, but I've had time to adjust."

"You look wonderful," Joanne told her. "I want to hear all about what you've been up to over the years. We'll have a nice sit-down tomorrow at the luncheon."

Alina nodded and smiled and moved on to John's father.

"Lina!" he boomed, a wide smile creasing his face. "Thank you for coming."

"Bill, I'm so sorry," she said, taking his outstretched hands. "I can't imagine what you're feeling right now."

"Can't you?" he asked gently, his blue eyes that were so much like John's meeting hers. "I'm sure it's very similar to what you're undoubtedly feeling right now. Shock. Grief. And bloody discomfort at all these strangers milling around."

Alina was surprised into a short laugh and Bill's hands tightened briefly on hers.

"Something like that," she agreed, pulling her hands away. "You haven't changed at all."

Bill tilted his head to the side and studied her for a second.

"You have," he said unexpectedly. "You look different. More...I don't know. Intimidating."

"Bill!" Joanne exclaimed, overhearing. "Stop it! You'll embarrass her!"

Bill raised an eyebrow and looked at Alina.

"Am I embarrassing you?" he asked. "I'm sorry."

"No, you're not," she assured him. "It's fine."

"See? She says it's fine," Bill told his wife as Alina turned away.

Her eyes fell on the gleaming black casket a few steps away and Alina felt her heart thump in her chest. The low drone of conversations faded into the background, and she sucked in a deep breath as her gut clenched. Suddenly her hands were trembling and she was having a hard time catching her breath. Memories chased themselves across her mind; hazy memories of a younger, happier John and a life so far removed Alina felt as if they were someone else's memories. Yet, they were hers. It was as if seeing Joanne and Bill had opened a floodgate, unleashing emotions carefully buried for years.

She could feel dozens of pairs of eyes watching her, waiting for her to walk up to the casket and say her final farewell. A hot wave rolled over her and the trembling spread from her hands to rest of her as she took a step toward the coffin.

Alina couldn't remember ever feeling so alone.

Then, suddenly, she wasn't.

A strong hand took one of hers and Alina glanced up into a pair of green eyes, filled with understanding. She swallowed and closed her fingers around Michael's. His warm clasp seemed to absorb the trembling from her hand and she took a deep, steadying breath. He didn't say a word, but held her hand and stepped up to the casket with her, shielding her from the curious scrutiny with his broad shoulders.

Alina stared down at John's impossibly still face, frozen in death. He looked at peace. Gone were the bruises and cuts that had marred his face and neck in the hospital. Gone were the habitually grim lines around his mouth, weary evidence of a career in federal law enforcement. Instead, he appeared to be finally at rest.

The trembling stopped and Viper felt herself grow calm once again. The grief that had threatened just seconds before receded, leaving her numb. John wasn't there. The shell left behind was simply that: a shell. The John she knew, and had loved, was gone. There was nothing more for her to do here.

Alina turned away from the casket, gently pulling her hand away from Michael's. She took one last deep breath and felt the haze clear from her mind, becoming aware of the low drone of conversation around her once again.

"Thank you," she said quietly, glancing up at Michael.

His eyes met hers and he nodded.

"You're welcome."

Alina moved into the crowds, her shoulders squared and her

back straight. One by one, old familiar faces from days long past stopped her, asking how she was and what she'd been doing all these years. As she moved further away from the gleaming casket, Viper never once looked back.

John was now where he always belonged: in her past.

Chapter Twenty

Alina watched from the shadows on the far end of the porch as Michael stepped out and looked around. He spotted her and moved along the wooden planks until he reached her.

"Had enough?" he asked.

"I had to get out of there before I did something I'd regret," she admitted ruefully. "I don't even remember half those people."

He chuckled and leaned against the railing next to her.

"You hid it well. I'm surprised you stayed as long as you did. Stephanie's looking for you. She wants to introduce you to Blake."

"That's not a good idea."

"I don't think she agrees," he said. "You might as well resign yourself. She's determined. Besides, I don't see that it can possibly make much difference at this point. He already knows who you really are and I can vouch for him. He hasn't told a soul. I don't see him starting now."

"That's not my primary concern," Alina said. "I've told you before. I'm dangerous company these days. The less he's involved, the better for him."

"He's a big boy. He knows the risks. He'll take care of himself."

"Where's Angela?" she asked, changing the subject after a moment of silence.

"I left her inside talking to someone she knows. Relax. Nothing can possibly happen in the middle of that crowd." Michael glanced down at her and Alina could feel him studying her in the darkness. "How are you holding up?"

"I'm fine."

"You're not fine," he said bluntly. "You can lie to yourself all you want, but I felt you shaking in there."

Alina was silent for a moment, watching as a couple came out onto the porch and went toward the other end, pulling out packs of cigarettes.

"I'm dealing with it in my own way," she said finally. "I'm used to death. It's part of my daily life. It's not his death that's the problem, it's the memories."

"The memories are a good thing. It's how he lives on in your life."

"I don't need him to live on," Alina said shortly. "I need him to be laid to rest."

Michael raised an eyebrow and opened his mouth to reply, but he never got the chance. Stephanie and Blake came outside and spotted them.

"There you are!" Stephanie exclaimed, coming towards them. "Why are you out here in the dark?"

"I needed some air," Michael said quickly, drawing an unreadable look from Alina. "It was getting hot in there."

"It's packed," Stephanie agreed with a grimace. "Alina, I don't think you've officially met Blake Hanover. Blake, this is Alina."

Blake nodded and held out his hand to her in the shadows.

"It's nice to finally meet you."

"Is it?" Alina softened her question with a faint smile and took his outstretched hand. "I wouldn't speak so soon, if I were you."

Blake grinned and looked into her face, unabashedly amused.

"At least I know you're not boring," he said. "I'm sorry we're meeting under these circumstances. I know John was close to you. I'm sorry."

Alina pulled her hand away smoothly and nodded in acknowledgement.

"Thank you," she said shortly.

"The breeze feels good out here," Stephanie said, turning her face into the wind blowing from the front yard. "It really is hot in there." She glanced around. "Where's Angela?"

"Inside," said Michael.

Stephanie frowned at him.

"You left her alone?" she demanded.

"She's hardly alone. There have to be close to a hundred people in there and, as far as I can tell, she knows them all."

"That's not the point," Stephanie muttered.

Michael sighed and straightened up.

"I'll go check on her," he muttered, heading toward the door.

"Thank you!" Stephanie called after him. She took his place next to Alina in the shadows and looked at her old friend. "How're you holding up?"

"I'm fine."

"I'm not. I feel like I've been hit by a truck," Stephanie said roundly. "We're going to Chickie and Pete's for wings and beer after this. You want to join us?"

Alina glanced at her, then at Blake.

"I don't think that's a good idea."

"Why? I haven't seen you in over a week. We need a couple hours to relax, especially after this."

"You guys go ahead. You've earned it," Alina said. She nodded to Blake. "Especially you. I hear you've been helping Steph through all this. Thank you."

"It's been no trouble," he said with a shrug. "I've lost enough friends to know how it feels. Besides, it's not all unselfish. I'm working out of the Philly office for a few days and Steph's been kind enough to put me and Buddy up. You remember him?"

He slid the mild jab in smoothly and Alina felt her lips curving in a grin.

"Of course I remember Buddy," she replied. "He's a big old teddy bear."

Blake grunted at that and Stephanie burst out laughing.

"Apparently not with everybody," she told Alina. "That being said, he's been nothing but friendly with me."

"It's strange, that," Blake said thoughtfully. "He took to you right away. That never happens."

"I beg to differ," Alina murmured, her eyes dancing.

"Walker!"

Someone called out suddenly, forestalling any response Blake may have been about to make. Alina turned to watch as a man waved and ambled towards them, somehow appearing to rush without actually hurrying. His sandy-colored hair refused to lay flat, sticking up towards the back, and wire-rimmed glasses perched on his nose. She raised an eyebrow as he approached. He had the bizarre air of a mad scientist and Viper instinctively knew she was looking at the forensic genius John had held in such high esteem. Her lips twisted as a sense of melancholy rolled over her. John had called him the basement gnome. She wondered if that nickname would now die with the Special Agent who coined it.

"Sorry to interrupt," he said, joining the small group in the shadows. "I was trying to find you in there. There's so many people!"

"Yes, it's a packed house," Stephanie said. "Matt, you remember Special Agent Hanover?"

"Yes, of course." Matt shook Blake's hand, his head bobbing awkwardly. "Hanover."

"Call me Blake," Blake said. "It's good to see you again."

"Wish it was for a happier reason," Matt said.

"Same. I'm sorry. Everyone liked John."

Matt nodded and pushed his glasses up on his nose.

"Yeah, they did. He was good people. I've been to three of these now and it's not getting any easier," he said, sounding bewildered. "I don't think it ever will."

"Matt, this is my old friend–"

"Raven," Alina interjected smoothly, holding her hand out. "Raven Woods."

Stephanie glanced at her, a look of consternation on her face at her almost-slip. While there was nothing that could be done about the many people from their past who knew Alina's real name, there was an unspoken agreement that all new people were introduced with her alias.

"Nice to meet you," said Matt, shaking her hand. "That's an interesting name."

"My parents were hippies," Alina said blithely.

"My parents were morticians," he told her. "I was named after the first client of their joint business."

Alina blinked, feeling the corners of her lips pulling irresistibly upwards. She repressed them firmly.

"I'm fairly confident I was named after a mushroom."

Blake erupted into a coughing fit.

"Remember that side project you gave me last week?" Matt turned his attention back to Stephanie, dismissing Alina and mushrooms from his mind.

Stephanie nodded and Viper stilled. Last week, before all hell let loose with Asad and his load of bombs, she had given Stephanie a white lab coat and asked her to have the basement gnome analyze it. It had been worn by the man she was convinced had killed John. She doubted he would find anything, but at the time, it was the only lead she had. Apparently, Matt was as good as the reputation that preceded him.

"Yes."

"Well I got something today. It isn't much, but there really wasn't much to work with. I managed to get some DNA off it, but I can't get a match on anyone. I've run it through all the databases we have and no hits. Without something to compare it to, it's useless. Now if you get another DNA sample and bring it to me, I can tell you if it matches the one I have, but that's about it."

"Then what did you get?" Stephanie asked with a frown.

Matt pushed his glasses up on his nose again.

"I told you, it's not much, but it's something interesting," he said, dropping his voice. "At least, I think it's interesting. The coat comes from Singapore."

Viper's grew still while Stephanie stared at him blankly.

"What?"

He nodded.

"Yep. I noticed the stitching was different from what I'm used to seeing on traditional lab coats, so I looked more closely at everything. It was the buttons."

"The buttons?" Stephanie repeated.

"Yes. There are millions of different buttons out there, all used for different things. Most of them are standard buttons, but these weren't," Matt explained. "I narrowed the material down to the South Pacific, and then worked to match the exact button. Singapore. Those buttons are only used in three factories in Singapore. The fun part? One of those three factories produces lab coats. I can tell you where it came from, when, and in what batch."

"That's crazy," Blake said. "You figured all that out from a button?"

Matt glanced at him.

"Of course."

"What's the name of the factory?" Stephanie asked, glancing at Alina.

"I wrote it down for you," Matt said, digging in his pocket. "I brought it with me so I could give it to you tonight. I didn't want to say anything in front Rob. You know, since it's off the books."

"I appreciate that," Stephanie murmured, taking the folded piece of paper from him.

Blake raised an eyebrow and glanced at her, but remained silent.

"Will this get you closer to figuring out what happened to John?" Matt asked.

"I hope so."

"Good." Matt pushed his glasses up on his nose once more and turned to leave. He went a few steps, then paused and looked back. "First the bomb residue from Syria and the Ukraine, and now a coat from Singapore. What the hell was John up to?"

"I wish I knew, Matt," Stephanie said grimly. "I wish I knew."

Matt nodded and studied her for a minute, then sighed.

"If you need anything else, let me know. I'll do what I can to help."

She nodded and he continued on, disappearing into the funeral home. Once he was gone, Stephanie handed Alina the folded piece of paper without opening it.

"You heard the man," she said. "The coat came from Singapore. Where did you get it?"

Viper took the paper and raised her eyes to Stephanie's, considering her for a long moment.

"Not Singapore," she said finally.

Stephanie rolled her eyes.

"You don't say," she muttered.

"Anyone care to clue me in over here?" Blake asked, looking from one to the other. "What lab coat?"

Stephanie looked at Alina and she shrugged.

"He already knows too much as it is," she said in answer to the question on Stephanie's face. "Go ahead and tell him. It can't make it any worse."

"That's comforting," said Blake.

Stephanie looked at him.

"Last week, Lina gave me a lab coat and asked me to have Matt analyze it, off the books. Matt already found the bomb residue on John's Firebird and gave me the results on a flash drive. He also told me he'd help any way he could if it meant finding out what really happened to John."

Blake looked at Alina, her face hidden in the shadows.

"Where did the coat come from?" he asked. "What does it have to do with anything?"

Alina was silent for a moment, studying Stephanie's face in the darkness. Now wasn't exactly the best time to tell her that her partner was murdered. Then again, would there ever be a good time? And did she really want Blake to know about this? Her gaze shifted to him.

"Stop thinking and just tell us," Stephanie said, watching her. "I have a right to know, being as it was *my* forensic wizard who pinpointed where the coat was made."

Viper was silent for a long moment, then she sighed imperceptibly.

"It came from Cooper Hospital," she said, raising dark, emotionless eyes to Stephanie's, "the day John died."

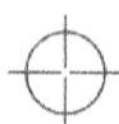

Angela glanced at her watch and looked around. While the throng had thinned considerably over the past hour, the large front room was still crowded and stuffy. If she didn't get some air soon, she was going to sweat to death. She'd find Stephanie or Alina and see if they wanted to go outside. Or, better yet, leave altogether and go to Chickie and Pete's for that beer.

Craning her neck, Angela scanned the crowds but they were nowhere in sight. She turned to leave the room and check the hall, almost plowing into someone as she did so.

"Oh!" she exclaimed, pulling up short and glancing up.

Trent looked down her, his gray eyes hooded. Dressed in dark pants with a black turtleneck under a charcoal sports jacket, he looked both relaxed and intimidating at the same time.

"Hello Angela."

Angela stared at him in surprise.

"Trent! What are you doing here?" she asked, falling back a step.

"I missed you at the office today. Jeff said you took a couple days off for a funeral," he said with a smile. "I wanted to offer my condolences."

Angela nodded, a feeling of disquiet washing over her.

"That's...very thoughtful of you," she said, forcing a smile. "I appreciate it."

"It's crowded," he said, looking around. "I don't think I've ever been to a viewing this packed."

"Yes, John was a good man."

Trent looked at her.

"Jeff said he was an FBI agent?"

Angela nodded, glancing toward the coffin at the front of the room. As she did so, she scanned the crowded room again, searching for a friendly face she could flag down.

"Yes."

"How did you know him?"

"We grew up and went to high school together. He ended up partnered with one of my best friends."

Trent raised an eyebrow.

"Really? Small world."

"It is around here," Angela said, looking back to him. "If you don't leave South Jersey to go to college, you pretty much stay forever."

"What happened? I mean, how did he die?"

"He was in a car accident."

"Oh my God, so it was unexpected!" Trent exclaimed.

"Yes. It's been quite a shock."

"I'm so sorry. How have you been holding up?"

"Well, as I said, it's been a shock." Angela glanced at her watch, wondering where Stephanie and Alina had disappeared to. She could really use an intervention.

"It must be hard being alone at a time like this."

Angela's head snapped up and she looked at him, startled.

"What?"

Trent raised an eyebrow innocently.

"You live alone, right? It must be hard to be upset and alone."

Angela stared at him, Stephanie and Alina momentarily forgotten.

"How do you know I live alone?" she demanded.

"You mentioned it in Miami. I'm sorry, have I upset you?" he asked, concerned.

"I…no," Angela shook her head. "I'm sorry. I think I'm just tired," she said sheepishly. "It's been a long couple of days."

"I can imagine," he said sympathetically. "If there's anything I can do…"

Angela shook her head and summoned a smile she didn't feel.

"Thank you, but I'll be fine," she assured him. "I just have to get through the funeral and then everything should calm down."

"When is the funeral?"

"Tomorrow."

"Are you staying with friends?"

Angela's brows furrowed into a faint frown.

"I…why do you ask?"

Trent shrugged.

"I don't know. I guess I just don't like the thought of you being alone at a time like this."

Angela's eyes narrowed slightly.

"I'll be fine."

"Why don't you let me take you out for a drink?" he suggested.

Angela felt her face grow warm as she scrambled in her mind to come up with an excuse, any excuse, to decline without sounding rude.

"Really, I'll be ok," she began, breaking off as Michael emerged from the crowds next to them. "Oh! Michael!" Angela exclaimed brightly. "There you are!"

Michael raised an eyebrow at the look of relief in her eyes.

"Sorry, I got distracted by…someone," he said, closing the distance to her side.

"Trent, this is a friend of mine, Michael," Angela introduced him. "Trent works for Trasker Pharmaceuticals. I met him in Miami while I was there on business."

"Nice to meet you," said Trent, holding out his hand.

Michael gripped it, his mind spinning.

"Trasker?" he repeated, managing to keep his voice level through sheer force of will. "Now why does that name ring a bell?"

"They're one of the largest pharmaceutical companies in the world," Angela told him. "I'd be surprised if you didn't know the name."

"That's probably it. I don't pay much attention to the business section, unfortunately. What are you doing up in Jersey?"

"Angela and I managed to put together a deal with her bank," Trent said easily, glancing at her with a smile. "It wasn't easy, but she pulled it off. I'm here to facilitate the transition of accounts."

"He makes it sound much more exciting than it really is," Angela said with a laugh. "I'm glad we could talk them into coming onboard, though."

"Did you know John?" Michael asked.

"No. I just came to offer Angela moral support."

Michael raised an eyebrow and glanced at Angela.

"That's thoughtful of you," he said. "It's been a shock."

"That's what I was just saying," said Angela. "Have you seen Stephanie? She's been the most torn up. I should probably get back to her," she added pointedly.

"I'll get going," Trent said. He looked at Angela. "If you change your mind about that drink, give me a call. You shouldn't be alone right now."

"She's not," Michael said smoothly. "We're keeping an eye on her. Don't worry."

Trent nodded.

"Good to know," he murmured. "It was nice meeting you, Michael. I'll see you soon, Angie."

Michael watched as Trent turned and made his way toward the front door. As he disappeared into the crowd, Angela exhaled loudly beside him.

"Thank God you came when you did," she told him. "That was the most awkward conversation of my life."

"What was he doing here?" Michael asked, looking down at her.

"I have no idea," she confessed. "I just met him last week. It's weird. I mean, who just shows up at a viewing? Where are Steph and Alina? I want to get out of here and go get a drink."

"I left them outside."

"Let's go get them, and get the hell out of here," she said, turning toward the door.

Michael followed her, his brows drawn together in a scowl. Why was someone from Trasker showing up at John's viewing? And how the hell did Angela get involved in all this? The break-in at her house suddenly seemed much more ominous and Michael was glad he had insisted on Alina bringing Angela to her house. While Viper brought along her own set of problems, at least her house was secured, and more importantly, Angela would not be alone.

Chapter Twenty-One

The muffled sound of a TV droned in the background from the adjoining room. The connecting door was open and the man sitting at a make-shift table glanced towards it, his dark eyes flashing with impatience. The sound of the canned laughter from the sitcom was grating on his nerves.

"I don't know how you can watch that rubbish," he called through the door. "It's not even funny."

There was no answer from the other room and he shook his head, bending over the table again with the soldering iron. Kasim Jamal very carefully held the end of a copper wire to a device piece and touched it with the hot iron, fusing it to the device. Once it was secured, he set the iron in its holder and sat back, stretching.

The table was covered with an array of parts that, once assembled, would combine to create one of his masterpieces. He sighed. That was what Asad used to call his customized bombs. Asad appreciated the patience and attention to detail that Kasim put into all his devices.

Now Asad was dead, murdered by the same assassin who had killed their beloved leader and mentor.

Kasim scowled and lifted his eyes to stare across the shabby motel room at the far wall covered in maps of South Philadelphia. Al-Jibad was gone, and so was Asad, but he could finish what they started. As long as he had breath, Kasim would continue.

His cellphone began ringing and vibrating on the scratched side table next to the bed and Kasim looked over in surprise. Standing, he crossed the room and picked it up. The screen told him the number was private.

"Hello?"

"You're still alive," a voice said. "Congratulations."

"I am not so easy to kill," Kasim replied. "Many have tried."

"Nasser is dead. His body washed up in the Potomac five days ago."

Kasim sank into a chair, his brows drawing together.

"I am not surprised. When we had no contact from him, we assumed he had been killed. How?"

"He was stabbed in the neck."

"Viper?"

"I don't think so," the voice said thoughtfully. "Nasser was killed at least four days before he bobbed up. Viper wasn't in Washington, DC."

"Then who?"

"I don't know. We don't have much to go on."

Kasim shook his head and rubbed his eyes.

"And the Viper?"

"Is hunting you. She won't stop until she finds you."

"She is welcome to try," Kasim muttered. "I will be ready."

"Don't be arrogant. She will find you, and she will kill you. It's what she's trained to do. Your only hope is to stay hidden until I can get you out of the country."

Kasim looked at the equipment and parts spread out over the table and around the room.

"And how do you suggest we do that?" he asked.

"It's quite simple. I know how Viper hunts. It's easy to avoid being found if you know what to avoid."

"I'm listening."

"Find a secure location and stay put," said the voice. "Somewhere that isn't isolated, but isn't in the center of the city. Somewhere no one will look twice or ask questions. Don't travel. Avoid airports, train stations, bus stations, any transportation hub. She'll be monitoring all of them."

"Cars?"

"Travel by cab. Better yet, use Uber. Don't rent a car. She monitors rental agencies as well." The voice paused, then continued. "I don't know how much she's figured out with the Casa Reinos Cartel. To be safe, cut off all contact with them. That goes for all your associates overseas as well. Viper has ears and eyes in just about every country. I can guarantee your known associates are being watched and listened to."

"If they can be found," said Kasim. "Many of them are in hiding."

"Don't risk it. Trust me. In fact, just stay off the Internet and out of chat rooms altogether. She's inordinately skilled in extracting information from the web. If you go online, she'll find you and backtrack your location before you even know you've been tagged."

"That's impossible," Kasim scoffed. "No one can pinpoint one person on the Internet."

"You're right. It's impossible. What does America know?" Sarcasm dripped from the voice over the phone. "I'll tell you what. You go online and log into one of your dark web sites. I'll set a timer. By the time it goes off, I'll have word of your death on my desk."

Kasim was silent, staring at the maps of South Philadelphia broodingly.

"If I do all this, everything you have said, then what?" he finally demanded. "How long do I hide like a rat?"

"Until I contact you and tell you it's safe to travel. I'm making arrangements. I can get you out of the country. You just stay down until I contact you."

"How do I know you will do it?"

"I got you over here, didn't I? I got you across the border, across the country, and right into their backyard. I'll get you out again. I just have to blind Viper long enough to move you."

Kasim sighed.

"Very well," he agreed. "I'll wait for your call."

Kasim hung up and set the phone down. He looked up as a shadow fell across the door.

"Well?" his companion asked, leaning against the door frame. "What's the plan?"

"We stay here for now. Stay offline. No contact with anyone, even the Cartel."

"And all this?" the man motioned to the bomb parts spread out through both rooms. "Do we continue?"

"Yes." Kasim stood up and walked over to the dresser to pour himself a glass of water from the tall bottle sitting next to the TV. "We continue. They think they can move us out of the country at their will. We stay. We finish what we started. We will not be manipulated."

The man raised an eyebrow.

"Manipulated?"

"Yes." Kasim drank some water, set the glass down and turned to look at him. "I will get a call when it is safe to move. Ha! As if I will be a puppet on a string."

"But if we have a chance to leave and go back to plan and try again, perhaps–"

"But we do not," Kasim said flatly. "I do not trust the West. It will never be safe to move. That phone call will lead us out into the open, where we will be exposed."

The other man frowned.

"Surely, if that was the plan, we would not have been fed all this information on Viper," he objected. "Why give us tools to hunt her if their goal is to send her after us?"

"I think the current plan is to use us as...what do they call it...bait?" Kasim asked. The other man nodded. "We failed in our mission, the mission we were brought here to complete. They have no need for us anymore, but they still want Viper. If Viper is hunting us, what better way to draw her out?"

The man slowly nodded in understanding.

"Then what do we do? If we cannot move now because Viper is hunting us, and we cannot move when we get a call to tell us to move, what can we do?"

Kasim smiled grimly and pointed to the huge map of South Philadelphia hanging on the wall.

"We build, and we continue. We are not pawns to be moved around at will. We are the tip of the sword, and we will strike at the heart of everything they hold close."

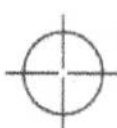

Kyle lowered his binoculars and glanced at his watch. The crowd at the funeral parlor was starting to thin out, but there were still a large amount of people milling around both inside and out. It wasn't the ongoing stream of people coming and going through the front door that held his attention, though. It was the small group standing in the shadows at the far end of the front porch he'd been watching for the past half hour.

He had no idea when the first one came out. It was almost as if they just materialized deep in the shadows. Kyle wouldn't have even known they were there if it weren't for the tall Marine from Washington. When he stepped out of the front door, Kyle watched as he looked around before heading down to the end of the porch. Even then, he still wouldn't have noticed the figure deep in the shadows. It wasn't until the Marine leaned on the railing that he realized he was talking to someone. No matter how he tried, Kyle could not get a clear look of the person so thoroughly concealed in the shadows. When the man wasn't completely blocking his view, the darkness seemed to be protecting the figure with its own curtain. It was infuriating.

A few minutes after the man came out, Agents Walker and Hanover joined them. Between the three Federal agents, the mysterious figure in the shadows was completely obscured and Kyle gave up trying to get a good look at them. Whoever it was, they would not be seen until they moved out of the shadows. When the Marine went back into the funeral home, Kyle thought he might get lucky and the figure in the darkness would shift, but no such luck. Agent Walker simply moved into the Marine's spot, partially blocking the figure, and there she stayed.

Kyle shook his head now and stretched. It was no use. If Viper was at the viewing, or had been at the viewing, he had missed her. He tilted his head thoughtfully as the Marine re-appeared in the doorway with the woman from the church. Perhaps he was following the wrong person. He firmly believed Agent Walker would lead him to Viper eventually, but perhaps his time would be better served with the Marine and the other woman. He certainly had nothing to lose. If they didn't lead him to his quarry tonight, there was always tomorrow.

Eventually, someone would lead him to Viper.

Viper glanced up to the flat screen hanging above the mantel as a loud tone echoed through the house. Michael's truck turned off the road into the trees and she dropped her gaze to her laptop. She had returned from John's viewing over an hour ago and changed into black yoga pants and a dark tee-shirt. Feeling much more comfortable, she had settled on the couch in the living room with her laptop to begin the tedious process of trying to find a chink in the Organization's cyber-armor. Hawk thought she was insane, and perhaps she was. Strictly speaking, he was right. She didn't *need* confirmation Kyle Anthony March was an asset working for the Organization. She wanted it, especially after learning the white lab coat hailed from Singapore.

If Viper was going to pursue one of their own assets, she damn well needed to know what she was up against.

The black pickup pulled onto the gravel and Alina listened to the powerful engine moving past the front of the house and pulling around the side. She sighed and closed the laptop, standing to carry it to the den in the front of the house. She had been hoping to get more work done before Michael and Angela returned, but obviously it had been a quick stop for wings and beer.

When the back door slid open and Michael and Angela stepped into the house, Alina was in the kitchen getting a bottle of water from the fridge and the flat screen above the mantle was dark.

"Lina, you should have come to Chickie and Pete's," Angela announced, dropping her purse onto the black granite bar and bending down to take off her four inch stilettos. "We had a good time. It was just what we needed. Blake is absolutely hysterical. Even Stephanie was laughing, and that's saying something."

"She seemed fine earlier," Alina said, sipping her water. "What do you mean?"

Angela shrugged.

"Something happened to get her panties all in a bunch," she said. "I don't know what. She didn't say, and I never really got the chance to ask. I'm going to get changed. Do you have any wine? I'd love a glass when I come down."

"Yes."

"Great!" Angela headed down the hallway toward the stairs. "Why don't you pour us some?"

She disappeared up the stairs and Alina looked at Michael. He came around the bar to join her in the kitchen.

"We need to talk," he said in a low voice.

Viper raised an eyebrow and watched as he went to the fridge, reaching in for a bottle of water.

"What does Angela do, exactly?" he asked, turning to face her as the fridge swung closed.

"What do you mean?"

"Her job. What is it these days?"

"She still works for the bank," Alina said slowly, studying him. "She's a Vice President now. She moved out of anti-money laundering into sales and operations over the winter. Why?"

"Because she's somehow become involved with Trasker," he told her grimly.

Viper stared at him, a chill running through her.

"What?"

He nodded, opening the water and taking a long drink.

"Someone from Trasker was there tonight. She met him in Florida, where they worked together to make some kind of deal between Trasker and the bank. Now he's here."

Alina set her water down on the kitchen island, her mind working furiously.

"What's his name?"

"Trent. I didn't get a last name, but I don't like the vibe I got from him. The whole thing feels off, but I can't put my finger on why."

"You mean, aside from the fact Trasker Pharmaceuticals is the company that manufactured an Ebola virus for distribution as an antidote for Anthrax?" Viper asked dryly. "Of course it's off. It stinks to high heaven. The question is how the hell someone found out who Angela was and, more importantly, that she knows me."

"It might not be about you," Michael said after a moment of silence. "It might be about me. I'm the one who's investigating their records. They could have found the connection to me."

Viper raised an eyebrow doubtfully.

"When was the last time you spoke to Angela before this weekend?" she demanded.

"Last fall," he admitted.

"Then I doubt this is about you."

"How could anyone from Trasker know who you are?" he argued. "And how could they connect you to her?"

"The same way people in Syria, Greece and Italy all knew who I was," she said shortly. "Someone told them."

Michael stared at her for a moment and ran a hand over his short hair in frustration.

"This is absurd," he muttered. "Why target Angela? Why not me? My connection to you is far from secret."

Viper was silent for a long moment. When she finally lifted her eyes to him, Michael felt a chill go through him.

"She's the weakest link," she said flatly. "Out of everyone, she's the only one without any kind of military or defense training. They know I'll protect her because she can't protect herself."

Michael blinked.

"You think this is all just to draw you out?"

"Someone broke into her house, ignored all the high ticket items, and went straight for her. They didn't look twice at anything, except maybe the cat. If she hadn't fought back, they would have taken her. Want to lay bets on what I would have done?"

Michael shook his head.

"If you didn't know about the Trasker connection, you would have gone after her," he agreed. "Hell, even if you did know, you still would have gone after her. So now what? She's here with you. It worked, only instead of you going to her, she came to you."

"They don't know that," she said slowly. "Not yet, anyway. Not unless you were followed."

"I wasn't."

Viper looked at him doubtfully, but let it go.

"You take care of Angie. I can focus on the threat if I know you've got her."

He nodded.

"Agreed. After the funeral, we'll keep her locked down here and I'll be able to dig into the Trasker files. I got the internal records, but there's a lot of data and it's going to take time to track down the connection between Trasker and the Cartel."

"And Mr. X?"

"So far, nothing out of the ordinary. I'm waiting on a call back from an old Marine sergeant who might be able to tell me something."

Viper nodded and was opening her mouth to tell him to keep on it when a loud tone echoed through the house once again, sending a chill streaking down her spine. Her head snapped around and she strode to the living room, picking up the remote from the coffee table and pointing it at the flat screen above the mantel. The TV came alive, displaying a 360-degree view of the property. The view was split into eight sections and one was flashing red.

Something, or someone, had tripped the perimeter.

Chapter Twenty-Two

Stephanie sipped her beer and stared blindly across the living room. She'd been feeling numb since Viper uttered those words on the porch at the funeral home.

"'*It came from Cooper Hospital the day John died.*'"

The words echoed in her mind, and Stephanie shook her head. At first, she hadn't understood the implication. She just looked at Alina blankly in shadows, wondering what she was talking about. It was Blake who sucked in his breath beside her as he realized what Alina was saying.

John's death wasn't because of the accident.

Stephanie fought back an almost overwhelming wave of frustration, taking a deep breath and trying to focus. Once Blake realized what was going on, he'd asked a few pointed questions. Alina answered them calmly and concisely. That was when Stephanie learned about the doctor wearing a white lab coat who disappeared as John went into cardiac arrest. That was also when Stephanie learned that potassium chloride was still part of an assassin's arsenal.

The door behind her opened and Buddy bounded in, shaking himself off inside the door as Blake followed, closing the door behind him.

"It's getting chilly out there," he said, flipping the deadbolt. "I thought it was Spring."

"They said a cold front was coming through tonight," said Stephanie absently. "It'll warm up again tomorrow."

Blake glanced at the beer in her hand and headed to the kitchen to get one for himself.

"You ok?" he asked over his shoulder.

"Define ok," she muttered, raising the bottle to her lips.

Buddy watched his owner disappear into the kitchen, and looked at Stephanie, sitting on the couch with her feet propped up on the coffee table. Deciding she was more settled, he ambled over and dropped his head onto her leg, gazing up at her with soulful brown eyes. Stephanie smiled and slid her hand over his head, scratching behind his ears.

"On a scale of one to five, how pissed off are you?" Blake asked, coming back with a beer in his hand.

"Ten."

He nodded and dropped onto the couch beside her. Buddy transferred his head from Stephanie's leg to Blake's lap, his hind quarters wiggling happily.

"You had no idea?" he asked.

"How could I? She never told me anything! She just gave me the coat and asked to have Matt try to pull DNA off it. She never said why." Stephanie shook her head. "I should have known something was up. She was too calm when John died, almost clinical. I wondered at the time, but I thought she was just in denial. Now it makes sense. She was furious, not calm. She knew someone went into the hospital and murdered him in cold blood."

A fresh wave of anger mixed with grief washed over her and she lifted the beer to her lips again, trying to force the emotions away before she started crying out of sheer frustration. She was tired of crying, tired of having red eyes and feeling like she'd been hit by truck. It was as if John had died all over again.

"Is she always like that?" Blake asked suddenly.

Stephanie looked at him.

"Lina?"

He nodded.

"Like what?"

"Well she dropped that bombshell, then didn't explain anything. Hell, she didn't even say why someone would want to kill John. She just told us about the doctor and disappeared a few minutes later." Blake shook his head. "I mean, what the hell?"

Stephanie let out a choked laugh.

"Yes, that's pretty much her SOP. She told us what she thinks we need to know. She's a woman of few words. It can be infuriating."

Blake was silent for a moment.

"She's not what I expected," he said finally. "I don't know what I was expecting, but that certainly wasn't it."

"I told you," Stephanie murmured. "You had an image of the devil in your head. She's not."

"No. She's worse," he said bluntly. "She hunts the devil, and it shows. It takes a lot to put me on my guard, but she did it with one look."

Stephanie nodded and looked at him sympathetically.

"She can be intimidating. She doesn't even know she's doing

it."

"That's what makes it so effective." Blake sipped his beer. "So, what now? John was murdered. It puts a whole new light on everything. Viper's known all along, and she didn't seem surprised to hear the coat came from Singapore. Do you think she already has a lead?"

"I would put money on it. She won't let someone get away with killing John." Stephanie leaned her head back on the couch tiredly. "I'm still trying to wrap my mind around it. Why kill him?"

"The bomb didn't work. It didn't kill him instantly, the way it did with the other racer, Dutch. Someone wanted to finish the job."

"But it makes no sense! Why kill a Federal agent? There's something else going on and I can guarantee Viper knows what it is."

"Ask her."

"Oh, I plan on it," Stephanie said grimly. "After the funeral tomorrow, I'm dragging it all out of her."

A low growl suddenly filled the living room and Stephanie lifted her head, stiffening. Buddy had curled up on the floor in front of the couch while they were talking, but now he raised his head, his attention focused on the front window. The fur at his neck slowly bristled, rising into pointed tufts, and another growl rumbled from deep within his throat.

Stephanie looked at Blake. He watched his dog for a second then stood, reaching for his firearm in the holster at his side. As he stood, so did Buddy, his teeth barred.

"What is it?" Stephanie asked, watching the large dog as he moved toward the window.

"I don't know, but it's not good," Blake replied, following Buddy.

Stephanie dropped her feet to the floor and stood up, setting her beer next to Blake's on the coffee table. Another low growl erupted suddenly into barking as Buddy lunged for the window. Blake reached out and moved the curtain aside to look out.

"I can't see anything," he said. "Can you hit the lights?"

Stephanie crossed to the light switch quickly, plunging the living room into darkness. As she did so, Buddy reared up onto his back legs, placing his front paws on the windowsill, barking.

Blake peered out the window, looking for the threat Buddy knew was out there. Suddenly, he stiffened.

"What the..."

Spinning around, he strode for the door, his Sig Sauer in his hand.

"What is it?" Stephanie asked sharply.

"Your car," he said shortly, flipping the deadbolt. "Someone's broken into your car!"

"What's going on? What was that god-awful noise?" Angela demanded, running down the stairs and down the hall to the living room.

"It's the security alarm," Alina said shortly, striding into the kitchen and opening a drawer under the counter. She pulled out a tablet and swiped it, typing in an access code. "Someone's tripped one of the perimeter sensors."

"What?" Angela looked from the flashing square on the flat screen to Michael, then to Alina. "What does that mean?"

"It means someone's on the property," Michael said grimly, turning his gaze from the TV to Viper. "Can we get a close up on that section?"

"Working on it."

Michael moved around the couch and went to join her at the bar.

"Where is that?" Angela asked, staring at the TV. "It's not the driveway."

"It's on the east side," Alina murmured, swiping on the tablet and tapping a camera view.

Michael looked over her shoulder as the flashing section on the flat screen displayed on the tablet, larger and in more detail. Viper moved the camera slowly, scanning the dark woods and underbrush for what tripped the security.

"I don't see anything," Michael said after a moment. "Could it have been a deer?"

"It's possible." Viper switched to the next camera. "They usually show on the plasma though."

She moved the next camera, scanning in a slow circle. It moved over a tree before continuing on, but Alina stopped suddenly and went back.

"There."

"Where?" Michael demanded. "I don't see anything."

Viper pointed to a shadow just barely visible beyond the tree and Michael sucked in his breath.

"I would have missed that."

Alina tapped the screen and the single view turned back to the eight sections visible on the flat screen. She scanned the other sections carefully. After tapping on two of them and searching for a moment, she returned to the multi-screen view and handed Michael the tablet.

"He's alone," she announced, turning away and pulling a black bag out from a cabinet under the bar. She reached inside and pulled out a pair of night vision goggles. "I'm going to take care of this. You stay with Angela and keep an eye on the cameras. If anyone but me gets to the yard, shoot."

Michael took the tablet with a curt nod. Angela watched as Alina circled the bar and headed for the sliding door.

"What are you doing?!" she demanded. "Are you nuts? You don't know who's out there!"

"I don't care who's out there," Alina said shortly. "Stay with Michael. You'll be safe here."

"What about you? You're not safe if you go out there!" Angela protested, her voice rising. "Can't we just call the police?"

Viper stopped with her hand on the sliding door and turned to look at Angela.

Angela's eyes widened at the look on her friend's face and she took an involuntary step backwards.

"It's not me you need to worry about." Viper shifted her gaze to Michael. "You know what to do."

He nodded, coming around the bar with the tablet in his hand.

"I've got her. You just take care of you."

Viper disappeared into the night. As soon as the door closed behind her, Michael strode over and flipped the lock.

"What the hell just happened?" Angela demanded when he turned around. "Why did you let her go out there?!"

Michael's lips twitched ever so slightly.

"I've learned not to question her," he said humorously. "Besides, it's not my call."

Angela stared at him in disbelief.

"What are you talking about? You're a Federal agent. You should have made it your call!"

Michael sighed and looked at her, at a loss. Angela didn't know who Alina really was, and it certainly wasn't his place to tell her. How was he supposed to explain to Angie that her friend was far deadlier than whoever was out there in the trees?

"She'll be fine," he said. "Trust me."

Stephanie followed close behind Blake as he went out the door, closing it quickly behind herself before Buddy could get out as well. A rash of barking vocalized his displeasure at the treatment, but Stephanie ignored him. She unsnapped her holster, ready to draw her Glock if needed. Blake was already halfway to her Mustang, his long legs covering the ground quickly, and Stephanie followed, casting a searching gaze around the small parking lot. No one was running away, and there didn't appear to be any suspicious cars. In fact, nothing seemed out of the ordinary at all.

Aside from the fact that her trunk was wide open.

"Why didn't the alarm go off?" Blake asked, holstering his weapon as he reached the Mustang and saw no one around.

"I may not have set it," she said, joining him. "I don't always. Nothing ever happens here."

She looked into her trunk and frowned.

"What?" Blake asked, seeing the look on her face.

"Nothing's missing," Stephanie said. "My Go Bag is still there, and so is the toolbox."

She leaned into the trunk and pulled the toolbox towards her, unsnapping the lid. All her tools were still inside, untouched.

"Maybe they didn't have time to grab anything before Buddy raised the alarm," Blake said, looking around the parking lot.

Stephanie pushed the toolbox back and reached for the bag she always kept in the trunk packed for unexpected all-nighters.

"That's strange," she murmured. "It's open."

Blake watched as she pulled the bag out.

"Someone went through it," she announced, looking up. "Son of a bitch!"

"Is anything missing?"

"No...doesn't look like it. What the hell?" Stephanie finished looking through it and looked up at him, her brows drawn together in confusion. "What were they looking for?"

Blake shook his head.

"You tell me. It's your trunk. What do you keep in here?"

"This is it," she said with a shrug. "I never keep anything excit–"

Blake raised his eyebrows as she broke off suddenly, tossing the bag aside and striding to the passenger's door. She opened it and reached in, pulling another bag from the backseat.

"What's that?" he asked, watching as she wrenched it open.

"It's the stuff from John's safe deposit box," she said, peering into the bag. "I forgot to take it into the house earlier."

Stephanie went back to the trunk where she could use the trunk light to see into the black bag.

"You left that in your car?" Blake exclaimed. "Steph!"

"I know! I don't know how I forgot..." her voice trailed off and she looked up, her face draining of color. "It's gone."

"What's gone?" Blake demanded.

"There was an external hard-drive. It's gone. So is the notebook."

"That's it? That's all that's missing?"

Stephanie finished going through the bag and nodded.

"Yes. Everything else is still here, including a stack of cash and a diamond engagement ring," she said. "What kind of thief leaves cash and jewelry behind?"

"The kind that isn't a thief," Blake said grimly.

Viper paused just inside the trees and pulled her .45 from her back holster, listening intently. The shadow had been just inside the perimeter. By now he would be closer. Her military-grade NVGs gave her clear vision in the darkness, casting everything in a green light as she started through the trees. She turned her head and watched a deer a few feet away move in the opposite direction. A startled opossum lifted its head as Viper stepped silently into its range of scent. It scurried under some brush to hide. She paused, then turned to her left. There was too much wildlife activity here. The threat had to be further to the left.

She moved deeper into the woods, her heartbeat steady, her senses focused on the trees around her. Viper excelled out here, both in nature, and in the darkness. Not only had she mastered the skill of moving silently through woods, which was no small feat, but she seemed to instinctively know how wildlife worked and she used it to her advantage. Pausing in the trees to listen, she noted the absolute silence ahead and to the left.

Viper smiled faintly and moved forward, listening to the night. Not a sound marred the silence. No owls hooted, no raccoons stirred, and no deer picked their way through the underbrush. Everything was still. She moved behind the trunk of a large, thick pine tree and peered around it, scanning the area slowly. On her second pass, she saw him.

He was standing between two trees, holding a thin flashlight pointed toward the ground. As she watched, he shone it around the area and started to move forward again. A loud pop echoed through the trees as he stepped on a dead branch and Viper grimaced. Stealth was not his forte, she decided, when he stepped on a clump of underbrush. There was no way this was a military-trained assassin.

Reaching up to her headgear, she clicked a button on the side and zoomed in on the man's face. He was wearing a turtleneck under a loose jacket and dark pants. Viper didn't recognize him from any of the numerous photos she'd been scrolling through for the past few days. Her fingers moved and she pressed another button, taking several photos of the stranger. If it wasn't one of hers, it had to be the guy from Trasker. He must have followed Michael and Angela from the viewing.

Viper's lips compressed and she moved out from behind the tree silently. He'd regret that decision soon enough.

She moved silently to her left, crossing through underbrush and moving behind another tree about twenty feet in front of him. If he stayed on his present course, he would have to pass her. Viper flipped the safety on and put her gun back into its holster. She bent and slid her combat knife out of her ankle sheath instead, holding it flat against the inside of her arm as she waited in the darkness. Her breathing was steady as she listened to him move through the night behind her. It was going to be a piece of cake.

Without warning, a loud screech ripped through the silence behind Viper, startling her. She moved swiftly from behind the tree and looked in the direction of the high-pitched sound. Viper stopped dead, momentarily stunned.

A large black shadow was diving from above, his claws outstretched, headed straight for the tall shadow moving through the darkness. It happened so fast that the intruder didn't have time to do anything but throw up his arms in a feeble attempt to protect his face. The warning shriek faded into the night as Raven's deadly claws made solid contact with his arm. Viper winced as her pet hawk closed his talons around the forearm, his wings spread for balance, and lowered his beak toward the top of the man's head. Ducking in panic, the intruder let out a howl of pain as he tried to shake the hawk loose from his arm. Razor sharp claws held tight as Raven landed a solid hit on the side of his head with his deadly beak and another scream of pain ripped through the night.

Viper put her knife away, and reached for the Ruger again. The element of surprise was gone. She took off the safety, watching as the intruder finally shook Raven free of his arm. Even from this distance, Viper saw that his jacket was shredded and the hawk's claws had ripped open his forearm. Blood poured out of his arm as the man turned and began to run back through the woods.

Raven swooped up into the trees before turning and diving down in an arc, coming in for another pass. Viper raised her gun, aimed, and cursed softly. There was no clean shot without risking her pet. She lowered her weapon and began moving swiftly through the trees.

The man was running flat-out now, weaving through the trees and tripping over the underbrush as he tried to dodge the bird of prey. Raven swooped down and landed a glancing blow to his head with his claws, arching away as the man ducked under a low branch.

Viper leapt over a rotting log and dodged between two pine trees, closing the gap between them. The man was almost to the edge of the woods now and she caught the glint of headlights beyond the trees as a vehicle passed on the road. She shook her head and slowed. She wouldn't catch him before he reached the road. She raised the gun again, planting her feet and taking aim. Raven was going in for another bombing run, his claws outstretched and his wings curved forward to give him leverage. She hesitated, then fired.

Raven shrieked and flew into the trees at the sound of the shot and the intruder stumbled, his whole body lurching forward precariously. He looked back wildly as her shot skimmed his shoulder, missing by barely a hair. Through some sheer force of will, he managed to keep his balance and broke out of the trees a second later.

Viper lowered her weapon and moved swiftly forward. She reached the tree line just in time to see him disappear into the trees on the other side.

"Damn!"

She slid the safety on and reached back to tuck her .45 into her holster as another car flew by on the road. A moment later, an engine roared to life. Viper watched from the shadows as a dark-colored SUV pulled out of the trees. The tires squealed as the man hit the gas and disappeared down the road.

Chapter Twenty-Three

Alina looked up as the door slid open and Michael stepped onto the deck, a beer in his hand. She was standing in the shadows at the far end of the deck with Raven next to her on the railing.

"Angie took herself off to bed," he told her. "She's not happy."

"I don't imagine she is," Alina murmured.

When she emerged from the trees, Angela had been on the deck with Michael, waiting for her. After assuring herself that Alina was alive and well, she laid into her, demanding answers; answers Viper refused to give.

"I tried to turn off the TV so she couldn't watch the cameras," Michael said, moving toward her slowly, keeping one eye on the black hawk next to her. "She wouldn't let me. When you pulled out your gun, I had no good explanation for her."

"I know." Alina turned away from the railing and went to sit in one of the Adirondack chairs. "She's suspected for a few months that I'm not what I say I am. All I can do is try to make sure she doesn't learn the full truth."

Michael looked at her for a moment, then lowered himself into the chair next to her.

"I don't know. At this point, maybe you should just tell her the truth," he said slowly. "Maybe it would be better."

Alina glanced at him, her face impassive.

"No," she said flatly. "Angela is in too much danger as it is."

"That's my point. It may be safer for her to know exactly what's going on. She's hell-bent on finding out. If we just tell her, it will stop her from doing something stupid."

Alina watched as Raven stretched and settled down again, staring out into the night with his hawk eyes.

"Too many people already know who I am and what I do."

Michael sipped his beer and fell silent. A brisk wind swirled along the deck and Alina zipped her black jacket up with a shiver. The night had grown cold, but she was reluctant to go back inside. She was filled with restless energy and being outdoors helped soothe it.

"Any idea who he was?" Michael broke the silence a moment later.

"I got a picture before Raven swooped in. I'll run it tomorrow."

"Do you think he was here for you or Angela?"

Alina shook her head.

"I don't know," she admitted. "He wasn't just passing through. He hid his vehicle in the trees across the road and didn't approach from the front. He was looking for the house."

Michael stared out over the back lawn.

"How the hell did he know where to look?"

Viper glanced at him.

"He followed you."

Michael looked at her.

"There's no way," he objected. "I would have noticed if I was being followed."

"Would you?" Alina raised an eyebrow. "It was late and dark. You could have been followed from the funeral home."

"I'm telling you, I would have known," Michael insisted.

Viper studied him for a long moment before reaching into her jacket pocket.

"Perhaps," she said. "But you *were* followed."

She held out her hand and Michael looked down to find a small tracking device in her palm.

"What the hell?!"

"This was on your truck. It was placed under the tow hitch. I found it a little while ago, while you were inside with Angela."

Michael stared at the device.

"How long was it there?" he demanded.

Alina shrugged.

"Not long. If it had been there for any length of time, there would have been an outline from dirt and dust settling around it. When I removed it, there was nothing."

She tucked it back into her jacket pocket and watched as Michael drained his beer.

"I led someone right here," he muttered. "Damn!"

Alina's lips curved faintly.

"Don't worry. He'll think twice before coming back," she advised. "I've deactivated it, so the GPS signal is lost."

Michael looked at her, his brows pulled together.

"What if he already passed the location on?" he demanded. "Hell, Lina, that guy could have been the one who took a shot at you and Damon!"

"Not possible. That shooter is dead."

Michael stared at her.

"What?"

"You didn't think I'd just let a sniper walk away, did you?" she demanded, amused. "Gunny, what do you take me for?"

"You could have told me that," he muttered. "I've been thinking this whole time they'd try again."

"Oh, someone will. Until I find out who's leaking information all over the place, I'm still a target. You can rest easy, though. The man Raven attacked wasn't one of them."

Michael rubbed his forehead.

"How can you be sure?" he asked tiredly.

"He wasn't a professional. He had no idea how to move quietly, and he was unarmed."

Michael dropped his head back against the chair with a groan.

"You fired at an unarmed man?!"

Viper's lips twitched.

"It wasn't a kill shot," she replied, amused again. "I was aiming for his shoulder. I wanted to stop him, not kill him."

Michael was silent for a long moment, staring up into the black sky.

"Do you think this house is compromised?" he finally asked.

Alina shrugged.

"Yes, but I won't know to what extent until I run the photo."

"Lina, I am so sorry," Michael said, turning his head to look at her. "This is my fault."

She waved a hand impatiently.

"It's not your fault. If anything, it's my own fault for coming back here. I knew the risks."

"And if they know where you are now?"

Viper stared out into the darkness, her lips pressed together in a thin line.

"I'll handle it."

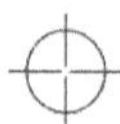

Alina stood at the window in her bedroom and stared out into the night. The house was silent, everyone asleep except her. She lifted her glass and took a sip of the vodka she'd poured before coming upstairs.

After Michael went to bed, she had retrieved her laptop from the den. The security breach tonight made one thing very clear: she was running out of time. She didn't think the intruder Raven shred to pieces was a professional, but Viper couldn't take the chance he was connected to the leak in Washington, especially after finding the tracking device on Michael's truck. She needed as much information as she could find on Kyle March, and she needed it now.

While she was hacking into the Organization's server, there was a person who could help on the ground. She was an old friend, and had proved over the years to be an invaluable asset. Trained by Mossad and stationed in Egypt, Reyna was one of the few people in the world whom Viper respected as a weapon in her own right. The woman was unbelievably skilled in gathering information.

Alina shook her head and took another sip of vodka. She wasn't sure if she had done the right thing in sending her contact an encrypted message asking for help. She didn't doubt Reyna would gladly assist, but Viper was leery about involving yet another person in this mess. She was rapidly running out of people she could trust, and if Kyle was indeed an asset with the Organization, then Reyna would quickly end up in the same boat as Alina. However, if Reyna could reveal how a dead man paid utility bills in Madrid, it would get Viper one step closer.

Alina turned away from the window and walked over to the bed tiredly. She set the glass on the side table and got into bed, slipping her .45 under the pillow. So many questions! And now she had to worry about Angela as well.

Alina's head sank into the pillow and she stared up at the ceiling. How did all this get out of control so quickly? First John, then Hawk, and now Angela. One by one, everyone around her was being targeted. Who knew so much about Viper?

And how the hell was she going to find them before they found her?

Kyle shook his martini shaker. The ice turned the metal cold, sending a chill into his fingers, but he didn't notice. He was staring across the room, lost in thought, as he went through the mechanical motions of preparing his cocktail.

He'd known that dog would be a problem.

He shook his head. He hadn't made a sound in the parking lot, but that pit bull had known he was there anyway. He'd finished going through the first bag in the trunk and was just opening the second one in the back seat when the barking began. He didn't have time to do a thorough search, so he had grabbed the two things that looked the most interesting. As it was, he barely made it away in time. Who would think the FBI could move that fast?

Kyle lowered his hands, pulling the top off the shaker and reaching for the metal strainer. It was the Marine who made it out the door in record time. He frowned and held the strainer over the opening, pouring his drink into a martini glass. Luckily, he'd been able to get away before he came out of the alcove. It was damn close.

Setting the shaker down on the bar, Kyle picked up his glass and took a sip before turning to move across the room to the couch. When Agent Walker went to the bank this morning, he was right behind her. He had been surprised when she joined an older man in the parking lot outside the bank. The surprise quickly turned to interest as he watched through the glass front of the building. The two met with someone who had every appearance of being the bank manager. A moment later, Kyle was inside the bank, waiting for a CSR to talk to him about opening an account, seated a few feet away from Agent Walker.

Kyle sipped his martini again and set it down carefully on the coffee table before sinking onto the couch. As soon as he had heard the words "safe deposit box," Kyle knew what was happening. The man in the hospital bed had had a contingency plan in place. He'd felt a moment of amusement in the bank, recalling the detailed instructions to burn John Smithe's condo down to the ground. So much for covering all the bases.

His eyes fell to the old, tattered notebook sitting next to his martini. The external drive was in the other room on the desk, connected to a laptop. It was surprisingly well protected and he hadn't broken through the security yet, but he anticipated getting through it by the morning. In the meantime, there was the notebook.

Kyle leaned forward and picked up the martini. Lucky chance, spotting that just as he was putting the bag back. If nothing else, perhaps it would give him some insight as to what kind of man he'd killed. He sipped his martini.

It was a strange thing. In the years he'd been doing this work,

Kyle never really gave much thought to his targets. They were simply names and faces in a file with a specific monetary amount fixed to them. Nothing more. Nothing less. And yet, this one had been much more from the very beginning. Since the first contact, everything about this job had been more: more money, more pressure, more precision, and now, more complicated. He needed to know more about his target than he'd been told, more about the person he was and the threat he posed. Kyle wanted to know everything he could about John Smithe because now Viper was involved.

A scowl crossed his face as he stared at the notebook broodingly, nursing his drink. An FBI target, two ex-Marines from Washington and a legendary assassin who some whispered was urban myth all combined to make...what? What the hell had he stumbled into when he blithely took a job that seemed too easy to turn down? He was all set to take care of Viper himself, but what then? Killing his adversary would save his own life, but what about the person who hired him? He was in possession of an external hard drive and a notebook that, unless he was very much mistaken, were the very items his employer wanted destroyed. Would killing Viper be enough? Or would they simply send someone else after him?

Kyle pursed his lips thoughtfully. Always assuming, of course, that they found out about the existence of the items in question. It was entirely possible that they never would. In that case, putting an end to Viper would put an end to all threat to himself. He could return home, continue with his life, and the entire situation here could play out as it saw fit.

He finished his martini and leaned forward to set the empty glass on the table. Who was he kidding? It was never that simple: witness two Marines and an assassin. His best option was to find out everything he could about Agent John Smithe. Then, and only then, could he make an informed decision about everything else.

Then he might have a snowball's chance.

Chapter Twenty-Four

Michael stepped out of the mother's room on the side of the altar, closing the door behind him. It was empty and secure. He glanced around the cavernous church and shook his head. There was just too much real estate. There was no way he could secure every alcove and entryway.

Blake emerged from the side antechamber where Michael had entered the day before and gave him a thumbs up from across the church. Michael nodded and turned to walk up the right side of the church toward another antechamber.

When he arrived this morning, Blake was outside on his cell phone, talking to his boss. After he hung up, Michael enlisted his aid to help him secure the church. At first Blake thought he was crazy. The funeral would be attended by a hundred Federal agents, all carrying side arms. What could possibly happen? It took some fast talking, but Michael managed to convince him by virtue of one word: Viper.

Now he suppressed a sigh, and stepped into the right antechamber, looking around. A door led outside here, as it did on the other side, and he opened it to glance outside. A set of cement steps led to the alley running between the church and school. Michael closed the door again and turned to go back into the sanctuary.

He didn't really know what he expected to accomplish, but Michael knew he had to keep Viper safe or Damon would have his head. Turning right, he continued down the side aisle towards the back of the church. He had the added complication of keeping Angela safe as well, or Viper would have his head on a platter. Michael shook his head. Either way, he would not win if something happened here today.

"Michael!"

Angela hailed him from the center aisle towards the front. He paused and she hurried up the aisle, crossing over to the right at the middle of the church where the front and back sections of the sanctuary were separated by a cross aisle. Her heels clicked on the marble floor.

"I thought you were with Stephanie and Joanne?" he asked, his voice echoing off the empty pews and marble columns.

"I was," she said breathlessly, joining him. "The hearse just arrived. Have you heard anything from Alina?"

Michael shook his head.

"No."

"Where is she?" she wondered, wringing her hands together. "She said she'd be right behind us. That was an hour ago!"

"She'll be here," he assured her. "Stop worrying."

"Easy for you to say," she muttered, turning away. "You don't have to listen to Stephanie threatening to break her legs if she doesn't show up."

"Why on earth wouldn't she show up?" he demanded, exasperated. "I don't understand why you two are freaking out so much. She'll be here."

His phone started ringing and he pulled it out of his inside jacket pocket, turning to stride toward the double doors at the back of the church.

"Don't forget to mute that!" Angela called after him. "Joanne will have a fit if it rings during mass!"

Michael waved his hand at her as he pressed on the heavy door nearest to him, stepping out into the vestibule.

"Hello?"

"And how's my favorite grunt doing this morning?" Damon asked cheerfully. "All pressed, dressed, and ready for a funeral?"

"Just about," said Michael, crossing the vestibule and stepping outside onto the front steps of the church. "I'm at the church now. How's the recovery coming? Will you be joining us anytime soon?"

"It almost sounds like you miss me. Are things that dull up there?"

"Hardly." Michael glanced at his watch. "I've got my hands full."

"I heard Angela moved in," Damon said, his voice sobering. "Anything new on that front?"

"Plenty, but there's not enough time to fill you in. I want to finish securing the church as best as I can before people start arriving."

"Is there anything I should know about?"

Michael sighed and ran a hand over his short hair.

"Someone breached the security perimeter last night," he said reluctantly. "Alina went out there but Raven beat her to the punch, literally."

There was a short silence.

"Raven?" Damon sounded like he was trying not to laugh.

"Oh, that's great!"

Michael felt his lips pulling into a grin despite himself.

"It was...interesting, to say the least."

"And the victim?"

"Got away."

Another silence ensued.

"Never a dull moment," Damon said finally, no trace of amusement remaining in his voice. "Anything else?"

"Not yet."

"Well keep me posted. Is she there?"

"She's on her way," Michael said, glancing at his watch again. "At least, that's what she said an hour ago."

"Do me a favor, gunny? If she shows up looking like a Kardashian, take a picture. I want to see it for myself."

Michael choked.

"What?!"

But he was speaking to dead air. Damon had already disconnected.

Alina stood in the side antechamber, scanning the crowded church. She'd slipped in through the side door facing the school, avoiding the line stretching out the front doors of the church. Her plan was to arrive at the last moment, and leave at the first opportunity once the mass was over. In doing so, she hoped to present the smallest possible window to anyone watching for Viper to make an appearance. There was no sense in making her situation any worse than necessary. If it wasn't for the fact Stephanie and Angie would both kill her if she didn't come, Alina wasn't sure she would have taken the risk. John was dead. He neither knew nor cared who showed up to his funeral.

Her dark eyes slid over the crowd slowly from her spot behind a column. Some of the faces she recognized from days long past, others she didn't know. Most were FBI or local law enforcement, a testament to John's popularity and standing in the community. Viper's lips tightened briefly. There were a lot of guns in this church. That shouldn't be a problem, but she couldn't help but reflect that it made it more complicated for her own security. More guns logically meant more opportunities for an assassin to shoot a target, and unfortunately, she was a potential target. After a moment of brooding, Viper set the thought aside. No point in creating a situation where there was none.

She turned her eyes to the front of the church, and the open casket placed before the steps leading to the altar. The line of mourners entered from the doors at the back of the church and filed down the far side of the church to the front, crossing in front of the pews to view John, then proceeding to their seats up the center aisle. On this side of the church, the front pew was reserved for the family. Alina could see Bill and Joanne, seated on the end next to the center aisle, with an aging couple next to them. The rest of the pew was obscured from her line of sight, but Alina assumed that Stephanie and Angela were in that pew, or the one behind. Joanne wouldn't have let them go far. She would have seated them with the family.

Alina hesitated to emerge from her protected spot in the alcove. John's aunt and uncle would be there, and his cousin Brett, if he was still alive and sober. What was left of the family nucleus was in the front of the church, and Alina was reluctant to join them. Somehow, it made it all so final. Someone coughed loudly, the sound echoing around the cavernous sanctuary and drawing Alina from her thoughts. It was time. She had to go join the others before Angie blew up her phone again.

With one last, searching glance around the filled church, Viper moved out of the alcove and headed down the side toward the front left of the altar. As she drew closer, she saw that John's aunt and uncle were indeed in the first pew, minus their son. Stephanie was also in the front pew with Angela beside her. Michael and Blake were sitting directly behind them, along with several other men in dark suits with the clear stamp of FBI on them. Alina's lips twitched despite herself. Same haircuts, same posture...hell, they even all had the same color suit – black. It was like an ad for Federal Law Enforcement.

Michael sat on the end, next to the side aisle. Her heels clicked on the marble floor as she walked and he turned to see who was approaching. A look of relief crossed his face when he saw her, followed closely by a look bordering on astonishment. She raised an eyebrow in question, her eyes meeting his.

"What?" she asked, drawing alongside him as he stood.

Michael shook his head, his lips pulling into a grin.

"Nothing," he said, his voice low. "I've only seen you in a skirt once, that's all."

"Don't get used to it," she muttered. "It doesn't happen often."

Angela turned at the sound of the voices and jumped up at the sight of Alina.

"Lina!" she exclaimed, moving out of the pew to greet her. "Finally!"

She ran an experienced eye over Alina and nodded in approval.

"You look amazing," she announced in satisfaction. "Joanne wants you with us. You can slide in next to Stephanie."

"I'll stay on the end," Alina replied, motioning Angie back into the pew. "I don't want to disturb anyone." *Or be trapped with no way out*, she added silently.

"Lina!"

Stephanie began to stand but Alina waved her down again as Angela resumed her seat. She slipped into the pew next to Angela and sat down.

"It's about time you got here!" Stephanie hissed, leaning forward so that she could see her. "Where the hell have you been?!"

"I was running behind. I obviously didn't miss much."

"No, they're still coming in," Stephanie answered, glancing back to gauge the line. "At least the line seems to be in from outside now."

There was a murmur and a 'psssst' from the other end of the pew. Alina leaned forward to see Joanne waving to her. She nodded back, smiled in greeting to John's aunt, and sat back before either woman thought to get up and come greet her properly. The less attention drawn to her the better.

"You look fantastic," Stephanie said, turning back to her. "Is that what Angie picked out?"

"Yes."

"I told you," Angela said, glancing at her. "She should let me dress her all the time."

"Is everything alright?" Michael inserted his head between Angie's shoulder and Alina. "You're late."

"Fine," Alina said, glancing at him. "Stop worrying."

"Why is he...why are you worrying?" Angela demanded. "I swear, Michael, you've been like a mama bear all morning. What's got into you?"

"You mean besides the visitor we had last night?" he asked.

Angela shrugged and turned to face the altar again.

"Oh that," she muttered. "I don't see anyone missing half their arm, so I think we're safe. Oh, good *Lord*! What is she *wearing*?!"

Alina glanced at her, raising an eyebrow at the look on her friend's face. She followed Angela's horrified gaze.

"Oh my...do you see this?" Stephanie hissed.

Alina not only saw, but was having a hard time not laughing.

John's ex-girlfriend was advancing on the open coffin. Leopard print had been exchanged for a more respectful, solid black. Dressed in a knee-length, sleeveless dress, she would have been unremarkable if it weren't for the neckline plunging clear down to her navel. The deep opening could have been overlooked if the gap was narrow, but it was not. The wide expanse of skin left exposed displayed much more than the pantsuit from last night and Alina heard a low chuckle behind her.

"Well, that's an interesting choice," Michael said.

"Interesting choice?" Angela gaped. "Joanne must be having a heart attack!"

"It will take more than that to give her a heart attack," Alina said, the faintest tremor in her voice.

Angela glanced at her suspiciously.

"Are you laughing?!"

Before Alina could acknowledge or deny, Nipples made her move toward the coffin. She sniffled and dabbed at her eyes with a black handkerchief. Tottering on stilettos higher than even Angela wore, she went to the side of the casket to say her final farewell. From Alina's vantage point at the end of the pew, she had a clear view of John's ex-girlfriend and she shook her head in bemusement. John couldn't have found a woman more different from Alina if he went to outer space and came back with a green-skinned alien. Part of her was absolutely horrified her successors had apparently all followed this same mold: fake boobs, fake hair and no brains to speak of.

"What the...oh no, she is not!" Angela exclaimed under her breath.

Alina stared transfixed as the woman reached the side of the casket and burst into uncontrollable tears. The sobs were loud and she made no attempt to try to smother them or keep it down. Within seconds, the sobs escalated into a wail and an uncomfortable hush fell over the front half of the church.

"For God's sake," Stephanie muttered audibly.

A black-suited usher from the funeral home moved forward silently, reaching her side in record time. He reached out to place a gentle hand on her arm, trying to turn her away from the coffin. He was murmuring something quietly and succeeded in leading the distraught woman a few steps away before she wrenched out of his grasp and turned back toward the casket.

Angela sucked in her breath and Stephanie let out an involuntary gasp as Nipples threw herself at the casket.

"NO!!" she cried, her voice echoing through the church. "John, don't leave me!!"

She draped herself over the side of the casket sobbing, her arms going over John's motionless shoulders. As her midriff made contact with the side of the coffin, the thin fabric of her dress proved no match for the silicone it restrained. Gasps filled the front pews as a large, round breast popped free.

Alina clamped her teeth down on her bottom lip to stop from laughing and clapped her hand over her mouth. Michael's head disappeared from behind her shoulder and she heard him burst into a muffled fit of guffaws.

"Good Lord!" Bill exclaimed loudly from the other end of the pew, standing.

Joanne reached up and pulled him down forcibly, her face bright red.

"Let the usher handle it!" she hissed. "Don't make it worse than it already is!"

"You can't get much worse than a boob smacking our son in the face!" he retorted, his voice booming through the church.

"Oh my God," Stephanie gasped, sinking down in the pew, her shoulders shaking.

To give the poor usher credit, he never once cracked the professional mask he wore as he once again approached the wailing woman. He smoothly positioned himself so that she was partially concealed as he gently pulled her off of John's lifeless body.

"For God's sake, tuck that boulder back in!" Angela muttered, watching as the usher tried to pry her away from the casket. "I don't need to see a bouncing Buddha at eleven-thirty in the morning!"

"Angie!" Stephanie whispered in a strangled voice.

"What? I don't!"

Alina felt herself losing the battle and her shoulders began to shake silently.

Realizing the woman was in no shape to address her wardrobe malfunction, the usher quickly removed his suit jacket and draped it around her shoulders. Fortunately, he managed to cover her before she faced a packed Catholic church. Unfortunately for the front row, he didn't get the jacket on before he turned her away from the casket.

"Oh *God*!" Angela exclaimed, slapping her hand over her eyes.

"At least it's perky," John's aunt announced in a stage whisper. "Could be worse. It could look like mine!"

"Roxanne!" Joanne exclaimed, horrified. "Really!"

Someone whistled behind them and Alina's shoulders shook harder. She watched through tearing eyes as the usher covered the offending mammary gland and led Nipples down the aisle and away from the casket. He had one arm firmly wrapped around her shoulders while the other hand held his jacket closed in front of her. She wasn't getting away again.

"Is it gone?" Angela demanded, her hand still covering her eyes.

"Yes," Stephanie said, turning her head to watch as Nipples was led away. "I think we're safe."

Angela dropped her hand and immediately twisted around in the pew, craning her neck to watch the exit.

"Did that really just happen?" Blake demanded from behind them, his voice shaking with laughter.

"Yep." Stephanie glanced at him, a grin tugging at her lips. "We like to keep our funerals interesting in New Jersey."

"This is better than Jersey Shore," Michael said, his eyes meeting Alina's as she looked back to check the progress of Nipples and the usher.

Her eyes were dancing.

"John would be very proud," she agreed.

"John's somewhere right now laughing his ass off," Stephanie said, overhearing. "I wouldn't put it past him to have planned this somehow!"

Alina returned her attention to the front of the church in time to see an older gentleman turn away from the casket and pause next to Bill, laying a hand on his shoulder in a motion of comfort. The line of mourners continued, the drama over, and the ordeal continued. As the last of the mourners paid their respects, Alina glanced up to the statue of Mary next to the lectern in front of her. The peaceful countenance and outstretched hands belied the absurdity of the scene that just took place, and Alina suppressed another chuckle. Stephanie was right.

If there was an afterlife, and John was in it, he was undoubtedly laughing at them all.

Chapter Twenty-Five

Alina glanced at her watch as she sat down. The mass was underway at last, with Father Angelo at the helm. He'd aged in eleven years, with silver gracing his temples, and new lines on his face, but his eyes were still every bit as warm and filled with wisdom as they had been the last time she saw him. Once he turned to face the congregation after the procession, his eye caught hers and he gave her an imperceptible nod. Alina was uncomfortable with the recognition. She'd been away for so long that it seemed unreal that people remembered her. She'd seen so much over the years, things that changed her down to her very foundation. Viper was an entirely different person from the heartbroken girl who went away eleven years ago. It felt as if no one should recognize her.

Her eyes shifted from the priest to the shiny black casket now closed before the altar. Inside was the very man she'd run from all those years ago, and now here she was saying goodbye. Alina resisted the urge to shake her head. There was no point in dwelling on it. The past was the past, and nothing could change the course that had led them here. John was killed by an assassin because of letters her brother wrote twelve years ago.

Everyone in the church believed John was killed by injuries sustained when his Firebird flipped and hit a tree during a night street race in the Pines. Only she knew the truth: that Kyle March had gone into John's hospital room and injected potassium chloride into his IV, inducing the fatal heart attack that killed him. Viper listened to Father Angelo recite the opening prayers of the mass, her mind back in the wide corridor of the hospital. If she'd arrived just ten minutes sooner, John might still...she stopped the thought impatiently. No. Kyle would simply have found another way, and they still would have ended up right here.

It was John's own fault, of course. If he'd just come to her with the letters, Viper could have taken on the investigation that got him killed, but he didn't. She frowned. Why hadn't he? Hawk thought it was suspicious, and it didn't sit well with Alina either. She had no answers, though.

"Will you stop scowling?" Angela hissed.

Alina glanced at her in surprise.

"Would you like me sit here grinning like a loon instead?" she whispered back.

"No. Just look tragically calm!"

Alina blinked.

"Good Lord," she muttered under her breath.

The congregation stood up as a hymn began playing and Alina stood with them.

"Who am I looking tragically calm for?" she asked Angela in a low voice.

"Everyone!" came the exasperated answer. "How many times do I have to tell you that everyone is watching you?"

"And how many times do I have to say that I don't give a flying–"

"*Ssshhh*!!!" Stephanie hissed, stopping Alina mid-whisper. "For God's sake, Father Angelo will hear you two!"

"Father Angelo can't hear anything up there," Angela retorted, falling silent nonetheless.

Alina felt her lips curving despite herself and repressed the smile firmly. As the hymn ended and they began to seat themselves again, Stephanie remained standing and moved past them out of the pew. Alina raised an eyebrow in question and Stephanie made a face.

"First reading," she whispered in explanation, stepping past Alina and out of the pew.

Alina grimaced in sympathy, turning her attention to Father Angelo as he recited another opening prayer, his voice booming through the crowded church. A stray lock of hair escaped from the chignon at the back of her head, and Alina raised a hand to brush it behind her ear.

A chill streaked down her spine and the fine hair on the back of her neck prickled in warning. Her hand dropped and Viper turned her head, casting a sharp glance behind her over the sea of faces.

Michael caught the look and raised his eyebrows questioningly. She shook her head imperceptibly and turned her head back, her lips pressed together grimly.

Something was wrong.

Every fiber in her being was suddenly and inexplicably tense, humming in warning. Viper had learned over the years not to dismiss her sixth sense, and it was screaming now. She shifted on the wooden pew, conscious of the holster strapped around her upper thigh holding a modified Glock G43. Thanks to Angela's wardrobe requirements, Viper's SR45 had been out of the question. Now, her skin crawling with warning, Alina wished she had the more powerful weapon.

The opening prayer was winding down and Alina watched Stephanie move forward to the lectern directly in front of her. Alina slid her eyes to the left. Mary the Blessed Virgin gazed tranquilly over the congregation, but it was the double-door exit drawing Viper's attention. With a quick glance, she gauged the distance to the exit, estimating the number of seconds it would take to clear it.

Stephanie mounted the shallow steps and moved behind the lectern as a hush fell over the church. Father Angelo fell silent and someone coughed in the back, the sound echoing through the sanctuary. All eyes turned to the left of the altar where Stephanie stood behind the tall, ornately carved podium elevated above the congregation.

Viper cast another glance around. Her heart was pounding now, thumping against her ribs almost painfully. She had to move! She was too exposed here in the front pew. There was nothing to protect her, nothing to shield her.

"A reading from the Book of Wisdom," Stephanie said, her voice strong and clear in the microphone attached to the lectern.

Alina forced herself to focus on her friend's face as she took a deep, calming breath. As soon as the reading was over and Stephanie returned to the pew, she would slip out of the exit doors and double back to the rear of the church. She would watch the rest of the mass there, where she could see everyone and no one was behind her.

"`The souls of the righteous are in the hand of God, and no torment shall touch them,'" Stephanie read, her eyes on the large book open before her. "`They seemed, in the view of the foolish, to be dead; and their passing away was thought an affliction and their going forth from us, utter destruction. But they are in peace.'"

A loud bang interrupted the reading as a kneeler slammed down, wood striking marble with sudden and irrepressible force. The sound cracked out like a shot, echoing through the church. Viper reacted on pure instinct, sliding off the pew and lowering her head toward the floor even as her brain registered the sound. It was just a kneeler, not a gunshot.

Then all hell broke loose.

Viper raised her head to see Angela staring, dumbfounded, straight ahead. She straightened up a bit and glanced over the waist-high wooden wall in front of her. Stephanie was nowhere to be seen, and the lectern had a hole the size of a golf ball halfway down the front.

The gaping hole looked black against the cream paint and the wood surrounding it had splintered from a high impact force. Alina twisted her head around, her eyes going straight to the only possible point of origin for a shot at that angle.

Michael straightened up from where he and Blake had also hit the floor with the sound of the kneeler, their years at war showing its toll as it had with Viper. He saw the mangled lectern and turned his brown eyes to hers.

"Where?" he demanded, knowing her thought process was already a few seconds ahead of him.

"The organ loft!" Viper answered, reaching under her skirt to pull the small gun out of her thigh holster. "I'll go out the door and cover the alley. You take the inside and flush him out."

"You're not going out there alone," Michael objected. "Blake can handle inside. I'm coming with you."

"It'll take both of you to keep track of him in this crowd." Viper stood up, her eyes icy. "I'll be fine."

"What? Wait! What are you doing?!" Angela cried, snapping out of her stupor. "Was that a gunshot?!"

"Yes." Viper grabbed her wrist and pulled her up. "Come with me!"

She turned and pulled Angela behind her as she stepped out of the pew. Panic was sweeping through the church as the words 'gun' and 'shot' echoed down the aisles. Michael and Blake raced up the side toward the organ loft in the middle of the church, their guns drawn. Viper glanced over her shoulder to see them go, then turned back toward the exit. Releasing Angela's wrist, she sprinted toward the doors.

Someone screamed and Viper registered a muffled 'pop' as the Virgin Mary's tranquil profile shattered. Angela shrieked behind her as the upper half of the statue blew into pieces, heavy cast ceramic flying in every direction. Glancing back, Alina registered the look of horror on Angie's face and she reached out to grab her wrist again, dragging her relentlessly toward the double doors. A second later, she hit them at a run, pulling Angela through behind her.

"Lina..." Angela gasped as the doors swung closed on the chaos erupting behind them. "I don't think...I feel…."

Alina turned and stared at the blood covering the side of Angela's face. As she did, Angela swayed before her eyes slid closed, and she fell into Alina's arms.

She caught Angela as she fell, her heart surging into her throat. Quickly moving to the side, she eased her down against the wall. Blood was everywhere, pouring from her temple and her shoulder. Alina quickly tilted Angie's head, examining the gash on the temple first. It was large and deep, but on the bone, missing the dangerous soft spot by mere millimeters. A wave of relief washed through her and she turned her attention to the blood on the shoulder. Ripping open Angela's blouse at the shoulder, she found a large chunk of the Virgin Mary embedded between her collarbone and neck.

Satisfied that neither of the wounds were life-threatening, Viper stood up swiftly and turned away. If she felt a twinge of guilt at leaving her friend unconscious in the alcove, it was quickly pushed aside.

A few seconds later, Viper was in the alley between the church and the school, running toward the steps where she entered the church earlier. If Michael and Blake did their job, the only exit available to the shooter would be that door. She could hear the commotion in the front of the church as people streamed out in panic. If the shooter made it to the crowds in the front of the church, there would be no stopping him. He'd disappear in seconds.

The door at the top of the flight of stone steps flew open and Viper raised her pistol, flipping the safety off as she did so. Blake emerged from the church and looked over the railing.

"Did you see him?" he demanded breathlessly.

She shook her head, lowering the gun.

"Damn! Where's Michael?"

"He went to the front of the church," he replied, jogging down the steps. "The door to the organ loft was open when we got there, so we split up."

Viper hesitated. Her instinct was to go to the front of the church where the mass exodus of mourners swarmed, even though she knew the chances of finding him in the crowd were slim. And yet, something gave her pause.

"Angela was hit by shrapnel from a statue," she told Blake, turning her dark eyes on him. "She's in the alcove in the far door, unconscious. Can you…?"

Blake was already nodding and turning to head down the alley toward the door she indicated.

"I've got it," he said over his shoulder. "You just find the bastard!"

Viper nodded and looked up at the church beside her. Logic dictated that he would follow the flow of people and blend in to disappear. He was a professional. He would have planned for the chaos, and planned to use it to his advantage. That was why Michael headed straight to the front of the church once he realized the shooter had already flown the nest.

The door above her opened and people began swarming out of the church. Viper glanced at the first wave of people coming through the door as she moved her pistol to her side, concealing it from their view. She glanced toward the back of the church. Michael was in the front, but he didn't know who he was looking for. With every second, her chances of catching the assassin slipped lower and, with a curse under her breath, Viper turned to move toward the front of the alley. Sirens were sounding in the distance now. She was almost out of time.

Viper had only taken a few steps when a streak of awareness shot down her spine and her heart leapt in reaction. She snapped her head around in time to see the far door where she exited a few moments before open. A priest stepped out, a cassock covering his black pants to mid-calf. Turning his head, he looked directly at her.

Viper's breath caught in her throat and an icy chill ran over her skin as she recognized the face from the corridor outside John's hospital room.

They stared at each other down the length of the alleyway for a charged moment before he turned and began to stride away from the church, heading toward to the parking lot in the back. Fury, hot and swift, rolled through her and Viper darted after him. She ignored the people streaming out of the side door of the church, running through them, her eyes on the priest. As she moved, Viper took a deep breath, pushing the anger aside. Emotion had no place here. He was an assassin who targeted her at a funeral, of all places. This was business.

By the time she had navigated the crowd, Kyle had disappeared from sight around the back of the church. With a low curse under her breath, Viper broke into a full sprint, flying down the alley. Her heart settled into the steady, rapid rhythm she knew so well and her senses tuned to everything around her. The smell of the old stone church beside her, the sound of her heels on the pavement beneath her, and the distant chaos ensuing from the church behind her all faded into the background, noted but set aside for the time being. The only thing that mattered was getting to the assassin before he disappeared.

She rounded the corner of the church, and emerged into the large parking lot, her eyes scanning the rows of parked vehicles.

There! A dark head was just ducking into a sedan at the far end of the first row.

Viper ran to her right, both hands on her pistol, her eyes on the late model sedan. The engine roared to life and it backed out of the spot quickly. Her eyes narrowed as she saw the driver's side window open and sun glinted off metal.

Viper dove between two vehicles on her left as the shot rang out. She hit the side of a black Cadillac Escalade as the bullet whizzed past. The Cadillac's alarm began shrieking and she ducked down, dropping onto her knees and rolling under the SUV as tires squealed and Kyle gunned the sedan. Viper settled on her stomach and waited, the gun pointed toward the expanse of pavement. A second later, the sedan's front tires came into view and she fired.

The shot was deafening under the Cadillac, but her aim was true. The bullet ripped into the front left tire and the sedan swerved as the vehicle pulled to the left. Kyle kept control, however, and the sedan skidded around the end of the row of vehicles, heading for the exit at the back of the parking lot.

Viper rolled out from under the SUV and jumped up, darting between cars to emerge into the wide aisle leading to the exit. She raised her pistol, firing three rapid shots. One hit the right taillight and another hit the back windshield, but Kyle was almost to the exit. She lowered her gun as the approaching sirens wailed less than a block away, watching as the sedan swung into the empty street.

He was gone.

Alina flipped the safety on and tucked the gun back into the holster on her thigh. She turned back toward the church as lights from the first police cars lit up the front of the alley between the school and church. Viper glanced at the crowds filling the alley and front of the church and turned to weave her way through the rows of parked vehicles to her right. Moving quickly, she passed the back of her old elementary school on her left, then the convent beside it. The parking lot narrowed and Viper used the trees along the edge to help shield her as she moved rapidly, emerging onto another side street. She turned right and went halfway up the street to where her black Rubicon was parked along the curb.

Kyle wouldn't get far before the tire she shot expelled all its air. He also stuck out with a shattered back windshield. He would dump the sedan as soon as he could.

Viper opened the driver's door and climbed into her Jeep. She started the engine, slamming the door closed behind her. With any luck, she'd find him before that happened.

Chapter Twenty-Six

Michael turned away from the ambulance containing Angela and Stephanie, pulling his cell phone out of his pocket. Blake was accompanying them to the hospital. Neither was critically hurt, but both had lost significant amounts of blood. Surprisingly, Stephanie was the worst of the two. The bullet in her leg was dangerously close to the femoral artery, prompting the medic to call ahead for the surgeon.

Michael tapped a button on his screen and lifted the phone to his ear, walking away from the ambulance as it slowly rolled down the alley into the parking lot. The phone rang twice before it was picked up.

"Yes?"

Relief washed through him at the sound of Alina's voice.

"Where the hell are you?" he demanded, his voice sharper than he intended.

"In Pennsauken. Our shooter dumped his car. I just finished going through it."

Michael raised his eyebrows.

"You followed him?" he exclaimed. "How did you find him?"

"I saw him leave the church. I couldn't stop him, but I slowed him down."

"Did you find anything in the car?"

"No. How's Angie?"

"On her way to the hospital with Stephanie," Michael said, walking toward the parking lot. "Stephanie took a bullet in her leg. Blake's with them. I managed to go through the organ loft before the cops got there."

"And?"

"Nothing. It was clean." Michael pulled his keys out of his pocket. "Where in Pennsauken? I'll come meet you."

"For what?" Alina sounded amused. "He's long gone."

"Hey, anything to get away from here. The only reason I'm walking free is because I have a badge that trumps the Feds. Everyone else is being held in the church until they can be interviewed."

"Go to the hospital and check on the girls." He heard a door close and an engine start. "Call me as soon as you have an update."

"Where are you going?" he asked, but there was no answer. She had already disconnected.

Viper disconnected and glanced at the torn piece of paper in her hand. It wasn't much, but it was enough. She dropped it into her cup holder and pulled out of the empty parking lot.

She had told Michael an outright lie. She'd found two things in the sedan, missed by the assassin when he dumped it. The first was the torn scrap of paper, extracted from between the driver seat and the carpeted floor board inside the door. It wasn't surprising Kyle had missed it. It was completely obscured by the frame under the seat. The other item was more obvious, and she had no good explanation for why the assassin would have left it to be found. Whether he was in a hurry, or simply didn't think it was something included with an older model sedan, he had failed to remove the GPS chip from the on-board computer.

Viper frowned, slowing for a stop sign. It was a rookie mistake, and one she hadn't expected him to make. Her eyes narrowed thoughtfully and she glanced at the chip sitting on the passenger seat. Why did he leave it behind? He had to know she was right behind him. Her lips tightened and she returned her gaze to the road. He'd ditched the car fast enough.

Alina turned right and headed toward the highway. The torn scrap of paper was part of a parking garage receipt. Unfortunately for him, the address was still visible.

Fury was simmering below the surface and Alina took a deep, steadying breath. Now was not the time for emotion, yet it was there, threatening. It was bad enough John's final send-off turned into a complete fiasco, but now Stephanie and Angela were both in the hospital, victims by association. Viper pressed the gas, accelerating with more force than necessary to pull onto Route 130.

When she came back to New Jersey, she knew the risks involved to herself. In her opinion, the possibility of getting one step closer to the invisible puppet master in Washington, DC outweighed those risks. What she hadn't taken into account was the toll on her friends, or the unexpected arrival of Michael and Blake. Because of that miscalculation, Stephanie and Angela were both caught in the crossfire. Not only that, Joanne and Bill had their final good-bye to their only son disrupted by the actions of the very assassin that killed him!

Viper veered off onto an exit heading toward Camden and the Ben Franklin Bridge into Philadelphia. Perhaps Hawk was right. Perhaps she should have stayed away from Jersey. As soon as the thought entered her mind, however, Alina shook her head. She came back to New Jersey with a plan, and that plan had not changed. Her hand tightened on the steering wheel. The plan was flawless, even with the unexpected additional players. She had to stop letting emotion get in the way. The plan was the plan, and the only way to keep them all safe was to follow it.

And kill the enemy so well-hidden in Washington.

Alina rubbed her forehead and flew along in the far left lane, speeding toward the tolls for the bridge. The letters Dave had sent John twelve years ago held all the clues to the identity of her arch-nemesis, but she was unable to decipher them without the attachments. Her hand dropped back to the steering wheel. Without the attachments, she had no way of pinpointing the traitor behind all of this.

The frustration and fury she'd been carefully repressing for the past two weeks tightened her gut, and made Viper's throat constrict. Not only did her brother die trying to get the information out to someone, but now that information was lost forever. John was dead, Hawk was shot, she was being hunted, and Stephanie and Angela were hurt and it was all because of her brother's curiosity and her job. Her lips tightened. It would all be for nothing if she couldn't figure out who was behind it. Kyle was just a pawn, another puppet on a string. It was the puppet-master she wanted.

Her phone broke the silence in the Jeep, ringing through the speakers and pulling Alina from her thoughts. She pressed a button on the steering wheel.

"Yes?"

"Go secure," Charlie's voice filled the Jeep.

Alina pressed a button on the screen of her phone.

"Done."

"What the hell just happened?" he demanded. "There was an active shooter at John's funeral?"

Viper's lips twisted humorlessly.

"Someday you have to tell me how you know everything," she said, switching lanes for EZ pass. "It can't have hit the news yet."

"It hasn't. Tell me what's going on."

"A sniper was in the organ loft," said Alina, slowing to roll through the toll booth. The light flashed green and she pressed the gas again. The bridge loomed ahead of her, and beyond it, the Philadelphia Skyline. "He took a shot, but missed and hit the lectern."

"You were the target?"

"Yes." Viper glanced over her shoulder and moved into the middle lane to cross the bridge. "Someone knocked a kneeler and I hit the deck. The round went over me. He tried again, but I was moving and he hit a statue."

"Did you see him?"

"Yes."

Silence greeted that and Alina was halfway across the bridge before Charlie spoke again.

"I'm assuming he got away since you're not telling me it's been contained."

"He did, but he won't get far."

"You sound confident. Why?"

Viper's eyes narrowed.

"When have I ever failed?"

Charlie chuckled reluctantly.

"Fair enough," he murmured. "You have a lead?"

"No, but I'm working on it," she lied. "Do you have any information on your leak?"

"Yes," he said unexpectedly. "It's worse than we thought. Assets are being targeted all over the globe."

"How many?" Viper demanded, approaching the end of the bridge.

"As of this morning, I have four confirmed dead and three missing," he said. "It's not just you anymore. I've warned the rest and they're going dark."

Alina swore.

"Is it confined to the Organization?"

"It appears to be. There are no signs of any other agency being targeted."

"Who have you pissed off, Charlie?" Viper demanded, turning right off the bridge and taking the exit to Center City. "Are you any closer to finding out if the leak is in our house or someone else's?"

"I am."

"Don't forget–"

"I won't," he said, cutting her off. "They're all yours when I have a name."

Viper nodded, navigating the narrow city streets of Philadelphia skillfully. She was skirting around the edge of Center City, cutting through neighborhoods of row homes pressed together just feet from the curb. When this all began and she was chased across Europe a few weeks ago, Charlie promised her he would send her when he found the leak. It was beyond business now. It was personal.

"What about Hawk?" she asked. "Is he safe where he is?"

"For now. I don't anticipate him staying put for much longer."

"He'll be safer on his own," Alina said, slowing for a red light. "No offense."

"I don't doubt that," he agreed. "It's not him I'm worried about."

Alina watched in her rear view mirror as a black sedan with tinted windows pulled up behind her. She glanced at the light as it turned green and pressed the gas.

"What's that supposed to mean?"

"I'm not happy with you being in New Jersey. You're too much of a target there."

"Only if they know where to look," she pointed out, approaching the next block and another red light. "I have my reasons. You know that."

Alina stopped at the light and glanced in her rear view mirror. The black sedan was still behind her. She frowned and shifted her eyes to her side mirror, watching as two youths in hoodies moved from the sidewalk into the street behind the Jeep. Her lips tightened as one crossed behind her while the other one started walking beside the Jeep. She glanced at the red light swiftly, then the black sedan behind her.

"I can't change your mind?"

Before she could answer him, something hit the window next to her. Viper turned her head incredulously to stare down the barrel of a semi-automatic.

"Hold on, Charlie," she said. "Give me a minute."

"Get out or I'll blow your head off!" yelled the youth.

"Is someone actually..." Charlie began, sounding dumbstruck.

"I think so," she answered, amused. "Hold on."

Viper undid her seatbelt and moved her hand to the door handle. She opened the door just enough for the unsuspecting, would-be car-jacker to shove the gun into the opening, pointing it directly at her. As soon as the hand holding the weapon passed the edge of the door, Viper pulled the door closed again, hard. She threw the Jeep in park, catching the semi-automatic as it fell. Moving swiftly, she released the door and spun sideways in the seat at the same time, kicking the attacker solidly in his chest. He stumbled backwards, lost his footing and fell onto the curb.

Viper followed him.

Before he could regain his feet, she was above him. The butt of his own weapon made solid contact with his temple and the car-jacker sank back on the cement silently. Spinning around, Viper started toward the back of the Jeep. The other half of the car-jacking duo was backtracking toward the black sedan. She raised the semi-automatic in her hand, watching as the back window of the sedan opened. The barrel of another gun appeared. Without breaking stride, Viper fired. Her shot was true and the barrel lowered abruptly as the weapon dropped from lifeless fingers. Reaching the back of the Jeep, she unloaded a stream of bullets into the front tires of the sedan as the driver threw it in reverse and hit the gas. The partner still in the road yelled, raising a pistol and pointing it at Viper.

"I'ma kill you, bitch!" he screamed.

He never got the chance to fire. One bullet entered his neck and the other went into his chest. The pistol dropped from his fingers as he fell into the road, dead. The sedan never hit the brakes as it sped backwards, the front tires flattening as they went.

Viper turned and went back to the driver's door, flipping on the safety as she went. She climbed back into the Jeep, tossing the gun onto the floor of the passenger side, and closed the door. Putting the Jeep back into gear, she hit the gas, crossing through the intersection and leaving three bodies behind.

"You were saying?" she asked, reaching for her seatbelt as she drove. "Something about changing my mind?"

"Do you go out of your way to look for trouble?" Charlie demanded. Whether his voice was shaking from amusement or anger, Viper wasn't entirely sure.

"Sad, isn't it?" Alina asked, turning left down a side street. "It just seems to find me."

"How many were there?"

"At least four, maybe five."

"How many are still alive?"

"Two."

A sigh filled the Jeep.

"That isn't exactly what I had in mind when I told you to take care of yourself up there."

Despite herself, Viper's lips curved in a grin.

"Maybe not, but we can't have it easy all the time, can we? That wouldn't be any fun."

Michael slid his phone into his jacket pocket and glanced at his watch as he strode up to the entrance of the ER. No sooner was he on his way to the hospital than Damon called. How he knew about the funeral was a mystery, but he did. He was short and to the point: how the hell did a shooter make it into the church? It had been a long time since Michael felt like a teenager taken to task by an irate adult, but Damon managed it within the space of half a minute.

Michael scowled as the automatic doors slid open and he went into the hospital. Alina's safety was his primary responsibility, and he'd failed. Never mind how or why, it was only by the grace of God himself that Alina still had a head on her shoulders. He shook his head. Of all the things that could have gone wrong, the would-be assassin was foiled by a church kneeler. A kneeler! He couldn't make that up if he tried.

A nurse behind the intake desk looked up as he approached.

"Can I help you?"

"I'm looking for two patients brought in a little while ago," he said, pulling out his badge. "Agent Stephanie Walker and Angela...oh god, I don't know her last name."

The nurse looked at his badge and turned to her computer.

"Walker?" she repeated, typing rapidly. "Did she come in...oh yes! Here it is. Gunshot wounds."

"That's the one."

"Mike!"

Michael turned in surprise as Blake came through a door at the far end of the room.

"It's about time you got here! Steph's gone into surgery, and Angela is getting stitched up." He glanced at the nurse behind the desk. "I'll take him back."

She nodded and turned to grab some papers off a printer behind her, dismissing them.

"How bad is Stephanie?" Michael asked.

"She lost a lot of blood, but she should be fine," said Blake, hitting a large, stainless steel button on the wall. The doors began to swing ponderously open. "At least, that's what the nurse said before they rushed her back."

"Was it really close to the artery?"

"Don't know yet." Blake glanced at him as they walked into

the bowels of the Emergency Room. "It's a miracle your girlfriend wasn't killed. If she hadn't hit the deck..."

"Trust me, I know. What about Angie?"

"They picked pieces of the Virgin Mary out of her head, neck, shoulder and chest, and stitched her up. She'll be fine."

Blake led him to the end of a wide corridor and they turned the corner. The smell of antiseptic and the sounds of medical equipment assaulted them, and Michael sighed. He hated hospitals.

"Where's the Black Widow?" Blake asked, leading him down the corridor. "Please tell me she had more luck than we did."

"Not really. She got eyes on him, but he got away."

"Damn! Who is this guy? What was he doing there?"

Michael glanced at him.

"You don't know?" he asked, surprised. "I thought you would have figured it out by now."

Blake stared at him blankly.

"Figured what out?"

Michael stopped walking and pulled Blake to the side of the hallway.

"I can't tell you much," he said, lowering his voice, "and I'm guessing Walker doesn't know much either, so this is strictly between us."

Blake nodded in acknowledgment.

"I came up here because I was asked to watch Lina's back. Someone's discovered her identity, and they're gunning for her."

Blake stared at him hard.

"How the hell did that happen?!"

Michael shrugged.

"That's what she's trying to figure out."

Blake ran a hand over his short hair.

"That's why she didn't want Angela staying with her," he said slowly. "Stephanie said she was going to get the story out of her later today. She doesn't know any of this!"

"No one does except me, and I don't know the whole story. I was told to make sure this didn't happen."

Blake shook his head.

"How the hell were you supposed to secure a church that size with no resources and no back-up?" he asked. "It couldn't be done. Even with a full team, there were too many people and too many exits." He paused for a moment, then shook his head again. "What kind of demented bastard hits a funeral, for God's sake!?"

"One who's desperate. He knew she would surface for the

funeral. It was the only time he was guaranteed a shot."

"And he took it," Blake muttered, turning to continue walking down the wide corridor. "This is turning into a circus. Does she have any leads?"

"Your guess is as good as mine," Michael said with a shrug. "She wasn't telling me much to begin with, and after this, it will be even less. In fact, I won't be surprised if she just goes dark and disappears altogether."

Blake looked at him.

"You think she'll run?"

"No," Michael sighed after a moment of thought. "I wish she would, but she won't. She'll stay and fight."

"Angela is in here." Blake motioned to the next room. "How much do we tell her?"

"Nothing," said Michael flatly. "Viper doesn't want her to know anything."

Blake nodded.

"Got it." He looked at him, and for the first time all day, a smile cracked his face. "Are you ready? She's not in a good mood."

Michael rolled his eyes.

"I took on the Taliban and insurgents in Iraq and Afghanistan," he muttered. "I think I can handle Angela."

Chapter Twenty-Seven

Robert Carmichael poured some soda from the half-empty two liter into a pink paper cup with Disney Princesses stamped on it. He set the bottle down on the paper tablecloth, also adorned with Disney Princesses, and turned to look over the back yard. Over twenty six-year-old girls swarmed around in the sunshine, dressed in their best princess dresses. Shoes had been discarded, tights were getting grass-stained, and shrieks of laughter filled the air as they ran in circles, engaged in some kind of game his sister had cooked up.

He sipped the soda and watched as his niece chased after a pink beach ball, her birthday tiara askew over her blonde curls. This was the last place he wanted to be spending his Saturday afternoon, but Rachel had made it very clear: show up or there would be hell to pay. So here he was, sipping warm soda out of a Disney Princess cup and listening to the screams of little girls as they played.

At least the FBI issue was on its way to being handled. It was a shame they didn't bite on the drugs though. Robert sighed inwardly. Honestly, who would think Hanover would have hidden cameras all over the house? He supposed he should have known something would go wrong. After all, everything had gone wrong ever since that first street racer got killed up in New Jersey. It was like someone had broken a mirror, or spilled some salt. The bad luck was going to end though. At least, for him. Not so much for Special Agent Blake Hanover. By the end of the weekend, Robert wouldn't have to worry about him digging around into anything except legal aid.

"Rob!"

Robert turned reluctantly to face a tall, red-faced man trudging across the grass towards him. He spread a wide smile over his face and moved forward, holding out his hand.

"Glenn!" he greeted his brother-in-laws' cousin. "Good to see you! How was Miami?"

"Busy," said Glenn, wringing his hand, "but productive. I'm glad to be home. Nothing like your own bed to sleep in."

"I hear that! How's Janet? And the kids?"

"Fine, fine. Everyone's fine. She's here somewhere. She got here early with Olivia. Knowing her, she's probably in the kitchen organizing more sugar for these rugrats." Glenn glanced at the paper cup in Robert's hand. "Good Lord, is that what we have to drink?"

"Afraid so."

"What's your sister doing? Trying to cause a riot of adults?" Glenn turned to head toward the tall blonde woman directing traffic in the middle of the rugrats. "I'm going to go say hello before Janet appears and collars me into helping with something. You know how it is!"

Robert nodded and watched as Glenn made his way through the crowd of mini princesses. Glenn was nice enough. He was certainly a family man who managed to endear himself to his sister, but Robert found him barely tolerable. He laughed too much. Men who laughed that much were suspect. No one had that much to be happy about, especially in today's political climate.

He glanced at his watch and wandered toward the patio where his brother-in-law was standing in front a grill, surrounded by half a dozen other bored husbands. It looked like the burgers were almost ready. With any luck, he could eat, they'd cut the cake, and he could high-tail it out of here. There were still a few things to wrap up at the office, and then there was the benefit dinner tonight. His assistant had reminded him again this morning of the importance of putting in an appearance. The public loved a philanthropist, and they needed the public on their side before the run to the mid-term elections. His assistant was worried about ratings and support numbers. Robert grimaced to himself. What his assistant didn't realize was that none of it would matter if Blake Hanover managed to uncover his connection to Dominic DiBarcoli and Trasker Pharmaceuticals. In fact, if the FBI agent dug deep enough that would be the least of their worries.

If the public found out about the Casa Reinos Cartel, all would be lost.

Viper sipped black coffee and set the cup down next to a laptop on the bistro table. She was seated in front of the window overlooking a busy city street just outside Chinatown. She glanced at the traffic outside, then turned her attention back to the screen in front of her.

She had reached the parking garage without any more excitement and her luck held when she discovered all the cameras were working, and recording to a server. The garage was perfectly placed in the city. The Convention Center, train station, and Chinatown were all within walking distance, as well as numerous hotels. There was no way of narrowing down where Kyle went from there unless she managed to get something off the cameras. To that end, she had parked in the garage and crossed the road to the coffee shop on the corner, where she proceeded to hack the security footage, not only from the parking garage, but also from the traffic cameras in the street. One way or another, she'd find out when Kyle was there, and which direction he went.

It wasn't much, but it was a start.

Her phone vibrated in her jacket but she ignored it, her attention focused on the black and white footage on the screen. The time had been missing, but the date was still on the paper. The receipt was from two days ago. She found the day on the server and began the tedious act of plowing through camera footage, looking for the sedan. Ironically enough, it wasn't the sedan that caught her attention first. It was Kyle himself.

Viper hit pause and stared at the grainy picture on the screen. It was definitely him, dressed in a black jacket and jeans, walking into the parking garage from the east side entrance. She tilted her head and studied him for a moment. He had a bag over his shoulder and a cup of coffee in his hand. Alina glanced at the cup of coffee next to her laptop and raised an eyebrow.

It was the same cup.

Her lips curved coldly. He was staying nearby. That narrowed the field down considerably. She pressed play and watched as he strode into the garage and disappeared into the elevator. Alina reached for her coffee again, watching the various floors until Kyle emerged from the elevator on the top floor and strode towards the sedan. A minute later, it pulled out of the spot and rolled toward the exit ramp. Sipping her drink, she watched as he circled down to the ground floor and pulled to the entrance. There he stopped and spoke to the employee, who nodded and passed him the infamous receipt.

Viper sat back thoughtfully. Why get a receipt if he had paid in cash? Surely he wasn't dumb enough to pay with a credit card? She picked up the torn paper and glanced at it. All that remained was the address, date and name of the business. No amount or form of payment remained. Her eyes went back to the screen and she pressed her lips together. If he had paid with a card, she could find out exactly where he was, and even what kind of toothpaste he used. They always paid cash. It was how they worked. So why the receipt?

The sedan turned right out of the lot and disappeared out of frame. Viper reached out and paused the footage, glancing at the time stamp on the camera. It was just after ten in the morning. She resumed and sped it up, sipping her coffee as the hours quickly rolled over, and countless cars came and went through the entrance. By the time she'd finished her coffee, the footage was onto the next day and the sedan had not returned. With a sigh, she closed out of the program and sat back in her chair, thoughtfully turning her attention out of the window.

He was staying nearby, that was apparent, and he had the option of parking in the street or utilizing the parking garage. She stared blindly at the traffic. He would want somewhere he could go unnoticed; somewhere that assured a high level of privacy. A hotel would be her first choice, followed very closely by a short-term, furnished rental. Unfortunately, both were abundant in the city, and narrowing it down would take time, time she didn't have.

Alina turned her dark gaze from the window and glanced to the back of the store and the two barista's working behind the counter. There was another way she could narrow it down.

All she needed was a name.

Michael looked up as Blake came back into the room. Angela was propped up in the bed, her phone in her hand, scouring the local news sites for updates. Her blood-stained clothes were in a clear plastic bag on a stool in the corner and the hospital scrubs she'd been given hung on her slender frame. A thick bandage covered the new stitches on her neck, and another was visible on her shoulder.

"How are you feeling?" Blake asked, looking at her.

"Like I'm ready to get out of here," she replied, glancing up. "I'm all stitched up and they gave me Vicodin for pain, so I'm not feeling much of anything right now. How's Steph?"

"She just got moved into a room. The doctor said the bullet barely missed her femoral artery. It's out, but she lost a lot of blood. When she fell, she clocked her head pretty bad. He wants to keep her for a few days to keep an eye on her."

"Oh, I bet she has something to say about that," said Angela. "She won't stay in for a bump on the head and a hole in her leg."

"I'm sure she will, once she wakes up," Blake agreed, "but she won't have a choice. I'm not letting her leave."

Angela grinned.

"Good luck with that," she said, going back to her phone. "I'll put money on Stephanie."

"I'll put mine on Blake," Michael said with a laugh.

"How about you?" Blake asked her.

"I'm just waiting for the doc to sign the discharge papers and I can leave. Although, I don't know if I want to now. Maybe I should stay with Steph."

"I don't think that's an option," said Blake with a grin. "It's not exactly a hotel. You can't just check in and out."

"Have you heard from Lina yet?" Angela turned to look at Michael, frowning when he shook his head. "Where the hell is she?!"

"I don't know."

"Have you heard anything about the shooting? Either of you? All the news is saying is that someone opened fire at a funeral and the shooter is still at large. How can that be all they know?"

Blake glanced at Michael and caught the look of exasperation in his eyes.

"The news isn't going to know any more than the police, and that's all the police know right now." He shrugged. "You have to give them time."

"This is absurd. Why would someone start shooting at a funeral anyway?! It's disrespectful!"

Blake bit his lip to keep from laughing.

"Mmmm," was all he could trust himself to say.

"I mean, who were they even aiming at?" Angela continued, oblivious. "Obviously they weren't a good shot. I mean, they hit everything except a person, thank God. Have you heard anything about a possible motive?"

"I don't know any more than you do," Blake said. "I left with you, remember? Mike, did you hear anything before you left?"

"Nope."

Angela looked from one man to the other, her eyes narrowed. They both stared back blandly, and the silence was suddenly very thick.

"What aren't you telling me?" she demanded after a moment.

Michael's eyebrows soared into his forehead in surprise.

"What?"

"Don't play dumb," she snapped. "There's something you're not telling me. What is it?"

"I don't know what you're talking about," Michael muttered,

glancing at his watch. "I don't know any more about this than you."

"You know something. You're not even remotely bothered by the fact that someone opened fire at a funeral. That means part of you was expecting it. And you've been spending more time looking at your phone, waiting for something, than you have been talking to me. It's Lina, isn't it? She's got something to do with this, and you can't get hold of her."

Blake was startled, and he was glad that Angela's full attention seemed to be focused on Michael at the moment. He looked at the woman in the bed, a new light of respect dawning in his eyes. She was proving to be a lot sharper than he had given her credit for.

"I'm just wondering where she's disappeared to," said Michael, looking up. "Forgive me if I'm a little concerned, considering that out of the three of you, she's the only one unaccounted for."

"I've called her three times," Angela admitted, the accusing tone leaving her voice abruptly. "It goes straight to voicemail. She's infuriating. What's she doing? I'm telling you, she knows something, just like you two."

"All I know is that when Steph wakes up, I have to somehow convince her to stay put for a few days," Blake said. "I don't know what else you think I should know, but that's my main concern right this second."

"What about her boss?" Angela asked after a moment. "He was there, right? Is he coming to see her? Maybe he can convince her."

Blake blinked.

"You know what?" he said, pulling out his phone. "That's not a bad idea. Rob will make sure she stays put."

"I'm good for some things."

"I hate to be the voice of doom over here," said Michael apologetically, "but isn't she on LOA? Rob can't order her to do anything if she's on leave."

"Actually, she's not anymore," Blake said, hitting speed-dial. "Rob mentioned it this morning before...well, before everything went down. She was supposed to go into the office tomorrow morning for a meeting."

Michael stared at him, his eyebrows drawn together.

"Just like that? She's reinstated with no explanation?" he demanded. "What kind of outfit do you Feds run over there?"

Blake glanced at him and held up his hand as he turned away.

"Yeah, Rob? It's Blake." He strode out of the room, the phone pressed to his ear.

"That will make Stephanie happy, at least," said Angela. "She's been miserable not working. Does it matter why?"

Michael shrugged, his face creased into a frown. A few weeks before, Stephanie was placed on administrative leave of absence following John's accident. There had been no clear explanation for the action, and Michael knew Alina had some suspicions regarding it. When John passed away, Rob used it as an excuse for Stephanie to remain on leave. Now, suddenly, she was back in the fold? No questions asked? Michael scowled. Something wasn't right and he didn't like it.

And what was more, he knew Viper wouldn't like it either.

Chapter Twenty-Eight

Late afternoon sun filtered through the trees as the black luxury SUV rolled along the deserted country road. This stretch of road was always quiet, cutting southwest through Northern Virginia, away from the bustle and craziness of Washington, DC. The driver was used to the route, having made the trip many, many times before. The green rolling hills on either side of the road with their ancient oak trees passed unnoticed by either the driver or the sole occupant of the back seat. The driver glanced at the clock on the dash, then in the rear view mirror. Soundproof glass separated him from his passenger and he noted that he was still engrossed in the flat screen TV. He returned his eyes to the road in front of him

In the back of the SUV, the lone occupant watched the news with only half his attention, his laptop open beside him. While he appeared to be engrossed, his mind was actually split between the updates on his laptop and the news on the screen. All that changed with a simple statement of breaking news. His brows furrowed in consternation as the newscaster switched to their sister-station in Philadelphia. There, a somber brunette took delight in reporting the terrifying ordeal at the funeral of an FBI agent that morning.

His lips pressed together grimly, the reports and updates on the laptop momentarily forgotten as she described how an unknown shooter opened fire inside a church during the funeral mass for Special Agent John Smithe. The shooter fired several shots, hitting another agent and shattering a large statue of the Virgin Mary. No one was killed, but two women were rushed to the hospital and three others were treated on-site for minor injuries. The shooter was still at large, and police and federal authorities were asking for any information from the public.

The passenger stared at the TV. Who the hell went to a funeral and opened fire? He shook his head and reached into the inside pocket of his suit jacket, pulling out his cell phone. What was this world coming to? People couldn't even lay the dead to rest without someone coming along and stirring up trouble. He swiped his screen and pressed a button, reaching up to slip his Bluetooth onto his ear. The image on the TV moved from the newscaster to footage of a large, gray stone, Cathedral-esque church.

"I'm standing in front of St. Peter's Catholic Church in Merchantville where, just hours ago, someone opened fire on mourners as they gathered to pay their last respects to Special Agent John Smithe," a reporter said, motioning to the church behind her. "This was no ordinary shooting. We're told the gunman was concealed in the organ loft, where he took at least three shots with a high-powered weapon. Those shots weren't random. Witnesses say the shooter didn't spray the crowd, but rather seemed to be aiming toward the altar. Thankfully, no one was killed in the attack."

The camera went back to the studio and the man picked up the remote, muting the TV as the phone in his ear connected.

"Hello?"

"It's me," he said, glancing out the windows at the sprawling countryside whizzing by. "Have you seen the news?"

"Not yet," the voice answered. "Why?"

"Someone started shooting at John Smithe's funeral this morning. Were you there?"

"No. I was in the ER all night. I've got staples in my head, and my arm is glued, stitched and bandaged from the wrist to the shoulder," the voice replied testily. "I'm high on pain meds. I wasn't going anywhere."

The man scowled.

"Trent, what the hell are you doing up there?" he demanded. "All you had to do was detain one woman."

"Have you ever been to Jersey?" Trent snapped. "They're all insane! The woman attacked me. She stabbed me in the neck and pushed me down a flight of stairs. I managed to get away without her seeing my face, but I still have three stitches in my neck and a concussion from that night."

"And your arm?"

Trent sighed heavily.

"She's not staying at her house anymore. She's been with some guy the past couple days. When they went to the viewing last night, I put a tracker on his truck and followed it. He lives out in the woods in the middle of nowhere. When I was trying to find the way through the trees, a damn owl attacked me."

The man felt his lips quiver.

"An owl?" he repeated.

"Yes. I assume it was an owl. What else flies around at night?

It sure as hell wasn't a bat. It clawed up my arm and split open my head, then someone shot at me!"

"What?"

"They missed. I got the hell out of there and drove straight to the hospital. It must have been the guy, unless someone was out hunting. I'm telling you, the people up here are a race unto themselves. The nurse at the ER wasn't even fazed. It's like people come in with shredded arms all the time."

The man was silent for a moment, staring out of the window thoughtfully.

"Who's this guy she's staying with?" he asked finally. "Her boyfriend?"

"No idea. I met him at the viewing. He sure seemed protective of her," Trent said slowly, "but he could be just a friend."

"Well that's a complication. Can you get her away from him?"

"I tried to talk her into a drink, but she didn't bite. That's why I followed them."

"Figure it out," said the man, his eyes falling back to the laptop as a new report came into his email. "I didn't send you up there to fail. I sent you to get her."

"I'm trying. What happened at the funeral? Who was the shooter?"

"They don't know. He got away." The man raised his eyes to the passing scenery again. "I don't like it though. Get the girl and get her to me. I don't know what's going on up there, but we're running out of time."

The man disconnected and pulled the Bluetooth off his ear. He tucked his phone into his pocket and turned his attention back to the TV. The news had moved on to weather conditions in the Midwest. His lips tightened angrily and he returned his gaze to his laptop.

This shooter complicated things. There was only one reason someone would hide in an organ loft with a rifle at John Smithe's funeral, and the fact that they missed presented a huge problem. Viper would disappear now. It was her only option. Any hope he had of finding her location was lost.

"Damn!"

Blake unlocked the door to Stephanie's condo and stepped

inside. Buddy reared up, planting his paws on his chest, his tail wagging furiously.

"Yeah, I know, boy," Blake murmured, rubbing his ears fondly. "Let's get your leash. It's been a long day."

Buddy ran in a circle and watched as Blake picked up his leash from one of the dining room chairs. As soon as he saw it, he tore around in circles again and barked. Blake laughed and hooked it onto his collar.

"Come on," he said, opening the door again.

Buddy bounded out of the house and dragged him through the alcove and down the sidewalk to the large, grassy courtyard next to the parking lot. As soon as he hit the grass, he went straight for a bush and kicked up his leg, relieving himself of a river.

The sun was fading and Blake yawned. What a day. Rob showed up at the hospital a few minutes after Stephanie woke up. A lively argument ensued when she realized that both her boss and Blake expected her to stay in the hospital. A grin passed Blake's face. They'd won in the end, but it was a hard win. Ironically, it was Angela who sealed it. She sailed in, discharge papers in hand, and laid such a guilt trip on Stephanie that she finally caved.

Buddy finally lowered his leg and turned to start sniffing around, wandering to the right. Blake followed, the grin fading. Rob was not happy about the events of the morning. Hell, none of them were, but Rob was particularly upset. Not only was one of his men dead, but now his surviving partner had a bullet in her leg. When Blake left the hospital, there was an agent standing guard outside the door of Stephanie's room, and another one at the end of the hall. They would rotate every twelve hours with another pair until Stephanie was released. Rob was taking no chances, and given what Blake now knew about John's death, he was grateful for the precaution. If Rob hadn't set agents to watch her, Blake would have stayed himself. In fact, that had been his plan until Rob arranged the guard.

Buddy crouched down, and Blake pulled a plastic bag out of the holder clipped to the leash handle. Stephanie knew the agents were there, and Blake got the impression she was grateful for them, even if she did tell Rob he was being ridiculous. She wasn't a stupid woman, she knew what happened to John, and knew how precarious her own position now was. She didn't know yet that the bullet in her leg was meant for her best friend. Blake shook his head.

When she found out, all hell would let loose.

Buddy finished, and Blake bent down with the plastic bag. What a complete mess the whole thing was! When he had left the hospital, Michael was grim, and Angela was almost fit to be tied. Neither had heard from the Black Widow, and both were getting dumped straight into voicemail when they called. Blake straightened up and tied a knot in the bag, turning to walk toward the green trash can at the edge of the courtyard, installed for just this purpose. Perhaps she had finally come to her senses and gone underground. Michael thought it was unlikely and Blake admitted he would be surprised himself, but it was certainly the most logical thing for the assassin to do. You couldn't be eliminated if you couldn't be found.

Blake dropped the bag into the trash and turned to walk Buddy across the courtyard and around the complex. How the hell did someone find out about Viper, anyway? Was there a leak in her organization? That was a chilling thought. His brows drew together as he walked, his lips tightening.

A few weeks ago, terrorists not only got into the country, but they managed to smuggle several bombs up the East Coast. They had infiltrated the largest pharmaceutical company in the country, and attempted a biological attack on the United States. Now the very assassin that stopped the whole thing was under attack. No one would ever convince Blake everything wasn't connected. What the hell was going on?

His phone rang in his pocket, interrupting Blake's musings. He pulled it out, glancing at the screen. His eyebrows raised in surprise when he saw his boss's number on the screen.

"Hey Ken," he answered, holding the phone to his ear. "What's up?"

"I heard about the shooting up there this morning. I'm checking on you. You ok?"

Blake frowned. While his boss was a good boss, he'd never been a mother hen to any of them. If one of his agents got hurt in the field, he was famous for asking about the blood loss. If it wasn't a critical amount, he didn't call.

"I'm fine. My suit didn't even get wrinkled," he said. "Did Rob tell you?"

"Yes, and it's all over the news. Did it really happen inside the church?"

"Yeah. The shooter hid in the organ loft."

"How's Agent Walker doing? She was shot in the leg?"

"She'll be fine. She's lost a lot of blood and has a concussion. She clocked her head on the marble floor pretty good. They're keeping her in for a few days to keep an eye on her."

"Thank God it's not worse. Rob said it was close to the

artery."

"Yes. She was lucky."

"Any ideas on the shooter?"

"No. He disappeared in the commotion."

"Who the hell opens fire at a funeral, for God's sake!?" said Ken disgustedly. "Especially one filled with Federal agents!"

Blake thought of Michael's words earlier. He said it was a desperate person, and Blake was inclined to agree.

"That's what we're all saying. It's insane."

Ken cleared his throat.

"Blake, I know you've had a long day, but there's something we need to discuss. Something's come up."

Blake stilled at the tone in Ken's voice.

"What is it? Did you find the guy who broke into my house?"

"Not yet. No one's seen him since Friday. We're still looking. This is something else." Ken paused, clearing his throat again. "What can you tell you me about a woman named Tina Ricci?"

Blake frowned.

"Tina Ricci?" he repeated. "Nothing. I recognize the name, but I couldn't tell you how. Why?"

"She was a witness two years ago on a case you worked, the Finaldi case. Remember it?"

"I remember the case but I don't remember a specific witness. We had no shortage of witnesses on that one. It took more time to sort out the witnesses than it did to track him down."

"Well, she remembers you. In fact, she's filing formal charges against you."

Blake stopped short, his brows snapping together.

"For what?!"

"Professional misconduct and sexual assault."

"*What*?!" he bellowed.

"The Prosecutor called me this afternoon as a courtesy," said Ken. "She claims you sexually assaulted her during the investigation."

"That's...that's ridiculous!" Blake sputtered, stunned. "I would never...I don't even know the woman!"

"Look, I know this is a lot to take in. I'm emailing you a photo and a list of the charges right now. Take a look at them, especially the photo. See if you even recognize her. It may just be some crazy who's fixated on you for some reason, or she could have you confused with someone else. Whatever it is, we need to figure out what's going on and come up with a game plan."

"A game plan?" Blake repeated, his head spinning. "How do

you game plan for this? It's a flat-out lie! I would never assault a woman, especially a witness, for God's sake!"

"I know, but unfortunately there are steps that need to be taken and procedures we need to follow. I have to place you on LOA until the charges can be investigated internally."

"Place me on...Ken, you don't honestly believe any of this, do you?" Blake demanded, his blood running cold.

"Honestly? No, I don't. I know you. I know you would never do the things she's accusing you of doing. Don't think I haven't noticed how quickly this is happening after someone planted a brick of heroin in your house, either. Trust me Hanover, I know the whole thing smells rotten. That's why we have to make sure we follow the procedures to the letter. We don't want to make this any more difficult than it already will be."

"Meaning?"

"Meaning if we do everything by the book, we have a better chance of convincing people of your innocence," Ken said bluntly. "You want to keep yourself as clean as possible so the mud they sling won't stick."

Blake ran a hand through his hair in frustration.

"What do I do?" he asked after a moment. "Do I come back to DC?"

"Right now, check out the email and write down anything and everything you remember about any interaction you may have had with her. Stay where you are for the time being. I'll have to tell Rob, of course, and you'll be on formal leave of absence starting tomorrow. God willing, we'll get this cleared up quickly."

Michael watched as Angela climbed out of his truck, moving stiffly. Once they left the hospital, she had dropped her façade. It was clear she was in pain and exhausted, but she hadn't shown any of that in the hospital. Grudgingly, he admitted she was a lot stronger than he gave her credit for. Not only was she careful not to worry Stephanie, but she did her part to make sure Stephanie stayed put under doctors' care. It was only when she got into the truck that the mask faltered.

"I don't see Lina's Jeep," she said, looking around. "Where the hell is she?"

"I have no idea," he said, closing the door behind her. He

looked at her purse, dangling from her hand. "Do you want me to take that?"

"I'm ok," she replied, glancing up at him. "It's not heavy. I just can't get it onto my shoulder."

Michael nodded and turned to walk across the grass with her toward the deck.

"How will we get in if she's not here?" Angela asked suddenly.

"I have a key."

She stopped and stared at him.

"What?! Why do you get a key and I don't?!" she demanded. "I've known her since we were six!"

Michael shrugged and laughed, going up the steps to the deck.

"I don't know what to tell you," he said over his shoulder. "She gave it to me last night, along with the security code if I needed it."

He reached into his pocket and pulled out his keys. He waved the small wand Viper had given him in front of the pad next to the sliding door and heard a faint click.

"Well, I like that!" Angela huffed, joining him at the door. "What if we didn't come back together?"

"I'm not letting you out of my sight," he retorted, sliding open the door and standing aside for her to enter. "She knows that."

"Why? It's not your responsibility to protect me."

"Alina made it my responsibility," he said, following her into the house and closing the door behind them. "Until you're not in danger anymore, my place is wherever you are."

Angela dropped her purse onto the dining room table tiredly.

"Do you really think I'm still in danger?" she asked. "We don't even know who it was that broke into my house. It could have been some random crack-head."

Michael pressed his lips together and was silent. He walked over to the bar and dropped his keys on the granite top before shrugging out of his suit jacket. Angela watched him thoughtfully.

"You know something."

He looked up in surprise to find her staring at him with an uncannily sharp gaze. Once again, Michael was forcibly reminded that Angela was not as dumb as she appeared.

"What?"

"Don't try to pretend. You and Alina know something you're not telling me," she said pointedly. "I don't appreciate you two knowing something about me that I don't even know myself."

"It's not about you..." Michael began, then stopped. He ran a hand over his short hair and sighed heavily. "I can't tell you. I'm sorry. If Lina wants you to know, she'll tell you."

"Fine." Angela picked up her purse and turned to stalk down the hallway running to the front of the house. "I'll take it up with her, if she ever comes home. I'm going up and getting changed."

Michael watched her go and went into the kitchen. He opened the fridge and gazed into it, his stomach growling. Glancing at his watch, he realized it was already past six and he hadn't eaten anything all day. For that matter, neither had Angela. He examined their options. There weren't any that didn't involve cooking. He closed the fridge and opened the freezer. All he could see was frozen meat, vegetables, ice, and a bottle of Ketel One. There was not one bag of chicken nuggets or a frozen pizza to be had.

He closed the freezer and turned to go out of the kitchen. Pulling his phone from his pocket, he swiped the screen. He didn't know where Viper was or what she was doing, but if she was coming back, she could damn well bring something to eat.

Michael typed a quick text to her and moved down the hall towards the stairs. Where was she anyway? She'd gone after the shooter, but when he spoke to her, she hadn't found anything. He paused at the foot of the stairs. Or had she? He scowled and started up the steps. If she found something, would she have told him? Michael didn't know anymore. Viper had never been very forthcoming with information, but Michael had felt a decided shift in the past few days. It was almost as if she didn't trust him.

He went into the spare room next to Angela's and closed the door. Crossing the room to the closet, he pulled out a hanger for the suit he had bought yesterday for the funeral. He'd get changed, go downstairs, and get back to work on Trasker. Trying to figure out what Viper was up to was akin to trying to decipher a dead language. It was never going to happen. Not for him, anyway.

Michael pulled a pair of jeans out of his open duffel bag on the floor. To be honest, he didn't even know if Damon had a good grip on what Viper was up to. She'd locked them both out, going her own way instead. He frowned and began undoing the knot in his tie.

When she had come to see him that night at his house, she was very matter-of-fact when she told him there was someone hunting her. She'd been calm, collected, and very clinical about the whole thing. Yet he'd sensed that under it all, she was furious. Not just at her agency for allowing her identity to be leaked, but at everyone around her for holding her back. Michael had no doubt in his mind that Viper was capable of attacking any threat head-on, but this wasn't her typical target.

He pulled the tie off and tossed it onto the dresser. Michael stilled as a thought occurred to him. Alina wasn't a stupid woman. She knew the threat she was facing, and she knew better than most how people in her line of work usually ended their careers. Last summer, when he met her again, she hadn't known if she would make it out of the situation alive. It wasn't until after it was all over that he realized just how much she had faced down her own potential death. If there was one thing he could say for the deadly assassin his best friend's kid sister had become, she had grit. Viper had the kind of grit that was rare these days. It was a kind of prosaic strength that allowed her to do what she did, safe in the knowledge that if she died, she was going on her own terms and taking a few more bad guys with her. She would give it all to fulfill the oath she had taken to protect the country, even with her own life.

Michael sucked in his breath and stared at his reflection in the mirror above the dresser as the cold truth hit him.

Viper didn't expect to make it out of this alive.

The realization crashed into him, rocking him to his core. She was keeping them all at a distance, making sure everyone knew exactly what they needed to know and not one detail more. Viper was moving them all into position so when the end came, they would be as minimally affected as possible. The less they knew, the safer they would be. She'd take the fall for all of them.

Michael sank down onto the side of the bed. He swore to Dave he would take care of her, promised to keep an eye on her. How the hell was he going to do that when he couldn't even keep a shooter out of a church? How could he protect her when he had no idea what was going on in her world?

His head lifted after a moment and Michael got up to finish changing. He would work on Trasker. He would find the link between Trasker, the Cartel and the terrorists. He would find out who brought the terrorists here, and who had the most to lose by them failing in their mission. Once he had a name, he would know who wanted Viper dead.

Then he could help her.

Chapter Twenty-Nine

Stephanie looked up as the door to her hospital room opened. The nurses had made their rounds five minutes before and the doctor wasn't coming back until morning. Her hand moved under the blankets to her Glock which Blake had slipped to her before he left. If she was going to be stuck in this bed, temporarily helpless, at least she had a way to protect herself.

Her shoulders relaxed and she lifted her hand from under the covers as Alina materialized, closing the door softly behind her.

"Lina!" she exclaimed. "You're ok!"

A faint smile crossed her friend's lips and she moved silently to the side of the bed, her eyes flicking to the monitors briefly before coming to rest on Stephanie's face.

"Of course I'm ok," she murmured. "Nice guard out there."

"I'm surprised he let you in," Stephanie said with a grin. "He's been a pain in the ass. The nurses changed shifts and he demanded ID from the new ones before he let them in."

"He didn't see me. How's the leg?"

"Fine. The bullet missed the artery, but I lost a lot of blood just the same. They say I also have a concussion. All in all, not enough to keep me here, but they're doing it anyway."

"And Angie?"

"Discharged earlier. They stitched her up, and sent her on her way. Where've you been?"

Alina sat in the chair Blake had pulled over to the bedside earlier.

"Busy," she said shortly. "Was anyone else hit?"

Stephanie shook her head.

"Not that I know of. I think there were some minor injuries from the statue. Angie got the brunt, but Father Angelo also got caught by some of it. I think a couple others did as well. I don't know for sure. I was out when it all happened. The last thing I remember is hearing a kneeler hit the floor and then pain shooting through my leg."

Alina nodded and Stephanie studied her for a second, noting

the rings under her eyes and the alertness in her shoulders.

"They said the shooter was in the organ loft," Stephanie said slowly, watching her. "He only aimed at the altar, didn't take any shots anywhere else. If he wanted to, he could have massacred half the Bureau today."

"He wasn't there for the FBI," Alina finally spoke, her voice void of any emotion.

Stephanie waited, but nothing more was forthcoming.

"Well, thank you Captain Obvious," she muttered. "Care to loop me in on what you know?"

"He was there for me."

Stephanie stared at her, her irritation forgotten with those five words.

"You? But…how? Why?"

Alina sat back and crossed her legs, meeting Stephanie's gaze calmly.

"Remember I said I wasn't sure it would be safe for Angela to stay with me?"

Stephanie nodded.

"And I said you were going to have to explain that," she said. "So explain."

Alina's lips curved briefly.

"Be careful what you ask for," she murmured half to herself. "There's something I haven't told you. I didn't think it was necessary, but after this morning, it's only fair to tell you so you can be on your guard. A few weeks ago, I was compromised. Someone leaked my identity, and I was pursued across Europe."

Stephanie's jaw dropped and she stared at her friend.

"What?!" she exclaimed. "How did that happen?"

"That's what I'm trying to find out. Last week they tried again. They missed me, but hit Damon."

"Oh my God!" Stephanie felt her heart drop and she stared at Alina, almost afraid to ask. "Is he...?"

"Dead? No, but only because of sheer luck. He should be dead. We both should be."

Stephanie sucked in some air and raised a trembling hand to run it through her hair.

"Where? What happened?"

"A shooter took a shot from a hotel window," Alina told her, ignoring the first question. "As luck would have it, a helicopter was passing. I think the spotlight blinded him. The round was off target."

"Is he ok? Where did he get hit?"

"In his side. He's recovering."

"Alina, why didn't you tell me any of this?" Stephanie demanded. "I could have helped somehow."

Alina looked amused.

"How?" she asked politely. "I was half a world away. Anyway, when I got back you were busy trying to deal with the funeral, and then Angie had her incident," she added quickly as Stephanie looked ready to argue.

"I still could have done something," Stephanie muttered, "even if only to be a shoulder to lean on. Hell, I know what Damon means to you, and we just lost John. Lina, you don't have to handle everything yourself."

"I'm fine."

The steel thread in Alina's voice warned Stephanie to back off and she sighed imperceptibly.

"So the shooter this morning is the same one who missed Damon?"

"No. That one's dead."

Stephanie looked at her, startled despite herself.

"How do you know?"

"Because I shot him."

Stephanie threw up her hands.

"Of course you did. Lina, I swear if I hadn't known you since we were five, I'd hate you."

Alina was surprised into a laugh.

"Why? Because I'm honest?" she asked, amused. "Why does everyone think I'd just let the man who shot Damon walk away?"

"Everyone?" Stephanie latched onto that. "Who else knows?"

Alina sighed.

"Michael," she admitted. "Before you get all pissed off, I had no choice. He had to know."

"Why does he have to know and I don't?" Stephanie demanded.

"He's working on something and it was pertinent knowledge he needed. That's all I can tell you."

Stephanie was silent for a long moment, staring across the room, her mind spinning. A lot of things were falling into place now, but more and more questions were emerging.

"The shooter this morning, do you know who it was?" she asked finally, turning her head to look at Alina.

"Yes."

"Is that where you've been all day? Looking for him?"

"Yes."

Stephanie nodded and dropped her head back on the pillows, staring up at the ceiling.

"They know where you live," she said slowly. "They know you're in this area."

"They knew John's funeral was in this area," Alina corrected her. "They knew I'd go."

Stephanie raised her head again, studying Alina's face.

"You're awfully calm about all this," she said. "How are you not freaking out right now?"

Alina's lips curved humorlessly, the smile not reaching her eyes.

"What's the point? I knew the risks when I came back for the funeral. My regret is that you were caught in the crossfire."

Stephanie waved her hand impatiently.

"I'm fine. What are you going to do?"

Alina raised her eyes and Stephanie found herself staring into Viper's cold, emotionless eyes. She shivered.

"What can I do?" she asked, looking away from those eyes quickly. That was a look she'd seen only once before, and one she never wanted to see again. "You can't expect me to just sit back and not help."

"There *is* something you can do," Alina said slowly. "It would help Angela."

"What?"

"At the viewing, there was a man she met in Miami. He followed her back. He works for Trasker Pharmaceuticals."

Stephanie gasped.

"What?!"

"His name is Trent Whitfield."

"You don't think...oh my God, you don't think Angie got involved with the terrorists somehow?!" Stephanie asked, her trembling returning.

"No, but she got dragged into something. He approached her at the viewing, then showed up in the woods outside my house."

Stephanie gasped again, her mind spinning.

"What?! Why didn't I know about this?" she demanded. "What happened?"

"He tripped the security. I went out and got a good picture of his face before Raven attacked him."

Stephanie choked, torn between laughter and outrage.

"Raven attacked him?"

For the first time since she came into the room, Alina grinned a genuine grin.

"Ripped his arm up and got a couple good hits to his head. He must have spent the whole night in the ER."

"How do you know it was him?" Stephanie asked after a moment.

"I ran the picture through a database this morning and got a hit."

"And we're not calling the police why?"

"If he's involved with Trasker and the terrorists, it's a little above the LEO paygrade," said Alina. "I want you to see what you can dig up on him. There might be something I can use."

Stephanie nodded.

"I'll start in the morning," she agreed. "Blake's bringing my laptop."

Alina nodded and stood.

"Thank you."

She turned to leave, then paused and turned back. Stephanie was surprised to see the old Alina she grew up with looking down at her.

"I'm sorry, Steph," she said softly. "I'm sorry I brought all this back here. If I could go back, I would never have returned to Jersey last year."

"Then I would never have seen you again," said Stephanie, reaching out her hand. "I'll take anything that happens if it means having you back again."

Alina took her hand and smiled wistfully.

"God, I wish it was that easy," she said in a low voice.

With those cryptic words, she was gone.

Stephanie watched the door close silently behind her, and leaned her head back tiredly. She hadn't missed the flash of pain in the dark brown eyes. Alina was getting tired.

And there was nothing Stephanie could do to help her.

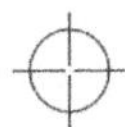

Alina emerged from the bathroom, refreshed from her shower, and moved into the bedroom. She had arrived home an hour ago, bearing pizza and beer. As Michael and Angela dug in, she came upstairs to shower and change out of the ridiculous black dress Angela had made her buy for the funeral.

She sat on the edge of the bed and pulled on her boots. Her stomach growled, reminding her that she hadn't eaten since the coffee shop. She had to eat something, and pizza was the most convenient, if not the healthiest choice.

Alina finished tying her boots and stood up, heading out of the bedroom. She tried to fuel her body well, taking care to eat only healthy, organic meats and vegetables. She limited her carbs and sugar, and tried to limit her fat as much as possible. Her two indulgences were her coffee and the occasional glass of wine. So far, it had served her well. Her body was a well-oiled weapon, and she took care of it accordingly. However, tonight there wasn't time to make something sensible. Pizza would have to do.

She jogged down the stairs and rounded the corner, striding down the hall. Michael was seated at the dining room table with his laptop, an empty plate and half-empty beer beside it. He glanced up from the screen when she walked down the hall.

"We saved you some pizza," he said. "I put it in the oven to keep warm."

"Thanks."

"Feel better?" Angela called from the living room.

Alina glanced over her shoulder. Angela was lying on the couch, watching the flat screen TV above the mantel.

"I wasn't feeling bad before," she said, heading toward the stove.

"Could have fooled me," said Angela, picking up the remote and switching off the TV. "You looked miserable when you came back."

"I wanted to get out of that dress," Alina muttered, opening the oven and pulling out the pizza box. "I'd had enough of heels for one day."

"Well, you looked fabulous," Angela told her, rising and picking up her empty plate. She carried it into the kitchen. "Where were you all day?"

"Busy."

Angela waited for her to continue. When she didn't, she rolled her eyes.

"That's enlightening," she said, opening the dishwasher to put her plate inside. "Busy doing what?"

"How's your neck?" Alina asked, ignoring the question.

"Hurts like hell. The pain killers are wearing off. I'm just going to take some more and go to bed. I'm wiped out."

"I can believe it." Alina took a bite of pizza, not bothering with a plate. Instead, she reached for a piece of paper towel. "You've had a long day. I stopped and saw Steph on my way back. She looks better than you do."

"Gee, thanks!" Angela said with laugh. "She should look better. She spent most of the day sleeping!"

"I don't think being knocked unconscious and then being under anesthesia counts as sleeping," Michael interjected humorously from the dining room.

"I would almost rather that than the fourteen stitches I got while I was awake."

"Look at the bright side," Alina said. "You'll have some awesome scars to show off."

Angela snorted and turned to pull a bottle of water out of the refrigerator.

"I don't want them. I've already got one. It's hideous."

Alina blinked and her lips quivered. If Angela knew about only half the scars Viper had collected over the past ten years, she'd have a conniption.

"Scars are sexy," Michael announced, seeing the look on Alina's face. He winked at her. "They show you've had an interesting life."

Alina was surprised into a short laugh.

"Speaking from experience?" she asked, taking another bite of pizza and leaning against the bar.

"Of course." Michael grinned. "I can't keep the women away."

"I don't think that has anything to do with scars," said Angela over her shoulder. "Scars are not sexy."

"Ouch!" Alina said. "Michael, you're out of luck."

"So are you," he murmured in a low voice.

Alina shot him a look, her eyes filled with laughter.

"Depends on who you ask," she retorted before she could stop herself.

"What are you two going on about?" Angela asked, walking around the bar and toward the dining room table where a plastic bag held a pill bottle and her discharge paperwork.

"Nothing." Alina finished her pizza and straightened up. "Go up and get some rest. You've earned it."

Angela picked up the bag with her pain killers and turned to head down the hall toward the stairs.

"I plan on it. I'll see you tomorrow."

Alina tossed the paper towel into the trash and turned to pull her tablet out of the drawer in the kitchen. She carried it over to the bar and sat on a stool, her head bent over the screen.

"What are you doing?" Michael asked after watching her a moment.

"Checking the perimeter," she said absently. "I'm not happy with one of the camera angles."

"They seemed fine last night," Michael said, standing up and walking over to stand next to her. "We were able to see everything we needed to see."

"For that side, yes," Alina said, glancing up at him. After a moment's hesitation, she turned the screen so he could see what she was looking at. "This is the back of the property. One of the cameras shifted, leaving a blind spot. See?"

Michael leaned down and studied the quadrant.

"Not much of a blind spot. There's only about two feet you can't see."

"How many feet do you think a trained assassin needs?" she asked him politely.

Michael looked at her and straightened up again.

"Point taken."

"I'm going to adjust it," Alina said, standing. "I switched off the sensors, so keep alert. There's no alarm on right now."

"After this morning, I don't think I've relaxed once," Michael said, going back to his seat at the dining table. "I'm certainly not going to start now."

Alina nodded and went to the sliding door.

"I'll be back soon."

Chapter Thirty

Viper moved through the trees quickly and silently, completely at ease in the darkness. The camera was on the back perimeter, at the edge where her property met the protected nature reserve. She noticed the camera angle change last night when they had their unexpected visitor. The most likely explanation was that a bird or squirrel knocked it. She pushed a low-hanging branch out of her way. At least, she hoped that was the cause of the camera shift. The alternative was much more unpleasant.

An owl hooted nearby as she passed and something moved in the underbrush, darting across her path and disappearing into a rotten, uprooted tree trunk. Alina smiled faintly, moving easily through the woods. The night creatures paid no attention to her as she passed through their midst, ignoring her as if she were one of them. She didn't bother them, and they disregarded her. It was a mutual appreciation.

Viper approached the camera a few minutes later and pulled out a Maglite, shining it up into the pine tree where the camera was mounted. Painted to blend perfectly with the tree, it was practically invisible until the bright light illuminated it. Alina pursed her lips. It had shifted slightly to the left and was hanging crookedly.

She pulled two metal loops with pointed ends out of her jacket pocket and switched off the light, tucking it into the outside pocket on her thigh. Using the loops as handles, she quickly scaled the immense tree until she reached the camera, some twenty feet above the ground. Once she was level with it, Viper pulled out the Maglite and switched it on. Examining the casing, she grinned suddenly and put the thin flashlight between her teeth, holding the light steady on the camera. She reached out and plucked a long black feather out of the corner of the camera. Definitely a bird, and her first bet was on Raven himself.

Alina straightened the camera, glancing down to estimate the angle she needed. She straightened it, adjusted it once more, and pulled the Maglite from her mouth, switching it off. Tucking it back into her cargo pocket, she reached into another pocket and pulled out her phone. Swiping the screen, she opened her security app and pulled up the camera. A moment later her phone was back in her pocket and she was backing down out of the tree.

She had just dropped onto the ground again, and was slipping the loops back into her pocket, when a shiver of awareness streaked down her spine. Her breath caught silently in her throat as her heart thumped in warning.

Viper spun around, swinging her right hand in a sharp arc. The side of her palm made hard contact with a wrist, raised defensively against her attack. Her brain registered the defensive block even as she turned her hand to grip the wrist, forcing it down by gripping two pressure points. As she pushed the wrist down with her right hand, her left fist drove into the assailant's kidney, eliciting a low grunt of pain.

Before she could follow up with another hit, strong fingers clamped down between her shoulder blade and her neck. Blinding pain shot down her arm and up her neck into her head. The pressure increased and she was spun around, her right arm pulled back and up behind her.

"Are you going to stop, or do we keep going?" Hawk demanded in her ear, his voice washing over her like molten lava.

Relief rushed through her, and Viper stilled. As soon as she did, Hawk released her arm and neck. Spinning around, she stared up at him, her heart skipping a beat.

"Hawk! What are you doing here?"

He looked down at her, a slow smile pulling at his lips.

"I was getting bored," he said with a wink. Then he grimaced and rubbed his back. "Did you have to go for the kidney?"

"That's what you get for sneaking up on me. You should know better."

"To be fair, I wasn't expecting to find you all the way out here," Hawk said. "What are you doing?"

"Adjusting a camera. I think Raven shifted it. He left damning evidence in the slats."

Hawk glanced up into the tree.

"Damning evidence?"

"A feather. Did you come on a bike?"

He nodded and motioned to his left.

"It's over there. I was going to walk to the house."

She tilted her head and studied him.

"How are you feeling?"

"The incision is sore from riding a motorcycle for four hours," he answered. "Otherwise, I'm fine."

"You shouldn't have come," she said in a low voice.

Damon stepped closer and looked down at her, settling his hands on her waist.

"You knew I would," he murmured, his eyes meeting hers. "I'm not sitting this out, especially after what happened this morning."

Alina felt lost in the shadows in his eyes, his musk surrounding her with comfortable warmth. She raised one hand to his shoulder and the other to his jaw, feeling his five o'clock shadow beneath her fingers, and all the tension of the past few days suddenly ebbed out of her.

"I know," she whispered.

Damon lowered his lips to touch hers softly, lingering for a long moment before he raised his head again. He raised a hand to trail his fingers along her jaw gently. His eyebrow raised slightly suddenly in question and he moved his hand to her neck. Sliding his fingers under a thin chain resting against her skin, he lifted a necklace out from under her jacket. As he did so, a slow smile curved his lips. The chain was fed through a silver eyelet, welded onto a twisted lump of metal. The bullet that nearly killed them both rested in the palm of his hand. Damon raised his eyes to hers.

"You're wearing it."

She nodded slowly.

"I'm going to put it on a bracelet when I have time. I'm not comfortable wearing necklaces, but it will do for now."

"Thank God he missed today," he breathed, pulling her close to him in a tight hug.

"Another lucky break," Alina said, resting her cheek on his shoulder. "Someone dropped a kneeler as he was taking the shot. It went through the lectern and into Stephanie's leg."

Damon rested his chin on the top of her head, absorbing that news.

"How is she?" he finally asked.

"Fine. They're keeping her in the hospital for a few days as a precaution." Alina raised her head and looked up at him. "This luck won't hold. This is twice now they've tried, and each time someone else takes the bullet. This has to stop."

Damon cupped her face in his palms, his eyes boring into hers.

"Then we'll stop it."

His lips settled on hers and she sighed into him. This was what she needed: Hawk's calm assurance and strength to lean on. The past couple of days had been wearing on her and tonight, on the way back from the hospital, Alina had finally admitted to herself that she was getting tired. She needed the support only Hawk could offer and, for the first time in her life, Alina wasn't afraid to admit it, or afraid of what it meant.

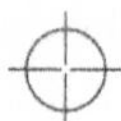

Michael looked up as the door to the deck slid open. His eyebrows soared into his forehead when Damon followed Alina into the living room. He stood up as Damon closed the door behind them.

"I was wondering if you would show up," he said, meeting him in the living room and holding out his hand. "Good to see you up and around."

"Someone had to come keep an eye on the circus," Damon retorted, a smile softening his words. He grasped Michael's hand firmly. "How are you?"

"Can't complain. How are you feeling?"

"Sore." Damon moved into the dining room, glancing at the laptop open in front of Michael. "I've had worse. How's it coming?" He nodded to the computer.

"Slow. I haven't had much time to focus on it," said Michael, sipping his beer. "I'm making progress, though."

Alina came out of the kitchen and handed Damon a bottle of water.

"Today wasn't exactly an easy day," she said. "He spent most of it at the hospital with Angie and Steph."

"Angie?" Damon asked, opening the water and taking a long sip. "What happened to her?"

"She got hit with shrapnel from a statue." Alina picked up the tablet she'd left on the bar and swiped it to examine the camera angles. "She got a few stitches, but she'll be fine."

Damon watched her for a beat.

"What happened, exactly?" he asked, pulling out a chair at the dining table and sitting. He turned to face her. "All I know is someone opened fire at the funeral."

Alina glanced at him, her lips twitching. She set down the tablet, satisfied the camera position was perfect.

"Oh, I'm sure you know more than that," she murmured, amused. "He was in the organ loft. His first shot went high through the lectern, where Stephanie was giving the first reading. His second shot hit a statue of the Virgin Mary as I passed it. Angie was behind me and took the brunt of the pieces in her neck and shoulder."

"Blake and I went straight to the organ loft," said Michael, leaning back in his chair. "He was already gone when we got there. I went to the front of the church and Blake went out the side. We thought we could catch him before he disappeared."

Damon glanced at him, his expression grim.

"How did he even get in the church?" he demanded. "I thought I made it clear–"

He stopped abruptly, but it was too late. Alina's eyes narrowed sharply.

"So that's why you showed up when you did," she said, looking at Michael. "He sent you."

Michael had the grace to look sheepish, but Damon looked at her squarely.

"Someone had to watch your back, and I wasn't in a position to do it."

Alina's lips tightened.

"I don't need a babysitter," she said coldly. "I'm more than capable of taking care of myself. All you did was send another target into the line of fire."

"I'm hardly just another target," Michael objected. "I'm trained to protect the President."

"Yet a shooter made his way into the organ loft," Damon said, turning his blue gaze back to Michael. "Care to offer an explanation?"

"Oh, for God's sake!" Alina exclaimed. "Don't be ridiculous. He couldn't lock down a church the size of St. Pete's without a full advance team, which he didn't have. Besides, the shooter was dressed as a priest. Even if he *had* been able to inspect every person who came into the church, a priest wouldn't have raised any red flags."

Damon's head snapped around.

"A priest?" he repeated. "You saw him?"

She nodded, getting up to go into the kitchen.

"He came out the back while I was in the alley between the church and the school," she said, opening the fridge. She returned a moment later with another beer for Michael, and one for herself. "He saw me. I managed to hit his car as he was leaving the parking lot. He dumped it on the other side of town."

Damon watched as she handed Michael the beer and seated herself across the table from him.

"Why do you get a beer and I get water?"

"Because I didn't just drive four hours on a motorcycle when I should still be in the hospital," she retorted. "And I'm mad at you right now. So no beer for you."

Michael choked back a laugh at the look on Damon's face.

"That's not a good reason," Damon muttered, but he sipped his water. "Did you find anything in the car?"

Michael looked at Alina, waiting for her answer.

"No," she said smoothly, opening her beer. "It was clean."

Damon raised an eyebrow doubtfully but let it go.

"The funeral was his best chance of you coming to him," he said. "Now he has to find you."

"Wait, you said he was dressed as a priest?" Michael asked suddenly.

Alina nodded, sipping her beer.

"Yes, why?"

"When I went with Angie to the church on Monday, I passed a priest coming out of the side door. He looked surprised to see me."

"What did he look like?"

"Dark hair, about five-ten, maybe a buck eighty," said Michael slowly. "He had dark eyes, maybe brown."

"That was him," Alina said decidedly.

"Son of a…" Michael glowered. "I was less than a foot away from him!"

Damon looked at him, a flicker of sympathy in his blue eyes.

"There's no way you could have known. Professionals aren't easy to spot."

"He was there the day before setting everything up," Alina said thoughtfully. "He likes to plan ahead."

"That will work to our advantage," Damon said, looking at her. "He'll have to improvise now."

Alina nodded, lost in thought.

Michael looked from one to the other and shook his head.

"I don't see how that's a good thing. He'll be unpredictable now."

A brief smile passed over Alina's lips and Damon chuckled.

"Trust me, there are only so many options left to him," he assured Michael. "He'll be far from unpredictable. If anything, he'll be easier to pin down."

Alina looked up.

"And I'll be waiting."

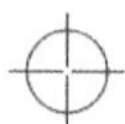

Alina looked up as the opening to her command center slid

open. Her eyes moved to the security monitor and she watched as Damon stepped into the opening. She returned her gaze to the screen before her and quickly minimized the window. When Damon entered the long room a moment later, she had a generic website open.

His hair was still damp from the shower, and he had changed into a pair of black sweatpants and an old US Navy tee-shirt. The fresh smell of shower gel entered the room with him, and Alina glanced at him with a smile.

"Feel better?"

"Much." Damon pulled out a chair next to her. "The gunny finally called it a night?"

She nodded, stretching her arms over her head with a yawn.

"Not long after you went up to shower. He took his laptop up with him. He said he didn't want to keep me up while he worked."

Damon grinned.

"Clearly he doesn't know you very well."

Alina shrugged.

"No rest for the wicked. We're all busy tonight."

Damon leaned back in his chair and swiveled to face her, growing serious.

"So tell me what really happened today."

Alina raised an eyebrow.

"You know what happened. He took a shot at the funeral and missed."

Damon studied her for a moment, his blue eyes sharp and probing.

"What about the car?"

"It was clean."

"Bullshit. You might be able to sell that to the gunny, but not me. What did you find?"

Viper stared back at him, her mask impenetrable.

"You're a pain in the ass, you know that?"

Damon grinned and winked.

"So I've been told. Were you able to trace the car?"

"No. It was rented through the airport, paid in cash. The name on the paperwork was a dead end," Alina said, turning to pick up a half-empty bottle of water.

"GPS?"

Alina glanced at him, her lips curving faintly.

"I'm running it now," she replied, sipping her water.

Damon frowned.

"You didn't run it earlier?" he asked, his brows coming

together. "Why? You could have caught him."

"I didn't need to." Alina set the water down and turned to face him. "I found a receipt for a parking garage in the car under the seat. It was easy enough to track him down."

Damon nodded, his brow clearing.

"What happened?"

"He's staying at a hotel in Center City, not far from Chinatown. He's been using a parking garage for the car, and he goes to the same coffee shop every day for his morning pick-me-up."

"That's sloppy. Did you get a name?"

"I got the name he's using, yes." Alina turned back to her computer and pulled up a database. "He's not completely careless. The only place he's used the name is at the hotel and the parking garage."

Damon shrugged.

"That just means he hasn't been anywhere else. He's been looking for you, not sight-seeing. What hotel?"

Alina glanced at him.

"Oh no." She shook her head. "You're not getting involved. You're going to relax and finish healing."

"Don't be ridiculous," Damon said, frowning. "I'm fine."

"No you're not. You'd still be in the hospital if it weren't for the fiasco this morning. I can't do anything about you checking yourself out, but I can make sure you don't throw yourself right back into the line of fire."

Damon snorted.

"I'm already in the line of fire just by being here. So tell me what you know."

"Hawk, this isn't your problem," said Alina, turning to face him again.

"This most definitely *is* my problem," he shot back. "I took a bullet for all this. That makes it my problem."

"No, that makes you collateral damage."

Damon's eyes narrowed and turned icy, his lips pressing together briefly.

"Did you really just say that?" he demanded softly.

Viper shrugged.

"Perhaps it was a bit harsh," she admitted.

"Oh, you think?!"

"My point is that you've already been shot over this. You've paid your dues. This wasn't your fight to begin with; you got caught in the crossfire, and now it's time to let me take care of it."

Hawk leaned forward, his eyes never leaving her face.

"This became my fight the second they came after you," he growled. "Now I'm only going to say this once. You don't have a monopoly on this one. Our Organization is under attack. They're not just coming after you, they're coming after all of us. One by one, our assets are being exposed and eliminated. We're all involved now. Either you loop me in, and we work together, or I walk out tonight and do it alone. Either way, I *will* be hunting this bastard down, and then I'll be going after the one in charge of it all."

Alina met him glare for glare.

"I won't have you on my conscience too. John already died over this. I don't need another death on my tab."

Hawk stared at her for a beat, his face impassive.

"That's what this is about?" he demanded. "You think John was your responsibility? You think I'm your responsibility?"

Her mask slid into place abruptly, and Viper stared back at him silently. Hawk ran a hand through his hair and got up impatiently. He paced to the end of the narrow room, then turned back.

"You know as well as I do, the odds of us making it out of this alive are getting lower and lower every day we wake up." He gripped the back of the chair he'd vacated. "We've never had much expectation of making it to a grand old age. Hell, we're lucky we've made it this far. I'm not your responsibility, just as you're not mine. But if we don't figure out a way to work together, we'll check out a hell of a lot sooner than if we stick together. Think about it! We've both dodged the reaper how many times now? If we're together, those odds only get better."

"If we weren't together in Singapore, you wouldn't have been shot."

"And you would be dead."

They glared at each other for a long moment, neither giving way until, finally, Viper's gaze wavered.

"We're stronger together," said Hawk softly. "We always have been. They knew it in boot camp, and Harry knew it in the training facility. That's why they all pitted us against each other."

"To control us," she murmured.

"Exactly."

Viper was silent for a long moment before she finally lifted dark eyes to his.

"He's staying at the Hampton Inn, near the Convention Center, in the city. He checked in Friday night."

Hawk stared at her.

"That was before you were here. No one knew you were back stateside!"

Viper nodded grimly.

"Exactly. So how did he?"

Chapter Thirty-One

Michael stared across the white Formica table at Blake, his coffee forgotten in his hands. The early morning diner crowd faded into the background as he tried to comprehend what he'd just been told.

"What?!"

Blake nodded, sipping his coffee.

"Ken called me last night. I don't even remember the woman."

Michael set down his mug and rubbed his face.

"Sorry. I'm trying to wrap my brain around this," he said, dropping his hands and shaking his head. "So, this woman you don't even remember is accusing you of...what, exactly?"

"Professional misconduct and sexual assault."

"That's the most ridiculous thing I've ever heard." Michael reached for his coffee. "When did this supposedly happen?"

"Two years ago. She was a witness on a case I was working. She claims I insisted on interviewing her alone, then followed and assaulted her a few days later."

Michael stared at him.

"And she's just now coming forward?"

Blake shrugged.

"The affidavit states she's been in therapy for two years and just now came to a place in her recovery where she can face the experience," he muttered. "The Bureau has no choice but to follow procedure. I've been placed on leave, pending a full internal investigation."

Michael drank his coffee in silence, his mind spinning.

"What the hell is going on?" he finally said, setting down his empty mug. "First someone plants drugs in your closet, now this. What the hell have you gotten yourself into?"

"I have no idea," Blake said, pouring more coffee into his cup from the thermal carafe on the table. "Believe me, I've been asking myself that since last night."

Michael took the carafe from Blake and refilled his own cup.

"Someone is trying to discredit you, and it's someone who doesn't know you very well. They're picking things completely out of character for you."

"They're picking things that will ruin my career."

"You pissed someone off," Michael agreed. "Any idea who?"

Blake gave him an exasperated look.

"Would you like a list?" he asked. "I can think of any number of people who aren't happy with me. I'm sure you could do the same. We're Feds in DC, for God's sake!"

Michael grinned.

"Good point. Ok, let's start with this woman. What's her name?"

"Tina Ricci. She's a political consultant."

"Of course she is," Michael muttered. "What firm?"

"She has her own practice, The Ricci Group."

Michael nodded.

"We'll start there," he decided. "Can you think of any reason she would have a bone to pick with you?"

Blake shook his head.

"None. This is all so surreal. How can I defend myself against a woman I don't even remember?"

"You don't," said Michael firmly. "You let your attorney defend you. You do have one, right?"

Blake nodded.

"I called him this morning. He's coming up tomorrow morning."

"Good. In the meantime, I'll add this Tina Ricci to my list and see what I can find out."

Blake looked at him, his face grim.

"For God's sake, be careful. We don't need you coming under fire as well. I can only handle one catastrophe at a time."

"Have you told Stephanie yet?" Michael asked after a moment.

"No. I'm going to the hospital after breakfast. I'm not looking forward to telling her. What if she believes it?"

"I wouldn't worry about that," Michael assured him. "She's not stupid. She'll realize someone is attacking you."

"I hope so."

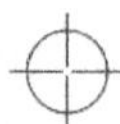

Viper glanced around the deserted hallway before bending over the door handle. A second later, she was rewarded with a faint click, and she slipped inside silently. She closed the door behind her and reached into her back holster to pull out the Ruger, listening intently. No sound marred the perfect silence.

When she left the house just after dawn, Hawk was still sleeping. Despite their conversation last night, Alina didn't tell him of her plans for this morning. What he didn't know couldn't bother him.

Viper flipped the safety off and moved forward, holding the gun near her shoulder. Kyle had checked into a spacious two-room suite, and the sitting area faced her at the end of the tiny entryway. Coming to the edge of the wall, Viper glanced around the sitting room, then peeked around the corner to see into the rest of the suite. It was empty.

A sofa was in front of her, facing a flat screen TV mounted on the wall across the room. Two arm chairs flanked a coffee table in the center of the sitting room, and a full wet bar and mini fridge were next to the TV. Wide double doors stood open on the other end of the wall, giving Viper a clear view into the bedroom. The bed had not been slept in.

Moving forward slowly, Viper crossed the sitting room to the bedroom, pausing at the open doors. There was no sound from within, and she scanned the bedroom slowly. The dresser was bare and the small desk in front of the window was clear.

Viper put the safety back on and crossed the bedroom to look in the empty bathroom. Plastic still wrapped the cups on the sink and the shower curtain was pulled back to expose a sterile tub. A basket on the vanity held an assortment of unopened shampoos and soaps.

Alina pressed her lips together and tucked her gun back into her holster, turning to gaze around the large bedroom.

Kyle was gone.

She wasn't really surprised. After she followed him out of the parking lot yesterday, he had to have known she would hunt him down. The problem, of course, was now he was in the wind again.

Alina crossed the room and systematically began to go through every drawer and closet, looking for anything that might have been left behind. She was just closing the last drawer when her phone vibrated in her pocket. Pulling it out, she glanced at the screen and frowned at the number displayed. Her eyes narrowed and she hesitated for second before sliding the phone back into her pocket, ignoring the call.

Turning to the king-size bed, Alina bent down to peer underneath. A moment later, she straightened up again. Even under the bed was spotless. She shook her head and went back into the sitting room. Housekeeping was not this good. Kyle had sanitized the place before he skipped out.

Less than ten minutes after she entered the suite, Viper was slipping back out the door. The sitting room was just as sterile as the bedroom. There was nothing left of the assassin who caused such a stir at John's funeral yesterday morning. He had disappeared.

As Alina closed the door behind her, her lips tightened grimly. While she would love to think Kyle had fled, Viper knew better. He had simply changed locations. His goal remained the same.

And now she had no idea where he was.

Stephanie looked up from her laptop as Blake came into the hospital room carrying a cup carrier with two large coffees in one hand and a large bouquet of flowers in the other. The Go Bag from the trunk of her car was slung over his shoulder.

"I've got coffee and the bag from your car," he announced, walking over to set the cup holder down on the side table near the bed. He dropped her bag onto the bed. "I stopped and got these for you. I thought they might cheer you up."

Stephanie accepted the flowers with a large smile.

"They're gorgeous!" she exclaimed.

Blake grinned and lifted one of the coffees out of the holder.

"I'm glad you like them," he said, taking them from her and handing her the coffee. "I didn't know if you like flowers, but I figured the room could use some color."

"I appreciate it," she told him sincerely, sipping the coffee. "And the coffee! I don't know what they have here, but it is *not* coffee."

Blake glanced around, looking for something to put the flowers into, then shrugged and laid them down on the table.

"Maybe the nurse has something we can stick these in," he said, picking up the other coffee and sinking into the chair next to the bed. "How are you feeling today?"

"I feel fine, but the doctor isn't happy. My white cell count went up overnight and he thinks there's an infection. They put an antibiotic through the IV."

Blake frowned.

"That's not good. See? It's a good thing you agreed to stay."

Stephanie glowered at him.

"Don't you dare say I told you so, or I'll throw this coffee at you!"

Blake laughed and held up his hand in mock surrender.

"My lips are sealed!"

Stephanie nodded and set her coffee down on the table, reaching for her bag. She opened it and reached into the inside pocket, pulling out a phone charger.

"Thank you for grabbing this," she said, plugging the charger into her phone. "My phone died overnight."

"No problem."

Blake got up and took the cell phone and charger from her, walking around to plug it into the outlet behind the side table. He laid the phone on the table within her reach and went back to his chair.

"Have you heard anything from Michael?" she asked. "How's Angela?"

"I met him for breakfast this morning. She's fine, I think. He said she was in pain last night, but took some meds and went to bed. I don't think he'd seen her yet this morning."

"Angie's tougher than she looks. She'll be alright." Stephanie reached for her coffee again. She glanced at Blake. "What's wrong?"

Blake raised his eyebrows.

"What do you mean?"

She smiled at him.

"I'm getting to know you pretty well, Blake Hanover. You look bothered by something. So spit it out. What is it?"

Blake hesitated for a second, then got up and walked over to the door. He said something to the agent on duty and closed the door. Stephanie raised her eyebrow as he crossed back over to the chair.

"It's that bad that you have to close the door?"

"I'd rather not take the chance of anyone overhearing, no," Blake admitted. "I got a call last night from my boss, Ken."

"Good! Did they find the guy who planted heroin in your closet?"

Blake shook his head, his face grim.

"No. He's disappeared. Something else has happened."

Stephanie watched him, a feeling of foreboding stealing over her.

"What?"

Blake looked at her, got up restlessly and began pacing.

"A woman filed charges of professional misconduct and sexual assault against me."

Stephanie's mouth dropped open.

"What?!"

"She was a witness on a case I worked two years ago. I don't even remember her, and I certainly never assaulted her."

"Of course not," Stephanie said immediately. "You're being attacked."

Blake stopped pacing and looked at her.

"You didn't even hesitate," he said, surprised. "How do you know I didn't assault her? I mean, I didn't, but what makes you so sure?"

Stephanie gave him an exasperated look.

"I may not have known you for long, but I think I'm a pretty good judge of character. You're not a predator. At least, not that kind," she qualified with a quick grin. "I have no doubt you were lethal enough in the Marines."

Blake nodded and resumed pacing.

"Well, I appreciate your vote of confidence. I'm going to need all the support I can get. I don't even know where to begin to defend myself."

"We can start by examining who would go through this amount of trouble to come after you." Stephanie sipped her coffee. "First the drugs, now this. Someone wants you out of the picture. Who?"

"That's the big question," Blake said, picking up his coffee from the arm of the chair. "Michael said he'll look into the woman, but I can't do anything. I'm not even allowed onto agency property."

Stephanie frowned.

"They suspended you?"

"Administrative LOA, pending an internal investigation," he said glumly. "I have an attorney coming up on the train tomorrow. Ken advised I stay put up here for the time being. Do you mind if Buddy and I stick around a little while longer?"

"Of course not!" Stephanie waved her hand. "You're welcome as long as you need to stay. Why isn't he making you go back to DC?"

Blake glanced at her.

"Honestly? Ken thinks the charges are bogus, but he has to follow protocol. I think he's thinking if I stay up here, I'm not presenting an easy target."

Stephanie fell silent, staring at the blanket thoughtfully. Blake continued to pace restlessly, drinking his coffee.

"After we stopped those bombs, when did you get back to DC?" she asked suddenly, looking up.

Blake paused.

"I don't know...I was here Sunday night, then Monday we were both in the Philly office," he said slowly, casting his mind back. "I left Tuesday morning to go back, so I must have gotten back in town around mid-afternoon. Why?"

"When was your house broken into?"

Blake looked at her.

"Wednesday night."

They stared at each other for a beat, then Blake whistled.

"You think this is all tied in with the terrorist attack?"

"It seems a little coincidental that the day after you get back into town, all this starts. And let's face it, that wasn't an ordinary terrorist attack. You've been working the Casa Reino Cartel for over a year, and they were involved in running the bomb parts up the coast. Then you interview Dominic DiBarcoli about street racers and he ends up dead the next day, in DC. When you get back home, someone plants drugs in your house. You don't think they're all connected?"

Blake stared at her, stunned, and pulled out his phone.

"I never even saw it," he muttered, hitting speed dial.

"Who are you calling?"

"Michael."

Stephanie raised an eyebrow.

"Why?"

"He's digging into Trasker Pharmaceuticals. If they're coming after me, he's next!"

Chapter Thirty-Two

Alina slammed the door to the Jeep, crossing the grass towards the deck. She raised an eyebrow as Damon emerged from the trees at the back of the yard and paused, waiting for him. He strode across the lawn, moving with a jungle-cat stride that emanated dangerous power. She watched him, wondering if she would ever get used to seeing him like this.

"Where did you disappear to at the crack of dawn?" Damon asked, his blue eyes meeting hers as he joined her.

"I had something to take care of. Where are you coming from?"

A laugh lit his eyes.

"I had something to take care of."

Alina grinned and turned to continue toward the deck.

"Touché," she murmured. "How did you survive Angela this morning?"

"As you can see, I came back. She has some very definite opinions, doesn't she?"

Alina choked back a laugh.

"You have no idea. She was convinced I scared you off."

Damon grinned and glanced down at her.

"I'd like to see you try."

Alina met his gaze and smiled.

"Don't tempt me," she murmured, reaching for the sliding door.

Alina stepped into the living room and glanced around. Angela was ensconced at the dining room table with her laptop, cellphone, headset, and soda, typing away. Michael was settled in the recliner, his laptop open, and earbuds in his ears. They both looked up as she came in.

"It's about time you showed up!" Angela exclaimed. "Where the hell have you been?"

Alina raised an eyebrow and walked over to drop her keys onto the bar.

"I wasn't aware I had to check in."

Angela flushed at the mild reproach in Alina's voice.

"You could at least send a text," she said less aggressively. "Michael and I were both trying to reach you all day yesterday, then you disappear again this morning."

Alina walked over to the cabinet and pulled out a mug, setting it under the spout of her coffee machine.

"As you can see, I'm fine," she said over her shoulder before hitting a button on the machine.

The loud noise of grinding beans filled the kitchen. Damon walked into the kitchen and got a mug out of the cabinet, joining her at the coffee maker.

"All I'm saying is that a text can go a long way," Angela called from the dining room.

"I'm starting to appreciate why Michael has headphones in," Damon murmured in her ear.

Alina nodded in wholehearted agreement as the grinder stopped and the machine began brewing espresso into her mug. Once it was finished, she pulled her mug out and moved over so Damon could make his. She sipped the coffee and turned to go over to the bar.

"How are you feeling?" she asked, sliding onto a bar stool.

"Sore." Angela stretched and sat back in her chair. "Have you spoken to Stephanie today? I tried calling but it went straight to voicemail."

Alina shook her head.

"I stopped and saw her last night. Her phone probably died. I don't imagine she had a charger with her."

"Michael won't let me go see her," said Angela with a frown. "I don't see why we can't go to the hospital."

"Because you promised you would stay put after the funeral," Alina said. "Nothing's changed. If anything, it's more important you stay here, out of sight."

Before Angela could argue, her cell phone rang. After glancing at the screen, she picked up her Bluetooth and hooked it onto her ear.

"Hello," she answered, turning back to her laptop.

"Where are we with Kyle?" Damon asked her in a low voice, leaning against the granite bar next to her with his coffee in his hands.

Alina glanced at him, hesitated, then sighed.

"He's disappeared. Checked out this morning."

Blue eyes studied her over the rim of his mug.

"You went to the hotel?"

She nodded.

"It was wiped clean, not even a hair left behind." She looked up at him. "And before you get up on your high horse, I didn't expect him to be there, so I didn't see the point in telling you."

Damon studied her in silence for a moment.

"Any idea where he went?" he asked finally.

"No."

"Fantastic," he muttered, drinking his coffee. "So, we've got him and this Trent guy in the wind and Kasim is still missing. Is there anything else I'm missing? Do you want to let a couple more out of Gitmo while we're at it?"

Alina grinned despite herself.

"If it was easy, everyone would do it."

"Now here comes your gunny. He doesn't look happy," Damon warned, straightening up. "I think things are about to get worse."

Alina turned to watch as Michael stood up, setting his laptop down on the coffee table. Damon was right. He didn't look happy. His lips were set in a grim line as he moved towards them.

"You went out early," he said to Alina, joining them at the bar. "You were leaving when I came down."

"You were up early, then," she replied with a smile.

"Blake called me at the crack of dawn," Michael said, leaning on the bar and crossing his arms over his chest. "Things just keep getting worse."

Alina frowned.

"Did they find the guy who planted the drugs in his house?"

Damon's eyebrows shot into his forehead.

"Wait, what?" he asked, startled. "The guy who did what?"

Michael looked at him, then Alina.

"He doesn't know?" When she shook her head, he turned his green eyes to Damon. "You know who Blake is?"

Damon nodded.

"I know of him. He's been tracking the Casa Reinos Cartel, and helped Stephanie with the bombs a few weeks ago."

"Right. Well, last week, someone broke into his house and planted a brick of heroin in his closet. He's got hidden cameras all over the house, so they have video of the person doing it."

Damon frowned.

"I don't like the sound of that."

"Neither did I," Alina said.

"It gets worse," Michael said. "Last night, a witness from a case two years ago pressed charges against him for unprofessional conduct and sexual assault."

Alina stared at him, her lips pressed together.

"I'm guessing he doesn't have a clue what this witness is talking about?" Damon asked after a moment of silence.

"Not the slightest," said Michael. "I know you don't know him, so you'll have to take my word for it, but the very thought of Blake doing anything like that is ridiculous."

Damon glanced at Alina to find her staring into her coffee mug, lost in thought.

"Is it a legitimate witness?" Damon asked, looking at Michael.

"Yes, but he doesn't have any memory of having even been alone with her. He's been placed on leave, and they're launching an internal investigation."

"So he's not working while they sort this out?" Alina looked up sharply.

"No."

Damon glanced at her curiously.

"What are you thinking?"

Alina glanced at Angela. She was still on the phone, typing and talking at the same time, engrossed in her work. Alina lowered her voice.

"That someone doesn't want Blake working right now, and perhaps for good reason. When he was up here, he linked the Cartel to Dominic DiBarcoli and helped track down the bombs. Hell, he witnessed one of the bombs detonating. He knows all about the link between Trasker and the terrorists. Then, he goes home and immediately becomes a target. Someone's getting worried."

Damon nodded, his brow clearing.

"They're afraid he'll uncover something in Washington."

"Or someone."

Michael looked from one to the other.

"That's really thin," he said. "It could just be someone he locked up."

Alina looked at him, suddenly amused.

"Do you still believe in Santa, too?"

"I'm just saying there are other possibilities. You don't always have to jump to the conspiracy theory."

"You haven't been around the block as much as we have," she murmured.

Damon finished his coffee and set the empty mug down on the bar.

"She's right. Odds are not in favor of this being orchestrated by a disgruntled inmate. At least things are starting to make sense now."

Michael snorted.

"I'm glad you think so. It's about as clear as mud to me."

"Let us worry about making sense out of it," Alina said. "You just keep working on Trasker."

"About that," said Michael, straightening up. "I found something interesting."

She raised an eyebrow questioningly.

"And that is?"

"I came across an investor list. A lot of people have invested heavily in the company, which is no surprise. I went through it, and a few names jumped out at me. On a hunch, I backtracked one of them to a shell company in the Florida Keys. You'll never guess who the CEO was."

"I don't have to because you're going to tell me," Alina said dryly.

Michael grinned.

"Dominic DiBarcoli."

"You're right," she said after a second of silence. "That *is* unexpected."

Damon raised his eyebrows and glanced at her.

"How so?" he asked. "We knew he was involved with Trasker. How is this unexpected?"

"It wasn't the name I thought would be the first one out," Alina said, picking up her empty coffee mug and standing up. "When did he buy stocks?"

"That's the best part," said Michael. "A month ago."

"That's convenient timing," Damon said. "Especially if you're expecting a sudden demand for their latest and greatest drug."

Alina circled the bar and carried her mug over to the sink.

"So now we know he was set to make money on the antidote."

"We know more than that," Michael said, turning to face her. "I know who put the money into the shell company to purchase the shares."

Alina spun around and looked at him sharply.

"It wasn't his own money?"

Michael shook his head.

"Not all of it. Only about a third of the money came from Dominic's firms. The rest came from an offshore account."

Damon and Alina stared at him, their attention arrested.

"Where?" Alina demanded. "What country?"

Michael blinked.

"Country? What does that matter?"

"What country?!"

"Singapore!" he exclaimed. "The money came from an account in Singapore."

Stephanie opened her laptop and powered it up, glancing across the room at the TV on the wall. A news anchor droned on, reporting on another wildfire in California, and she shook her head. As much as she hated watching the news, the alternative daytime soap was worse.

Blake had left over an hour ago, the nurse had unearthed a vase for the flowers, lunch had been and gone, and she was finally able to turn her attention to Trent Whitfield. Once her laptop loaded, Stephanie opened the FBI database and cracked her knuckles while she waited for her VPN credentials to verify and the software to launch. Her mind wandered to Blake, and the witness accusing him of sexual assault. Her lips tightened and she shook her head.

What an absolute crock. Her blood was boiling on his behalf. Stephanie admitted that she perhaps didn't know Blake as well as she would like, but she knew him well enough to know she had never once felt uncomfortable with him. The idea of him assaulting anyone would be laughable if it wasn't so serious. He could lose his career over this! Who the hell was this woman, and why was she so determined to destroy a man's life?

Blake said Michael would see what he could find out about the witness. He wouldn't even give her the name. Stephanie's lips twitched. Blake wasn't stupid. He knew if he gave her the name, she'd start poking around.

Stephanie turned her attention back to the laptop screen as the database opened and she quickly set Blake and his troubles out of her mind. She'd worry about him later. Right now, she had to find out what she could about this Trent Whitfield, and why he was suddenly Angela's shadow. Why did he show up at the viewing for a man he'd never met? And why did he drive out into the Pine Barrens looking for Angela?

Stephanie paused thoughtfully. Alina said he was attacked by her hawk. Birds of prey were no joke. If Raven did his job, Trent would definitely have spent the rest of the night in the ER. Typing rapidly, Stephanie forewent the national database for a moment, turning instead to the local hospitals. About half an hour later, she found what she was looking for. Trent Whitfield was admitted into the Virtua Emergency Room in Voorhees at 1:05am Tuesday morning with severe lacerations.

"Well, that's that," Stephanie murmured. "He was definitely the one Raven attacked."

She minimized the screen and went back to the federal database.

"Alright, Trent Whitfield. Let's see who you are and why the hell you're here."

"Son of a--!" Damon exclaimed. "You're sure?"

Michael stared at him, then looked at Alina.

"Of course I'm sure. What's the big deal with Singapore? You both look like you've seen a ghost."

"Let's just say Singapore is getting to be a sore spot," Alina said. "You said you had a name?"

Michael nodded.

"It took some digging, but I was able to trace the account back to someone in Washington, DC," he said, lowering his voice. "That's what I was doing when you came in. The account belongs to Senator Robert Carmichael."

Alina frowned.

"Senator Carmichael?" she repeated. "You're sure?"

"Why do you two keep asking if I'm sure?" Michael demanded, disgruntled. "This is what I do. It's why you have me doing it!"

"I don't think that was a name she was expecting either," Damon explained, watching Alina's face.

"How does Carmichael connect to Dominic?" she demanded, looking at them. "How do they even know each other?"

Michael shook his head.

"I have no–" he stopped abruptly, his eyes widening. "Of course!" he exclaimed suddenly. "That's who it was!"

Alina and Damon stared at him.

"Care to clue us in?" Damon asked, amused.

Michael looked at Alina.

"The night before the bombs, remember?" he demanded. She

shook her head blankly and he sighed. "I stopped here on my way to Brooklyn. I told you I'd met Dominic DiBarcoli at a fundraiser in DC."

Alina nodded slowly.

"Yes," she said. "You were there for your boss. I remember now. What of it?"

Michael shook his head and made an impatient noise.

"I couldn't remember who introduced us. It was Robert Carmichael. Senator Carmichael introduced me to DiBarcoli."

Chapter Thirty-Three

Angela pulled the headset off her ear and looked around, stretching. Michael was in the recliner, his ear buds in his ears and his laptop open on his lap. A legal pad rested on the arm of the chair, covered in notes, arrows and numbers. Standing, she closed her laptop and glanced at her watch. The afternoon was half gone already, most of the day spent on conference calls. Angela sighed and walked over to the recliner.

"Hey!"

She poked Michael. He looked up and pulled one of the earbuds out of his ear.

"Yeah?"

"Any idea where Lina is?"

Michael looked around, then shrugged.

"Nope. I've been focused on work. Did you try upstairs?"

"Not yet. What do you think about dinner?"

He raised an eyebrow and glanced at his watch.

"It's a little early for dinner."

She sighed loudly.

"I don't mean to eat now. I mean, what do you want for dinner?"

Michael shrugged and put his earbud back in.

"I have no preference. I'm ok with whatever everyone else wants."

Angela rolled her eyes and turned away, heading down the hallway toward the front of the house.

"Mr. Personality," she muttered under breath.

She got to the end of the hallway and glanced into the front room on her way past. Alina was seated at the desk in front of the window, engrossed in something on her laptop.

"There you are!" Angela exclaimed, stepping into the den. "I was just going to check upstairs for you."

Alina looked up, raising an eyebrow.

"What's up?"

"Nothing." Angela wandered around the room restlessly. "I just need to stretch my legs and clear my head for a minute."

Alina smoothly closed the laptop as Angela glanced over, and turned to face her.

"How's the pain?" she asked.

Angela grimaced.

"I'm toughing it out. I've been on conference calls all day, so I didn't want to be all loopy from Vicodin. I'll take one later. Have you heard from Stephanie?"

"No."

"She texted me a little while ago. Her white blood count shot up. They have her on an antibiotic now."

Alina frowned.

"That's no good."

"No. She doesn't seem concerned though. She just wants to get out of there." Angela wandered over to the bookcase on the back wall and picked up a book absently. "Where did you go yesterday?"

Alina raised an eyebrow, an amused smile pulling at her lips.

"What makes you think I went anywhere?"

Angela looked at her in exasperation.

"I may have fainted, but I'm not an idiot. You left the church to go somewhere, and it wasn't the hospital. What was so important that you ran away, leaving your two best friends bleeding and unconscious?"

As she spoke, Angela grew more agitated. Alina looked at her for a moment.

"I certainly wasn't running away," she said dryly.

"Then what were you doing? And don't tell me you had something to take care of. I'm tired of hearing that from you."

"You really don't want to know, Angie."

Angela's face developed a decidedly mulish expression and she glared across the room at Alina.

"Yes I do!" She lifted her hand and pointed at her accusingly. "You're hiding something. What is it? Was it Mr. Hunk O' Mysterious? Is that where you were?"

Alina stared back at her, her face impassive.

"What good will it do if I tell you?" she finally asked. "What will change? How will it affect your life?"

"I won't be pissed off anymore, for starters! And maybe I'll have a better understanding of what the hell is going on around here."

"You know what's going on," Alina said calmly. "Someone tried to attack you, and someone else opened fire at John's funeral."

"And Michael just happened to come visit at the same time, and now Damon shows up as well," Angela retorted. "The last time everyone was here like this someone stole fifty-six million dollars from the banks and a North Korean terrorist got his brains blown out."

"You know about Jin Moon?" Alina was surprised. "I didn't think you watched the news."

"Of course I watch the news. I'm not uneducated. I scan the headlines on Facebook every day! The point is that when everyone comes here together, bad things happen. And more and more, you seem to be in the middle of it all."

"That's an unfortunate coincidence."

Angela snorted inelegantly.

"Coincidence, my ass. The other night you took off into the woods on your own without thinking twice. More importantly, Michael let you! I wasn't happy about you not explaining, but I let it go."

"Clearly not," Alina interjected, amused again.

"But I am *not* letting yesterday go," Angela continued, ignoring the interruption. "What was so important you didn't wait to see if Steph and I were ok? We could have been dying for all you knew!"

"You weren't dying," Alina said, exasperated. "I checked you before I left. None of your wounds were life-threatening."

"See? How do you know that?" Angela pounced. "How do you know about random injuries? Why do you have guns all over the place? Why do you have a security system to rival the White House? And *where the hell did you go yesterday*?!"

Alina studied her for a long moment, then sighed.

"I went after the shooter. I saw him leave the church, and I thought I could catch him."

Angela stared at her, her mouth gaping.

"You…you thought...why…" she stammered. "Why would you do such a thing?!"

"It seemed like a good idea. No one else was going after him. Someone had to do something."

"Someone…and that was you?! Are you insane? He had a gun!"

"So did I."

"I don't care if...wait, what?!" Angela looked as if her head was going to fly right off her shoulders. "You took a *gun* to a *funeral*?!"

"This sounds like a great conversation I'm missing," Damon said from the doorway, his voice shaking.

Angela swung around to face him.

"Did you know about this?!" she demanded, her voice rising to an octave that made Alina wince inwardly.

"Know about what?" he asked innocently, leaning against the doorjamb and crossing his arms over his chest.

"About her carrying guns to funerals?"

Damon looked at Alina, laughter dancing in his blue eyes.

"Really? How Pulp Fiction of her," he drawled.

Alina glared at him.

"Don't encourage her."

"You know what?!" Angela threw her hands up in the air. "I'm done. If you don't want to tell me what the hell is going on, fine. Whatever. I'll find out eventually. You know I will."

Angela stalked past Damon and down the hallway toward the living room, muttering the whole way.

Damon watched her go and turned to look at Alina, a grin pulling at his lips.

"Will she?" he asked.

Alina sighed.

"Probably. Angie was never one to suffer secrets."

"Is that going to be a problem?" he asked, the grin fading as he advanced into the room. "I came in and stopped you from giving her too much information for a reason."

Alina looked up at him.

"How much did you hear?"

"Enough to know that you already told her too much."

"As far as she's concerned, it wasn't enough," she pointed out with a grin. "She'll be sulking for the rest of the night."

"Better that than yet another person knowing too much about you. Now, more than ever, you have to watch yourself. You know that. We can't trust anyone; even people you've known your whole life."

Alina stood up, meeting his gaze squarely.

"Are you trying to chastise me?" she demanded, amusement in her eyes. "Because I'm not feeling guilty, so you're not trying hard enough."

Damon shook his head.

"Laugh all you want, but too many people already know who you are, what you do, and where you are. Don't add Angie to that list. It will only make it more dangerous for her."

"It's already dangerous for her," Alina retorted. "Maybe even more so because she doesn't know the truth. Regardless, I'm not telling her anything she hasn't already figured out for herself. She knows I carry. She saw it the other night."

"You didn't have to tell her you went after Kyle!"

Alina grinned.

"True, but did you see her face? Totally worth it."

Damon chuckled.

"Was it worth her sulking?" he asked, dropping the lecture for the time being.

"Maybe not," Alina said, turning toward the door. "Luckily, I know how to make amends. How do you feel about Italian?"

Stephanie leaned her head back against the pillows and rubbed her eyes. Her mind was spinning, and her head hurt. On the surface, Trent Whitfield appeared to be a normal, average executive. He excelled in college, graduating with honors, and kept going up from there. Trasker hired him four years ago, luring him away from a competitor with a much larger salary and better weather. He settled down in Miami easily. He was dedicated to his job. His fellow executives liked him and played golf with him on the weekends. Trent Whitfield was unexceptional in every way, except one: he couldn't seem to settle on a place to live.

Stephanie rolled her head to loosen her neck and opened her eyes to stare at the ceiling. In the past four years, he had moved four times. Each year he signed a one-year lease on a luxury condo, and at the end of each year, he failed to renew it.

Her curiosity piqued, Stephanie examined the four properties more closely. She was on the second development when she stumbled across the newspaper article about the missing woman. She had disappeared without a trace from the building. No sign of forced entry to her condo, or of a struggle. Her body showed up four months later in a dumpster about three blocks away.

One by one, Stephanie uncovered three other women, all reported missing from their buildings, and all showing up dead months later. The most recent victim had surfaced in an alley just three weeks ago. The police had no leads and no suspects in the murders, and the case was open and ongoing. So far there was nothing to link any of the women together.

Except Trent Whitfield. All four women disappeared from their building while he was living there.

Stephanie shook her head and reached for her cell phone. It could be nothing, but there was only one way to be sure. She scrolled through her contacts until she found the name she was looking for, and dialed.

"Special Agent Thomas," a tired voice answered.

"Hi Lenny, it's Stephanie Walker. How are things in sunny Florida?"

"Raining right now," Lenny said cheerfully. "How's my favorite Yank doing?"

"I've seen better days. I'm laid up in the hospital right now."

"That doesn't sound good. What happened?"

"I got shot in the leg."

"Wait…I heard something about a shooting," Lenny said slowly. "What was it? I heard it on my way in this morning…"

"John's funeral," Stephanie supplied helpfully.

"Oh good God, that's right!" he exclaimed. "I'm so sorry!"

"Thanks. Not quite the send-off we were hoping for."

"And you were hit? Are you ok?"

"I'll be fine. They're keeping me to monitor an infection. Hey, I was calling to see if you could help me out with something."

"Sure. What do you need? I still owe you for that thing last year."

"There's an ongoing MPD investigation down there. I think it might tie into something unofficial I'm working on up here," Stephanie told him. "Do you know anyone over there?"

"Hmm…not that I'm on speaking terms with," he said thoughtfully. "What's the case?"

"Four women have disappeared in the past four years. Their bodies show up a few months later."

"Well, it's not ringing any bells, but that doesn't mean anything. You think it might tie into something up there?"

"Maybe. I'm just following a hunch."

"Well, send me the deets and I'll see what I can dig up," Lenny decided. "You said it's unofficial?"

"Yes. It's something I'm looking into for a friend," Stephanie said. "I'm emailing you what I have now. They all went missing from their condo buildings, and the same tenant was present each time. It's probably nothing, but I'd like to make sure."

"Sure thing."

"Hey Lenny, how soon can you work on this?" Stephanie asked, clicking send on the email. "It's time sensitive."

"You caught me at a good time, Steph," he told her. "I just wrapped up a case yesterday, so I've got a little extra time. I'll see what I can find out and let you know in the next day or two."

"I really appreciate that," she said earnestly. "Give me a call as soon as you have something."

"Will do. And Steph? I really am sorry about John. I know it must be hard right now."

"Thanks, Lenny."

Stephanie disconnected and rested her head back against the pillows with a tired sigh. The empty feeling inside, that had been weighing on her like a rock since John died, suddenly seemed more pronounced. Not only had his funeral been ruined by someone shooting up the church, but now she was stuck in the hospital, helpless and alone. Lenny said it must be hard, but he had no idea. Everyone thought John had died in a freak accident. They didn't know the truth.

Stephanie reached out and closed her laptop, lifting it up and sliding it onto the table next to her bed. She picked up the remote to the TV and turned it off, then laid back and closed her eyes. There was nothing more she could do right now, and she was suddenly very tired and very discouraged. If nothing else, a nap would help alleviate the almost overwhelming feeling of emptiness, at least while she was asleep.

Chapter Thirty-Four

Michael stretched and stood up, setting his laptop on the coffee table. He plugged in the charger and turned to head into the kitchen for a bottle of water. Angela was still ensconced at the dining room table, a can of Pepsi at her elbow and her laptop open before her. She looked up as he passed by.

"Where is everyone?" he asked.

"I don't know," she said, reaching for her soda. "Alina said she was going to pick up dinner, and I have no idea where Damon disappeared to."

"Dinner?" Michael paused, looking interested. "Do we know what she's getting?"

Angela shook her head and stood up, carrying her empty soda can into the kitchen to throw it away.

"All she said was she wouldn't be long. I hope she's not because I'm starving."

Michael opened the refrigerator and pulled out a bottle of water.

"I won't lie. I've been so busy I didn't even realize I'm hungry."

Angela looked at him.

"You've been working non-stop with your headphones on all day. I'm not surprised."

"You're one to talk. You've been on the phone all day."

Angela grinned.

"True," she admitted. "I've had back-to-back conference calls, and people keep calling to check on me. They all heard about the shooting."

"Have you heard from Joanne?" he asked, opening the bottle and taking a long sip. "How is she?"

"She called me last night." Angela leaned on the counter and shook her head. "She was beside herself. By the time they were all allowed to leave, she and Bill simply couldn't handle the burial. The funeral home held John overnight and they buried him today, just family. She wanted me to go."

"What was your excuse?"

"That I was all stitched up and in a lot of pain," Angela said with a shrug. "I didn't lie, but I didn't know what to tell her. I mean, I wasn't about to tell her someone broke into my house and is still after me."

"Fair enough." Michael turned to move out of the kitchen. "Does Stephanie know about the burial?"

"I assume so." Angela followed him. "Joanne said she and Bill stopped by the hospital last night to see her. I'm sure she told her then."

"What a nightmare," Michael said, shaking his head. "It's bad enough they had to bury their son, but then to have his funeral turn into a complete circus. I can't begin to imagine how they feel."

Before Angela could reply, Michael's phone began ringing and he pulled it out from his jeans pocket. He glanced at the screen and looked at her.

"It's my boss. Sorry."

Angela waved her hand and went back to her laptop.

"No worries."

Michael hit accept and turned to go toward the sliding door outside.

"Hi Chris." He opened the door and stepped onto the deck. "What's up?"

"Just checking in," said Chris Harbour. "I got your email about the shooting at the funeral. When I approved you going up there for a few days, I didn't think I'd have to worry about your safety."

Michael chuckled.

"You and me both. It's been a crazy couple of days. Thank you for understanding and letting me come. I'm glad I'm here."

Chris cleared his throat.

"About that," he began, and Michael repressed a sigh.

"What happened?" he asked, resigned.

"Nothing," Chris hastened to assure him. "At least, nothing as dramatic as what you've been dealing with up there. I have to ask you to come back tomorrow for a few hours. You can go right back, but some there's something I need to review with you in person."

Michael frowned. Chris was aware Michael's phone wasn't secure, and that someone was listening to all his calls. The fact that he was being intentionally vague was warning enough that he'd come across something important.

"I can catch the train from 30th Street Station in Philly," he said slowly. "I'll have to check times, but I can probably get there by eight. What time do you need me?"

"Eight is fine. I'll meet you at the station."

Michael glanced at his watch.

"I'll book the ticket now and email you the confirmation."

"I'm sorry to ask you to come back last minute. I know it's a lot."

"Don't worry about it. It will give me a chance to grab some fresh clothes from the house."

"I'll see you in the morning."

Michael disconnected and stared at the lengthening shadows in the yard. Chris knew he was investigating Trasker. He'd given him full reign to concentrate on finding out how they got involved in the attempted biological attack. If he was calling him back to DC, it could only mean Chris found something involving Trasker. Michael frowned and turned back to the house.

He just hoped all hell didn't break loose while he was gone.

Viper looked up as the door to the deck slid open and Hawk stepped outside, a bottle of beer in his hand. Raven stirred on the banister beside her, watching through black eyes as Damon walked over to the chair next to her. Once he was seated, Raven turned his attention back to the deep shadows in the trees. Alina smiled faintly. Her two hawks were getting used to each other.

"Why are you out here alone?" Damon asked, glancing at her. "There's still plenty of food left in there."

"I've had enough."

"You barely ate anything," he said, sipping his beer. "That was an absurd amount of food."

Alina smiled.

"Tarantella's is good for that. They're a family-style mom and pop place. Best Italian around here."

"It *was* really good," he admitted, "and Angela is talking again, so you were right."

"Chicken Parm is the quickest way to Angie's heart," she said with a laugh. "And the wine didn't hurt."

"You still haven't said why you're sitting out here all alone."

Alina glanced at him and reached down to pick up her wine

glass from beside her chair.

"It was getting too loud in there. I needed some quiet."

Damon looked out over the dark lawn in silence for a moment.

"What do you know about Senator Carmichael?" he asked finally. "You were surprised he was the money behind Dominic."

"I don't know any more than what I looked up this afternoon. Democrat from California. He's been in office for eight years, and is one of the bigger opponents of immigration reform. If he has his way, the border will never be secured. He wants higher taxes on oil, and he's pushing for absurdly strict gun reform. All in all, just about what I'd expect from a Californian."

"But not the name you expected to hear in connection with Dominic DiBarcoli and Trasker."

She looked at him.

"No."

Damon nodded.

"Another red herring?"

"Or another pawn."

They fell silent again for a moment.

"This is getting more and more tangled with every thread we pull," he muttered. "Now we have a link between Dominic, Carmichael, and Trasker, but to what end? What does any of this have to do with our leak?"

"I don't know, but they're connected. I'm sure of it."

"Has Michael made any progress on that other project?"

"Not that he's said. In his defense, he's been a little distracted the past few days."

Damon ran a hand through his hair and leaned his head back.

"I still don't like him working on it. It's too risky."

Alina glanced at him.

"Risky for him or me?"

"Both, but mainly you. Don't take this the wrong way, but the gunny's safety is not my primary concern right now."

Alina smiled faintly and sipped her wine.

They fell silent again, each sipping their drink, lost in their own thoughts.

"Have you made any progress on Charlie's firewall yet?" Damon asked.

She shook her head.

"I'm working on it. It's tricky."

"You knew it would be. I hope it's worth the effort."

Alina shrugged.

"We'll find out."

"Why bring in another professional?" Hawk wondered, staring into the night. "Especially one of our own?"

"John was investigating what happened twelve years ago. It's possible Kyle was involved in that situation."

He looked at her sharply.

"He was active then?"

Alina nodded.

"Just barely," she replied. "He was deployed the same year Dave was killed, but according to his file, he arrived a couple months later."

Hawk pressed his lips together and fell silent. Viper glanced at him. He didn't need to voice what he was thinking. She had already thought the same thing. Records and dates could be altered.

"Tell me about Asad," he said suddenly.

Alina raised an eyebrow.

"What about him? You already know everything you need to know."

"Not everything," he said softly, looking at her.

Alina felt her cheeks flush and was grateful for the shadows. She didn't pretend not to know what he meant. There was no point. He knew she hadn't told him the full story.

"Asad is dead," she said, her face emotionless. "That's all you need to know."

"Something made you furious," Hawk said calmly. "He said something. Got under your skin."

She studied him in the darkness for a long moment, debating what to tell him. Hawk was notorious for having ice water in his veins, but Viper wasn't convinced he would be quite so impartial if he knew just how much Asad had known about her.

"He was surprisingly chatty in the end," she said finally, sipping her wine. "I had to encourage him, but once he got started, he took pleasure in showing off what he knew."

Hawk looked at her sharply.

"What did he know?"

"Quite a bit. He knew where I lived in France, for one thing."

He scowled.

"How the hell did he know that? *I* didn't even know until you told me!"

Alina looked at him and sighed.

"It gets worse. He knew things no one else knows."

Hawk stared at her apprehensively.

"Like what?"

"He knew about an incident that happened with my brother when we were kids, something no one outside the family knows," she said.

Damon was silent for a long moment.

"Obviously, someone knows," he said at last.

"Oh, he was being coached," Viper said matter-of-factly. "I suspected it as he talked, but when he let that one out, I was positive. I pulled the ear bud out of his ear after I slit his throat."

"Well, that's just fantastic. He was being coached in real time by the same person who wants your head on a platter and you never saw fit to tell me?!"

She shrugged.

"What difference would it make?" she asked practically. "There's nothing you can do. I sent them a message. They know I'm coming for them."

Hawk shook his head and finished his beer.

"Head games," he muttered. "That's all that was."

"Yes."

"How did they know you would find Asad?"

"Honestly? I think when their whole plan went pear-shaped, they wanted me to get to Asad. They used me to tie off their loose end."

Hawk nodded slowly.

"Of course," he breathed. "They didn't have to worry about him because you'd take care of it. But what about Kasim?"

Viper grimaced.

"Well, that's where I'm stumped," she admitted. "Why let him go? And why come after me before I've hunted him down? Why not let me eliminate him as well before trying to blow my head off?"

"I asked you in Singapore if you thought Kasim could be planning another attack and you said no," he said, looking at her. "Are you sure about that?"

Their eyes met in the shadows.

"No."

He nodded.

"That's what I thought," he murmured. "That could be why they let Kasim go."

"And that's why I need to find him."

"You've got nothing yet?"

"No. I'm monitoring everything but so far, nothing."

Hawk was silent for a moment.

"What about that racer Tito?" he asked. "What's the story with him?"

Alina finished her wine and set the glass down.

"He was on his way to meet Asad," she said slowly. "I forced him off the road. I heard the explosion a few minutes later. That wasn't me."

Hawk looked at her.

"What do you mean it wasn't you?" he asked, startled.

Alina shrugged.

"I shot his front tire and he hit a tree head-on," she told him. "The worst I did was force him into a potentially fatal collision. When I searched Asad's farmhouse later, I found the detonator. He also had a computer with tracking software installed on it."

"So, Asad blew Tito's car when it was within range," Hawk murmured. "He was tying up loose ends."

"Exactly."

"I'll tell you this much, I can't wait to find the son-of-a-bitch who organized all of this. Not that I'm opposed to Tito's untimely demise, or Dominic's, or Asad's, but I want to know who allowed all this to happen on our side of the line."

"You and me both," Viper muttered. "Have you had any luck with Jordan Murphy?"

"I have, but it doesn't help us much," he said, dropping the subject of Asad and Tito. "He's definitely dead, and he was dead long before those utility bills were paid in Madrid."

"I already knew that."

He shot her an amused look.

"Do you want to hear this or not?" he asked.

Alina grinned.

"Are you going to tell me something I don't already know?"

"Keep it up and I won't tell you anything."

Alina chuckled.

"Go on. Amaze me."

"He was back for almost a year when he was killed in a car accident. The police on the scene decided it was a straight-forward drunk driving crash. Jordan's blood alcohol level was .117."

"That's pretty drunk. So what's the catch? I can feel one coming."

Damon nodded.

"According to his sister, Jordan never drank," he told her. "In fact, he was so anti-drinking that he drank Sprite for the champagne toast at her wedding."

Viper raised her eyebrows.

"Well, isn't that interesting. How did a teetotaler end up drunk as a skunk?"

"If we believe his sister, he didn't. She insisted her brother was killed but no one listened."

Alina glanced at him.

"Where is she now?" she asked softly.

Damon met her look steadily.

"She died unexpectedly two months ago. She went in for surgery on her thyroid. While she was in the hospital, she had a sudden heart attack."

Viper stared at him, a chill streaking down her spine.

"What?"

He nodded grimly.

"And guess who she had a long phone conversation with a few days before her surgery?"

She looked at him silently, waiting to hear what she had already guessed.

"Special Agent John Smithe."

Chapter Thirty-Five

"Damn."

Alina exhaled silently, staring through the darkness. Even though she had known it was coming, hearing her suspicion confirmed was still jarring.

"Whatever got your brother killed, also made Jordan a target," said Damon.

"And his sister, and John," Alina added.

"Someone's going through a lot of trouble to make sure the past stays there. It doesn't really help us much, except to confirm everything is linked together."

"I've got a contact of mine seeing what she can find out about Madrid," said Viper after a long moment. "That might shed some light on something. Now we know it definitely wasn't Jordan in Spain, but she can confirm who *was* using his name. It's a start."

Hawk glanced at her.

"I hope she's more discreet than John. Everyone who asks questions about Jordan Murphy ends up dead."

"She hasn't failed me yet."

"Viper, please be careful. This bastard knows a lot about you. It's not safe to use known contacts."

Alina was silent for a long moment, staring out over the lawn.

"She's not a known contact," she said at last. "I've worked hard to ensure no link exists between the two of us. It would be fatal for both of us."

He glanced at her.

"How so?"

Viper turned to look at him.

"Let's just say her reputation is such that everyone in the Middle East has a price on her head, for one reason or another. I have nothing but utter respect for the network she's managed to build."

Hawk studied her for a moment.

"Another agency?" he finally asked.

Viper smiled faintly and didn't answer. He sighed.

"At least that's one person we don't have to worry about. "You understand my concern?"

"I do," she said quietly.

"Viper, how does someone know so much about you?" he asked, his voice low. "You said Asad knew about something that happened with your brother when you were kids. How the hell did someone find out about it?"

"If I knew, we wouldn't be having this conversation. It would all be over."

Damon shook his head.

"I've said this a few times and I'll keep saying it. You can't trust anyone, especially those closest to you."

Alina glanced at him and he held his hand up to forestall any comment she might make.

"Listen to me. Asad knew about the house in France. Fine. The leak in our Organization could be responsible for that. But something involving your life when you were a kid? No one knows those things. No one except the people who were there. Whether you want to admit it or not, there are only a couple of people who know personal things about you and your brother. The only way someone could pass that information on to Asad is if they heard it from someone who was there."

Alina knew he was right. She'd known ever since that afternoon when Asad uttered the words that convinced her he was being coached. She could count on one hand the number of people who knew about that incident with Dave.

"I'm keeping an eye on all of them. There's only so much I can do while we unravel all this."

Damon sighed.

"I know. We just need to be vigilant."

"Harry called me this morning," Alina told him after a few moments of silence.

Damon glanced at her, his eyebrow raised.

"What did he want?"

"I don't know. I didn't answer. I was in the middle of searching Kyle's hotel room."

"He didn't leave a message?"

"No."

Damon frowned.

"I haven't heard from him since we stopped the bombs," he said. "Charlie isn't keeping him updated. Now he tried calling you? What the hell is going on?"

Alina shook her head.

"I don't know, but if he calls again, I'll have to take it. The problem is who will be listening."

Damon looked at her.

"I don't like any of this," he muttered. "Are you sure you won't disappear?"

"Yes," she said with a short laugh.

The door behind them slid open and they both turned to watch as Michael came out onto the deck.

"I cleaned up the food and put it away," he said, walking over to lean against the railing. "Angela just went up to bed. She said to say good night."

Alina nodded.

"Thank you for cleaning up. You didn't have to."

Michael smiled.

"I know. What are your plans tomorrow? Will either of you be around?"

Damon raised an eyebrow.

"What's going on?" he asked.

"I have to go down to DC," Michael told them. "I'm catching the six o'clock train from 30th Street station."

"What happened?" asked Alina, watching him.

"Chris called. He wants me down there tomorrow. I think he's found something for me about Trasker. I'm only going for the day. I'll be back tomorrow night."

"We'll handle Angela," Alina said. "Be careful. If it's Carmichael causing the drama down there, it's only a matter of time before he realizes Blake isn't the only threat."

Charlie looked up from his heart-healthy omelet as a shadow fell across him. He was seated in his favorite diner at his usual table, tucked back in the corner where he had a good view of the entire dining room, but no one had a good view of him. He looked up into Harry's face and nodded.

"Good morning," he said, waving Harry into a seat. "You're late."

"I didn't see your message until I got to the office," said Harry, sinking into the chair across from him and leaning his cane against the table. "Is that...egg whites?" he demanded, aghast.

Charlie smiled faintly.

"I'm watching my cholesterol," he said calmly. "Have you eaten?"

"With the birds," he said cheerfully, flagging down a waitress. "I'll have some coffee, though."

He ordered coffee and waited until the waitress disappeared again before turning his gaze back to Charlie.

"What's so important that you invited me to breakfast?" he asked, settling into his seat comfortably. "We usually meet for coffee later in the day."

"You've heard about what happened in New Jersey?" Charlie asked, glancing up.

"Hard not to," he grunted. "It's been all over the news. Not everyday someone walks into a Fed's funeral and starts shooting. Have you spoken to her?"

Charlie shook his head.

"No."

Harry stared at him.

"She's alright, though?"

"I presume so."

"You presume...dammit man, you don't know?!" Harry exclaimed, startled out of his habitual calm.

Charlie looked at him, amused.

"If she wasn't, I would have heard," he said. "I'm sure she's fine."

That soothed Harry a bit.

"Do you have any idea who or why?" he asked, his voice returning to normal.

"I have a few ideas, but nothing confirmed yet. "Agent Walker was hit."

Harry sighed heavily.

"How badly?" he asked.

"She's in the hospital. The bullet went into her leg. I'm told it just missed her femoral artery."

Charlie fell silent as the waitress approached with Harry's coffee. She set it down, glanced at Charlie's cup and took it away with a promise of a fresh cup.

"Well, hell," Harry said after she'd gone. "How's she doing?"

"She'll be fine." Charlie finished his omelet and reached for a slice of whole wheat toast. "The other one was also hurt."

Harry raised an eyebrow.

"The other one?"

"The other friend," said Charlie. "Angela Bolan."

Harry's face cleared.

"Oh yes! The banker. What happened to her?"

"A couple lacerations from a statue, nothing more. She was treated and released."

Harry was silent for a long moment.

"Viper will be furious," he said finally. "She'll go after the shooter."

"Undoubtedly. I wouldn't place bets on his survival rate at this point."

"Do you think she has any leads?"

"It's Viper. You trained her. What do you think?" he asked dryly.

Harry grinned.

"Valid point."

The waitress returned with Charlie's coffee, set it down with a smile, and left again.

"Well, I can only think of two reasons someone would walk into an FBI funeral and hide in the organ loft with a rifle," Harry said, sipping his black coffee. "The most likely one is they were there for Viper."

"And the other?"

Harry shrugged.

"They were there for one of the other agents in attendance. Given the presence a few weeks ago of a terrorist who wanted her dead, I'm going with the former."

"Have you found anything new on Kasim?" Charlie looked at him. "You've had enough time."

Harry scowled.

"He's disappeared. We can't find any trace of him. I'm confident he hasn't slipped out of the country, but beyond that...I've got a team working around the clock. He'll pop up somewhere, but until then, we're blind."

Charlie sipped his coffee, watching Harry over the rim.

"I'm not happy that someone knew enough to know where Viper would be yesterday," he said after a moment, lowering his cup. "Do you think the DHS is compromised, or should I be looking elsewhere?"

Harry shook his head.

"I think more than just Homeland is compromised," he said slowly. "I've been finding informational leaks from other agencies as well. But none of the people I'm watching have clearance high enough to know about the existence of Viper or any of your assets."

Charlie studied him.

"And yet someone does," he said softly.

"Are you sure the leak is on our side?"

Charlie nodded.

"Yes."

Harry sighed.

"Then I'll keep looking. It's damn touchy, though. The levels you're talking about don't take questioning well. What about you? How are you faring on your end?"

"I'm getting close," said Charlie unexpectedly. "I think they're getting help from other agencies. I want to know our two departments are handled before I tackle any of the others."

"Obviously," Harry agreed, nodding. "I'll see what I can get for you. Give me until tomorrow night. I've got something set up. If they take the bait, I'll know exactly who we're looking at by then."

"Good."

Charlie lifted his coffee cup again and Harry watched him thoughtfully.

"Why is Viper still here?" he asked. "Why haven't you sent her overseas?"

"I don't want her in the field while assets are dropping like flies," Charlie told him, his gray eyes arctic. "I don't want any of my people out there, but they already are. All I can do is keep them moving and hope for the best. She's safer stateside."

"And Hawk?"

"He's been briefed on the risks. He's watching his back."

Harry shook his head.

"I'll tell you what," he said in a low voice, "when I find out who's behind all this, I'll kill him."

Charlie looked at him, a faint smile toying on lips.

"I doubt very much you'll be in time."

Michael glanced at his watch and pulled out the clean phone Alina had given him. Striding to the curb, he raised his hand to hail a cab. Chris met him at the station when his train came in and they went to breakfast. Over eggs, bacon and toast, his boss told him what was so important that he had to catch an early train down. Now, as a cab pulled to a stop and he climbed in the back, Michael's lips tightened. It was not a good development.

He gave his address to the driver and sat back as the cab eased into traffic. Looking down, he dialed Alina and held the phone to his ear while it rang. After three rings, he disconnected with a low curse before the voicemail picked up. Michael stared out the window, debating, before finally calling Damon. If he couldn't get Viper, Damon was the next best thing. Someone up there had to hear what he learned this morning before something else happened. They'd all had enough excitement for one week.

"Yes?" Damon picked up after the second ring. "Don't tell me you're in trouble already."

"Not me, you guys," Michael retorted.

There was brief beat of silence, then a soft sigh.

"Well that does not sound good, gunny."

"It's not. Is she with you?"

"No."

"She's not picking up. Do we know she's ok?"

"I'm sure she's fine." Damon sounded amused. "She's navigated through worse territories than South Jersey. What happened? Are we expecting trouble?"

"I just talked to my boss," Michael said slowly. "He had dinner last night with an old friend of his, who is also a Vice President at Trasker."

Damon whistled.

"Nice. What did he find out?"

"Ever since the incident with the antidote, he and two other VP's have been trying to find out how the hell an Ebola virus was introduced into their pipeline," Michael told him a low voice. "They determined only a handful of executives had the opportunity and ability to make the substitution."

"And?"

"They've been doing a secret internal audit of their computers and network usage. They narrowed it down to two prime suspects."

"And you have the names," Damon stated. "I have to say, gunny, you never cease to amaze me."

"I'm not done yet," Michael said dryly. "Trent Whitfield is one of those names."

Silence greeted that for a long moment. When Damon finally spoke, there wasn't a trace of amusement left in his voice.

"You're sure?"

"They are. They're just waiting for him to come back from his business trip."

Chapter Thirty-Six

Alina glanced at her watch as her phone vibrated again. She left the house an hour ago. Since then, she had three missed calls. This would make four.

"You'd think it was the damn apocalypse," she muttered to herself, lifting a case of Pepsi into the red cart. "How the hell do they all function when I'm not here?"

She pulled her phone out and glanced at the screen, ready to hit the ignore button. Alina paused when she saw that it wasn't a phone call at all, but an incoming encrypted message. She raised an eyebrow and swiped the screen. The message was from Reyna, her contact in Egypt.

Alina slipped the phone back into her pocket and pushed the cart to the next aisle to grab a box of frosted Pop-Tarts. Honestly, she didn't know how Angie could consume all this sugar. She looked at the next item on the list and shook her head. Bagels. She should have known.

Reyna was working faster than Viper had anticipated. She hadn't expected to hear from her until tomorrow at the earliest. The size of the message told her Reyna included attachments, and large ones at that. They would have to wait until she returned from her supply run.

When her phone vibrated again a few minutes later, Viper's lips tightened in annoyance. She pulled her phone out again and glanced at the number.

"Yes?"

"You sound annoyed," Damon told her, sounding gratingly cheerful himself. "What's wrong?"

"My phone hasn't stopped since I left. I'm ready to turn it off."

"I know Michael called. Who else?"

"Stephanie, Angie, and now you." Alina paused next to a display of cleaning sprays and picked up a bottle of multi-purpose lemon-scented cleaner, tossing it into the cart. "How do you know Michael called?"

"He called me when he couldn't get you. He had not-so-glad tidings."

He paused and Alina waited. When he didn't continue, she sighed.

"Do you want me to guess?"

"His boss had dinner with one of the VP's of Trasker last night. Turns out they've been running an internal software audit on all their execs with access to switch the Ebola virus with the antidote," he told her. "They narrowed it down to two names, and Trent is one of them."

Alina's brows drew together in a scowl.

"Damn. That's a problem."

"Yep."

"I'm just finishing up, then I'll be back." She steered the cart toward the check out.

"Viper," he said in a low voice, "it's no coincidence he came after Angela."

"Oh, I know," she said grimly. "At least now we know what his endgame is. The question is who's behind it."

Hawk watched through his binoculars as a pit bull bounded out of the door, a tall, brown-haired man behind him. The dog would have cheerfully kept going but for the leash pulling him up short as his owner locked the door behind them.

Hawk studied Blake Hanover thoughtfully. He knew who he was, knew he was an FBI agent in Washington, DC who was in the Marines with Michael, and that he'd helped Stephanie not only a couple weeks ago with the bombs, but also last fall with the North Korean hacker. He knew Blake had declared war on the Casa Reinos Cartel. The man obviously had guts, and Viper liked him. That was good enough for Hawk. Viper didn't take to people easily, if at all. Their line of work didn't exactly foster trusting relationships.

Blake turned away from the door and headed across the sidewalk to the grass courtyard, waiting as the dog kicked up his leg in front of a bush. Damon lowered the binoculars and glanced at his watch. It was almost noon. The morning had been spent babysitting Angela and scouring the local hospitals for Trent Whitfield. His patience paid off when he came across not only his name in Virtua's database, but also his temporary local address. Trent was at an extended stay hotel in Mt. Laurel.

Blake and the dog began moving again and Hawk lifted his binoculars again to watch as he led the dog across the parking lot to a black Challenger. He opened the passenger's door and the dog jumped into the backseat, circling on the seat twice before sitting down. He closed the door and circled around to the driver's side. A moment later he was pulling out of the lot.

Once the Challenger disappeared down the road, Hawk lowered the binoculars and tucked them into his jacket pocket. He got off his motorcycle and started across the large grass courtyard. He didn't know how long Blake would be gone, but he was glad he took the dog. While Hawk had worked around animals before, he preferred not to. Unlike Viper, he didn't have a magical way with them.

Stephanie's front door was closing behind him a few minutes later.

He looked around, noting the dog bed near the couch, and moved through the living room to the dining room. Stacks of papers and file folders on the table illustrated just what Stephanie was in the habit of using the dining room table for, with a noticeably empty spot the size of a laptop in front of one of the chairs. Damon glanced into the kitchen and turned and went down the short hallway. On the left a door led to a spare room that was half storage. The door across from it opened into a bathroom. Damon glanced into both, then continued to the door at the end of the hallway. This was clearly Stephanie's bedroom. After a quick glance around, he returned to the dining room and began systematically going through the papers spread over the dining room table.

If Viper knew he was here, she would be furious. Someone was hemorrhaging information about her and Hawk wasn't discounting any possibility. While she was limited by a sense of loyalty and friendship, Hawk was not. He was doing what needed to be done. Until they found the leak, everyone was a suspect.

And that included Special Agent Stephanie Walker.

Damon made quick work of the dining room table, moving on when he was finished. He did a cursory turn around the living room, then headed back to the bedroom. His lips pressed together grimly as he thought of Kyle in the organ loft at the funeral. His gut tightened, as it did every time he allowed himself to think about the assassin with Viper's head in his crosshairs. If it wasn't for the freak chance of a kneeler slamming, Viper would be dead, her head blown apart with a single round.

How the bloody hell had it all come to this? Two months ago he was in the old Soviet bloc, secure in his mistaken belief that the only way their cover could be blown was if they themselves blew it. When Harry summoned him back to the States to watch Viper's back, he knew something was wrong, but he never dreamed they had a leak.

He stepped into Stephanie's room and looked around. It wasn't neat, but it wasn't a disaster either. There seemed to be a kind of organized chaos, kept under control by the fact that Stephanie clearly didn't spend a lot of time in her bedroom. He went to the closet first, his attention drawn to the safe. Crouching down, he examined it for a moment before reaching into his pocket and extracting a pair of latex gloves. He pulled them on and bent over the safe. It was a standard dial combination safe and he had it open a few minutes later. He moved a stack of ammo boxes and three pistols, reaching for a pile of folders underneath. He began flipping through them, scanning the contents quickly.

As soon as Viper told him she was made in Damascus, he knew they had a serious problem. Even so, he was inclined to believe it was isolated to Viper, until Singapore. The stitches in his gut and the dull, throbbing ache from the surgery and his cracked rib were a constant reminder someone meant business, and that business affected the entire Organization.

Hawk finished going through the folders and set them aside. He pulled a metal box out of the safe and opened it, finding a stack of cash, a passport, birth certificate, social security card, and old driver's licenses. Shaking his head, he closed the box and replaced everything in the safe exactly where he'd found it. Closing it, he spun the lock and stood up, looking around the closet.

Clothes hung from the wrap-around railing, and shoes and boots were haphazardly balanced on two shoe racks. A stack of clear storage tubs took up one corner, holding what looked like linens. He turned to leave the closet and was just stepping out of the door when something caught his eyes. A black bag had slipped and fallen to the side, trapped between the wall and the clear storage tubs.

Hawk raised an eyebrow and reached for the bag, frowning when he felt items inside. Carrying it out of the closet, he set it on the bed and looked inside. He pulled out a large manila envelope and glanced inside. Cash. Damon frowned and glanced back at the safe. Why did she have what looked like a couple thousand dollars in cash outside the safe? Especially when he already knew she kept cash *inside* the safe?

He set the envelope aside and reached in to pull out a folder.

Damon flipped it open and his eyebrows soared into his forehead when he found himself staring at John Smithe's birth certificate.

"What the..."

He sorted through the documents in the folder, all John's, the frown growing. Why did Stephanie have all John's personal and confidential identity documents? And why weren't they destroyed in the fire that destroyed everything else?

Hawk set the folder down, his lips settling into a deep frown, and reached into the bag again to pull out a long, white envelope. His fingers felt something hard inside and he opened the envelope, tipping it. A diamond ring fell into his hand.

Damon held it up, examining the ring. The band was white gold, twisted to look like vines. The vines separated and came up to hold a decently sized diamond solitaire.

The realization came to him suddenly and Damon stared at what he instinctively knew was Alina's engagement ring. Why did Stephanie have it?

Hawk dropped the ring back into the envelope and stared at the small stack growing next to the bag. Why did Stephanie have any of this?

He looked in the bag and saw a couple boxes of ammo and pulled out a Beretta. Beyond that, the bag was empty. Damon dropped the gun back into the bag and picked up the white envelope thoughtfully. This was all John's. Yet, it was in Stephanie's closet. He pressed his lips together thoughtfully, staring at the collection of items. What joined them all together? It appeared to be a fairly random assortment. Cash, gun, ammo, old diamond ring, personal documents...not exactly a collection you would keep in a bag in a closet.

Hawk's eyes narrowed suddenly and he gathered the folder and envelopes together, putting them back into the bag. It wasn't a collection you would keep in a closet, but it was certainly the types of things you would keep in a safe; or a safe deposit box.

Damon put the bag back where he'd found it and quickly went through the rest of the bedroom. Nothing else of interest presented itself and he left the bedroom a few minutes later. He glanced at his watch, noting how long he'd been in the apartment, and went into the spare room. He did a quick, thorough search of the storage half of the room, then headed out of the condo and back to his motorcycle.

Why did Stephanie have the contents of John's safe deposit box in a bag in her closet? More importantly, why hadn't she told Alina about the ring? If nothing else, wouldn't she want to give her old friend the option of keeping it? Yet, Damon was positive that Alina knew nothing about any of it.

Hawk climbed onto his motorcycle and pulled on his helmet. Was that everything? Or was there something else that wasn't in the bag? Hawk stilled and stared unseeingly across the parking lot. Something like an external hard-drive with attachments sent by Dave Maschik from Iraq twelve years ago?

Alina pressed her lips together and closed her eyes, counting slowly. When she reached ten, she opened her eyes. The offending sight was still here.

"Angie!"

Her voice bellowed through the house.

"Yeah?" Angela's voice was faint and muffled by the floor between them, coming from the dining room.

"You want to come explain this?" Alina yelled down the second floor hallway.

There was a long pause, then she heard Angela's footsteps coming down the hall from the back of the house.

"Explain what?" she called from the bottom of the stairs, her voice much louder now.

"My bedroom."

Alina waited as Angela came up the steps and rounded the corner.

"Oh that!" Angie exclaimed, coming down the hallway towards her. "I'm just trying to help you out."

Alina felt her eyelid start to twitch.

"Help me out with what?" she bit out.

Angela joined her in the bedroom door and looked surprised.

"Getting laid, of course!" she said. "I honestly don't know what's wrong with you, but you have a perfectly delicious man who just keeps following you everywhere, and he slept on the couch last night!"

Alina stared at her for a beat.

"What?"

"He did! I came down for a drink of water in the middle of night and he was asleep on the couch in the living room. Enough is enough. The tension between you two is insane."

Alina turned her attention back to her bedroom. She didn't think she'd ever seen so many candles in one place. Every available surface was covered. It didn't end there, unfortunately. Somewhere, somehow, Angela had unearthed just about every red pillow in the house and artfully arranged them on the bed, turning it into something out of a bad porn film. On her bedside table, a bottle of wine and two glasses were arranged next to a large, empty bowl.

"What's the bowl for?" Alina heard herself asking, even though she was sure she didn't want to hear the answer.

"Strawberries," said Angela promptly. "That's why they were on the shopping list this morning. I'll fill the bowl before I go to bed so they're all ready for you."

"Oh for God's sake."

"And I put massage oil on the dresser," she continued with a wink. "If you don't get laid tonight, he's a monk."

Alina's other eye joined the first in involuntary muscle spasms and she raised a hand to pinch the bridge of her nose.

"Oh trust me, he's not a monk," she murmured under her breath.

"What?"

"Nothing. Take it all down. I don't need your assistance in my love life, thanks all the same, and I most certainly do not need strawberries and massage oil."

"But–"

"No!" Alina's voice hit a decibel she rarely used and she felt the iron control on her patience slipping. "This is ridiculous! I don't have time for this."

"That's the problem! You have to make time! Lina, I don't know how long it's been, but you're clearly in a dry spell. It's not natural to go too long without sex, especially when you have a gorgeous Hunk O' Mysterious just hanging around with nothing better to do!"

"Nothing better…" Alina stared at her old friend, speechless.

"I know if I thought he'd look twice at me, I'd throw myself at him," Angie continued, unaware of Alina's struggle beside her. "I really don't understand what your issue is. And don't give me any bullshit about working relationships or not having time. Everyone has time for sex. Even the President has time for sex."

"Oh really? You've discussed it with him?"

Angela glared at her.

"Don't get sarcastic with me," she snapped. "I'm trying to help you here."

"You can help me by removing all of this from my bedroom," Alina retorted, turning to go down the hallway toward the stairs. "I'll take my chances with the dry spell."

Alina closed the door and crossed the den to the desk, sinking into the chair and dropping her face in her hands. Her shoulders began to shake on their own and she closed her eyes as laughter welled up inside her. Candles and strawberries! Good God, she probably would have mounted a ceiling mirror if she'd had the chance! Viper imagined the look on Hawk's face if he walked into the room alight with all those candles and her shoulders shook harder.

Angela was right. Damon did sleep on the living room couch last night. What she didn't know was that Alina spent the night in the command center. Damon went upstairs when he couldn't keep his eyes open any longer, and decided to crash on the couch until she came up. The problem was that she didn't come up until dawn. By then he was awake, and stiff, and not too happy about falling asleep on the couch.

Alina lifted her face from her hands, staring out the window across the front lawn. If Angela had even an inkling of what was going on, she would forget all about her obsession with getting Damon and her together for the long haul. If she even suspected half of what was going on, she'd realize what a bad idea it was.

And it *was* a bad idea.

No matter how she looked at it, this new relationship with Hawk was dangerous. It was distracting to them both, and it only served to underline the inevitable fact that they were not likely to make it out of this alive. They had both used up their nine lives long ago, and were existing on borrowed time already. Now, with someone in Washington determined to see her dead, that time was running out. It didn't matter that when she was with Hawk she was probably the happiest she'd ever been. It couldn't last simply because *they* couldn't last much longer. Sooner or later, someone would catch up with them. If it wasn't Kyle, it would be someone else. There was no shortage of mercenaries out there, professionals who made their living the same way she did. Eventually, her number would be called. The best she could hope for was that she went out fighting, and took a few of them with her.

A wave of melancholy crashed over her and Alina frowned. She had always known this life was a lonely one, but somehow Damon had managed to partially convince her it didn't have to be. And part of her still had hope. Hope that she would find the bastard in Washington before he found her, or Hawk. Hope that they would have more time together; time to share the cities they loved so much with each other. Hope that they could build enough memories to last a lifetime, however long that lifetime may be.

Unfortunately, hope never did count for much in her world.

Viper sighed, opening her laptop. She had work to do. She didn't have the luxury of sitting here dwelling on what could have been, or what might be. Reyna had sent her information, and she had to evaluate it to see if it shed any light on the mystery surrounding Jordan Murphy and Dave's death.

She was surprised at how quickly Reyna got her information, even though she'd worked with her enough in the past to know how efficient the agent was. Once she contacted her, Viper knew she would be on the ground in Madrid within twenty-four hours. The speed with which she got actionable information once she was in place was what impressed her.

Alina began a security scan of the encrypted zip file and opened the accompanying email, skimming it quickly. She raised an eyebrow as she read. Jordan Murphy had spent six months in Madrid on a medical visa, paying rent and utilities on a one-bedroom flat in the heart of the city.

"Pretty impressive for someone who was already dead," she murmured.

The medical procedure was listed in the official records as a clinical trial for acute sinusitis up to and including reconstructive surgery on nasal passages. Reyna went on to state the real purpose of the procedure included more than just the nose. Jordan Murphy had full reconstructive surgery.

Viper was far from surprised. If you had the money and the inclination, plastic surgery was a popular option for people like her. It was the ideal way to disappear, as long as you could guarantee the records would never see the light of day. Unfortunately, that could rarely be guaranteed, as evidenced by Reyna finding the sealed records for Jordan Murphy.

The security scan finished on the encrypted file and Alina opened it. Reyna found the file in the archives of a medical warehouse. How she had located it, or gained access, was never explained, but she did note in the email that the records were scheduled to be destroyed next month. Reyna had simply scanned the whole file and sent it to her, leaving the original in the warehouse.

Alina clicked through pages of typed notes, detailing the surgery and recovery, scanning through until she reached a page with a photo attached. She sucked in her breath, staring at the photo of Jordan Murphy taken before the procedures began.

Viper was staring at the same face from the photo attached to the application for the Organization.

She was looking at Kyle Anthony March.

Chapter Thirty-Seven

Michael followed a tall blond, waiting while she opened the office door. She stood aside and Michael nodded in thanks before stepping into the large, corner office. Two of the four walls were glass overlooking the city and a large modern desk was positioned in front of one of them. A woman with dark hair a maroon tailored suit rounded the desk, coming towards him with her hand outstretched.

"Special Agent O'Reilly!" she exclaimed, a smile crossing her face. "We met a few weeks ago, didn't we? I believe it was at the annual Veteran's dinner?"

Michael smiled easily, grasping her hand.

"That's entirely possible, Ms. Ricci. Forgive me if I don't recall. I did quite a few events in a very short period of time. I met so many associates of associates I lost track."

Tina Ricci laughed and waved him toward a cozy sitting area off to the side.

"I know the feeling well," she said, moving to seat herself in an overstuffed armchair. "I got the impression you were saturated with new faces that night. If you're not here to follow-up on a chance acquaintance, what can I do for you?"

Michael seated himself in the chair opposite her.

"I'm hoping you can help me with something I'm working on. I've been told you're the woman to see."

One perfectly manicured eyebrow arched and a confident smile crossed her lips.

"Well, that depends on what you need," she said lightly. "The Secret Service is always welcome to any assistance it's within my power to give."

"My office has been asked to investigate the security of a few senators who were targeted by malicious and, at least in one instance, threatening correspondence. It seems some of the security measures in place are failing, causing potentially dangerous lapses," Michael explained. "Various items are making it through the security and into the hands of senators without being scanned and vetted."

"How alarming!" Tina exclaimed, her eyes widening. "What kinds of items?"

"Letters, photos, and in one isolated incident, an actual pipe bomb."

"Good Lord!"

"Exactly. So you see, it's imperative I narrow down the source of the vulnerability and correct it as soon as possible."

"Yes, of course. But I'm somewhat at a loss to see where I can be of help. I'm hardly in the security business."

Michael chuckled.

"I know," he said. "However, one of the targets was a client of yours last year. His campaign hired your firm. I was hoping you might be able to give some insight."

"I can certainly try," she said slowly. "Although I don't work personally with every client anymore. There are just too many. Who was it?"

"Robert Carmichael."

A flinch crossed the woman's face and Michael felt a twinge of satisfaction. His gut instinct had been right.

"Senator Carmichael?" she repeated. "Yes, I did work on that personally. He's such an influential figure on the Hill that it warranted my personal attention. What did you want to know?"

"Actually, it's not about him," Michael said smoothly. "It's about you."

Both eyebrows soared into her forehead and she gave him a politely blank look.

"Me?"

"Yes. In particular, why your firm didn't charge him for three months of intensive services."

The blank look turned to one of outrage instantly.

"How do you know that?" she demanded, her long red nails gripping the arms of her chair. "Our client records are strictly confidential!"

"I'm sure they are," Michael said agreeably. "I didn't look at them. I looked at his, and not one payment has ever been made to this firm, even though you've provided services multiple times. In addition, and this is really what I found fascinating, Senator Carmichael's campaign records actually show several donations originating from you personally around the same time your firm did work for him."

Tina stared at him, her lips pinched together unpleasantly.

"It's perfectly legal and acceptable for me to support political candidates," she said after a moment. "There's nothing wrong with that."

"That's true," he conceded, his eyes watching her closely. "It doesn't explain why your firm didn't charge him for services rendered."

She waved a hand impatiently.

"I don't know what you're talking about," she announced, a faint tremor marring the perfect tone of her voice. "All our clients are billed. His office probably just hasn't paid it yet. Unfortunately, it does happen. Now that you've brought it to my attention, I'll be sure to look into it."

"Oh, I already have. Not only has Senator Carmichael not paid anything to your firm, but when I added up your campaign donations, he seems to have collected over forty-eight thousand dollars from you in the past year alone. Now, I know I'm just a Marine-turned-Secret-Service, but that does seem a little excessive, doesn't it?"

"Look, I don't know who you think you are," Tina began, but he ruthlessly cut her off.

"Before you get yourself all bent out of shape and say something you'll regret, why don't you take a moment to think. I'm not trying to embarrass you or make things worse, but I think you're being blackmailed, Ms. Ricci. I'd like to help you."

Damon stepped into the living room and looked around. Angela was in her usual spot at the dining room table, but there was no sign of Alina.

"Where's Alina?" he asked, closing the door behind him.

Angela looked up.

"Last I saw, she was in the den," she said, nodding down the hallway. "Tread carefully. She's not in a good mood."

Damon glanced at her, his lips twitching.

"Why doesn't that surprise me?" he wondered. "I'll take my chances."

Angela shrugged and went back to her laptop.

"Good luck."

Damon started down the hallway. The door at the end opened as he did and Alina emerged from the den, a frown on her lips. When she saw him, her face lightened somewhat.

"I'm just going to make some coffee," she said, heading

towards him. "Do you want some?"

"I'm fine." He turned to follow her back to the kitchen. "How's it going here?"

Alina shrugged and pulled a clean mug from the cabinet, setting it under the spout of her coffee machine.

"Nothing too exciting going on," she said, hitting the button and turning to face him. "Trent tried to call Angie a little while ago. I stopped her from answering. Other than that, all's quiet on the Western Front."

"I still don't see why I couldn't answer," Angela called from the dining room. "It's not like he can do anything through the phone."

Alina closed her eyes briefly in exasperation and Damon grinned sympathetically.

"It's not a matter of him doing something to you over the phone," he said, turning to look at Angela from the kitchen. "It's a question of not acknowledging him."

"He's a work associate," she said, getting up and coming over to stand on the other side of bar. "I can hardly *not* acknowledge him! Besides, we don't even know for sure that he's dangerous."

"Yes we do!"

Damon and Alina spoke in unison and Angela blinked, looking from one to the other.

"We do?"

Alina sighed.

"Yes, we do," she said tiredly, walking over to the bar while her coffee brewed into the mug behind her. She pulled out her phone and opened a photo, turning it for Angela to see. "He's the one Raven attacked in the woods the night before John's funeral."

Angela stared at the photo taken from Viper's NVGs and her mouth dropped open.

"Why am I just hearing this now?!" she exclaimed, looking up.

"Because John's funeral happened," Alina muttered, taking the phone back. "Forgive me if someone shooting up the church pushed Trent to the back of my mind."

"Why was he here?" Angela asked after a minute, her brows drawn together in a frown. "I don't get it. How did he even know where I was?"

"He followed you," Alina said, turning to go get her coffee mug from the coffee maker.

"Why?"

Damon glanced at Alina, his eyes hooded, waiting to see what she would say. Anything was too much as far as he was concerned, but

Angela was waiting for some kind of answer.

"I don't know," Alina lied. "When I find out, I'll be sure to pass it along."

Angela stared at her for a beat.

"I doubt that," she muttered. "You don't tell me anything anymore. Not that you ever told me much to begin with since you came back from Timbuktu, or wherever you were for ten years."

"What difference would it make?" asked Damon logically. "You're here, where you have a reasonable chance of being protected. How does knowing why someone is targeting you change anything? You're still being targeted, and you're still better off here than anywhere else."

Angela glared at him.

"That is such a male thing to say!" she exclaimed. "I'm just supposed to sit back and not ask questions, is that it?"

Damon looked startled.

"That's not what I meant," he protested. "I'm just pointing out how not knowing the answers doesn't affect you one way or the other right now."

Angela looked at Alina, sipping her coffee with an unholy look of amusement on her face.

"Are you listening to this?" she demanded.

Alina nodded.

"Mm-hmm."

"Do you agree with him?"

"It doesn't matter if I agree or not, I'm not the one that said it," she said with a grin. "I know better."

"Damn straight you do," Angela muttered, turning and going back to her laptop. "Don't think you're off the hook, though! First the candles and strawberries, now Trent. You're keeping me in the dark, Lina, and you know I don't like that!"

"Candles and strawberries?" Damon asked, raising an eyebrow.

"It's nothing you need to know about," said Alina, carrying her coffee out of the kitchen and down the hall. "Come into the den. I want to show you something."

Damon grabbed a bottle of water from the refrigerator and followed her, unscrewing the cap as he went.

"Is it going to make me happy or irritate me?" he asked, stepping into the den behind her. "I'm getting tired of bad news."

"Did you get some while you were out?" Alina asked, glancing at him.

Damon shrugged.

"It wasn't good news."

"Are you going to share?"

"Not yet." He held up a hand when she opened her mouth to object. "When I know what it means, I'll share. It might not be anything."

Alina glowered at him briefly.

"That sounds suspiciously like you're trying to keep me out of the loop. Didn't we just have a rather heated conversation about this the other night?"

Damon grinned.

"Was it heated?" he asked, a devilish twinkle in his bright blue eyes. "I think I would have remembered that. The last heat I remember was in Singapore."

"Not that kind of heat," she muttered, a reluctant grin pulling at her lips. "All anyone thinks about around here is sex. Don't you start, too."

"Too?" Damon latched onto that word. "Who else is thinking about it?"

"It doesn't matter." Alina opened her laptop and motioned him over. "I found out what Jordan Murphy was doing in Madrid. Or at least, what the person claiming to be Jordan Murphy was doing."

Damon walked over to look over her shoulder.

"Who's that?" he asked, looking at the photo on the screen.

"That is Kyle March before he had reconstructive surgery in Madrid."

Damon looked at her sharply and sucked in his breath.

"How the hell did Kyle get Jordan Murphy's name?" he demanded. "The two weren't in the same unit. Hell, they weren't even in the same country at the same time!"

"I've been thinking about it all afternoon," Alina said, sitting back in her chair and spinning to look at him. "The short answer is I don't know. There has to be a connection between Kyle and Jordan somewhere, but I don't know where. You're right. Their military careers never crossed and, as far as I can tell, there was no connection outside the military either. Kyle was born and bred in Rhode Island, and Jordan came from Kansas. There's nothing to connect the two."

"And yet something obviously did," Damon murmured thoughtfully. "Kyle must have known Jordan was dead when he was in Madrid. He wouldn't have taken the risk otherwise."

Alina nodded.

"The more I find out, the more questions I have," she said. "Why did he use the alias of a real person?"

"Your contact found this?" Damon asked, glancing at the photo on the screen. "How?"

"She accessed the medical warehouse and found the records. They're scheduled for destruction."

"Anything from her since?"

"No. She's on her way back to Cairo. I told her to get out before anyone realized she was there."

Damon nodded.

"That's the best course. I do question how she found the information so quickly."

Alina laughed.

"That's why I use her. She's amazing. Sometimes I think she has more contacts than Charlie."

Damon drank some water and looked down at her.

"Have you heard from Charlie?" he asked.

She shook her head.

"No."

"What the hell is he up to?"

Alina closed the laptop and stood up.

"I don't know, but he better be finding that leak for me," she muttered. "Are you planning on staying here for a while?"

Damon raised an eyebrow.

"I can. Why?"

"I found Trent's hotel. I'm going to pay it a visit. The sooner we remove that threat, the better for all concerned."

Damon grinned.

"Getting tired of the full house already?"

"You have no idea."

Damon grabbed her wrist as she passed him.

"Be careful," he said simply when she glanced at him questioningly. "If he's the one who switched the antidote, he's got more to lose than just his job."

Viper smiled coldly.

"Oh, I know," she said softly, "and I intend to see that he loses it."

Chapter Thirty-Eight

Viper glanced up from her magazine in the hotel lobby as the elevator opened and Trent strode out. He was wearing a high turtle neck, and his right arm was heavily bandaged and in a sling. He didn't look around, but went straight through the lobby to the front desk. He spoke to the person behind the counter for a few moments before turning to leave through the front doors. Viper turned her eyes to the desk, watching as the employee typed into the computer. She watched him for a moment thoughtfully, then closed her magazine and glanced at her watch.

Standing, she moved toward the elevator, tucking her magazine into the oversized tote bag slung over her shoulder. Honestly, Alina didn't know how women carried bags like this around all day. They were large, heavy, and got in the way of everything. However, it served a purpose for her right now in portraying an image. Not one employee in this hotel would remember the bored guest waiting in the lobby for someone.

The elevator opened and Viper stepped into it, pressing the button for the eighteenth floor with her knuckle. She kept her head down and angled away from the camera in the corner, focusing on her phone in her hand. When the doors opened, she never looked up from the screen as she stepped out of the elevator and turned left. As soon as she was halfway down the silent corridor, Alina tucked it into her pocket and lifted her head, going straight to Trent's door. She bent over the handle and was inside a moment later.

Unlike Kyle and his two-room suite, Trent occupied a standard, no-frills, queen room with adjoining bath. It was small, functional, and would take all of ten minutes to search. Alina pulled out a pair of gloves, sliding them on as she looked around.

The room wasn't a mess, but it was certainly feeling the absence of housekeeping. The bed was rumpled and unmade, the trash can needed emptying, and towels were tossed on the floor in the bathroom. A rolling luggage bag lay open on a chair with clothes half in and half out. An assortment of pill bottles littered the dresser and Alina picked one up, glancing at the prescription. Percocet. Another was amoxicillin. She put them back and turned to the suitcase. Nothing of interest there, she decided a minute later. Turning, she went over to the small, functional desk and looked down. A cord hung out of one of the drawers, plugged into the outlet on the wall. Alina reached out and opened the drawer, raising an eyebrow when she saw the slim laptop inside.

Viper pulled out the laptop and sat down, opening it. There was no password protection, and a second later she was opening his email. Scanning it quickly, the only item of interest she found was a receipt for a pair of train tickets to Washington, DC. She pursed her lips thoughtfully and closed out of the email. On the desktop was an unnamed folder and she clicked on it. Opening the first image file, her breath caught and her eyes narrowed sharply. She was staring at a photograph of Angela's house.

Viper opened all the photos in the folder, shaking her head when she finished.

"That's not creepy at all."

There were over thirty photos of Angela, her house, her car, and a whole set of Angela and Stephanie out to dinner. Viper stared at them and her lips tightened. These were surveillance photos. Trent must have started watching her the night he got into town. Alina tilted her head, studying one of the photos of Angela and Stephanie at dinner. Something was nagging at her memory. Something with Stephanie...her head straightened suddenly. The car! Angela came out of work to a flat tire, and Stephanie went to get her. That must be the night they were at dinner.

Viper's lips thinned unpleasantly. After looking at the photos, there was no doubt in her mind Trent was the one who slashed Angela's tire. He was probably hoping for a quick and easy grab while she was stranded by the side of the road. Unfortunately for him, Stephanie came to the rescue before Angie ever left the safety of the parking lot.

Viper pulled a flash drive out of her inside jacket pocket and plugged it into the laptop, copying the files over quickly. Trent was targeting Angela, but why? Why was Angela so important?

And why the hell did he just buy two train tickets to Washington, DC?

Michael filed off the train with the rest of the passengers, glancing at his watch as he stepped onto the crowded platform. It was rush hour and the commuter traffic was heavy as men and women hurried to get home. Michael followed the wave to the escalators and rode it up to the main hall, his head up and his eyes alert. He didn't care much for crowds and his time in combat made him uncomfortable with noise over a certain decibel, both of which were out of control during rush hour in 30th Street Station. Since rejoining the civilians in the city, he'd learned to keep his head up and his eyes moving. It helped keep the anxiety at bay.

Michael looked up at the sea of humanity in the main lobby as the escalator ascended. It was just before he reached the top that he saw him. First it was just his profile, but then the man turned his head to look behind him, affording Michael a full view of his face. It was a face Michael had spent hours studying a few weeks ago while he was trying to track him down. It was a face that Michael doubted he would ever forget.

It was also a face that was supposed to be dead.

Michael pushed past the man in front of him as the escalator reached the main floor and quickly moved through the crowds, keeping his eyes on the back of the head a few yards in front of him. How was it possible? His mind raced as he kept the man in sight. Asad Jamal was dead, killed by Viper a few weeks ago. Yet, there he was in front of him, moving through the crowded 30th Street Station.

His lips tightened, and he watched as Asad passed through an exit and onto the street. What was going on? First one of the terrorists floated up in the Potomac, now here was another one who was supposed to be dead. Did Viper know he was still alive? Where was the third one? And what were they still doing here?

Michael pushed through the exit and looked up and down the crowded sidewalk. He caught sight of him half a block down, walking rapidly with his head down. Michael turned and started after him, keeping within easy distance in the steady foot traffic. It was much less crowded on the street, and Michael felt some of the tension leave his shoulders. The fresh air felt good on his face, and he fell into a steady stride as he followed Asad down Market Street. He reached into his pocket to pull out his cell phone, pressing speed-dial and holding it to his ear as he walked. The phone rang once and went straight to voicemail. Viper wasn't picking up. He put his phone away and glanced at his watch. If Asad led him to the other one, he had to alert someone. Viper was the preferable choice. Failing that, he would have to call in reinforcements in the form of Blake and Stephanie, and that was something he didn't want to do.

One block turned into two, and then three. After fifteen minutes, Michael was beginning to wonder just where Asad was going. Market Street was wide and busy, and the evening traffic was heavy, but Asad just kept striding along the sidewalk, heading east. The only time he paused was near City Hall, where he stopped to look up at the impressive facade before continuing on and turning onto Filbert Street. Here the foot traffic was lighter, and Michael allowed the distance between them to extend. He needn't have worried. Asad never once looked back, crossing to the next block without slowing his stride. He turned the corner at 12th Street, disappearing from view, and Michael broke into a run, closing the gap quickly and rounding the corner a minute later. He was just in time to see his quarry disappear into the Reading Terminal Market.

Michael hurried to the entrance and went inside the busy indoor farmers market, looking around quickly. He frowned, scanning the area before beginning to move through the market slowly. After a few minutes, he gave up and let out a low curse.

Asad had disappeared.

Stephanie jolted awake when her phone began ringing. She looked around, disoriented, trying to find the source of the noise.

"Here." Blake's deep voice cut through her sleep haze and she looked over to see him holding out her phone. "It slipped down the side and I grabbed it before it fell."

"Thank you," she murmured, taking the phone. "Hello?"

"How's the leg?" Lenny asked cheerfully.

"Umm...fine...I think," said Stephanie, shifting to sit up higher on the pillows. "I can't really feel anything right now."

"Hey, take it while you can," he told her. "When I got shot in the shoulder, I thought it was a walk in the park until I went home and didn't have the good drugs anymore."

"Great. Something to look forward to."

"I've got some news for you. It looks like there might be something in that hunch of yours. I talked to the sister of one of the victims, and the best friend of another. They both told me almost the same thing."

"What's that?"

"The victims were friendly with a man in their building. When I showed them Trent's picture, the one recognized him. The other said she never saw him but she knew the name was Trent. Both victims really liked him and thought he was a nice, sweet guy. Now, that in itself isn't much."

"It's not," Stephanie agreed. "So they knew him. He lived in their building, after all."

"It gets better," Lenny assured her. "Turns out both victims ended up having a problem with their garbage disposals. Guess who offered to help?"

"The sweet, nice neighbor?"

"Bingo. He was very helpful. They were both thrilled not to have to call a plumber or handyman. But here's the best part. When police interviewed everyone in the buildings after the disappearances, Trent denied ever having met either of them. His statements claim he was rarely home because he traveled extensively for work."

"That's not enough to hang him, but it's a start. What about the other two victims?"

"I'm checking them out tomorrow. I'll let you know what I find out. I just wanted to let you know you were onto something. I hope it helps."

"It does. Thank you!"

Stephanie disconnected and stared across the room frowning.

"What's wrong?" Blake asked, looking up from his tablet.

"That was Agent Thomas from Miami," she said, setting the phone down on the bed beside her. "I called him yesterday. Turns out this Trent character has lived in four different condos in the past four years."

"He's having trouble settling on one?"

"Apparently. The weird part is that in each of those four buildings, a woman disappeared in the year he was there."

Blake frowned.

"That seems a little coincidental."

"Exactly. So I asked Lenny to look at the metro files and see what he could find out," Stephanie said, reaching for a bottle of water on the table next to her. "He did even better. Today he actually talked to friends of two of the victims. Turns out both victims knew Trent, and liked him. He fixed both their garbage disposals for them."

"What a nice guy."

"Yep. A real stand-up neighbor. Except when the police interviewed everyone in the buildings, he said he never met either of the victims."

"And that's where it unravels," said Blake. "They always do something stupid, like lie about something that's easy to check. Did the police ever find the women?"

"Yes. Their bodies turned up months later."

Blake shook his head with a frown.

"And there are no leads at all?"

"Nope. All four murders are still unsolved."

"If we presume Trent is the killer, and that he's targeted Angela, why change his MO now? Why target someone who lives states away? That makes no sense."

"I know." Stephanie sighed, capping her water. "None of it makes sense, but something isn't adding up, and he's right in the middle of it."

"You have to tell Michael," Blake decided. "They should know what we're thinking."

Stephanie nodded and reached for her phone.

"You're right," she agreed. "I'll call Lina. She's the one who asked me to see what I could learn about Trent."

Blake raised an eyebrow.

"She did? When was this?"

"The other night. She stopped by to see me."

Blake watched as she lifted the phone back to her ear.

"I'm a little surprised she asked for your help."

"I'm not," said Stephanie, glancing at him. "As much as she hates to admit it, she's only one person and she can't do everything alone."

"From what I've seen, that doesn't stop her from trying."

"True enough, but something's changed. I'm not sure what, but she's changed. She's being more distant and focused. This is how she was when she first came back, only it's worse than it was last year."

Blake considered her thoughtfully.

"What do you mean?"

"I don't know, really. It's just a gut feeling I got when she was here the other night. I can't really explain it." Stephanie lowered the phone. "She's not answering. I'll try again in a few minutes."

"Do you think she's working on another terrorist attack?"

Stephanie shrugged.

"I don't know. She's working on something, and I think it's tied in with John, but who knows."

Blake frowned.

"What the hell did John get himself into?"

Stephanie looked at him.

"That's what I've been asking myself for the past three days."

Damon walked into the kitchen, glancing at Angela. She was bent over her laptop in the dining room. He'd give her this: she worked hard. She'd been on the phone for most of the afternoon, alternating between the laptop and pacing.

"You almost done for the day?" he asked. "It's five-thirty."

"I'm just finishing up," she said with a yawn. "That last call just about killed me. It was a forty-minute conference call that could have been a one paragraph email."

Damon grimaced and opened the fridge to look inside. He was so glad his job did not involve conference calls. For that matter, calls of any kind were rare in his profession. His lips curved suddenly in amusement. What would Viper do on a conference call? God help them all!

"Any idea when Lina will be back?" Angela asked, closing her laptop and standing up to stretch. "What are we doing about dinner?"

"No, and I don't know," he said. "There's a bunch of food leftover from last night."

Angela visibly brightened and rounded the bar to join him at the fridge.

"I'll reheat the chicken parm," she decided, reaching for the large aluminum tray of chicken and spaghetti. "Do you want some?"

"I'm good."

"Suit yourself."

Angela set the tray on the stovetop, reaching over to preheat the oven. She jumped when a loud tone echoed through the house.

"What the hell?!" she exclaimed, staring at the stove as if it was a bomb. "Why is the oven so freaking loud?!"

"It's not the oven," Damon said grimly, striding over to the cabinet where Viper kept the tablet that was hooked into the security system. "That's the security perimeter."

"Why is it on?" Angela demanded, spinning around and looking up at the dark plasma above the mantel in the living room.

"I set it after she left," Damon said shortly, pulling out the tablet and swiping the screen.

"You know how to use it? Why?"

"Because I have a similar one at my house. Go pull the curtains over the windows in the dining room and across the sliding door."

Angela gaped at him.

"What? Why?"

He glanced at her and she shivered at the look on his face, hurrying to do as he'd asked without another word.

Hawk scrolled through the security quadrants quickly. After Viper had left, he set all the perimeter alarms except the driveway, knowing that when Viper or Michael returned, they would come that way. Whatever set the security system off, it was not them. He stopped when he came to the quadrant flashing on the east side of the woods.

"It's done," Angela said from the living room. "Now what?"

He tapped the flashing area and began scanning through the frames slowly.

"Come away from the windows," he said absently.

Angela came over to the bar and watched as he studied the tablet.

"It's not Alina or Michael?" she asked. "You're sure?"

"Yes."

Hawk stopped when he saw the figure moving through the trees.

"Son of a bitch," he muttered. "He just doesn't give up."

Angela stared at him.

"It's him, isn't it? It's Trent."

"Yes." Damon looked up and she shivered again. "And he came prepared this time."

Hawk set the tablet down and strode across the living room to the fireplace. Angela watched him reach up into the chimney and gasped when he pulled out a sawed-off shotgun.

"What do you mean he came prepared?" she demanded.

"He's armed," he said shortly, opening a wooden box on the mantle and pulling out a handful of shotgun shells. He fed two into the barrel, snapping it closed with a practiced flick of his strong wrist. He dropped the rest of the shells into one of his pockets and headed for the sliding door. "Stay here. Stay away from the windows and keep this door locked until I get back. I'll knock once, then twice. Don't open that door for anything else."

"Wait!" Angela cried, running after him. "What if he's not alone?"

"He is."

"What am I supposed to do?"

"I just told you." Hawk moved the curtain and slid open the door. "I won't be long."

"Wait!" Angela called again.

He paused and looked back impatiently.

"What?"

"For God's sake, be careful! Alina will kill me if anything happens to you!"

His lips twitched.

"Is that so?"

"Yes. She's head over heels for you, you stupid man. I swear, the two of you are trying my last nerve!"

That made Damon grin as he turned to step out the door.

"I'll be sure to tell her," he said. "Lock this behind me, then get into the hallway and stay there with your back to the wall. I'll be back soon."

Chapter Thirty-Nine

Hawk moved through the trees swiftly and silently, the shotgun in his hands. His heart beat steadily, settling into a rhythm as he moved to intercept Trent. Angela was worried about what Alina would do if he got hurt. Hawk's lips tightened and he glanced up into the trees. He was more worried about what she would do if Trent used the gun he was carrying on her bird. He had to get to him before Raven realized he was back.

The light was fading, and the shadows were deepening quickly as he moved through the underbrush, making no sound. He paused, listening, and went forward again. A moment later, he heard a branch pop about twenty yards to his left. Hawk moved and caught sight of Trent a moment later, picking his way slowly through the trees, coming towards him.

Hawk stood silently behind a tree, waiting as the man walked a few feet past him. He moved then, silently approaching him from behind. A loud screech rent the air and Hawk stifled a sigh. Raven was here.

Trent raised his arm, his gun aimed directly at the black mass diving out of the trees.

Hawk moved like lightening to close the distance between them, one eye on the descending hawk and one eye on Trent. He brought his right forearm down hard on Trent's arm, forcing it aside just as Trent pulled the trigger.

The shot echoed deafeningly through the trees and Raven shrieked. Trent swung around and Hawk's hand clamped around his throat. He glanced up in time to see Raven disappear into a tree and he turned his cold, blue eyes back to Trent.

"You're lucky you missed the bird," he growled.

Trent snarled and tried to raise his gun as Hawk slammed the butt of the shotgun into his wrist. The gun went flying into the underbrush as the joint audibly cracked. A second later, Hawk's right fist landed solidly in his gut. He grunted and doubled over, the wind knocked out of him with the force of the blow. As he did, Hawk sliced his hand into the side of his neck. Trent let out a strangled cry of pain and Hawk brought his elbow down on his temple swiftly.

Trent fell forward to the ground, unconscious.

Hawk bent over him and pulled the high turtleneck away from his neck. His lips thinned grimly when he saw the thick gauze bandage taped to the side of his neck. Releasing the sweater, he straightened up and stared down at the unconscious man at his feet.

Trent Whitfield had certainly seen better days. He looked like the walking wounded. Aside from the bandage on his neck, he had staples in his head and bandages covered his forearm. Now, thanks to Hawk, he also had a broken wrist, and would have a concussion if he ever came to.

Damon leaned the shotgun against a nearby tree and sighed. He had to move him and, by the looks of it, Trent was no light-weight. The branches in the trees above rustled suddenly and Raven glided by to perch on the lower branches of a pine tree. His shiny black eyes looked at Damon and he bobbed his head.

"Yeah, yeah, yeah," he muttered. "I did it for her, not you."

Raven shook out his feathers and stared at him, undisturbed. Damon shook his head and bent down to hoist Trent's inanimate form over his shoulder. Pain ripped through his side and shot up his ribcage. Hawk grimaced, dropping Trent with a low curse. Clearly, he wasn't moving him anywhere. He wasn't healed enough to lug two-hundred plus in dead weight anywhere without causing more damage than it was worth.

Damon glared at the unconscious man, frustrated by his inability to clean up his own mess. Finally, he bent down and undid the belt around Trent's waist, pulling it off and testing it. It was a good, strong, leather belt. He glanced at the shoes on Trent's feet and nodded when he saw the laces. It would do. It only had to hold until Viper returned.

Five minutes later, Trent was tied upright to a slim but sturdy tree. The leather belt was secured around his middle, while his hands were tied to the tree above his head with one of the shoe laces. The other shoe lace secured his feet to the base of the tree trunk. Damon stepped back, breathing heavily, to survey his handiwork. He didn't have a gag, but he supposed it wouldn't matter. If Trent woke up before Viper got back, the odds were low on anyone hearing him. The road was over a quarter mile away, and the nearest house was Viper's.

Hawk turned to leave, grabbing the shotgun as he passed it. He strode over to the underbrush where Trent's pistol landed, bending to pick that up as well. As he walked away, Hawk glanced back to see

Raven still sitting on the low branch, his black eyes on the unconscious Trent.

Damon grinned.

God help him if he woke up and tried to move while Raven was there.

Alina pulled the Shelby around the house, the tires crunching on gravel, and the engine growling low. She pulled up beside the detached garage and cut the engine, getting out of the low car as a loud rumble preceded Michael's F150. It pulled around the house and Alina watched as he pulled the truck up next to her Mustang. Walking around the back of the black pickup, she waited for him to get out of the cab.

"You're just getting back?" she asked as he climbed out.

"Yeah," he said, pulling his laptop from behind the driver's seat and slamming the door. "It was a long day. How about you?"

"No one got shot, so I guess that's a good day," she replied, turning to walk across the grass with him. "Everything ok in DC?"

Michael glanced down at her.

"Yes, for now," he said. "Damon told you what it was all about?"

She nodded.

"Yes."

"Then you know it's no coincidence Trent came after Angela," Michael said in a low voice as they mounted the steps to the deck.

Alina's face hardened.

"Oh, I know."

Before Michael could say anything, the sliding door slid open and Angela flew out.

"Thank God you're both here!" she exclaimed. "He came back! Trent came back!"

Alina and Michael stared at her.

"What?!"

"Where is he?"

They spoke in unison and Angela looked from one to the other.

"It's all over now, but I was terrified," she admitted, leading them into the house. "Damon made me stay inside and told me to stay in the hallway, away from the windows."

Damon looked up from where he was stretched out on the couch.

"It was the safest place," he said, sitting up. "He was never going to get this far, but better safe than dead."

Alina watched as he stood up slowly, almost painfully, and her eyes narrowed suspiciously. Her gaze dropped to his side and she strode forward, rounding the end of the sofa. Reaching out, she lifted up his tee-shirt before he could stop her and an ice pack fell to the floor at their feet. Her eyes raised to meet his.

"What the hell did you do?" she demanded.

"Nothing a little ice won't fix," he retorted, starting to bend down for the ice pack.

She beat him to it, swiping it up and pushing him back down on the couch.

"Sit," she commanded, handing him the ice.

"What's wrong?" Angela asked, staring at them. "Why are you so worried about a little bruise?"

Alina glanced at her.

"It's not a little bruise," she replied, turning to cross over to the bar. "He just had surgery and he has a cracked rib."

Alina dropped her keys onto the bar and rounded the island to go to the fridge.

"What!?" Angela swung around to glare at Damon. "I didn't know! I wouldn't have let you go out there if I knew that!"

"Then it's a good thing you didn't know."

Michael grinned at the look on her face and went over to sit in the recliner.

"I don't think that's what she wanted to hear," he said.

"Did you know?" Angela demanded, turning her attention on him.

"Yes."

She threw her hands up in the air and made a noise suspiciously like a hiss.

"Why am I *always* the last one to know everything?!" she cried. "And why did you go after Trent if you knew you were hurt?"

Her fiery gaze went back to Damon and he shrugged.

"I'm fine," he said. "He needed to be handled."

"And?" Michael prompted before Angela could respond. "What happened?"

"He was handled."

"Where is he?" Alina asked again, joining them all in the living room and handing Damon a bottle of water and two liquid gel capsules.

"Don't argue, just take it."

He grinned and took the Advil, tossing them back with the water, his blue eyes never leaving her face. Alina wasn't sure how she felt about the look in those eyes.

"He's tied up in the woods," he said after he swallowed. "I'll need you to give me a hand."

"You tried to carry a dead weight?!" she exclaimed. "No wonder you need an ice pack, you idiot!"

"He's *dead*?!" Angela shrieked. "What do you mean he's dead?!"

Michael choked back a laugh as Alina and Damon stared at Angela.

"No one said he was dead," Damon finally said with a frown. "What are you talking about?"

"Why would he tie up a dead man?" Alina added, her brows furrowed. "That's a waste of time."

"But you just said–"

"Dead weight, not dead body!" said Alina as she realized the confusion. "As in, unconscious, dead weight."

"Oh."

"Do we plan on leaving him out there indefinitely?" Michael asked from the recliner, his feet up. "How long has he been there?"

Damon shrugged and glanced at Angela.

"I don't know, maybe an hour? What do you think?"

"More like forty minutes," she said thoughtfully, looking at her watch.

"Then I doubt he's still out," Alina said. "What are you planning on doing with him?"

"He's going to turn him over to the police," Angela said before Damon could open his mouth.

Alina's eyebrow soared into her forehead and she looked at Damon, clearly amused.

"Is that so?" she asked.

"That is not what I said."

Angela looked at him with wide eyes.

"Yes it is!" she argued. "You said justice would take care of him. When I asked what that meant, you said the proper authority would handle it."

Michael started coughing in his recliner, his shoulders shaking and a hand covering the bottom half of his face. Alina felt a grin pulling at her lips and sternly repressed it.

"I'll go make sure he's ready for delivery," she said, her eyes dancing.

Damon began to stand and the laugh left her eyes. She shook her head and held him down with a hand on his shoulder.

"Oh no you don't," she said. "I go. You stay."

"Don't be ridiculous," he objected. "I know where I left him."

"Then you can tell me."

Michael sighed and lowered his feet, standing.

"This is where I think I step in," he announced. "As the ranking Federal agent present, I'll take care of him."

Damon and Alina looked at him.

"Your rank means exactly nothing to me," she said bluntly. "Trent's mine."

Michael's green eyes met hers squarely and his jaw hardened.

"We'll discuss this outside," he said shortly. "He's probably awake and could be gone, for all we know. We need to get moving."

"He might be awake, but I can guarantee he's not gone," Damon said, a grin on his lips.

Alina saw it and crooked an eyebrow curiously.

"Only one way to make sure," Michael said, turning toward the door. "Where is he?"

Damon was silent for a moment, then sighed.

"Head southeast," he told them. "He's tied to a tree about halfway to the road."

Alina nodded and followed Michael to the back door.

"Angie, make sure he doesn't do anything stupid, like let a couple terrorists out of Gitmo, until I get back," she said over her shoulder, drawing a laugh from Damon.

She stepped onto the deck and closed the door behind herself.

"Why would he let terrorists out of Gitmo?" Michael asked, his eyebrows raised.

Alina smiled faintly.

"Why not? What's a couple more? We're already in for a penny, might as well go in for a pound."

Michael glanced at her and they descended the steps, starting across the grass toward the trees.

"How is he?" he asked seriously. "That's the first I've seen him acknowledge the injury."

"He's healing," she said shortly. "He'll be fine."

"You're worried about him," said Michael. "Why? I'm sure he's had worse."

Alina glanced at him.

"I know he has, but I need him to be as close to one-hundred percent as he can be. Anything less will get us both killed."

"You're not talking about the shooter from the church."

"No."

Alina pulled a long, thin Maglite out of her jacket pocket and switched it on as they stepped into the dark trees.

"What can I do?"

"You've already done it. You found the connection between Dominic and Trasker. The rest is on us."

"Don't be ridiculous," he muttered, following her as she weaved through the pines. "Let me help. I'm a trained weapon at your disposal. Use it."

"Don't be so quick to jump in the fight, gunny. There's no guarantee you'll make it out again."

"There's no guarantee I'll make it through tomorrow either, but I'll still get out of bed."

Silence greeted that and Michael dropped it with a sigh. They moved through the woods quickly and a few minutes later the light fell across a figure tied to a slender tree trunk.

Trent appeared to still be unconscious, his head slumped forward. Alina frowned, moving forward. She played the light over his body. He was still tied securely and she bent to look at his face.

"He's still out?" Michael asked incredulously. "What the hell did he do to him?"

Alina looked up from beside him.

"I don't think this was him," she said dryly.

She stood up and shone the Maglite around the trees until she lit on a large, black hawk, settled in a tree not far away.

"What...again?!"

"Appears so." A thread of amusement was in Alina's voice as she lowered the flashlight back to Trent. "It's not deep, but it's right on his temple. It would have been enough to put him under again."

"He's lucky he's still got his eyes," he muttered, joining her next to Trent.

They both looked down at the unconscious man.

"I can't let you take him," Michael finally said. "I need to get answers out of him."

Alina glanced at him.

"And you don't think I can get information out of him?" she asked, amused again. "Gunny, have you met me?"

"So far, all we have on him is an attack on Angela and possible tampering with production at Trasker. That hardly falls within your jurisdiction."

"I don't have a jurisdiction. I'm not bound by red tape."

"No, you're bound by international law," he shot back, "and you're stateside."

Alina pursed her lips.

"Actually, we have something else on him," she admitted after a minute. "Stephanie called me in the car. It looks like he'll soon be the prime suspect in four unsolved murders in Miami."

Michael stared at her.

"What?"

"Four women, all from buildings he lived in, disappeared. Their bodies were later recovered. The police have had no leads, until now."

"And Stephanie thinks it was him?"

"Not just Stephanie, but another agent down there."

Michael ran a hand over his short hair.

"What the hell?" he exclaimed. "How do you guys manage to attract these people? For God's sake!"

"It wasn't me this time," she protested with a laugh. "It was Angie!"

"Even worse!" He looked down at Trent. "You're definitely not getting him now. This is an FBI issue. I'll take him, question him, then hand him over."

"And he'll be out and free in twenty-four hours."

"Maybe so, but he'll be alive to stand trial," Michael retorted.

"True enough," she conceded sheepishly. "I can't make that guarantee if I interrogate him."

"I know."

Alina looked down at Trent thoughtfully.

"I'll let you take him on one condition," she said slowly.

"I wasn't asking your permission," said Michael wryly, "but what's your condition?"

"Find out how the hell he knew to target Angie."

Chapter Forty

Angela settled herself in the recliner with her glass of wine and looked at Damon. He was sitting up on the couch with his feet propped on the coffee table, ankles crossed. He had a tablet in his lap and was scrolling through something, his attention focused on the screen. She sipped her wine, studying him over the rim of the glass.

"Is there a reason you're staring at me?" he asked, not lifting his eyes from the tablet.

"Just wondering why you had surgery," she said readily. "Why aren't you taking pain killers if you're still in pain?"

Damon raised his head and looked at her.

"Why would I take drugs when I can still function?"

She shrugged.

"Why fight pain when there are other options?"

"I wouldn't call this pain," he said, turning his attention back to the tablet. "More of a mild inconvenience."

"What did you have surgery for?" she asked a moment later. "You didn't say."

Damon sighed imperceptibly and looked up again.

"I was shot."

Angela's mouth dropped open.

"What?!" she exclaimed. "When?"

"Last week."

"What happened? And why aren't you in the hospital? When I was shot, I was in the hospital for two weeks. Where were you shot?"

"In my side."

Angela waited expectantly, frowning when no further information was forthcoming.

"How did Lina know?" she asked, trying a different tack. "I mean, it's not like you work together. You're in Homeland Security, and she's a private consultant."

Damon shrugged, remembering that Angela still believed he worked for the DHS.

"We're friends," he said evasively. "I told her."

"What's the story with you two?" Angela asked, sipping her wine. "You sure visit a lot, but you never stay long, and it's weeks or months before you come back."

Damon crooked an eyebrow.

"Why so interested?" he asked.

"Why are you both so secretive about it? I can't make it out. What's the big deal?"

He smiled faintly.

"I think you're the only one making it a big deal," he said. "It's not much of a mystery. We both travel extensively and our schedules don't line up often."

Angela pursed her lips and tilted her head.

"Do you ever plan on not traveling extensively?"

He raised an eyebrow.

"I assume you're going somewhere with all this? I'm sure my future travel plans aren't that interesting to you."

She shrugged.

"I'm just thinking, you're not getting any younger and opportunities like the one staring both of you in the face don't happen all that often. If you keep leaving Lina alone for months at a time, there's no guarantee she'll be here next time you roll into town. I'm not trying to be the voice of doom or anything, but that's the truth. You two have something special going on. You should grab it with both hands and not let go."

Damon studied her for a long moment.

"How long did it take you to think up that speech?" he asked finally, his blue eyes dancing.

"I just came up with it," she said with a grin. "How was it?"

"Good," he admitted. "A little extreme, but good."

Angela sipped her wine.

"I have my moments."

The door to the deck slid open and Alina stepped into the living room, closing the door behind her. Angela turned in the recliner to look at her.

"Where's Michael?" she asked, looking behind her.

"He's taken Trent into custody. He's driving him to the field office in the city," Alina said, glancing at her glass of wine. "Is there any of that left?"

"Yes. The bottle is on the counter in the kitchen."

Alina nodded and went into the kitchen.

"You let the gunny take him?" Damon demanded, getting up

and following her into the kitchen.

"I didn't have much of a choice," she said, pouring herself a glass of the red wine. "Stephanie called. It's looking like he's been a very bad boy, and it is definitely FBI jurisdiction now. Michael is going to question him about Trasker, then turn him over to the Feds."

Damon opened the fridge and reached in to pull out a bottle of beer.

"Since when did jurisdiction ever stop you?"

"Since I have other issues to worry about," she said, sipping the wine. "They can take him. We've got bigger fish to fry."

"What did he do?" Angela called from the living room. "And will you two come back in here where I can hear?"

Alina grinned and turned to walk around the bar into the living room, Damon close behind. She found his presence behind her comforting and sighed silently. She wasn't sure she wanted to get used to having him around.

Rounding the sofa, she sank onto it and set her wine glass on the coffee table. She bent to undo the laces on her boots, pulling them off as Damon settled down next to her.

"Well?" Angela prompted.

Alina glanced up at her as she pulled the second boot off.

"Are you sure you want to hear?"

"No, but tell me anyway."

Alina set the boots aside and pulled her feet up onto the couch, curling comfortably into the corner. Damon handed her the wine glass, and she smiled in thanks.

"I asked Steph to see what she could find on Trent," she told Angela. "Turns out he's moved four times in four years. In each place he's lived, a woman disappeared. Their bodies turn up a few months later. It's an ongoing investigation and there have been no real leads, until now. Stephanie had an agent start interviewing people who knew the victims. Two of them knew Trent, yet he denied having met them when the police interviewed him. He just jumped to the top of the suspect list."

Angela stared at her.

"Do you mean to tell me, you think Trent is a...is a..."

"Serial killer?" Alina provided helpfully. "Yes."

Angela gulped and lifted her wine glass, draining it. She got up wordlessly and went into the kitchen for a refill.

"I think she's taking it well," Damon said. "Considering you just kind of dropped it on her."

"She asked!"

Angela came back a moment later.

"And he was in my house? Are we sure it was him that night?"

"Yes. I saw the bandages on his neck where you stabbed him," Damon said, sipping his beer. "I mean, unless someone else stabbed him in the neck in the past few days."

Angela sank down into the recliner, looking stunned.

"Oh my God. I could have been...he could have–"

"Yes, but he didn't," Alina said briskly, not liking the look on her friend's face. "No point in worrying about what could have happened and didn't."

"Why me?" Angela asked, sitting back with her wine. "What made him come after me?"

Alina glanced at Damon and saw the warning in his eyes.

"I don't know," she said smoothly. "He's been watching you since he got up here, though. He's got hundreds of surveillance photos of you on his computer."

"What?!" Angela shrieked. "How do you know?"

"I saw them," Alina said calmly. "I went to his hotel and went through his room. Not only are there photos of you and your house, but he also has shots of you and Stephanie having dinner."

Angela shivered.

"That's just terrifying," she said, drinking some more wine.

"Please tell me you have copies of those?" Damon asked.

"Of course."

"Why? Why was he following me? Was he planning it all along?" Angela demanded. "This is unreal. I mean, you hear of this stuff happening, but you never think it will happen to you!"

"I think your flat tire was him," said Alina. "I think he was counting on you not seeing it and getting stranded at the side of the road."

Angela gasped.

"He was there!" she exclaimed. "That night! I came out of work and saw the flat, and he just kind of appeared out of nowhere. He offered to drive me home, but Stephanie was coming. I thought he was just being overbearingly chauvinistic when he insisted on trying to help."

Alina sipped her wine, tamping down the fresh surge of anger welling up inside her. If it wasn't for pure chance, Trent could have taken Angie before she even got back. Her lips tightened grimly. Angela would have been gone before Viper realized she had become a pawn in the Trasker mess.

"If Trent is the one behind the break-in, can I go home now?"

Angela suddenly asked, drawing Alina away from her thoughts.

Alina shrugged.

"Yes, if you want. If you don't, you're welcome to stay longer."

Angela stared into her wine glass thoughtfully.

"I'll see how I sleep tonight," she said after a moment. "This is a lot to take in. If I have problems sleeping, I might stay a few more days."

Alina studied her for a moment, then nodded.

"You're welcome as long as you need to stay."

"He'll be locked up, right?" Angela asked suddenly, raising her gaze to hers.

Alina's eyes hardened.

"Oh, he *will* be taken care of," she assured her, her voice like ice, "one way or another."

Senator Carmichael stared across the room at the paneled wall opposite, his mind clamoring to grasp what he'd just read. It didn't seem possible. This morning, everything was going perfectly according to plan. Now, ten hours later, everything had fallen apart, and he had no idea when, how, or why.

He stood up, his legs feeling weak, and walked around his desk to the sideboard where a decanter and glasses sat on a silver tray. Special Agent Blake Hanover was supposed to be suspended, and his cases turned over to another agent; an agent who would not look twice at an upstart businessman from New Jersey who used street racers to run product up and down the coast. Robert picked up the decanter, his hand trembling, and splashed some whiskey into a glass. As of this morning, Hanover was out of it, and it was clear sailing. The decanter landed on the tray with a click and he lifted the glass to his lips.

Now he had no idea what was going on.

Robert turned and staggered back to his desk, sinking into the leather chair with his whiskey. Three hours ago, Tina Ricci had abruptly contacted the FBI and dropped all the charges against Blake Hanover. She then called her attorney, who was on Carmichael's payroll, and informed her that it was all a terrible misunderstanding. She said she had confused Hanover with someone else, and she had dropped the charges. Two hours ago, her attorney went to her office, only to find that Ms. Ricci left earlier and didn't return. A visit to her townhouse in

Georgetown and a chat with her housekeeper elicited the information that she had departed for the airport on an unexpected business trip. As of half an hour ago, there was still no sign of check-in at any of the major airlines for Tina Ricci and no reservation could be found under her name.

She had disappeared.

Robert drained his glass and ran a hand through his graying hair before setting the empty glass on the desk. He dropped his head into his hands.

It was all over. Without the charges, Hanover would be reinstated, and his investigation would continue. It would only be a matter of time before he caught someone in the Casa Reinos Cartel. He came close four days ago. Carmichael got wind of it just in time, and the cartel member was the victim of an unfortunate boating accident off the Cuban coast. If Hanover got one of the Casa Reinos, he was done. They wouldn't hesitate to give him up as the one who paved the way, allowing them to move their product up and down the coast at will. In fact, Carmichael had already been warned by the head of the Cartel. If he didn't get Agent Hanover in line, they would make sure he came down with them.

Robert raised his head and stared at the picture of his wife and daughter on his desk. The scandal would engulf them. Chloe was starting Princeton in the fall. It would destroy her.

The Senator sat behind his desk for a very long time, staring into space, before he finally reached for his phone. It took three rings and he was getting ready to hang up when the call finally connected.

"Good evening, Senator."

"Sanders," Robert greeted Tina's PA, forcing his voice around the tightness in his throat. "I've been trying to reach Ms. Ricci all day. Can you tell me if she took any phone calls that might have upset her at all? I'm worried about her."

"Not that I'm aware of, Senator," the woman answered thoughtfully. "She had visitors in and out of her office all morning, then she canceled all her appointments and calls for the afternoon. She didn't seem upset, just preoccupied."

Robert frowned.

"Did she give a reason for clearing her schedule?"

"No. After the last meeting, she simply canceled everything and left."

"Last meeting? When was that?"

"It wasn't a scheduled meeting. A Federal agent came to the office. He called ahead, but showed up within the hour. I think it was about one in the afternoon...yes, it was just after lunch."

Robert's blood ran cold.

"Federal agent?" he repeated. "How strange. What was his name?"

"Oh Lord, let me think," she said. "It was an Irish name. Give me a minute...it's right there...Agent...Reilly...O'Reilly! That was it. Special Agent Michael O'Reilly. He was Secret Service."

"Hm. How odd. Well, thank you, Sanders. If you hear from her, would you please ask her to call?"

"Of course, Senator."

Robert disconnected and opened his laptop. His fingers trembled as he typed the name into the Secret Service directory. A second later, he was looking at a picture of a red-headed man with a short military haircut and a square chin. He scanned the short bio attached, his heart dropping. Another Marine. So much for the brief flare of hope it would be someone he could manage.

"Well, let's see who you are," he muttered.

Ten minutes later, his face was pale and he sat back in his chair. It had gone from bad to worse. Agent Michael O'Reilly had subpoenaed the internal records for Trasker Pharmaceuticals. If Blake Hanover was a thorn in his side, Michael O'Reilly was a damn bayonet. Testimony from a drug cartel could be discredited. Hard evidence from Trasker's own records was a death knell.

Robert stared at the screen blindly. There was no way out. There was no way to squirm out of this. He was going to crash and burn. Once O'Reilly went through the logs, he'd find Carmichael's involvement and there would be no talking his way out of it.

He was finished.

Chapter Forty-One

Alina came out of the bathroom with a towel wrapped around herself and glanced at the bed. Damon was sitting up, propped against the pillows, his phone in his hand.

"You're awake," she said, going over to the dresser and opening a drawer. "How are you feeling?"

"Better," he said, his eyes dropping to her long legs. His lips curved wickedly. "If you come over here, I'll show you."

Alina flashed a grin over her shoulder and closed the drawer, turning to go into the walk-in closet.

"If I go over there, we'll never get to work."

Damon grinned and swung his legs out of bed, standing and stretching. His ribs were sore and he grimaced at the flash of pain.

"How's your side?" he asked, walking over to the closet.

The towel was on the floor and Alina was dressed in loose, black cargo pants. She'd just finished pulling on a tank top when he leaned against the door frame.

"It's fine," she answered shortly, not meeting his gaze.

Damon frowned, his brows snapping together in suspicion.

"Show me."

She looked at him in exasperation and bent to scoop up the towel.

"Don't be silly," she muttered, dropping the towel into the hamper and pushing past him. "It's nothing."

He grabbed her wrist swiftly and pulled her back to him.

"Then humor me."

Brown eyes met blue and she glared at him. He just smiled at her maddeningly.

"Either you do it or I do, sweetheart."

Alina sighed loudly and pulled up her shirt. Damon raised an eyebrow and looked at her side. When he raised his eyes again, the laughter was gone.

"You got stitches."

"Yes."

"Why?"

"It was infected," she said, lowering her shirt. "It got beyond what I could treat. I had to get it cleaned out."

He frowned and followed her into the bedroom, watching as she went over to the bedside table and picked up her Ruger, slipping it into her back holster.

"How bad was it?"

Alina glanced at him and dropped her gaze again.

"It was bad," she admitted. "I left a piece of metal in there when I pulled the slug out."

"What did you tell the ER?"

"I didn't go to the ER. I went to a private doctor. I told him I was hunting and someone caught me by accident."

Damon sighed and went over to her, slipping his arms around her waist.

"We're a hot mess, you and I. We're the walking wounded."

She nodded and touched the stitched up wound on his side. The ribs above the puckered skin had turned a lovely shade of deep purple and the swelling was noticeable. Suddenly Alina was overwhelmed by a crushing feeling of defeat. Raising her eyes to his, she lifted her other hand to the side of his face.

"How much longer do you think we can hold out?" she whispered. "How much more can we take?"

Damon stared back at her steadily.

"As long, and as much as it takes. We'll do what needs to be done."

He lowered his lips to hers, and Alina leaned into him. He was right. They would do what needed to be done, and they would do it together.

Blake nodded in greeting to the agent outside Stephanie's door.

"Morning, Lou," he said. "How's it going?"

"Can't complain, and it wouldn't do much good if I did."

Blake grinned.

"Ain't that the truth."

He walked into the room and raised his eyebrows in surprise at the sight of Michael and Angela.

"What are you guys doing here?" he asked. "I thought you

were on lockdown."

"Not anymore," said Angela cheerfully from the chair next to Stephanie's bed. "It's all over!"

"Trent tried to get to Angela again yesterday," Stephanie said. "He ran into..."

Her voice suddenly trailed off and she looked at Michael in sudden confusion.

"A friend of Alina's," he finished smoothly. "He helped keep an eye on things while I was in DC."

Blake raised an eyebrow and looked from Stephanie to Michael to Angela.

"A friend?" he repeated.

"They've known each other since boot camp," Angela offered, blissfully unaware that Damon's existence was classified information. "They're more than just friends. They just won't accept it."

Blake's other eyebrow joined the first and he looked at Michael.

"Is that so?" he drawled. "Your girlfriend cheating on you, Mike?"

"She's not my girlfriend," Michael continued the old argument good-naturedly.

"Does he have a name, this friend?" asked Blake.

"Damon," Angela answered before either of the others.

"Damon, huh?" Blake looked at Stephanie. "Would that be the same Damon who took care of the driver in Washington a couple weeks ago?"

She had the grace to look uncomfortable.

"Yes."

"So what happened yesterday?" Blake asked, returning to the main topic and dropping the subject for the time being.

"Trent showed up and Damon intercepted him," said Michael. "When I got back, he was still unconscious. I took him to the field office in the city and spent most of the night interrogating him."

"And?"

"He broke around three in the morning. He confessed to killing all four women in Florida, plus three more no one knew about. Angela became a target when he met her in Miami."

"Son of a bitch!"

"My thoughts exactly," Stephanie agreed. "Michael transferred him to us this morning. We'll send him down to the Miami office, and he'll face trial there."

Blake looked across Stephanie's bed to Angela.

"You must be relieved."

"Yes. Michael's taking me back to my house. We just stopped here to tell Stephanie everything. It's been an insane couple of days. I'm looking forward to getting my cat home and just trying to get back to normal."

"I bet," he murmured.

"What time is your attorney coming in?" Stephanie asked, looking up at him.

Blake grinned.

"He's not. He called me an hour ago. All charges were dropped. The woman said she got me confused with someone else."

Stephanie's face lit up.

"Oh, thank God! That's wonderful!"

Blake looked at Michael.

"I'm not sure it's God I have to thank," he said, his eyes meeting Michael's. "What happened in DC yesterday?"

Michael shrugged.

"I may or may not have stumbled across some information involving Ms. Ricci and Senator Carmichael."

Blake's mouth dropped open.

"What?!"

Michael nodded.

"Carmichael has been blackmailing her for over a year. I managed to convince her it was in her best interest to drop the charges and let me handle Carmichael."

Blake stared at him.

"You mean to tell me that Carmichael was behind this?" he demanded. "He made her press the charges?"

"Yes."

"Why? What does he have against me? I've never even met the man!"

"You're investigating the cartel," Michael said. "I found a connection between Dominic DiBarcoli and Carmichael. If you get hold of one of the cartel, I think they'll give up Carmichael's involvement in the smuggling network you've been after."

Blake cursed under his breath.

"I had a trap set up for one last week," he breathed. "He didn't show, and a few days later his body floated up near Cuba."

"You were getting close," Stephanie said thoughtfully. "So he came after you. That's why everything was designed to discredit you. If you tried to pin anything on him, it would be the word of a senator against a disgraced agent."

Blake looked across the room at Michael.

"I owe you one, brother. Thank you."

Michael smiled and stood up.

"No need to thank me, and no need to owe me. We've been through enough together. If we can't watch each other's backs, what good was it?" He looked down at Angela. "You ready to get going?"

She nodded and stood up.

"Yeah. I don't want to leave Annabelle in the truck much longer." Angela bent down to hug Stephanie. "I'll stop by tomorrow. Any word on when you're getting out of here?"

"Not yet," Stephanie said with a grimace. "They're still pumping antibiotics into me. Are you sure you'll be okay on your own at the house?"

"I'll be fine," Angela assured her. "I feel really good about it today. I just want to get back into a normal routine as soon as possible. I'm going to work from home for a couple days while I'm on these pain killers."

Stephanie nodded.

"If you need me, call."

"Will do."

Blake watched as Michael and Angela departed, then moved over to the chair she'd vacated.

"Have you heard from your boss?"

"Not yet. I expect they'll still have to do an internal investigation, but without the charges, I don't see it going anywhere." Blake looked at her. "What did the doc say?"

"My numbers still aren't where he wants them. So another day of the antibiotics, and then more blood work. Now that Trent's taken care of, I have nothing to work on, and nothing to keep me busy. If they keep me much longer, I'll go crazy."

Blake grinned.

"Well, if you're looking for something to keep busy, you can always help me with the cartel while I'm waiting to be reinstated."

Stephanie looked at him, surprised.

"You want help?"

Blake shrugged.

"Sure. I've worked with you enough that I'd rather it was you than anyone else. At least I know you won't screw it all up."

Stephanie considered him thoughtfully.

"Rob won't let me take on any cases until I'm out of here and back at work," she said slowly. "If you're serious, I'd love to work on it. After the bombs and those drivers, I want that cartel shut down as much as you."

"Then we'll get to work. We can't have you laying around being lazy," he said with a wink. "Not when there's so much fun to be had working with me!"

Viper looked up when she heard the ding from the server in the other room. She set down the sharpening stone and long deadly blade, and stepped out of her armory into the command center. One of the monitors was blinking a message: *Access granted.*

A faint, satisfied smile crossed her lips and she pulled a chair over to the computer, seating herself. She pulled out a dual ended USB cord and plugged one end into the desktop and the other into an external drive connected by a separate cord to a laptop that she rarely used. Once everything was connected, Alina turned her attention to the screen and pulled the keyboard towards her on the counter.

"Alright, Charlie," she murmured. "Let's see what you know about Kyle Anthony March, aka Jordan Murphy."

If Viper felt any twinge of conscience at successfully hacking into the Organization's server, she resolutely pushed it aside. Desperate times, and all that.

She opened up the drive directory and began scanning the drives, looking for the one that housed all the asset files. Viper knew it would be encrypted and hard to find, but after ten minutes of searching, she found it. After another thirty minutes, she had it decrypted. She clicked it open and found herself looking at a list of seventy-five folders, all numerical. Alina frowned. She wasn't surprised the assets were assigned by numbers rather than names, but it made it significantly harder to find Kyle's folder.

Viper studied the folders. The numbers weren't dates, or ages, or even military ID numbers. They appeared to be completely random, but she knew that couldn't be the case. Each number had to relate to the asset in some way. She pursed her lips and began scrolling through the list of folders, looking for any numbers she recognized as pertaining to herself. That would give her a clue as to the naming convention, and help narrow down which of these folders belonged to Kyle. While she could simply open them and go through them one by one, Viper hesitated to do so. While she was fully prepared to violate Kyle's privacy, she wasn't ready to intrude on anyone else's. She knew she would be furious if someone went through *her* file without authorization.

It was about halfway through the list that Viper stopped and studied a number that jumped out at her. The two-digit year of her birth initially caught her attention, but the four digits following it held it. A reluctantly impressed smile pulled at her lips, and she scooted down to the computer a few feet away to open Kyle's military file. A moment later, she was back to scrolling through the list of folders. She found the number she was looking for toward the bottom of the list.

Clicking open the folder, she reached for her bottle of water. Kyle's file was smaller than she was expecting and she frowned, opening the first folder. Most of it was his military file, with some background reports and assessment reviews. She opened the next folder, scanning through medical records. Viper raised an eyebrow when she saw he had had tuberculosis as a teenager, leaving him with weakened lungs. The report noted that the condition had not caused asthma, and he was physically cleared. She closed out the medical history a few minutes later. Not surprisingly, there was no mention of the reconstructive surgery in Madrid.

Alina stretched and drank some water, opening the last folder. She frowned when she saw only one file inside. Clicking it open, she scanned his progress reports from the Organization's training facility. When she was finished, she sat back, stunned. Kyle had never completed the training course! Halfway through, his psych evaluations had deteriorated, and the last notation was from Charlie, discharging him from the program.

Kyle Anthony March had never become one of them.

Viper rubbed her eyes. Fantastic. A mercenary who was partially trained by the Organization. She didn't know which was worse: a fully trained assassin on a par with herself, or a partially trained one, forced to complete his training on his own in the field, without the benefit of oversight from a team of veterans. At least she could predict what another asset would do in any given situation. Kyle was a wild card.

Alina sat forward again, copying his entire folder onto the external drive. When it finished, she went back to the home folder. While she was here, she might as well copy her own file. It certainly wouldn't hurt to have a little insurance. She initiated the copy, hesitating for a moment before searching for Hawk's. He would be furious if he ever found out, but she grabbed it anyway. She had no intention of reading it, but if things went badly, they might need proof that they both were on Team USA, even if that particular team was unaware of their existence.

She was just getting ready to close out of the drive when another number caught her attention. Alina frowned and stared at the number below the folder. It took a full minute for her to realize why the number was so familiar to her. When she did, she sucked in her breath and felt her skin go cold as a wave of shock rolled over her. Her breath caught in her throat, and Alina felt as if her heart had stopped for a few seconds. The number swam before her eyes for a moment, then her heart pounded in her chest. It couldn't be.

It wasn't possible.

Almost in a daze, Alina clicked on the folder. It was filled with at least twelve sub-folders. She clicked on the first folder almost fearfully, not wanting to look but knowing that she must. Even though she knew what she would find, part of her hoped against hope she was wrong. The file opened and she stared at the military history on the screen. Her stomach dropped out of her and her face went hot, then cold again.

Alina reached for her water, her hand trembling, never taking her eyes off the military ID photo attached to the file. She knew what she would find as soon as she saw the number under the folder. She knew she was opening something she didn't want to see. It didn't seem to matter, didn't seem to lessen the gut-punching effect of seeing the proof before her.

Dave Maschik had been an asset in the Organization.

Chapter Forty-Two

Hawk looked around the room, closing the door behind him silently. The suite was on the ground floor of an extended stay hotel about twenty minutes from Medford. While Viper was focused on hacking into the Organization, using every available minute for that purpose, Hawk hadn't forgotten about the assassin responsible for the stitching in his side and the chaos at John's funeral. Last night, while she was sleeping, Hawk found him.

He moved across the living room, glancing into a small kitchenette. The coffeemaker was empty, but the smell of coffee still hung in the air. The kitchenette looked spotless. He glanced around and went into the bedroom. The bed was made, and the door to the bathroom was open, giving him a clear view of a vanity with towels folded and stacked neatly on the end. Everything was neat, clean, and almost sterile in appearance.

Damon frowned and moved back into the living room. He watched Kyle leave in a black Honda Pilot five minutes before and Hawk didn't know how long he had before he returned. He moved quickly, going through the couch, the pressed-wood entertainment center, and the kitchen cabinets. Aside from almond milk, half a hoagie, and a case of soda in the refrigerator, and coffee in one of the cabinets, there was nothing. He went back into the bedroom and crossed to the queen-sized bed, bending down to check under it. A rolling bag was stowed next to a slim black case secured with a combination lock.

Damon pulled out the rolling bag and flopped it onto the bed, unzipping it. He carefully sorted through clothes and plastic Ziploc bags with toiletries and medical supplies, placing everything back as he had found it when he finished. He was just closing the bag again when he saw the zippered pocket on the inside of the flap.

He opened it and slid his hand inside, feeling an envelope. Pulling it out, his eyebrows soared into his forehead. A single name was scrawled across the front: Viper.

Hawk flipped the unsealed envelope over and pulled out a single sheet of paper. A scowl gathered on his face as he read the letter quickly.

Viper,

If you're reading this, it's all over. Obviously, this was not the ending I was hoping for, but I try to prepare for the unexpected. I admit that with you it has been challenging. My congratulations on a fight well-won. I wish I knew how it ended. I know with you it would not have been easy.

I'm leaving you a parting gift. Consider it a token of my respect. I stumbled across a hard-drive, taken from a safe deposit box kept by Agent John Smithe. I believe you knew him, so I'm passing it on to you. I've left it somewhere only you will find. You're the only one I trust to handle what's on it.

All respect,

Kyle

Hawk refolded the letter and tucked it into the inside pocket of his jacket. He zipped up the luggage and slid it back under the bed. After a second's hesitation, he grabbed the locked case and turned to leave the hotel room swiftly. His mouth settled into a grim line as he crossed the parking lot.

The son of a bitch was going after Viper *now*.

That was the only explanation for the sterile state of the hotel room and the letter left where she would find it, just as he had. The assassin knew it was going to end today, one way or another.

Hawk got onto his motorcycle, securing the case on the back, and pulled his helmet over his head. Kyle had a ten-minute head start. The motorcycle roared to life and he hit the throttle, jumping the curb and pulling into traffic. He weaved through the lunch rush skillfully, ignoring the honks and hand gestures. As he sped down the highway, Damon tried not to consider that he had killed targets in much less time than ten minutes. It only took a second to pull a trigger, as he well knew.

Hawk's jaw tightened, and calm focus overtook him as he slipped into working mode. Viper was as skilled as anyone in the game. She would be ready for Kyle.

And if she wasn't, Hawk would make damn sure that Kyle never made it back to the hotel.

Michael pulled into an empty spot in the parking garage and glanced at his watch. After settling Angela back in her house with her cat, he had crossed the bridge into Philly to the field office. Trent was transferred into the FBI's care that morning, but Michael still had paperwork to fill out. He opened the door and climbed out, pulling his laptop from behind his seat before slamming the door and beeping the truck locked. He sighed, turning to head toward the elevator. This was not how he had planned on spending his day, but he was glad that Trent was off the streets and Angela was safe. Now if only he could get Asad off the streets as well. Michael's head snapped up and he caught his breath.

Asad!

He pulled the clean phone out of his pocket and dialed quickly. Between questioning Trent and taking Angela home, Michael didn't have time to warn Viper that Asad was still alive! The call connected and he listened to it ring once, twice, and three times. Pressing his lips together, he disconnected before her voicemail could answer. He would try again later. If he still couldn't get her, he'd call Damon.

Michael had just slipped the phone back into his pocket when his regular phone began vibrating. He rolled his eyes, fishing in his other pocket. He finally got it out, glancing at the screen. He frowned, pressing accept on the unknown number.

"Hello?"

"Is this Agent O'Reilly?" a male voice asked.

Michael's frown grew.

"Yes, it is."

"This is Senator Carmichael."

Michael's jaw dropped and he stopped short of the elevator alcove, standing near the wall.

"Senator! This is a surprise."

"Is it?" Robert asked dryly. "I doubt that."

"What can I do for you?" Michael asked after a moment of silence.

"Are you in Washington? I'd like to meet with you."

"I'm not, actually. What's on your mind?"

"I understand you've been given access to Trasker Pharmaceutical's records. I think we both know what you found. I want to discuss it."

"There really isn't anything to discuss," said Michael carefully.

"Oh, but there is. There's much more to this than you know. It's larger than me and Dominic DiBarcoli."

Michael stilled.

"I'm listening."

"I was Dominic's liaison. I met him and gave him instructions, guided him through the labyrinth of Washington, DC, and helped fund certain endeavors. You know about that by now. When he died, Dominic took a lot of information with him: information that some people believe died with him."

"I sense a but."

"I know it all," said Robert simply. "The information didn't die with Dominic. I'm the one who gave it to him."

"Why are you telling me this? You know I'm Secret Service. Anything you tell me can be used against you in court. You know that."

"I understand. I'm willing to tell you everything."

Michael sucked in his breath.

"You want to turn state's evidence," he said in sudden understanding.

"In exchange for protection for me and my family. What I know is...very sensitive."

"How sensitive?"

"Agent O'Reilly, I'm a United States Senator. Not much has the power to intimidate me, but this does. How much do you know about that attempted terrorist attack a few weeks ago?"

"Quite a bit. Enough to know they had help."

"Yes." Robert paused for a long moment. "That help came from Washington."

"And you know who's responsible?"

"Not only who's responsible, but how and why." Robert paused again. "Can you guarantee me and my family's safety?"

Michael ran a hand over his head.

"I can't guarantee anything until I've spoken to my boss, and we've met," he said. "If what you're saying is true, we'll work something out. When do you want to meet? I can be in the city tomorrow."

"Call me when you get into DC. I'll send you my personal cell number. It bypasses the aids and comes straight to me. I'll tell you where to meet me."

Robert disconnected and Michael frowned, lowering the phone and staring across the parking garage. Was it possible? Could Carmichael know the identity of the leak in Washington? If so, Michael might be able to help Viper after all.

Viper raised her head sharply when a red light silently started flashing above the stairwell leading to the kitchen. She slid to another PC, opening her security system. As soon as the database opened, her lips tightened into a grim line. The security protocol she had coded into the backup fail-safe had been activated.

A chill streaked through her and Viper got up quickly, spinning around to stride into her armory. She grabbed the combat knife she'd been sharpening earlier and slid it into the knife holster at her ankle. She strode to the stairwell, closing her laptop as she passed. That security protocol could only be activated one way. Someone had hacked into her security system, making the security perimeter useless, and disabling the audible alarm. As far as the main system was concerned, nothing was wrong. It was only the back-up system that had recognized the intruder.

She hit the button on the wall and the opening above slid open. She pulled out her phone and switched to the back-up security app as she mounted the steps swiftly. When she had set up the security system, Viper had intentionally put it on its own server, completely autonomous. Now she was glad she had taken the extra precaution. The hacker only had access to her security server, nothing else.

Viper lifted the five quart sauté pan off the magnet on her kitchen island and the structure slid over the opening to her command center. She hung it on the pot rack and turned her attention to the phone in her hand. While the main system was unaware of any breach, the back-up system knew exactly where the threat was located.

She knew who it was. She'd been waiting for him, expecting him. The reverse tracker in the GPS she took from his sedan told him exactly where she was, and she knew that when she left Philadelphia the day she took it.

Viper had known something was wrong when the GPS was still in the rental car. While she was in the coffee shop across from the parking garage, she had realized just why he left it behind. When she got back to the Jeep, she debated taking the GPS to her safe house in Old City. She had a full house, with Angela and Michael both in plain sight. Any attack on her would involve witnesses, and possibly additional causalities. However, if the assassin was as reclusive as most in their profession, he would wait until they were not there to strike. In fact, Viper had gambled on it. In the end, she decided to bring Kyle to her.

And there was no doubt in her mind he was here now.

Alina crossed the living room to the mantel and opened the

box with the shotgun shells. She pulled out an extra magazine for her .45, tucking it into a pocket on her right thigh within easy reach. Turning, she strode to the sliding door.

It was time to end this.

Charlie looked up from the laptop in front of him when the light began flashing silently on his desk phone. He sighed imperceptibly. His staff knew not to disturb him unless it was urgent.

"Yes?"

He pressed the speaker-phone button, returning his gaze to the screen in front of him.

"I'm sorry to interrupt, sir, but I have Bill on your secure line. He says it's urgent."

Charlie raised his eyes and picked up the handset.

"Put him through."

"Here he comes."

There was a pause, then Bill spoke.

"Hello?"

"I'm here. What's the problem?"

"Remember when you asked me to monitor Senator Carmichael?"

"Yes."

"I just intercepted a phone call he made from his office," Bill told him. "He called a Secret Service agent, name of Michael O'Reilly. You know him?"

"I'm aware of who he is," said Charlie with a frown. "Is he assigned to the Senator's office?"

"That's the thing," Bill said, a note of excitement in his voice. "He's not. In fact, he's not assigned to anyone's office. He works under Chris Harbor and specializes in fraud. He's the one who tracked down the missing money in DHS last year."

"I'm aware of that," Charlie said gently. "Why did Senator Carmichael call him?"

Bill paused and cleared his throat.

"He claims to be willing to give O'Reilly evidence relating to Trasker Pharmaceuticals. He wants protection in exchange for turning states evidence against someone in Washington. The inference was that it's someone higher than him on the food chain."

Charlie sat back in his chair and was silent for a moment.

"Send me the transcript of the conversation," he said finally.

"Already done," Bill replied. "And I put someone on Carmichael."

"No," Charlie said slowly. "Let's not do that just yet. Call them back."

There was silence for a beat on the line.

"Are you sure?" Bill asked finally.

"Bill, how long have we worked together now?"

"How long...err, well let's see...about four years, I guess."

"In four years, what has led you to believe that I am ever 'not sure?'" Charlie asked, his voice deceptively soft.

"I...well…nothing. I'm sorry. I'll call the asset back."

"Thank you."

Charlie hung up and opened his secure email. He read through the transcript silently and sat back in the chair. Charlie stared across the room for a moment before pushing his chair back and standing up, closing the laptop automatically as he did so. He turned to walk over to the massive window behind his desk. DC was bathed in afternoon sun, and Charlie slid his hands into his pockets, staring out over his city thoughtfully.

So Carmichael was spooked. Understandable. Everything he had worked for all his life was about to be ripped away from him, spoils in the invisible war raging in the highest echelons of Washington. He had received his hand, gambled, and lost. Dominic DiBarcoli's death was just the beginning, causing his world to unravel strand by strand. With every attempt he made to repair the damage, it simply got worse.

Charlie wasn't surprised that Carmichael was attempting to exchange information for security. He was desperately trying to mitigate the damage as best as he could. But really, where did the man think he could hide? He was a United States Senator, not some two-bit thug from the Bronx who ended up working for the wrong family. Senators couldn't just disappear.

Not without him.

Charlie absently watched the traffic on the street far below. When Viper had asked him to push through the subpoena to give O'Reilly access to Trasker's files, he was hesitant. She presented a compelling argument, however, and he agreed. If anyone could find something in those files, it was Michael O'Reilly.

Apparently he'd come through as promised.

His lips tightened ever so slightly, and he stared out the window without seeing the cars or people below. Carmichael thought he could outrun his involvement, but Charlie knew better. No one had made it out of this alive so far, and the death toll was only going to go up from here. Too many people were learning too many things. Now everyone was trying to do the right thing.

Charlie shook his head. God save him from civilians trying to do the right thing. It always ended badly, and never had the good results they so naively expected. While it was laudable, and even commendable, to want to adhere to a set of moral and ethical standards largely ignored by the majority of humanity, it rarely worked out for the best. Do-gooders were more likely to cause widespread harm than they were to do good, and therein was the terrible irony.

He turned away from the window and looked at the closed laptop on his desk. If he didn't get this mess sorted out soon, Washington would get hit with a wrath the likes of which it had never seen. His lips curved unexpectedly in amusement. If Viper was unleashed, they wouldn't know what hit them. Just as quickly as the smile came, it was gone. If Viper descended on DC, no one would be left standing in the end.

Charlie strode back to his desk and opened the laptop, settling down in his chair once again. Viper was being patient right now, but it wouldn't last. She was distracted by Kasim, and by the shooter at John's funeral. When those distractions were gone, her patience would end, and Hawk would be right by her side.

He had to wrap this up before that happened.

Chapter Forty-Three

Viper watched as Kyle silently moved through the trees. Dressed in dark brown pants with a green and brown camouflage jacket, he blended perfectly with the wooded area. A slender rifle bag hung across his body and Viper noted the slight bulge at his side, indicating a sidearm. He had come prepared.

She was perfectly still above him, settled in the branches of an old maple tree that had sprung up amid the pines, still with her combat knife in her hand. Viper watched as he drew closer, not a muscle stirring, her heartbeat steady and her deadly gaze focused on the assassin below.

Viper was perfectly comfortable in the woods. Both she and Hawk excelled in jungle warfare, a skill not many in the Organization were able to master. She had used it to her advantage many times, and it was one of the reasons she had ultimately decided to bring Kyle to her property instead of leading him away from her home. She had the advantage here, and she had every intention of using it.

Kyle was almost below her now, passing through the trees, his attention focused before him rather than above. She waited until he was directly underneath her, patient and silent. As soon as his shoulder was below her, Viper struck, swinging skillfully from the branch. She released her hold on the tree limb as she swung down, her feet hitting his shoulder blades and pushing him forward. He stumbled, lost his balance, and fell. As she landed behind him, Viper grabbed the strap to his rifle bag with one hand, slicing it off his body with her knife. Before he hit the ground, the rifle was flying through the air to land in the trees, well out of reach.

Kyle hit the ground hard and immediately rolled over. Viper looked up from the crouch she'd landed in, anger rolling through her unexpectedly as she stared into the eyes of John's killer.

They studied each other for a charged moment, each weighing the other and determining the best course of attack.

"So the rumors are true."

Kyle spoke first, his voice deep, sounding almost surprised.

Viper raised an eyebrow questioningly, forcing the almost blinding emotion burning inside her aside. She didn't respond, but waited to see if he would continue.

"We heard you were a ghost," he told her, raising himself into a crouch. "You have quite a reputation."

"I promise it doesn't do me justice," Viper assured him, her voice an icy wave.

Kyle smiled.

"That remains to be seen. Why are you here? You could be anywhere."

"I could ask you the same thing."

Kyle shrugged.

"We both know why I'm here. You saw me at the hospital. You recognized me."

"You recognized me first. How?"

He sighed, watching her combat knife warily as she flipped it casually into the air, catching it again smoothly without taking her eyes from his.

"John Smithe said your name right before he died," he told her calmly. "Viper isn't exactly a common name. You're a legend. When you looked back in the hall, I knew it was you."

Viper stared at him, her face an emotionless, cold façade. Inside, she was shaken. If John voiced her codename as he was dying, then he knew exactly what was happening. Any lingering hope she may have had that he never knew what hit him was extinguished. He knew he was dying, and knew he was powerless to stop it. And so he uttered the one name he knew would avenge him.

Alina hadn't thought it was possible for the rage inside her to burn any hotter, but she was wrong.

"Why John?"

Kyle seemed surprised.

"Because I was paid, of course. A rather large sum, as a matter of fact. Much more than an FBI agent should have warranted. I should have taken heed to that old adage, if something's too good to be true, it usually is."

"Who paid you?"

"I have no idea. I keep all my transactions anonymous."

Viper studied him. He was telling the truth. There was no need for him to lie, and she could see it in his eyes. He had no idea who hired him. Frustration mounted inside her.

"Not the best choice this time," she murmured.

He shrugged.

"Well, live and learn. It was almost worth it to meet you, though. I really thought you were a myth."

"As you can see, I'm real enough."

"Tell me, what happened in Singapore? How did you get the drop on Wesley?"

"He made a mistake."

Kyle raised an eyebrow.

"What was that?"

"He missed."

Her lips curled into a snarl and she lunged toward him, her blade aimed for his throat. Before the knife could find its mark, Kyle blocked the blow, his forearm slamming against her wrist. The knife flew out of her hand, landing harmlessly a few feet away. Suddenly disarmed, she countered by slamming her left fist into his jaw, snapping his head back to slam into the ground. He absorbed the blow as he lifted his leg, planting his knee in her gut and forcing her off him.

Neither of them stopped moving, each fighting with a ferocity well matched. While Kyle was larger and stronger than Viper, she had speed and agility on her side. She rolled away from him, sweeping out her foot as he pulled his sidearm from his holster beneath his jacket. Her boot heel slammed into his wrist, eliciting a howl of pain as the bone cracked and the 9mm went skidding into the underbrush.

She sprang to her feet, but before she could deliver a blow to his temple, Kyle swung his leg, wrapping it around one of hers and pulling. Viper felt her leg give and braced herself for a hard landing. She hit the ground and rolled, dodging his arm as it slammed down where her throat had been seconds before. Swinging up to her knees, she straddled him, reaching for his throat. Too late, she realized her mistake.

Kyle grabbed one of her arms and turned towards it. In doing so, his leg moved up, trapping her opposite arm between his thigh and shoulder. Viper rolled with him, gaining just enough slack that when he applied pressure with his thigh, her arm wouldn't snap in half. She sucked in her breath, preparing herself for what she knew was coming.

The loud pop of her shoulder dislocating echoed in her head as red hot pain seared though her shoulder and down her arm. Crying out in pain, Viper twisted her torso, using the sudden limpness of her right arm to her advantage. She brought both knees up, bracing them on his chest and forcing him back as her useless arm slid out of the arm block. Blocking the pain from her mind, she kicked out, using his own body-weight to put some distance between them.

Realizing he'd lost his dominant positioning, Kyle suddenly

rolled away from her. Their grappling had brought him within reach of the discarded 9mm and he reached for it now. The fingers of his good hand closed around the handle. Turning onto his back, he fired.

Viper's boot made contact with his forearm as he pulled the trigger. The shot was deafening as the bullet went wide of her head, missing her and hitting a tree. Once again, the gun skidded out of his hand. Before he could lunge for it, Viper came at him from the side. Leaning over him, she hooked her arm under his, forcing it upwards and pulling his shoulder up off the ground. As she did so, she lifted her leg over his head and brought her knee down on the other side, straddling his head, facing his feet. Kyle hooked his arm over hers, rendering her arm hold useless, and clamped it to his chest as he struggled to get out of the hold she had him locked in. Viper felt her hold on his arm slipping and she pulled back, trying to break his grip, but Kyle was stronger and the grip wouldn't budge.

Changing tactics, Viper leaned forward and clamped her hand around her right wrist, effectively trapping Kyle's arm in a lock while his other arm was trapped at his side. Her right arm was useless, but she could use it to stop him from rolling out. Pain coursed through her again, and Viper knew she only had a few seconds before her arm gave out completely. Leaning her weight forward over his torso, she felt his head rise from the ground under her as her body weight forced his shoulders up. As soon as she felt them rise, she pivoted on her knee and slid her ankle under his neck, rolling back and onto her side. Her bottom leg slid under his neck and she hooked her other one over the top of his throat, trapping him in a scissor choke while still maintaining her arm lock.

Kyle reached up to pull at her leg, but it was too late. In a surge of adrenaline and pain induced strength, Viper contracted, squeezing her legs and arms together. Burning pain seared through her and she cried out as she used every ounce of strength she had left to choke the struggling man between her legs. Sweat poured down her face and her breath came hard and fast as his struggles slowly weakened until Kyle finally went limp beneath her, unconscious.

Viper held the position for a few seconds more, then slowly relaxed. Releasing her arms, she braced her weight on her good arm and released her legs, pulling her bottom leg out from under his neck. As she removed her other leg and came to her knees, Viper reached behind her and pulled out her .45 in one smooth motion. Standing unsteadily, she backed up a step, aiming at his chest. Before she could squeeze the trigger, Kyle stirred. He was coming around.

Viper stood over him, watching as his head moved and his eyes opened. They widened at the sight of the .45.

"This is for John, you son-of-a-bitch," she said coldly.

Viper fired a bullet directly into his heart, watching as his mouth opened in shock and his eyes began to glaze over.

She squeezed the trigger again, sending a round into his forehead.

"And that was for Hawk."

Hawk climbed off his motorcycle and glanced at the Jeep parked in front of the detached garage. She was home. Part of him had hoped, during his frantic ride from Kyle's hotel, that Alina had left the house. No such luck.

Damon turned and started across the grass toward the house, listening for any sound out of the ordinary. His body was tense, his senses tuned, waiting for the first indication that Kyle was here.

A muffled gunshot echoed out of the trees behind him and Hawk spun around, breaking into a run. Of course! Viper would have gone out to meet him, not remained a sitting target in the house.

He entered the woods, moving swiftly through the trees in the direction of the shot. He listened as he ran, straining for any sound to give him a hint as to where they were. His blood ran cold when he heard Viper cry out, the sound much closer than he expected. It was a long, drawn out cry, filled with pain.

His heart pounded, surging into his throat as he turned toward the god-awful noise. He rounded a hollowed out log and clump of underbrush, his chest tight as he found it suddenly hard to breathe. If she was dead when he got there- Damon blocked the thought as it presented itself. She couldn't be. He wouldn't allow it! Hawk pulled out his Beretta, flipping the safety off as he emerged from behind a group of trees. The scene in front of him made him stop short.

Viper stood over the assassin, her gun pointed at his chest. He was coming around, and Hawk watched Viper's face as she waited for him to open his eyes. This was the Viper Hawk remembered from years past. There was no trace of the Jersey Girl, only the icy, stone-faced killer. But it was her eyes that gave him involuntary pause. They were blazing with a fierce fury barely contained. Hawk realized this Viper wasn't the emotionless weapon he was used to. This one was a trained assassin who was seriously pissed off.

The gunshot rocked the woods, echoing through the trees with deafening precision, followed almost immediately by a second one.

Relief slammed through Hawk, robbing him of breath, as Viper lowered her left arm. He slid the safety back on his gun and took a step toward her, raising his hands when she swung her .45 up again to point directly at him.

"It's me!" he exclaimed, sighing when she lowered her weapon.

Viper seemed to sag before him, the icy, lethal look on her face fading as he came toward her.

"For God's sake, Hawk," she muttered. "Stop creeping up on me!"

She switched on her safety and slid her gun into her back holster, glancing at the body on the ground. Hawk watched as her face grew shuttered and her lips tightened.

"One down," she said, almost to herself.

Damon put away his Beretta and walked toward her, noting her right arm hanging limply at her side.

"Your arm..."

She raised her eyes to his.

"My shoulder is dislocated," she said, turning away from Kyle. "My own fault. I didn't give him enough credit and realized it a second too late."

Damon grimaced.

"Have you dislocated it before?" he asked, reaching for her limp arm.

"Yes."

"Try to relax," he said, lifting her forearm gently until it was parallel with the ground. He pressed her bicep against her body and glanced into her face. "Are you ready?"

Alina met his gaze and nodded, locking onto his blue eyes.

"Do it."

Damon nodded and rotated her forearm away from her body, his eyes on her face. Keeping one hand on her forearm, he moved his other to her upper arm and began to rotate it back away from her torso. A second later, her shoulder popped back into the socket as she gasped softly. Damon gently moved her forearm across her body and pulled her to him, his arms going around her. She sagged against him as he rested his chin on the top of her head.

"How did you get him down?" he asked, his eyes going to Kyle's body. "I know he didn't just lie there and let you shoot him."

"I got him in a scissor choke," she said, her voice muffled against his chest. "I didn't think I'd be able to hold it with my shoulder done for, but I managed it."

Damon pulled away and looked down at her.

"That's my girl," he murmured softly, a warm glint in his eyes.

He lowered his lips to brush them against hers gently before straightening up and pulling away.

"What are you going to do with him?" he asked.

For the first time since he came upon her, a smile pulled at Alina's lips.

"What any self-respecting Jersey girl would do," she answered. "Dump him in a landfill."

Damon handed Alina a glass of wine and sank onto the couch next to her, a bottle of Yuengling in his hand. She took the wine gratefully. The sun had set before they returned from disposing of Kyle's remains, and by the time they entered the house, Alina was drained and exhausted. Her shoulder throbbed, her legs hurt, and her body felt like she'd been dragged backwards through a hedgerow.

"How did he find you?" Damon asked, turning sideways to face her and stretching his arm along the back of the couch behind her head.

Alina glanced at him sheepishly.

"I told him."

Damon raised his eyebrows.

"You what?"

"Not directly," she clarified. "When I found his car after the funeral, I took the GPS chip."

"Yes, I remember. That was sloppy of him."

"That's what I thought, at first. Then I realized the reason it was left was because he wanted me to find it."

Damon sucked in his breath.

"Of course," he breathed. "He put a reverse tracker in it."

"Bingo."

He studied her.

"And you knew this before you came back here?" he asked softly.

Alina smiled at the look of disbelief in his face.

"Yes. I wanted to bring him to me. The easiest way to get to a target is to bring them to you."

"You're insane," he said, lifting his beer to his lips. "Absolutely insane."

"If you really thought that, you wouldn't be smiling."

"I'm smiling because it worked," he retorted. "That doesn't change the fact it was reckless. What if he'd showed up while Angela and Michael were here?"

"Hawk, take a minute and think," she said tiredly, leaning her head back against his arm. "If you knew the location of a target, and that target had several strangers with them, would you attack? Or would you wait until the extras had left the building?"

A reluctant grin pulled at Damon's lips.

"I'd wait," he admitted.

"Exactly."

"Did you crack the firewall yet?" Damon asked after a few moments of silence.

Alina nodded, glancing at him.

"Yes. He wasn't one of us."

Damon stared at her.

"Then what's the story with the entrance application?" he demanded. "You said it was ours!"

"It was." Alina leaned forward and set her empty wine glass on the coffee table. "He never made it out of training. Charlie terminated him before he finished. He was deemed too dangerous after a few psych evals."

Damon's brows snapped together sharply.

"He was psychotic?"

She nodded.

"Charlie didn't want to risk it."

Damon let out a low whistle.

"So he was an assassin without a cause. A mercenary. How did he know about Jordan Murphy?"

"I have no idea. That's still a mystery."

Damon frowned thoughtfully.

"You said Jordan Murphy was a member of your brother's outfit, right?"

"That's right."

"And we know Dave was killed by someone over in Iraq," he said slowly. "Is it possible Kyle met the person who killed your brother along the way?" He shook his head almost immediately. "No. That wouldn't make any sense. Why would the topic even come up?"

Alina leaned back and turned to look at him.

"There's something else," she said, her voice low. "When I was looking for his file, I came across another one."

Damon raised an eyebrow questioningly.

"Why do I get the feeling I'm not going to like this?"

"Kyle wasn't one of us, but Dave was."

Hawk stared at her, his face suddenly impassive.

"Say that again?"

Alina sighed and rubbed her eyes.

"Trust me, I'm still trying to wrap my head around it," she muttered. "Charlie got hold of him while he was in Iraq. Those letters from him to John? Dave was investigating all that for Charlie. It's in his file. When the tour was over, Dave was scheduled to move into an intelligence slot until his enlistment was up, then on to the training facility."

Hawk was silent for a long moment before he drained his beer and leaned forward to set the empty bottle next to her glass. He sat back, stretching his legs out, and laid his head back.

"What you're saying is that Charlie knew he had a problem twelve years ago," he muttered.

"I think so. When Dave was killed, he lost his lead."

Hawk stared up at the ceiling silently, his lips drawn into a grim line.

"Everything was fine until John resurrected the investigation," said Alina after a few moments of silence. "Once he started poking the bear, it woke up. I have the letters, but without the attachments, it's impossible to figure out who we're after."

Hawk turned his head to look at her, his gaze shuttered.

"This is where I can help," he said slowly. "I might know something about that."

She raised an eyebrow, foreboding stealing through her at the look in his eyes.

"What?"

Instead of answering, Damon reached into the inside pocket of his jacket and pulled out an envelope.

"While you were hacking that firewall today, I went to search Kyle's hotel room," he said, handing it to her. "I found this."

Alina frowned and took the envelope, turning it over. A cold chill went down her spine at the sight of her codename scrawled across the front. She glanced at Hawk and pulled out the single sheet of paper, reading it swiftly. Shock rolled through her as she read, and when she finished, she raised her eyes to his.

"John had a safe deposit box?" she whispered, her throat feeling tight.

Damon hesitated for a second, then nodded slowly.

"Yes."

Alina stilled at the way he said that one word. Staring at him, she slowly sat up.

"You knew," she stated.

"Yes."

"How?"

"You're not going to like it," Hawk warned softly.

Viper stared back at him, her face impassive.

"Tell me."

"I found the rest of the contents in Stephanie's bedroom closet."

Chapter Forty-Four

Stephanie looked up when she heard the agent speaking outside her door. Blake had left about twenty minutes before to take Buddy out and grab his laptop from the house. She'd been reading through old case files connected to the Casa Reinos while he was gone, trying to familiarize herself with the deadly cartel. She paused to listen now as Lou spoke to another man outside her door. If she didn't know better, she'd think Lou sounded almost in awe.

"I'll have to see your identification," he was saying apologetically. "I'm sure you understand."

The answer was muffled and unintelligible, but the voice was deep. Her attention caught, Stephanie stopped trying to read what was on her screen and instead strained to hear the conversation.

"Thank you, sir," Lou was saying, "I'll just tell her you're..."

He was interrupted by that low voice again, and a shadow fell across the doorway. Stephanie raised her eyebrows questioningly as a man stepped into the room, waving Lou away.

"I'll just introduce myself," he said over his shoulder. "No need for you to leave your post."

"Yes, sir."

The man turned his attention into the room, and Stephanie found herself staring into a pair of piercing brown eyes. The man was tall, at least six foot, bald, and had the distinct bearing of ex-military. He carried a cane in his left hand and as she watched, he leaned on it, studying her.

"Agent Walker?"

"Yes." Stephanie closed her laptop. "And you are…?"

The man smiled faintly and moved into the room towards her.

"You can call me Harry. That's what everyone calls me."

Stephanie gasped.

"Wait!" she exclaimed suddenly, recognition dawning in her eyes. "You're–"

"Yes, yes," he cut her off, waving his hand as if he could wave away his name. "Call me Harry. Do you mind if I sit?"

Stephanie swallowed and leaned over to put her laptop on the table beside her.

"Please do." She pulled herself up higher against the pillows piled behind her and watched as Harry lowered his bulk into the chair beside the bed. "I'm sorry I'm a mess," she said, running a hand through her hair self-consciously.

Harry looked at her, a smile playing about his lips.

"How's the leg?" he asked.

"It's fine," Stephanie said, bemused. "How did you know?"

"I'm familiar with the situation," he said, leaning his cane against the arm of the chair. He studied her thoughtfully. "You're very lucky. I understand it came close to nicking the artery."

"Yes, it did." Stephanie stared back at him for a moment, then took a deep breath. "I'm sorry, but what are you doing here?"

She inwardly winced at her own bluntness, but Harry smiled.

"I've been following your career for some time now," he said, crossing his legs and sitting back as her jaw dropped open. "You needn't look so surprised. You're one hell of an investigator. It was bound to get my attention."

"Thank you?" she ventured.

He nodded.

"However, that's not why I'm here. I'm here to discuss a topic close to, I think, both our hearts. I'm sorry about your partner, by the way. Agent Smithe, wasn't it?"

She nodded mutely, her mind clamoring to keep up with him.

"My sincere condolences. It's never easy losing a partner. I wish I could say it gets better with time, but that's not the case." Harry shook his head and glanced toward the door. "What's the agent's name out there?" he asked suddenly.

Stephanie blinked.

"Lou."

"Lou!"

Harry bellowed toward the door, making Stephanie start. Lou's head appeared around the door instantly.

"Sir?"

"Close the door and don't let anyone disturb us. We won't be long."

Lou nodded and reached in to grab the door handle, pulling it closed behind him.

"There. Now we won't be interrupted," said Harry, settling back in the chair.

"You said you wanted to discuss something?"

He nodded.

"Yes. Well, more a some*one.* Alina Maschik."

Stephanie stared at him, her heart pounding. Harry looked relaxed enough in the chair, but she was uncomfortably aware of his sharp gaze studying her every expression. How did he know about Alina? More importantly, *should* he know about Alina? Someone already knew too much about the assassin. The man sitting across from her was very well known all over the country, by name if not necessarily by sight. He was the Assistant Director of Homeland Security, a national hero, and had been in Washington long enough to become a household name. Why was he in her hospital room asking about Viper?

Harry sighed faintly.

"I can see you have some concerns. I suppose that's understandable. Perhaps I should explain."

"Please do," Stephanie said, reaching for her water bottle.

"You know who I am, which means you know what my current position is?"

"Yes."

"Good. Before I held my current position, I was, among other things, an instructor," Harry told her. "I trained Viper."

Stephanie's mouth dropped open and she stared at him, stunned.

"You...you mean..." she stammered.

"So you see, I probably know more about her than you do at this point. Your loyalty is commendable, but misplaced in this instance. I assure you, we both have the same interests at heart."

"How did you know...?"

Harry grinned.

"I read people, my dear," he said gently. "It's what I do. You were wondering if I should know anything about Alina. You were weighing my identity against the fact that you know someone tried to kill her at John's funeral, and you were wondering if you can trust me."

Stephanie gulped down some water, flustered at how accurate his evaluation was.

"Guilty as charged."

"I believe we both have her best interest in mind, and that is why I'm here," said Harry, the smile fading from his face. "How much do you know?"

She shook her head.

"Not much," she admitted. "Only that someone leaked her identity, and she was chased out of Europe a few weeks ago. This week a sniper tried to take her out at John's funeral. Whoever leaked her information knew she would be there."

"Quite." Harry was silent for a moment, studying her. "Now tell me what you think," he finally instructed.

Stephanie raised her eyebrows.

"What?"

"Come now, Ms. Walker," he said. "You're an intelligent woman. I know you have some thoughts of your own. What are they?"

Stephanie considered him thoughtfully for a moment, then sighed.

"I don't know what to think. Alina doesn't tell me much, for obvious reasons. I don't know anything about her work, nor do I want to. If someone's leaking identities at that level, it has to be someone in the government who has some serious security clearance. I know I can't get past her military dates of service when *I* look her up. The fact they showed up at John's funeral means they knew she would be there, so they know about us and where she came from. Hell, they must know she's in Jersey."

Harry nodded slowly.

"Agreed on all points. I'd like to add a thought, if I may. Her location may have become obvious when the two of you worked together to prevent that attack a few weeks ago. The terrorists who planned it are known to Viper, and Viper is known to them."

"You think that's when it happened?" Stephanie asked, her brows drawn together thoughtfully. "You think that's when they pinpointed Jersey?"

Harry shrugged.

"I think it's a possibility. Right now, everything is possible until proven otherwise. That's why I'm here."

Stephanie raised an eyebrow.

"What do you mean?"

"We're working around the clock to find the leak. However, I'm not convinced Viper is safe, even here. As you said, they're now aware of New Jersey and her ties here. We need to make sure her location is not compromised anymore."

Stephanie stared at him.

"How do we do that?"

"We work together, Ms. Walker, until the threat is gone. You're in a position to help me protect her."

"How?"

"Whoever's behind this seems to know where she will be before she goes there," Harry said slowly. "If we can predict where she will be, I can have surveillance ready to go. Perhaps, just perhaps, we can reverse the tables and catch them before they kill her."

Stephanie scowled.

"You want me to spy on my best friend?" she demanded.

Harry shrugged.

"If that's how you want to interpret it. Personally, I look at it as possibly saving her life."

"Oh, please. Be serious," she muttered.

"I am. Deadly serious."

Stephanie looked up, startled by the tone in his voice.

"Ms. Walker, you have to understand that we're working against an invisible enemy, a ghost," he told her grimly. "If we don't find him before he finds Viper, she *will* die. Do you understand? It isn't a possibility, it's a fact. They won't stop until she's dead."

Stephanie stared at him in silence for a long moment, her skin prickling with goosebumps at the thought. Finally, she sighed silently.

"Tell me what you need me to do."

Fury surged through Viper, hot and fierce, propelling her off the sofa and across the room. She reached the mantel, then turned to pace angrily to the sliding doors and back again. Hawk watched her, loathe to say anything that might set off the powder keg.

"So Agent Walker's been keeping secrets," she hissed, turning to do another lap. "Why the hell would she do that?"

Damon was silent as she stalked back.

"What did you find?" Viper demanded, turning to pin him with a sharp look.

"A mix of things," he replied. "There was some cash, all his personal identification papers, a Beretta with some spare ammo; things you'd find in a safe, or safe deposit box."

"That's it?"

Hawk met her gaze steadily.

"There was also an engagement ring."

That startled her and Viper's mask cracked.

"An engage–" She stopped, then cleared her throat. "Was it white gold with a twisted band?"

He nodded slowly and she shook her head.

"Damn fool," she muttered. "Why the hell did he keep it?"

"Maybe he wasn't ready to let go," Damon suggested softly. "I know I wouldn't be."

Alina looked across the table and met his blue eyes. Her flare of anger dissipated with those words and she felt her body sag. She sighed and walked back to the couch, sinking onto the cushion beside him.

Without a word, Damon put his arm around her shoulders and she leaned into him, resting her head on his strong shoulder. The heat from his body enveloped her and Alina felt the tension flow out of her. She leaned against him silently for a few moments, content to absorb the strength and comfort he offered.

"If Stephanie cleaned out John's box, how the hell did Kyle get his hard-drive?" she finally broke the silence.

"I don't know."

She sat up and looked at him.

"What made you search her house?"

"I told you, I don't trust anyone right now. Someone knows too much about you. I wanted to make sure she was clean. As it turns out, she wasn't."

Alina's eyes narrowed and her lips tightened. In a moment, the look passed and Hawk knew Viper had set the emotion aside. There was no time for it. She would deal with Stephanie later.

"And now Kyle's left it for me," she said, picking up the discarded letter. "I wonder how he got it, and if Stephanie even knows it's gone."

Hawk glanced at the letter.

"He cracked it," he said. "He said you're the only one he trusts with what's on it. Whatever it is, it's big enough that Kyle realized how dangerous it is."

Viper looked at him.

"If it's the missing attachments," she said softly, "they hold the key to bringing down the bastard trying to kill us all."

Hawk's eyes met hers.

"What's the plan?" he asked simply.

"We do what we do best. We do our job."

Epilogue

Washington, DC

A black SUV pulled to a stop at the curb, and the engine idled for a moment before shutting down. The driver's door opened and a detective climbed out, a large paper cup of coffee in one hand. Flashing lights lit up the street and several neighbors crowded on their front porches, watching the show unfolding before them. The detective shook his head and slammed the door, rounding the front of the vehicle to walk up the driveway and towards the hub of all the activity. Why did these things always happen just when he was about to sit down and relax? The call came in just as he'd settled onto his couch to binge-watch the last season of Game of Thrones.

He held up his badge for the local police officer standing guard.

"Evening," he said.

"Good evening," the police officer replied, glancing at his badge. "Go ahead. He's around back."

The detective nodded and ducked under the crime scene tape, striding around the side of the house to the back. He was greeted by a bevy of activity. His forensics team was already there, securing the area, while one of their medical examiners knelt beside a prone figure on the grass.

"What do you have, Frank?" the detective asked.

The medical examiner glanced up.

"Hi Joe," he greeted him. "Sorry about Game of Thrones."

Joe grinned.

"Who told you?"

"Carl mentioned it," Frank said, motioning to one of the forensics team. "He said you'd be pissed to be pulled out again."

"I'm not happy, but I hadn't started yet," said Joe, pulling on latex gloves. "So what am I looking at?"

"It's pretty straight-forward," Frank said, getting to his feet. "He came out of the house to take the trash down. On his way back, someone stabbed him. The blade went in just below his sternum and pierced his heart. It's a very precise wound."

Joe looked at him, frowning.

"Same as Dominic DiBarcoli?" he asked sharply.

Frank nodded.

"I was wondering if you'd recognize it," he said. "I won't know for sure until I get him on the table, but it appears to be the same. Since that murder is still unsolved, I know you'll want my report as soon as possible. I'll get it to you as soon as I'm finished."

Joe nodded and looked down at the body. It was on its side, facing away from him.

"Is it OK to take a look?" he asked.

Frank nodded.

"Yes. I've finished my initial examination."

He stepped back and watched as Joe crouched down beside the body. He glanced up before touching the body.

"You'll need to make it a priority," Joe told him. "Given the victim's identity, by morning we'll have the Secret Service and everyone and his mother breathing down our necks."

Frank nodded.

"I've already called autopsy and told them to have everything ready. I'll get started as soon as we get him back."

Joe nodded.

"You're a good man, Frank. Don't let anyone tell you different."

Frank snorted.

"Tell that to my wife after I call to tell her I'm not coming home."

Joe grinned and turned his attention back to the body beside him. He sighed.

"Let's take a look at you," he murmured, "then we can get started on letting you rest in peace."

He reached out and rolled the body onto his back.

Senator Robert Carmichael stared lifelessly up at him.

Other Titles in the Exit Series by CW Browning:

Next Exit, Three Miles

Next Exit, Pay Toll

Next Exit, Dead Ahead

Next Exit, Quarter Mile

Next Exit, One Way

Next Exit, No Outlet

Other Titles by CW Browning:

The Cuban (After the Exit #1)

The Courier (Shadows of War #1)

The Oslo Affair (Shadows of War #2)

Night Falls on Norway (Shadows of War #3)

The Iron Storm (Shadows of War #4)

Into the Iron Shadows (Shadows of War #5)

When Wolves Gather (Shadows of War #6)

Games of Deceit (Kai Corbyn #1)

Close Target (Kai Corbyn #2)

Available on Amazon

About the Author

CW Browning was writing before she could spell. Making up stories with her childhood best friend in the backyard in Olathe, Kansas, imagination ran wild from the very beginning. At the age of eight, she printed out her first full-length novel on a dot-matrix printer. All eighteen chapters of it. Through the years, the writing took a backseat to the mechanics of life as she pursued other avenues of interest. Those mechanics, however, have a great way of underlining what truly lifts a spirt and makes the soul sing. After attending Rutgers University and studying History, her love for writing was rekindled. It became apparent where her heart lay. Picking up an old manuscript, she dusted it off and went back to what made her whole. CW still makes up stories in her backyard, but now she crafts them for her readers to enjoy. She makes her home in Southern New Jersey, where she loves to grill steak and sip red wine on the patio.

Visit her at: www.cwbrowning.com
Also find her on Facebook, Instagram and Twitter!

Made in the USA
Las Vegas, NV
24 July 2023